The CRUMPLED LETTER

The CRUMPLED LETTER

A Belle Epoque Mystery

ALICE QUINN

TRANSLATED BY ALEXANDRA MALDWYN-DAVIES

Previously published as *La Lettre Froissée (Une Enquête à la Belle-Époque)* by Amazon Publishing in France in 2017. Translated from French by Alexandra Maldwyn-Davies. First published in English by AmazonCrossing in 2018.

Published by AmazonCrossing, Seattle

www.apub.com

Amazon, the Amazon logo, and AmazonCrossing are trademarks of Amazon.com, Inc., or its affiliates.

ISBN-13: 9781503904361
ISBN-10: 1503904369

Cover design by Shasti O'Leary Soudant

A woman knows how to employ fleeting time in pursuing gentle amusements.

—Nicolas Boileau, *Satire X, Sur les femmes* (1693)

We have both fallen from one excess into another, and love has flown away. Bon voyage!

—George Sand, *Monsieur Sylvestre* (1866)

Never is a coffin seen in the streets, never any funeral trappings, never is a death-knell heard . . . In each hotel Death has its secret stairs, its confidants, and its accomplices.

—Guy de Maupassant, *Afloat* (1888)

Prologue

Cannes, France
February 1884

In the distance is the sea and the sound of the waves, and in the cellars of the Hôtel Beau Rivage, the domestic staff sleep in their quarters.

In her room, a young maid stares at a vial filled with amber liquid. The girl's face is youthful, fresh. Her pink cheeks are plump. The tone of her skin is delicate. Glistening with a fragile spark, her worried eyes shine.

The weak light from the sconce-held candle illuminates her hands, reddened by her daily cleaning tasks, as she lifts the vial to her lips.

She swallows the concoction in one definitive gulp. Her face twists into a grimace. It tastes so bitter. Her lips are dry, chapped. As she attempts to put the vial down, her hand drops. She lets go, and the vial falls to the floor.

She retches, bubbles of spittle forming as she regurgitates some of the foul liquid. She wipes at her mouth with her handkerchief. She is ashamed. The shock shows in her eyes . . . then the pain . . . then a sense of suspicion, followed lastly by understanding.

She grips her white apron just above where the hotel's initials are embroidered in blue on the pocket. *HBR.*

She clutches her stomach, releases the pressure, and falls to the floor, letting go of the handkerchief, which floats under the bed and rests on the ground.

Her striped white dress creates waves as she is dragged along the floor by the most brutal of hands. Dark-red tiling, pink marble steps, a graveled pathway. She is now in the garden, her body being hauled along the neatly manicured lawn.

Her feet are elegantly clad in black goatskin ankle boots with fine ivory buttons, a marked difference from her lowly maid's uniform. Leaving a trace in the grass, the pretty points are no longer polished, but scuffed and grubby.

Lampposts dot the grounds. The night is peaceful, in contrast to her desperate attempts to grab hold of anything she can . . . earth, stone, grass. Her work-worn nails, although cut short, are ripped to the quick as she digs at the soil.

Waxy saliva continues to foam at the corners of her cracked lips.

Her eventual scream pierces the hush of the night air.

With a final jerking motion, her body is now inert, left abandoned just below a tamarisk tree.

She remains conscious a little while longer. She hears hurried footsteps leaving the scene. She stares up at the sky but doesn't really see it. She can't focus now. Perhaps she is in a state of shock. How swiftly she has darted through life—as fleetingly as a shooting star.

The moon shines down upon her flushed face. She looks so serene beneath her mask of suffering.

And so it is, dear reader, as an invisible spectator that I, Miss Gabriella Fletcher, have repeatedly imagined this most dreadful event. It is a story that found me through a chance encounter.

Who knows what really happened that night?

Yet it seems the images I describe here are forever burned into my mind's eye.

This isn't something you will have read about. The story never made the dailies for reasons you will soon come to know. But I have had the mixed fortunes to learn of the details behind this case, the elements hidden from the public.

It is now time this story was told.

1

LES PAVOTS

The very same morning of this hideous crime, without having the foggiest idea that my destiny was tied irrevocably with that of this poor young girl, I walked at a brisk pace under the strong winter sun. I had my own worries and demons to chase, you understand.

Clasping a torn-off piece of newspaper, I crossed the passenger footbridge over the railway line at the town station. It was dusty underfoot. February tends to be a clear and dry month in this part of the world, and this one was no different, for there had been no rain for several weeks.

I was coming from my dreary boarding house, from a room I had been calling home for nine months now, since my hasty departure from the residence of Lady Sarah Clarence. It was my refuge, somewhere to lick my wounds, a place to hide away from my humiliation and distress.

Lady Sarah . . . No, I mustn't think about her. Not now.

I scurried along the coastal streets toward the Villa les Pavots, the address in the advertisement. It stated,

Seeking an educated and distinguished member of staff for the giving of astute cultural advice and guidance. Please apply directly and in person to Mademoiselle Filomena Giglio, Villa les Pavots, Chemin Vicinal Saint-Nicolas.

Perhaps this was my destiny, here on this very page, between an endorsement for an anticonsumption tincture and a proposal to acquire a townhouse on the Croisette. I had no idea how much this meeting would turn my life upside down. It was one of those defining moments.

So, this Filomena woman must be the governess of the house? Possibly Italian?

I took off my gloves and hat. It was quite a steep climb up to the villa, and I wanted to feel a little more at ease. My hair was tied up in a braid and was starting to come loose, partly because I was perspiring and partly due to the swift sea breeze. My hair, which has been described as strawberry blonde, fell into strands about my unadorned neck and ears. Fortunately, I was wearing a dress that cleared my ankles, which meant it stayed free of the dust and dirt from the streets just that much more.

I was walking through a newly constructed neighborhood, not far from the Boulevard de la Foncière, which, until recently, had been deeply entrenched in the countryside. Real estate speculation had provoked an economic crisis in the region, and bankruptcy was now rife among the local population, particularly in Cannes.

Who could have guessed that what was nothing more than a small fishing village just a few decades earlier would become a city brimming with unscrupulous profit seekers?

Banks closed down, shops were selling goods at a loss, and families taken in by the illusion of it all lost their very honor.

But here, just next to the main boulevard, traces of the old life could still be spotted. The divine scents of olive trees, tiny orange groves, and oleanders filled the air despite the coal fumes from the nearby train station.

I strode past the Mon Plaisir private hotel on my left and the convent on my right. The small coastal road took me as far as the monumental Hôtel Central. As I passed the majestic gateway in front of the gardens, I came upon a group of very slight, pale children—orphans, I imagined—walking two by two in their matching black capes. At the front of the line, two energetic nuns bounced along the pavement. I stopped, wiped my brow, and continued uphill.

And then there it was. The Villa les Pavots.

It was a very à la mode structure with a balcony on the second floor. There was no shortage of this type of architecture along the coastline. I hate the style and find it to be out of place in the Mediterranean. The home looked just like a chalet you'd find in the Alps, but added to it were English bow windows—of all things! A tasteless ragtag mixture with a mawkish edge, an attempt at being charming, which I found reeking of desperation.

The rosebushes were already blooming, on account of the mild weather. Although adding an artistic grace to the building's facade, the roses, too, were unnaturally sophisticated for this part of the world.

A vehicle was *in situ*, and how magnificent it was! A stunning landau in a modern canary yellow. Not far from where I stood was another fashionable little mode of transport. A spanking-new phaeton was parked in front of the main entrance. Two uniformed domestic staff were to-ing and fro-ing hurriedly between the vehicle and the house, shouting out to each other as they did so.

They were carrying bags and cases and attaching them to the back of the carriage. The horse whinnied nervously.

I could hear loud voices emanating from above. I peered up to the balcony and saw that the windows leading out to it were wide open. I could hear a woman, her cries far from stifled. Her voice was strident, with an intonation that could only be described as unladylike. Could this same woman be the mistress of such a house, tasteless as it was? Her manner was rough, to say the very least.

"You've never given a damn about me, have you, Eugène? You're just going to leave me in the lurch?"

Good grief! What was this place? Had the master and mistress abandoned their home? Were these servants I heard? Were they stealing everything in sight?

And then a man's voice—a timid, sheepish whimper.

"Don't take this so badly! I beg you, please, Filo, a little decorum!"

Filo? As in *Filomena*. So it *was* the woman who'd placed the advertisement.

"I'll be back, I promise you, as soon as I've won a medal. My parents will be at ease then. They'll be proud of me."

This was an educated man. I could tell by his diction. He seemed young, well brought up, and he wasn't losing his temper despite the insults being hurled at him.

"What about all those pretty words yesterday? All that talk of love? Was it just nonsense?"

"Please, my darling, calm yourself. I cannot allow them to disinherit me. If I must go all the way to Madagascar to avoid just that, then I'll do so. I have no other choice!"

"But you could die!"

"Oh, this war against the Merina monarchy is nothing but a joke, Filo! We'll make mincemeat of those cowards!"

Sometimes, we have an inkling of what fate may have in store for us. And here, I don't know why, these words cut me to the core. This fellow was bad news through and through. I knew it.

"Charlatan! That's what you are! This war suits you! As if it's the adventure of a lifetime with a capital *A*! You speak such filthy lies!"

Ah! The woman had the same intuition as I'd just had! I smiled.

I took my cigar box out of my handbag and searched for my matches. I had a quarter of a cigar left. I'd been saving it, making it last indefinitely, or that was my intention, at least. Unfortunately, the tobacconist hadn't given me credit for some time. I'd asked him to send the note to Lady Sarah, but it must have been returned unpaid. I found my matches, and as I lit the stump of my last cigar, I hesitated. Perhaps the smell would give a poor impression. I didn't care enough, though, and I gave in to my whim.

The thought of not getting this placement didn't overwhelm me with torment. Now that I had spent the final centime Lady Sarah had sent me out the door with, this placement was my last card, and I was playing it with a certain sense of fatalism. I was putting myself decidedly in the hands of Providence.

If I found myself on track for a new venture in life, I would cling to it, but only half-heartedly, passively, without enthusiasm, and with little hope. This is because I had lost my taste for life when I lost Lady Sarah. If I didn't get this post, all that was left for me was to finish the task I hadn't managed to complete the night before—letting the waters overtake me and forever ridding this world of the bitter Gabriella Fletcher.

A black cat unexpectedly fled from the front doors and rushed between my feet, almost knocking me off balance.

As I puffed on what remained of my smoke, I continued to listen in while observing the villa more attentively. An abundant garden lay to the front, boasting a palm tree, a banana plant, a japonica, and the rosebush that stretched up to the second-floor windows, all in bloom. Farther toward the front gate, I could see a canopy swing, an ornate octagonal pergola with an invasive *muscat* trellis. To the left of the entrance sat a wrought-iron bench with a few scattered wicker chairs. To all this was added a double iron gate, pathways covered with grit and chipping, marbled stone steps up to the front door, and a zinc porch awning covering them.

There was a new smell about the place. Even the earthenware tiles—decorated with bright-red poppies and the name of the villa:

Les Pavots—were shiny and looked as if they had been placed there only recently.

I knew the Villa les Lotus in the Russian quarter, as I'd visited its incredible Japanese gardens. Despite my ineptitude in the sport, I'd been invited there to play a game of mixed-doubles lawn tennis with Lady Sarah Clarence—*my* Lady Sarah—against Jean de Persigny and his sister, Marie. But that was before my fall from grace.

I'd never heard of the Les Pavots and for good reason. The house wasn't quite up to the standard to which I had become accustomed. In fact, compared with where I'd been, it looked like a custodian's lodge.

I heard a door slam. Footsteps. Eugène, or at least I assumed it was he, scurried out of the building. He was moving quickly, almost running.

I'd guessed correctly. He was young, around twenty or twenty-five. In order to give me something to do with my hands, I took out my father's watch, which I kept on a chain in a little pocket on my bodice.

I sensed something moving above my eye line. A slip of a girl who appeared to be in her early twenties stepped out onto the balcony and leaned over the balustrade. She had unkempt spicy brunette hair and was wearing flimsy indoor clothes in complete disarray—pink voile with organdy layering and sky-blue ribbons fluttering in the breeze.

"That's right! You get out of here! Go! Go and hide behind your parents! You gutless craven!"

Gutless craven? She had an unexpectedly wide range of vocabulary, this one! I chuckled as I leaned against the gate and watched the scene further unfold. The actors in this drama were so focused on their exuberant lines that I doubted they would notice me.

"Come, Lola," said the young man, now having stopped and turned back toward the girl. "Pull yourself together. You're going to regret saying all that. I don't wish you to forget how comfortably off you'll be!"

Lola? Hadn't he called her Filo earlier? Were there two women up there? This was some complicated business I was getting myself into!

He sighed. "My dear Filo, you do tire me so."

Ah! It was the same woman!

"I am my own master," he continued. "Do not assume that I obey my father. You have no idea of the sacrifices I have made, nor would you appreciate them."

As he turned and crossed the front courtyard, he gained a spring in his step, clearly pleased with himself.

Filo, Lola—I had no idea—burst into tears quite dramatically. She cried out in broken sentences, her sobs making her hard to understand.

". . . rental records . . . cheating . . . you I want . . . how can you . . . lie . . ."

But Eugène was no longer listening. He walked past me and jumped up into the driver's seat of his carriage without giving me a second glance and seized the reins.

"Farewell, my darling! I have no doubt you will be treated like a queen during my absence! Stop your braying, woman. You'll wake up the good sisters!"

Lola let out a piercing scream, and a sudden downpour of jewelry fell into the garden below.

"Here! Take your gifts! I don't want them anymore!"

She was aiming some of the pieces directly at Eugène, but he was beyond the open gate by this point, and they all fell into various flower beds.

Eugène cracked the whip. The horse broke into a canter and headed downhill at a breakneck speed, kicking up a cloud of dust as it left. As I reached the end of my cigar, I stubbed it out under my flat walking shoe and then patted myself down. It was now my turn to enter the fray.

I approached the front door just as it opened, and a woman in her fifties appeared. She wore a standard cloth dress with a dotted pattern and an apron of questionable cleanliness. Her chestnut hair was poorly styled into a bun at the back of her neck, and streaks of gray could be seen at the front. She had a pasty complexion, but her cheeks burned red. Her countenance showed a serious appetite for life despite her negligence when it came to dressing. She was startled when she saw me, for I hadn't even had time to knock. She took a step back.

"Yes? Can I help you?"

I showed her the piece of paper in my hand. "I'm here about the position."

"Oh, I see. Well, you're a brave one, I must say, huh? They're hardly queuing up for this job! The position is still open. Wide open at that!"

"Really? Yet, the announcement was published over a day ago."

"Don't fret yourself about that. Let me pick up this lot outside, and I'll show you where to go." She stepped out into the garden, bent down, and started to gather the jewelry and place it carefully into an elegant box she held in her hands.

I felt obliged to help her. I followed and studied the ground, finding a pearl necklace in among the flowers, too light to have been genuine, and a ruby bracelet that shone like tinted glass.

As I lifted my head to hand them over to the servant, our eyes met. My eyes met *hers*. Filomena Giglio's eyes, observing me from the balcony. Light, bright, and piercing. *Oh my, my!* This was something I hadn't expected. Her eyes were green—or were they turquoise? They were eyes that certainly didn't seem to fit with the voice I'd heard, nor the language she'd used, nor her age, nor her general comportment. These eyes seemed to express experience, a degree of frankness, and, most importantly, intelligence. The sort of emotional intelligence that is a rare find indeed. Perhaps this hypnotic stare was nothing but a ruse, but whatever the case, I was struck by her, and this was unsettling beyond measure.

She blushed the color of a damask rose and rushed back indoors. This broke the spell. A shiver went down my spine, and yet I was warm. I failed to understand what had just happened.

"Follow me. Your name? Mine's Rosalie," said the maid.

I rummaged up my sleeve and pulled out my visitor's card. "If you would be so kind as to announce the presence of *Miss Gabriella Fletcher.*"

"Announce the presence of . . . ? Ha! That's a good'un! I won't be making any formal announcements! Wouldn't even know where to start!"

She laughed as she took the card from my fingertips. I followed her through the entrance hall, taken aback by the decor and furnishings. I felt an unforeseen rush of contradictory and disturbing feelings.

The hallway was dark and perhaps appeared more so following my time spent outside in the bright winter sun. We walked past a ravishing Louis XVI sideboard with a host of everyday objects scattered along the surface: an enamel ewer filled with cloudy water, a percale washcloth with traces of pinkish makeup rubbed into it, and a bouquet of flowers in a vase that had most certainly seen better days. There was a strange odor of face powder mixed with an orange-blossom fragrance, sweat, and stagnant water.

What I had witnessed earlier between Eugène and the lady of the house had made me smile, but it now seemed to feel more poignant. It must have had something to do with that look she gave me. It had awakened within me the memory of my departure from Lady Sarah.

Feeling so utterly miserable and dragging my heavy carpetbag behind me, I'd turned back and hoped, nay begged, for a final gesture, a smile, a simple nod, maybe even a word: *No, don't leave, it was nothing but a silly farce, a lovers' tiff, it was to test you, to see how you would react!*

I would have accepted that the cruelest of jokes had been played upon me, whatever it took, if she would have just allowed me to stay with her. How I'd begged, how distressed I'd been. Especially as I'd just witnessed Filo . . . Lola . . . Mademoiselle Giglio . . . go through the very same experience before her Eugène upped and left.

I tried to clear my mind of any thoughts of Sarah and of my encounter with those icy waters the night before. I had to focus on my reasons for being there: the position, the advertisement.

And at that moment, as I was following Rosalie up a dark, cold, and dubious-smelling stairwell, I asked myself the following questions: Had destiny held out its hand to show me what I already knew? To revive my deep feelings through the heartbreak of this Mademoiselle Giglio? Why was I here and not forever resting in the dark waters?

2

Filomena Giglio, or "Lola"

As we reached the landing, I quickly returned my hat atop my head. It was a boater, which I knew was unusual for a woman, but I was in no mood for flowers and frills and fashion. I never was and had never been.

Rosalie opened a door and said, "I am announcing the presence of someone! An English someone!" She gave me the jewelry box, handed back my card, and stepped to one side to let me pass. She then plodded back down the stairwell, stomping her feet as she went.

I could still hear her muttering, "I can't be doing with all this! I've got a ratatouille on the stove . . ."

Members of this household were clearly accustomed to familiar, almost vulgar language, and the relationship between Mademoiselle Giglio and the maid/housekeeper/cook—whoever she was—seemed very relaxed.

I felt intimidated as I stepped into the room. I didn't take in much detail at first. The only thing I really noticed were three long freestanding cheval mirrors arranged as if to give the impression of a large mural. The setup was such that as soon as someone entered the room, the first thing she would see was an illusion of three people . . . but it would be the same person from three different angles. Of course, in this case, it was the reflection of the young woman from the balcony. Three of her.

The aroma of citrus fruits had hit me as soon as the door had opened. Even though the window was letting in fresh air, the perfume was strong, almost suffocating.

Somewhat troubled by her threefold reflection, I turned toward the real woman, the one in the flesh. She stood to my right next to a pink velvet chesterfield. She had covered the floaty outfit I'd seen earlier with a blood-red kimono boasting an orange-and-pink floral print. Her satin skin, the way she moved, the sparkle in her eyes . . . She mesmerized me the way a snake mesmerizes its prey.

Between the fireplace and the window, there was an Edison phonograph, the latest trend, surrounded by cylinders covered in waxy paper. I'd seen something like it before. Lady Sarah had had a friend in London who'd acquired one.

The demoiselle stared at me. She wasn't anywhere near as slight as I'd thought. In fact, she was a voluptuous, full girl, her curves generous under her kimono. A true French beauty.

Her thick hair looked wild but silky, almost animallike. Her eyes were like two deep emerald lakes, so alive. Her mouth curled into a mischievous, wide smile. This was a mouth made for laughing, singing, seduction. There was something irresistible about her, something that held me captive. Her gaze rested on me, and I found myself holding my breath. Several seconds later, as I gulped down some air, I wondered whether she'd noticed how taken I was with her.

I lowered my head, waiting for her to speak. Everyone knows, when interviewing for a position, the mistress of the house speaks first to explain exactly what she is seeking, and then the applicant asks questions about the terms and conditions of the post.

I knew my place.

But not a peep came out of this woman's mouth. She appeared indecisive. Was she wondering what I was doing there? And yet, Rosalie had made it more than clear. She must have still been caught up in thoughts of Eugène. Or she was expecting me to say something? But I had no idea what.

I handed over the box with her cheap costume jewelry in it. As if reading my mind, she said, "Yes, I know, they're not worth anything. But they were gifts, you see?"

Her physical charm was now matched, magnified even, by her voice. It was like water flowing from its source. So natural and bright.

"I don't suppose I'll ever get over this," she said. "I'm not just in pain here. It's so much more than that, believe me. Yes, I know that it's fairly inconvenient, this whole being *jilted* business, but it's infuriating too! The truth of it is, I loved that man. I fell for him the first time I ever saw his face. And it was so endearing, the way he courted me. It was wonderful! He was nothing like that friend of his, that horrid Philémon. What a boor! I thought I might have managed to hit Eugène with a couple of bracelets just now. Even though I know they're worthless metal, the sentimental value counts, doesn't it?"

I didn't know what to say. Was I to echo her using the same familiar tone, as if we were old acquaintances? Or was I to maintain my reserve and prove that I was more than capable of fulfilling my functions with discretion?

I opted for something between the two. "I believe sentimental value to be superior to financial value," I replied flatly. "It is the reflection of the heart, and—"

"Enough! No need for flattery with me. It's of no use. You've seen everything here, and you haven't fled. Bravo! I take my hat off to you! You're the one I need."

"Um . . ."

"To be honest, I do wonder if you have any idea what you have gotten yourself into here. You look too good to be true. What on earth has made you apply for the position here?"

"I don't understand. I . . ." She had rendered me speechless.

I beheld the room again. It was easier than speaking. I noticed several things I hadn't seen when I'd first entered. On the table was an ashtray brimming with the stubs of cigarillos, cigars, and lipstick-marked cigarettes. Alongside it were dozens of cosmetic pots, hairpins, and garters.

Striped pink-and-yellow stockings lay stranded in a pile in the corner, and a red satin corset had been strewn on the floor behind one of the armchairs. The color of the corset alone told me all I needed to know about where I was and what this girl did for a living.

My eyes met hers. Her cheeks tinged a delicate shade of pink, and she said pensively, "Oh! I see you've just realized what . . . Listen, all things considered . . ."

She sat down and invited me to do the same.

I took off my hat and gloves. This was becoming a bit of a habit now. I carefully removed my outer coat so it wouldn't crease, folded it, and placed it over the back of my chair. Before sitting, I gave her the newspaper advertisement I was still holding. It was now dry but had been fairly damaged after it had had a thorough soaking the night before.

She took it gingerly. "How odd! This paper . . . What happened to it?"

"It inadvertently took a bath," I said in as light a tone as I could muster, but my voice betrayed my pain.

"I see," she said, smiling kindly and observing me more attentively. But she couldn't possibly have guessed.

I coughed, a little embarrassed by the attention.

She continued, "Well, that's quite unusual, isn't it? So, what happened to you? How did you end up here?"

She wasn't speaking of my mode of transport, I was sure of that!

I don't know how she managed it, but the way she spoke to me, the compassion in her voice, forced all my emotions to the surface. My voice trembled, and I had trouble holding back the tears. "I lost my position in unfortunate circumstances . . ."

"Hushhh, hushhh now. Stop! Please don't continue any further. I know you're about to lie to me."

I understood that what she was attempting to do was spare me the embarrassment of a flood of tears that I would regret.

She added, "I trust you have all the qualities I'm looking for. You've been fortunate enough to have been well educated. You're . . . English? From a good family, I presume? You enjoy sports, you've lost your fortune, and you're all alone in this cruel world. I also suspect that you've been through some particularly difficult events recently, but that you've lived through worse. I might add that your particular tastes when it comes to . . . affections of the heart . . . No, that would perhaps be going too far. I don't wish to be indiscreet. I want you to look kindly on me. This is how it should be. I am sure we will look kindly on one another. Listen, it's all very well seeking paid employment, but your current situation isn't as bad as mine, believe me. You'll be better accepted in this town than I am, I'm sure."

My mouth dropped open. I was amazed at how directly she spoke. I didn't want her to see how shocked I was, so I did my best to keep my British stiff upper lip, but I couldn't help glancing quickly in the mirror to see if there was anything about my appearance that had given me away so easily. I attempted to explain myself. "An excellent education? Yes. I suppose so. My manners, the way I sit . . . Is that what you mean?"

"Exactly. Don't look so worried. It's glaringly obvious. You folded your coat so carefully. You were perhaps ever so slightly offended that a maid didn't take it from you before you put your derrière so tentatively on that chair. Were you scared you were going to catch something sitting down? Syphilis, perhaps?"

That was pure provocation, and I didn't like it. It was not the time or place to respond, but why willfully use such words as *derrière* and *syphilis*? Was she trying to embarrass me? Force my hand into leaving? If that was her intention, then I was certain she'd fail. She wasn't going to get the better of me. Whom did she assume she was dealing with? Some gutless woman fallen on hard times?

"You've come from money. I can tell by the quality of the fabrics you're wearing. Yes, the shades are somewhat those of a schoolmarm—black and white, very tiresome—but the fabric! Taffeta, raw silk, Calais lace. Where's the twill? The cheesecloth? Simple cotton from the colonies? Nothing of the kind for Mademoiselle . . . ?"

"Fletcher. Miss Gabriella Fletcher."

She winked at me. "I'm sure there's more to your name than that. There always is with the *petite noblesse*. Come on! Out with it!"

I said reticently, "My father was Baron Fletcher of Ramsey. That makes me the Honorable Gabriella Fletcher."

"Ha! The Honorable Gabriella Fletcher. It wasn't hard to guess! It's all in the details. You're high bred! Your shoes. Refined leather, but solid. And the laces are so masculine. You've been brought up high, but not too high. You don't play by the rules. I'm right, aren't I?"

I shook my head, annoyed. But she launched into it again. "You've no money, or you wouldn't be in this position. Plus, you obviously didn't even have enough to take a cab here. You're covered in dust. You're not a true aristocrat, though! If so, you wouldn't be seeking employment like this."

I bit back at her arrogantly: "Is the examination over?"

She smiled and continued. "You're priggish, but that's more than likely something to do with your nationality. We *Cannois* find that accent of yours a little pretentious. You couldn't have been aware of this, but what might have been your undoing elsewhere works in your favor here."

"Oh, really?"

"Yes. Your fake good manners. Your wanting to make a good impression just to get a job. Your stiff attitude. Your forced pomposity.

Despite all that, I sense you're a real tough woman. I bet you'll give me a run for my money, Miss Honorable Fletcher. You're hired. That's if you want me as your mistress, of course. I can tell you're starting to ask yourself some serious questions about this house, aren't you?"

"Well . . ."

"Yes, I know, you don't have to give me your answer straightaway. I also feel it important to be frank with you. No one else has yet applied for this position." She giggled a little. "My reputation must have seen them off! It's easy enough to find out about me, you know? You didn't ask around beforehand?"

"Um, no. I . . ."

"Ah, I see," she whispered. "I understand a little better. Anyone would have told you, Miss Fletcher. Before you present yourself, you should try your best to become informed of the moral stature of the master or mistress of the house." Her giggle turned to a fit of laughter. "Well, now you may consider yourself informed. I hope we will become friends. I feel as if we are already! I've adopted you! I want none of this *madame* and *mademoiselle* lark. Call me Filomena. No, Filo. Erm, no. Lola. What do *you* think?"

"What do I think of what?"

"Of Lola as a name? Do you accept that a demoiselle of my standing can use a nom de guerre? It's a question that's been bothering me for a while. I need to make a decision. I'm employing you for help with this sort of thing, you know? I'm utterly incapable of deliberating on a subject for too long. Especially anything serious. So? Your view on the matter?"

"I consider Lola to be a most excellent choice for your . . . *situation*. It's short, it sticks in the mind easily. It's piquant. It's lively and exotic."

"Sold! And what of your remuneration? I propose sixty francs a month initially. You will, of course, be lodged and fed, your clothes will be laundered, and so on. You'll make some serious savings, won't you?

Your appointments will be variable and will obviously increase with the more guests I receive. You see, in my profession, there are often surprises. But I'm no dolt! You haven't asked a thing about the arrangements yet. Go ahead! Ask your questions! I'll answer to the best of my ability, and then we can move on to something else."

She shouted, "Rosalie, bring up some tea! English people drink tea!"

What she'd said had taken me by surprise, and the unanticipated yelling had made me half jump out of my skin. This position wasn't going to be restful, that was a certainty, but it would do me some good. In a setting such as this, I'd have no time to brood or to dwell on dark thoughts. This would all be new to me, and there'd be enough happening to occupy my mind. I quickly thought of some questions one should ask when being interviewed professionally.

I stared into the distance, avoiding eye contact, and asked, "How many servants do you have here?"

"Two. Rosalie, the poor thing, lost her work as a cook in a private home in Nice when they cut down on their domestic staff. These are hard times, you see. That was three years ago. It was around that time that Eugène was having this place built for me. Nice, isn't it? The second member of the staff is Gustave. He's a good man. He repairs everything, empties the midden, and takes care of the vegetable plot and the horse. Oh yes! Can you believe it? I have a carriage and a horse! Isn't it wild?"

"You don't have a lady's maid?"

A crisp laugh preceded her response. "Someone to do my hair and dress me, you mean? Well, Rosalie helps me with my corsets, and I have a hairdresser who comes to the house. I paint my own face. I prefer it that way. I even make my own products. Any other questions?"

"Of course! I haven't really said anything about my expectations of you! I mean, I haven't told you why I placed the advertisement. Actually, it's you who will define my expectations and my needs."

"Meaning what?"

"It's simple enough. I don't want to be hearing jeers and mocking tones everywhere I go. I sometimes get confused with the names of writers, painters, and musicians, let alone their works, and I haven't the faintest idea whether they've been dead for an age or whether they're still in the land of the living."

"So, you need a . . ."

She let out a sigh of relief. "You've got it. You're perfect. What do you think?"

I was just about to reply that I had nothing to lose when she added, "No, don't tell me your decision just yet. Wait until you've had your tea. I hope Rosalie remembers to bring a few biscuits."

She smiled at me. It was somewhat exaggerated, as if she wanted to win me over. I thought that she had probably done much of the same as a child when she wanted to get around the teacher if she'd been naughty.

I really wanted to laugh, but I held it in. I didn't want her to think I was mocking her in any way. I couldn't believe how my fortune had changed in a single afternoon. It felt as though an enormous weight had been lifted from my shoulders. This house was a notch below what I'd been expecting, but I liked it. Was it because this fresh young woman was so contrary in character to Sarah?

She was still observing me, still hoping to convince me that she knew how to behave in a way that becomes a mistress of a house such as this.

"Have we done everything correctly? Let's draw this to a conclusion. Do you have a letter of recommendation from your former employer?"

I felt my face redden. Lady Sarah hadn't given me anything. She hadn't even glanced at me as I'd left, let alone furnished me with a reference! I doubt she could have imagined my current circumstances. I pretended to search through my bag. There was nothing in there but tissue paper and matches. She could see I was getting more agitated by the second.

"It's of no matter," she trilled. "I don't believe in certificates and letters of recommendation and the like. I believe in people's eyes."

I was starting to understand her. She came across as a little feather-brained, but was it an act? Because some of the nonsense she came out with was actually quite meaningful. She was subtler than one would give her credit for. And she had an exceptional gift when it came to reading the human subject.

I looked her straight in the eye and was about to speak when Rosalie opened the door, strode heavily footed over to the leaf table by the window, and banged down a laden silver tray.

At the very same moment, someone rang the bell outside.

3

AN UNEXPECTED MESSENGER

Lola, because that's what we'd decided Filomena Giglio would be known as from now on, startled out of her seat and scurried toward the balcony.

"Oh! A visitor!"

Rosalie mumbled to herself as she watched her mistress almost knock the cups and saucers from the tray with her hasty movement. And these were no ordinary cups! These were rococo *de Sèvres*.

"What's the point in using the good service for just any old body!" she complained. She grabbed the teapot by its handle and lifted it with force.

How brutal! I couldn't stand the idea of something happening to such a stunning object, so I placed my hand gently on her arm.

"Leave it, I'll do it."

Lola barked, "Yes, Rosalie! Just go and open the door! For who knows better how to serve tea than an Englishwoman? Come over here, Miss Fletcher! Come and take a gander at the man. Perhaps he's someone you know?"

"I doubt that," I retorted.

Rosalie left the room, slamming the door behind her. I joined Lola on the balcony, but made sure I stayed back a little.

A man waited below. He was not very tall, but upright and with a robust figure. He was peering down the hill as he tapped his foot impatiently. He seemed lost in thought, staring over to the Hôtel Central and its stunning gardens. The way he stood almost to attention gave the impression he was a military man.

His light-brown hair, with a reddish tinge, curled naturally over his forehead. Above the rebellious hair on his upper lip was a straight nose and below it a small mouth, wide chin, and the thick neck of someone who labored. And yet the way he held himself and his dress were quite the opposite of your typical workingman.

A delicately woven jacket in anthracite gray with fine stripes fitted snugly over his colossal shoulders. He looked like a finely dressed cart horse.

He held a bowler in his left hand with a pair of butter-colored leather gloves and a gold-headed cane. So he'd decided to take off his hat and gloves just as I had. A good idea when making that climb!

Without warning, and before I could stop her, Lola started waving and shouting out to him.

"Hey! I'm up here! Who are you? Who are you here for?"

He looked up. The movement was swift, as if he'd been stung by a bee. He smiled at us.

"Hello there! I'm here for a Mademoiselle Giglio. I've been sent by a neighbor of mine. A Monsieur de Bréville."

"Sweet Jesus! Eugène's friend is here!" cried Lola. "Thank God! I thought it might be something to do with that vulture Philémon!" Then she shouted, "Rosalie! What are you doing? Why haven't you opened up for this gentleman? He's a friend of Eugène!"

She spun around and dashed back inside. She tapped at her cheeks in front of the mirrors and pawed at her hair.

"Should I tie it up or have it hanging loose?"

I didn't give her an answer, because I could tell she wouldn't hear a word. She was prey to a great sense of agitation.

"Eugène has sent him along with his apologies . . . He wants to come back, but he dare not . . . He's sent his friend over as a scout to find out my feelings . . ."

As she daubed red lipstick over her sumptuous mouth, I returned to my seat and set about serving the tea.

"Sit down calmly," I said, "and get ahold of yourself."

My soothing voice had the same effect as I imagined plying her temples with cold water would. She stared at me as she approached the table, sat down with force, and straightened her back. She opened her satin kimono, which was barely covering her anyway, and smoothed it down to remove any creases.

"You're right," she snapped. "You see? You're definitely the right one for me."

Rosalie shuffled in and moved aside quickly for the man who walked in ahead of her. She was holding out a card behind his back and roared in her strong accent, almost as if mocking the guest, "Because I must announce people now, allow me to inform you of the presence of . . . this beautiful man, Guy de Mopassaaane, a man who writes letters."

He walked farther into the room and bowed, to which I responded with a slight nod and Lola with a flurry of eyelashes as she tapped her fingers together feverishly.

"You write letters?" Lola said. "Have you got one for me?"

I interrupted quickly, "No, Lola. Rosalie means to say Guy de Maupassant, homme de lettres. It means he has a certain level of education."

"I understood. I was just joking!" Lola exclaimed, getting to her feet and managing to save herself at the same time. "Take a seat, my good fellow. Let me present my friend Miss Gabriella Fletcher. She's English. I'm the young lady you're looking for."

The man who Rosalie had announced so glibly took the chair offered by Lola but first rotated it before sinking into its soft folds. He had turned it away from the mirrors.

"You'll forgive me," he said with a light tone. "I detest seeing myself."

"Really?" asked Lola. "It's my *raison d'être*."

"Oh? My view is that they fog the mind. They make me lose the very notion of my own self. I no longer recognize Maupassant. It's as if I am another. Sometimes, it is as if I am no one at all. I find it very troubling, so I look in mirrors as little as possible."

Guy de Maupassant was here? I was in the same room as one of the best-selling authors of our time?

I was a great fan of his works and so felt a little . . . shy? I'd spent so many moments of happiness with his short stories and poetry. This was a true delight. I felt Maupassant had a very particular aura. He knew how to describe the human soul and condition with a complete absence of moral judgment, which I found to be very much worthy of respect.

"So you've studied. You're an homme de lettres? What is your subject area?" Lola questioned in a worldly voice, which caused Maupassant to smile.

"I'm a journalist. I chronicle. And sometimes, I write stories. I even managed to get down a novel last year."

"A novel!" exclaimed Lola, genuinely impressed.

"Yes, *Une Vie*," I said with respect. "It's a beautiful book, Monsieur de Maupassant."

"Have you really read it, or are you just being agreeable?" he asked.

"Yes, I've read it," I said, annoyed. "I know it hasn't been easy for you to sell. Your publishers censored it, didn't they? Hachette, if I remember? Wasn't it illegal to sell it in train stations for some time?"

He howled with laughter and cried out, "Quite right! They tell me they found a frightful amount of scandal within those pages. Did you know that they own the moral rights on all book contents that they sell? Something to do with protecting the heads of the family. Luckily their consciences soon disappeared once the sales figures started pouring in. As soon as *Une Vie* proved itself to be the huge success it was, they lifted the ban, and copies started to sell from train stations. And Silvus—the humorist, do you know him?—openly ridiculed them! It was hilarious!"

"How so?" asked Lola.

He declared in a booming voice, imitating the comic, *"The danger for passengers isn't that the train derails. No, indeed, the danger for passengers is that everyone will spot their blushes as they try to covertly read* Une Vie.*"*

This little scene amused Lola, and she clapped her hands heartily.

"I remember you!" she said. "You were in the newspapers this winter! You set fire to your bedchamber, and the fire brigade had to intervene!"

"That's right," he boasted. "I'm the inflammable type!"

"I've read your stories, the work of your quill," I insisted, annoyed at the frivolous turn the conversation was taking.

"I'm flattered. It's such an odd phenomenon: when a book knows success, it is considered good taste to have a copy in one's library, to offer it as a gift, to quote it when and wherever possible . . . but reading it does not necessarily enter the equation."

"I'll remember that," replied Lola. "It's what I'll do, in that case. So, if this book of yours is famous, Monsieur de Maupassant, I must acquire a copy as soon as possible. You'll sign it for me, won't you? As a matter of fact, I remember hearing quite a lot about you when I posed for Jules. It was back in 1881, before I moved in here with Eugène."

"You pose?" he said, his eyebrows raised.

"Sometimes. At least, there was a time when I did so quite frequently. When passing painters would see my portrait hanging in Numa Blanc's window down on the Croisette, they would come and ask me. But hours and hours without moving, sometimes on one knee or leaning on my elbows . . . it can quickly become a torture! Such a *bore!*"

"This portrait you speak of—is it in his boutique's window display? It must be a thing of wonder!" declared Maupassant ironically, ready to mock her further, no doubt sensing she was showing off about her beauty.

"Oh no, my dear! It's terrible! Numa Blanc visited the enfleurage workshop at the Erhmann perfumery, where I was working at the time. He was completing some research for some illustrations he had to do. He chose me out of everyone there! I assume it was largely to do with the fact that my corsage was open due to the heat and that I'd lifted my skirts a little. He took me as I was, with no style to my hair and my clothes in complete disarray. All over town we went—to all the famous fashionable spots: in front of the palace, along the promenade, to the Suquet, the grandiose villas, and all the way to the top of the hillside."

"That's quite original! Outdoor portraits?"

"He said that photographs should be taken in open spaces, as is the case with paintings, and that we shouldn't be confined to a studio. He gave me a franc per shot and a ton of bonbons."

"You weren't paid so handsomely!"

"Is that a joke? We must have taken at least thirty shots over two Sundays, which meant I earned more than six months' salary in just two days compared to the perfumery. But the glory didn't really start pouring down until he enlarged the picture and displayed it in his boutique on the Croisette. He did it using daguerreotype with the Suquet in the background! He received several requests from artists passing through Cannes. And that's how I became a model. I left the perfumery and rented a room of my very own on the Rue Grande."

"You stayed a model? That's your profession, is it?"

"Well, they said they were painters at first, you see. But it was just a name they gave themselves. They used it as a pretext to meet the young girl in the window. And . . . erm . . . then I met Eugène." She sighed as she uttered this last part.

"And you posed for the notorious Jules. For which painting?"

"Do you work for a bureau of investigation or something? Or is it for your next novel? It was an illustration for a perfume label. But in the end, it was used for everything—soaps, perfume, powder—and I didn't see a sou! He paid me just the one time! Scoundrel! Anyway, I just wanted to say that I remember hearing your story about the whores who go to holy communion. It was you who wrote that, wasn't it?"

He acquiesced with a half smile.

"Would you like to come and sit here next to me?" she simpered with a tone meant to imitate the manners of a worldly lady, a little like when a young child plays tea parties with friends.

"How could I refuse such charming company?" Maupassant said, raising his eyebrows and moving over to join Lola on the divan.

He didn't waste time, that one! His eyes lit up as he beheld us in turn. It seemed he enjoyed our contrasting appearances. The younger one—half-dressed, bathed in colors, and reeking of strong perfumes, the scents of a night of passion mixed with orange blossom and pomade. Then there was me, the austere redhead with the English accent, covered from head to toe in black and white with a muscular, rather masculine frame.

A reticence came upon us. We watched one another without uttering a syllable. The lightly dressed younger lady, showing off her figure to its best advantage, devoured the gentleman with her eyes. In turn, he stared fixedly at the more severe of the two women, in other words—me. If I could tell anything by a look, it was that he was yearning to break open my hard outer shell.

As for me, I admit I was taking pleasure contemplating the many expressions bestowed upon the pretty face of Lola and wondering if their number was infinite.

And so, the love triangle began.

Someone had to interrupt this strange intermission. It couldn't be me. It wasn't my place, was it? Yet this state of limbo was starting to feel eternal, so I broke it abruptly.

"You said you were here on behalf of Monsieur de Bréville?"

A smile from Lola. "How do you know Eugène?" she asked.

"Eugène? I can't say that I do, really. No, this isn't a message from Eugène."

"Well, who is this Monsieur de Bréville who sent you?"

"Ah, well, it's Edmond. Eugène's father. He is one of my neighbors at Étretat, and knowing that I was heading down to Cannes, he took advantage of the situation and gave me this missive. And very grateful I am, too, for it has given me the chance to meet—"

"His father?" interjected Lola, turning pale.

"Oh, where's my head?" said Maupassant. "Here. This is the letter I was asked to give you. I hope it's good news!"

Lola grabbed the slightly thick envelope and stared down at it for what seemed like minutes without daring to open it. I could sense how bereft she was. She held it out to me.

"Open it, Miss Fletcher. I can't do it."

For want of a letter opener, I took a butter knife from the table. After wiping remnants of grease onto a serviette, I used it to open the envelope. Several banknotes fell out as well as a notelet. Lola's cheeks reddened, but she had the reflex to catch the money before it all fell to the floor.

"Should I read it?" I asked.

"Go ahead."

I read aloud:

"'Mademoiselle, you will understand from this letter that all accounts priorly held by my son, Eugène, have now been blocked. The banknotes herein are intended to cover any immediate costs. I hope to never hear from you again.'"

Maupassant clambered to his feet, shocked. He made a compassionate gesture, his hand touching Lola's shoulder, and then he moved away with discretion.

I remained seated, confused by what I'd read. There were several thoughts racing through my mind. *That's a lot to take in for a young girl like Lola. So much . . . and all at once. Her lover leaves, and now she's bankrupt? How similar our stories are! How unbelievable is this!*

Lola was as still as a rock. Her face remained without expression. She then took the letter from my hand violently, tore it into dozens of pieces, and threw them into the air.

Maupassant and I watched nervously.

Lola opened the door and bellowed down the stairs, "Rosalie! Bring up some champagne! It's time to celebrate my new life!" Her tone and furious expression betrayed her. She didn't really want to celebrate anything.

"At least they've compensated you handsomely, haven't they?" Maupassant ventured.

"Just shut up! You call this compensation after everything he promised me? Mere scraps! You're just like him, I'm sure of it! Just like all men, in fact! Cowards and cheats! Nothing heals the wounds of a scorned woman, Monsieur Maupassant! I wonder if he knew about all this when he left earlier."

"I truly believe that these actions were performed behind his back," I said.

Maupassant exchanged a glance with me, not knowing whether to laugh or become angered at the accusations. But Lola hadn't finished with him yet.

"Don't be surprised if I consider all you men to be alike. You were in on it! You knew about this! Cowards—the whole lot of you!"

"B-but . . . ," stammered Maupassant, refusing to abandon his good manners. "This is a little *farcical*, isn't it? I played no part in this."

It was at this point that Rosalie entered with a bottle of champagne and three crystal flutes. Lola snatched the bottle and opened it without hesitation—it was clearly a habit. She flooded the glasses and thrust one on the both of us before raising her own.

"Monsieur de Maupassant and the Honorable Miss Fletcher of Ramsey, let us make a toast to my glorious new life! New beginnings! The house is still mine! My spoils of war!"

She swallowed the golden liquid in one gulp and within seconds had a second glass in hand. She stepped over to one of the armchairs and plonked herself down. I suspected she was so mortified, so humiliated, that it would be some time before she was able to forgive Maupassant for bearing witness to this entire sorry story.

I had to admit, I felt relief. I had noticed that she was starting to carry the smallest of torches for this man, and the fact that the situation had taken an about-face pleased me immensely.

4

Assume Positions

After dipping his mustache into his drink and then searching in vain for a clean napkin on the tray, Maupassant gave up the idea of speaking to me with dry facial hair and asked, "And you, Miss Fletcher? Are you enjoying some days of rest here in our beautiful France?"

I took this to mean: *What in the devil's name is a woman of social standing doing in a house of ill repute such as this?*

I smiled. "I'm desperately seeking a position, and Mademoiselle Lola has had the good grace to be sensitive to my distress. We have just concluded my interview, and I'm to be appointed with a trial period."

"Chic!" cried out Lola. "So, you accept? Now *this* is something to celebrate."

"Lola," observed Maupassant. "That's several times I've heard that name now. I thought you were called Filomena Giglio?"

"She needs a nom de guerre if she is to succeed in her profession, don't you think?" I retorted.

"In her profession?" he repeated, eyeing me insistently.

My cheeks flamed, and I felt quite the fool. But Lola picked up where I'd left off.

"As my grandmother would say, 'If you can't see 'em off, rip 'em off.' It's an old Italian adage. Or maybe just a little saying of hers. I don't suppose she meant me to be ripping off my clothes, though."

We all giggled nervously and clinked our glasses together.

"Let us all say we agree on the name Lola, then! And we should perhaps consider changing the Giglio part too. We need to find you a good French name. Something royal, even!" said Maupassant.

"Why not?" said Lola.

"This morning, just on my way over here, I crossed the paths of three members of royal households who weren't a patch on you. Neither in terms of beauty, nor audacity, and even less so where repartee is concerned. You say you read very little, but your conversations are far more original than theirs, and your vocabulary is devilishly colorful! What fools they appear in comparison!"

"This will change," I affirmed. "Lola will start reading more! She is set to become the most cultured courtesan in the region."

"So, Miss Fletcher, that's your function here, is it?" asked Maupassant. "How ever did you get such an idea?"

"Mademoiselle Giglio put an advertisement in the newspaper."

"Yes. If I want to get ahead in business, the work of Miss Fletcher is a necessity. I see artists, merchants, leading industrialists, real men of the world. When I say 'see,' you understand my meaning, naturally. These are gentlemen, of course, and I need to be able to hold my own in a conversation with them."

"Is a conversation a strict requirement?" mocked Maupassant.

"Well, I never! Don't vex me! I wish to retain my clients in the long term, and I need ways of building up a loyal friendship base. I have come to recognize that these men hold educated ladies in great esteem, and I would like to be esteemed. That's where Miss Fletcher comes in. She's going to help me become estimable."

"Like some sort of . . . advisor? A cultural consultant?"

"Yes. I need to know how to keep house, how to receive guests, just as a lady would."

"Now I better understand!" said Maupassant, turning to face me. "This is the business I'm in. If I am to write properly, I must dissect."

A shiver ran down my spine.

"You're scaring me!" Lola tittered nervously.

"Humankind is certainly conducive to study in this town! Princes, princes, princes everywhere! No sooner had I stepped foot on the Croisette than I met three in a row! France? A republic? I appreciate that, but in Cannes, there is a concentration of royalty. Ousted, lost, forgotten. All those poor crowned heads come here to play host to their guests. It's so much easier for them to do so upon shared territory. And where there are princes, there are royal enthusiasts. They like to collect royal invitations, like we would pick mushrooms! It becomes an obsession to have a title at their table at least once a season—whether that be a prince, a grand duke, or Wales himself! This is the world I look upon.

"But there are also heaps of musicians, painters, writers. And lest we forget, the frail and the dying parading themselves down the sunny promenade. What a bleak sight! They alone are worth a detour to this town. And in their wake, in the tails of theses comets, we have spies, swindlers, thieves, impostors . . . You see? There is plenty to entertain here! And I deny myself nothing! Certainly not for my current project, in any case."

I fell into a fit of mirth. "I can hardly wait to read your next novel!"

"Reading is a waste of one's time," declared Lola.

"But just now you said that reading would be an advantage in your line of work!" reasoned Maupassant.

"I never said any such thing! It was Miss Fletcher. But knowing the content of books, the names of authors and characters, and how to talk about them would be beneficial. It would certainly be enough for my needs."

Maupassant bore a condescending and superior expression that irritated me profoundly.

"What's the point in that snobby little smile of yours?" I asked. "If you, too, had spent your childhood at school learning to stitch rather than *dissect*, you'd be in the exact same position. What do you believe girls are taught in schools?"

"A proponent of *women's suffrage*!" exclaimed Maupassant. "I don't know if you've got yourself a good bargain in engaging her, Mademoiselle Giglio. She will make your world a topsy-turvy one with her Utopian and revolutionary ideals. In a town as conservative as this, you could well lose your clientele."

"Don't worry on my behalf," answered Lola. "I believe she's right, but I'd never say as much. Not in company. I know how to navigate this town's waters. If I didn't, I'd still be living with my mother in her wretched little abode."

Her laugh was loud and clear. She rose from her chair and poured herself a third glass. She could hardly walk straight. As she paced the room, staggering as she did so, she added, "So let's resume the situation. I'm free. Unattached. Without capital. But with my house."

"Are you sure the house is yours?" I asked.

"Yes. Eugène had it built especially for me."

"Well, that's a piece of good news, at least," said Maupassant.

"Yes. All that's left for me to do now is to go on the attack, make my name famous, and gain the respect of everyone around."

Maupassant got to his feet and set his glass on the cluttered table. "Mesdames, I must take my leave of you. My brother, Hervé, and I are roaming the hills this afternoon, before the Compagnie Foncière come along, subdivide everything, and sell it all off. I like to accompany him as often as possible in order to avoid his spending his time elsewhere, getting further into debt that he'll never manage to repay. Would you give me permission to pass by tomorrow and ask after your well-being?"

"With pleasure, but not before three in the afternoon, if you please."

"Much obliged! I hope to be of service to you."

His eyes fell upon me for longer than I was comfortable with when he uttered this last sentence. I pretended not to have understood his innuendo.

Lola was prompt to say, "I'm sure you'll be very useful! For example, if you have invitations, whatever the time or date, you could let me know of them. If it's in a respectable place, I could make the most of it, could I not? There might even be a free meal in it, and I could meet all sorts of people! I just have to show myself."

Maupassant bowed. "Precisely! In fact, this evening at the Beau Rivage . . ."

Lola's eyes lit up. The Beau Rivage was one of the most magnificent palaces on the Croisette. Only the very well-heeled went there, with its incredible galas and concerts. It even had its own private theater. You had to either be invited or know someone in the "in crowd" if you weren't a client of the hotel itself. I doubted that Lola would ever be admitted entrance. There were a few lounges and private game rooms that were forbidden to women.

"I don't believe Mademoiselle Giglio could—"

I didn't have time to finish, as Lola cut me off. And that's how I learned a new lesson in the art of being a courtesan.

"You are mistaken, Miss Fletcher. I do go there from time to time. To the restaurant, I mean to say. The hotel manager, Hector Maurel, is an old acquaintance. He was once the maître d' at the Hôtel de l'Univers on the Rue de la Gare. He calls upon me when a gentleman is dining alone. My role is to guide him into choosing the most expensive delicacies, into drinking as much champagne as possible, and helping him avoid . . . boredom . . . just as women are expected to do in some of the lower-standing clubs and cabarets. I went there when Eugène was visiting his parents. What's happening there this evening, my dear Guy?"

"A recital with extracts from *Fanfreluche*. Jeanne Granier herself is honoring us with her presence. I have been asked to join them at Prince Radziwill's lodgings. Men are allowed to bring female guests, as we have taken a private room for supper. A way of getting around going to the concert! I hate music."

Lola clapped. It seemed to be something she indulged in every time she felt jubilant.

"You could both join me," added Maupassant. "I'll cause a scandal with you two. They'll simply have to bow down before me when they witness my powers of seduction."

I could tell he was speaking for my benefit. He was proud to have swung the evening his way. He struck a virile pose and readied himself to show us off in front of his friends.

It was out of the question that I attend such a soirée. My social decline, my lack of money, my absence of support, my obligation to work, the rumors about my liaison with Lady Sarah—all this had set me so far apart from the *real world*. I considered myself to be déclassé, without class. Yet I had clung to my honor. I guessed there were limits to how much people were willing to compromise.

It was one thing to notice a person's wardrobe eccentricities or their unusual politics, but to openly rub shoulders with them alongside a known prostitute and a man reputed for his scandalous adventures with women? It was a difficult task indeed. One would have to have been born a princess to get away with such things.

"Who will be present?" asked Lola.

"Riou will be there. He's Verne's illustrator. Also Cortelazzo, the director of the theater on the Rue d'Antibes. Oh yes! And I believe my friend Paul Saunière is expected, but *shhhh*, he's going incognito. He is such an amusing fellow! He always has numerous anecdotes about Dumas fils. He was his secretary, you know?"

"Chic! Such company will give me a kick up the derrière! I might even get a chance to sing for the director of the theater! Are you coming with us, Miss Fletcher?"

I felt embarrassed. It was as if Maupassant had challenged me.

"Goodness gracious! I should think not. You are so kind, and I appreciate your thoughtfulness, but employees should not socialize with their mistresses in the evening. It would do you no good turn, mademoiselle. I should stay in my position as unseen mentor. Let's not confuse our roles. We're already playing around with the standard codes of behavior," I replied.

Lola winked at Maupassant. "How well brought up she is! What she means to say is that she doesn't wish to be seen with the likes of us at such a frivolous soirée! She must be envisioning the debauchery!"

Maupassant howled with laughter and seemed to regard Lola with newfound respect, as though he'd been taken aback by the unpredicted honesty of a friend.

I felt my cheeks redden, slightly ashamed at my thoughts having been revealed. And yet I shouldn't have been so amazed, for since my arrival, Lola had demonstrated quite brilliantly her capacities to unmask.

5

A Soirée at the Beau Rivage

It was such a mild and pleasant evening in the gardens of the Hôtel Beau Rivage that Lola hadn't bothered fastening her short ruby-colored velvet cape, and there was an added bonus in that she was able to show off her décolleté to its best advantage.

Maupassant had come over to pick her up in his cab, and I watched them pull away.

I wasn't aware then that their evening at the Beau Rivage was about to transform my entire existence. Of course, what happened—as with a great many other scenes in which I'd played no active part—was recounted to me by my friends a few hours later. I will try to give as faithful an account as possible. But please forgive me, dear reader, if some details are merely surmised. If this is the case, it is simply so I am able to better arrange the facts when putting pen to paper.

Mademoiselle Lola had opted for a dark-crimson outfit that evening. Her muslin dress boasted a deep V-neck, and she wore no necklace. Her carmine satin gloves covered her arms up to the elbow. Her hat was the pièce de résistance, her head burdened under the weight of its dozens of crinkled silk flowers. The purplish hue of her headpiece highlighted the tone of her bronzed skin and her red-chestnut hair, which was looking a little fatigued that day.

She felt both dazzled and stunned by the evening in which she was avidly participating.

The Hôtel Beau Rivage was one of the most famous buildings on the Croisette. The palace had undergone renovations that summer, and the rooms now offered en suite bathrooms with hot water. They were among the most prestigious apartments on the seafront. The hotel was also one of the first to be installed with hydraulic elevators, with only specially trained men authorized to operate them.

On gala nights, the whole place was lit up with thousands of lights. The decor was like something out of a fairy tale, and added to that came the dresses, flowers, and jewels of the female guests. Lola was awestruck by the stunning lanterns, the opulent retiring rooms, the sophisticated conversations . . . She felt as if she were really someone in this town, thanks to Maupassant. He had become like a soothing balm to the heart, particularly following the day's disappointments.

They left a good while after the others, hanging back for some time in the private rooms where they'd dined. As they crossed the gardens, she held on to Maupassant, who walked to one side of her, putting all her weight on his arm—admittedly not much—with Paul Saunière holding her by the other elbow. She was a little woozy. The writer was hale and hearty, having not drunk much alcohol.

"You promise you'll walk me all the way home?" whined Lola.

It was two o'clock in the morning, and she felt that finding her own way home in such a state was beyond her capabilities. She was worried she'd end up in a ditch by the side of the road or walking the streets endlessly, and it wouldn't do for a girl like her to be walking the streets.

"Why in the devil didn't we bring your carriage?" moaned Maupassant.

"I let Miss Fletcher use it for her move."

"Let us take her back to her place," said Saunière, "and then we'll take a tour down on the Rue du Redan and have a nightcap at yours."

"Behold the sky!" said Lola. "Those stars! And can you see the lights from the Beau Rivage shimmering on the surface of the sea? That's *something*, is it not?"

"It would be a lot more fun if the odors from the Foux were a little more distant. It's awful when the wind comes inland," complained Maupassant.

"I can tell you don't know the Poussiat neighborhood!" she replied.

Lola was about to add how vile the pittosporum were smelling that season. Her eyes searched among bushes as she tried to seek evidence to prove this point when she spotted an object sticking out from the tamarisk foliage.

"Watch out! Don't trip on this thingamajig here! I don't want to be sprawled out all over the ground!"

The men paused in front of the object in question, forcing Lola to stop in her tracks. But it seemed as if time had slowed down.

Not one of them wanted to admit what they saw.

The object sticking out from under the bush was a foot.

A small, delicate, fine foot.

The foot belonged to a female and was clad in soft black leather boots with ivory buttons, a little scuffed on the toe. But if there was a lady's foot in front of them, then there had to be a second foot somewhere . . . and legs . . . and a torso . . . all concealed under the bush? The alcohol—or the shock—slowed their thinking.

What was the body of a woman doing hidden on the grounds of the Hôtel Beau Rivage? They surveyed each other in astonishment, a slight panic in the air.

"That's a woman's foot," said Maupassant, stunned.

"Has she fainted?" asked Saunière, his tone hopeful, as Lola dived into the bush without a care to her dress, to find out the exact nature of this impromptu turn of events.

She came back out, white with shock. "She reeks of absinthe!" The practical side of her nature had returned in an instant. She'd sobered up. "We need to pull her out from under there."

And she bent down and started pulling at the foot.

"Stop!" hollered Maupassant theatrically. "We don't have the right to touch her or anything within the vicinity of the body until the authorities have been called. What if we were to make invalid something that could be used as evidence?"

"What are you talking about? Why the drama? Perhaps she needs help!" cried Lola.

Both men went to lend a hand, and the poor woman's body, which had already been dragged a considerable distance, by the look of it, was dragged just that little bit farther to below one of the gas lamps on the pathway. Lola let out a scream.

"That's a hotel uniform," said Maupassant. "Note the embroidered monogram. *HBR*. A chambermaid!"

"It's . . . it's . . . ," Lola stuttered.

"Do you know her?" asked both men in unison.

"Yes. She's my friend," Lola stammered, her voice completely broken. "Clara. Clara Campo. She's from the Suquet, like me. She used to live two doors away from me. We've not been in touch for a while. But she . . . Two days ago, I was supposed to . . ."

The body was so clearly visible that Lola felt torn apart. She took a few steps back to try to distance herself from her feelings. Tears flooded down her cheeks. It was impossible to control them. She took out a lace handkerchief, which she usually kept in her pocket to simulate emotion in front of men, and dabbed at her eyes frantically. She walked back to the body, her hands clasped together tensely.

"Please tell me she's not dead! It's not serious, is it? She's just fainted, hasn't she? What's wrong with her? Has she fallen unconscious through drink? Has she had an attack? Perhaps she's hungry?"

Saunière and Maupassant exchanged a look.

"Lola," said Maupassant, seizing her by the shoulders. "Calm yourself. I'm afraid I think your friend . . . is no longer with us."

Lola leaned in. "Clara! It's me! Wake up!"

Clara's face looked shrunken, frozen in an expression of suffering. There was clearly no point in Lola's hoping. She recognized the rigid pain on that face and gave up.

"Her mother . . . What will I tell her?"

She took Clara in her arms and started to shake her, not able to let go. Her loud sobbing made Paul Saunière uncomfortable, fearful of attracting the attention of passersby. Maupassant gripped Lola's elbow and helped her to her feet. She moved in toward him, her face dripping with tears, and buried her head in his chest.

It took several moments before her crying subsided. A tormenting bitterness ravaged every inch of her body. It felt as if her sadness knew no bounds. Sorrow and remorse weighed heavily upon her mind. But another thought was invading these sensations: she couldn't help seeing herself there, lying on the ground, lifeless, hidden under a bush, in Clara's place. With her ungloved hand, she closed the young chambermaid's eyelids.

"She was so pretty, wasn't she?"

She lifted her head, dried her tears, and made a more concerted effort to bring her emotions under control. She dusted off her dress and scanned the horizon and nearby surroundings. Maupassant followed her eyes, paying close attention to what she might be seeing. Marks on the gravel and on the grass, traces that seemed to come from the entresol on the side of the hotel. He bent down and scrutinized Clara's face, as if she were about to speak to him.

"What are you doing?" asked Saunière.

"It's all in the details. These things are important."

As Maupassant moved in closer to the young girl's face, he wiped a little saliva from the corner of her mouth onto the end of his finger and then put it to his nose. He sniffed. With the shock brought on by the sight of the body, Saunière turned away and vomited into a flower bed.

"She was young," said Maupassant. "How can one simply die like this? When one is so young and in presumably perfect health? That said, the stench of absinthe means she most certainly must have drunk a bath of the stuff!"

"She didn't drink," said Lola. "I know she didn't. I don't know why she smells of it."

"Was it an accident?" asked Saunière. "Did she fall and crack her skull?"

"Yes, well spotted," said Lola with a sharp and mocking tone. "She walked out here all alone and then threw herself under this bush by accident."

"Are you being ironic?"

"Of course I'm being ironic," Lola snapped.

"It's a strange position to be found in, all the same. It looks as though someone definitely wanted her body covered up," declared Maupassant.

"Of course they did! It's as clear as a bell! Someone hid her here! This is a murder we're dealing with!" shouted Lola in a rage.

Bursts of laughter could be heard coming from the Croisette. Paul Saunière felt a further wave of anxiety come upon him.

"It's getting late. Someone will find us here!" he whispered.

"If the police find me at the scene of a murder, there won't be much of a chance for me!" Lola said. "I'll be imprisoned immediately, maybe even sent to the hospital, and then they'll card me. I'll have no choice in the matter. And then my entire family—even you gentlemen—will suffer for it. I'm sorry to have to tell you that. The scandal would be too much."

Paul Saunière glowered. "But . . . but . . . ," he stammered. "I couldn't survive something like that. I'm here incognito this evening. I can't be named. What are we going to do?"

"Quiet," interrupted Maupassant with determination. "We simply have to be organized."

"You cannot possibly understand!" persisted Lola. "I'm already in the firing line. The reason my name has never gone down on one of their lists is because I've been living under protection up to this point. I've been sheltered by my artist friends and by my Eugène. I've never practiced my professional activities on the street, but this would be a scandal nonetheless. And I can assure you that I have no need to be the center of such infamy."

"Nor do I, believe me!" exclaimed Saunière, his voice showing both astonishment and outrage. "I remain unknown in these parts! And that's how I like it!"

"As far as I'm concerned, it is quite the contrary. The publicity would serve me well," boasted Maupassant. "It would allow me to sell even more copies of *Une Vie*, and that can only be a good thing. So I'm the only one here willing to stay with her. Lola, go and wake the manager. I seem to recall you saying you two are acquainted."

"Yes. Maurel. Hector has only been managing the place since the beginning of the season back in September. He's not going to appreciate this, that's for sure!"

"Get a move on, then, Lola. Go and wake him, and Paul and I will stay with Clara. Paul, if someone comes, you can move on discreetly."

Lola shivered and pulled her cape farther around her shoulders. She moved at a brisk pace toward the now poorly lit main entrance of the hotel.

6

PANIC AT THE HOTEL

Poor Lola, despite her heartfelt pain and reticence to get involved, felt a strong desire to take action. She hoped to enter the hotel unnoticed and make her way to Maurel's apartment on the fifth floor via the majestic main staircase.

The entrance hall was deserted at such an hour. They were among the few who had stayed so late, and all other guests were long departed. There was just a single soul sitting behind the reception desk. The night concierge, half-asleep at the counter, reared up abruptly, almost military style, and waved at her, asking her at the same time what he could do to help.

He was elegantly dressed, and only his receding hairline put him at around the age of fifty. He had brown hair and a ruddy complexion, was close shaved, and didn't wear one of the fancy mustaches that was so à la mode among the men that year. His pearly gray uniform with its golden buttons was gaping a little at the front, showing that he was a man who wasn't a stranger to a good plate of food.

His eyes were gentle, and Lola immediately felt she could trust him. She whispered, "I have to see Hector Maurel now. One of the chambermaids has been found under a bush in the gardens. She's dead."

She didn't want to give any more information, that it was Clara and that Clara was known to her. The more neutral she remained in terms of her comportment, the better it would be for her.

"A chambermaid?"

The concierge scanned her from head to toe and stared, eyebrows raised, at her flamboyant red outfit. Lola realized she'd been labeled for what she was, and she knew from experience that her word was never taken as being credible as soon as she was identified in this way. He was wondering whether he could believe her, especially given what she was saying was rather shocking.

"Is something about my appearance troubling you?" she asked.

Whenever she was angered, her childhood accent would reemerge, the accent of the backstreets of the Suquet and her school, La Ferrage.

"Are you from Cannes?" asked the concierge.

"Yes, why?" Lola retorted impatiently.

He appeared reassured. "Me too. Come, let me take you to see the manager. If what you say has indeed happened, I don't have the where-withal to cope with it!"

He dropped a little card onto the counter: "Momentarily Absent." He lit an oil lamp and whispered, "There's no gas for us servants. We're supposed to use oil when the guests have gone to bed."

He hurried toward the stairs, and Lola followed him, her skirts rustling as she moved. Instead of going up the main staircase, the concierge jumped down the first few steps leading to the basement.

"We're going down? Doesn't Maurel stay up on the fifth floor?"

"Yes, but it's best if we go straight to the housekeeper with this. She's the one who must make the decision."

Despite his attempt at self-control, his voice sounded shaky, desperate almost. Once they'd reached the bottom of the stairs, they walked down a long corridor, past large and smaller cupboard doors with a range of signs: "Lighting," "Coal," "Laundry," "Ironing," "Linen,"

"Silverware," "Porcelain," "Glassware." A right turn led them to the servants' quarters, with men and women in separate corridors.

They stopped in front of a door with the inscription "Madame Davies." Three quiet knocks from the concierge were followed by a sleepy voice with a strong English accent, "Yes? Who is there?"

"It's Amédée, Madame Davies. I must ask your advice because something has just happened, and we need to wake up the manager."

"One moment, please."

Scuffling noises could be heard before the key turned in the lock.

The housekeeper, Madame Davies, grumpy upon waking, held a candelabra as she appeared in her thick white flannel nightgown buttoned up to the neck. Her round head was covered with a lace nightcap tied under her chin, and her gray hair was fastened into a plait that hung the length of her back.

"What's happened, my man, at this—?"

Before she could finish her sentence, she'd spotted Lola and started taking in some of her distinguishing features. Her pursed lips were evidence enough that she, too, categorized people and knew exactly where to place Lola—under "objectionable reputation."

This disagreeable welcome intimidated Lola more than Amédée's stares, and she didn't feel she could retaliate. But it didn't stop her from blurting out, "It's one of your chambermaids. Clara Campo!"

Zut! Too late! She'd said it! The dead girl's name. This was proof that Lola knew her. She was supposed to have remained a bystander. She always went that little bit too far. She never knew when to bite her tongue.

"Clara?" asked Amédée, clearly upset.

Lola continued, aggressively, "Yes. She's dead. My friends and I found her. We'd just had supper, and we were walking in the gardens. It was such a lovely moonlit night, but her foot . . . her foot was sticking out of a bush. We absolutely have to wake Maurel."

"We have to wake the manager," said Madame Davies, as if Lola hadn't just said as much.

And she marched off without closing the double door behind her. Amédée pushed Lola out of the way so as not to lose his position just behind the housekeeper. Lola followed behind, muttering, "That's just what I said!"

Madame Davies, although fairly plump in stature, didn't take the hydraulic lift, but rather started the long climb up a staircase to the fifth floor. She ascended at a fair pace, only showing signs of fatigue on the fourth floor, where she started to slow a little. They all arrived on a plain, undecorated landing, slightly out of breath, in front of the doors leading to the manager's apartments.

He wasn't sleeping and opened up to his guests, fully dressed, with a cigar in hand. Just one look at them told him something serious had transpired. Although he recognized Lola at once, he gave the impression he'd never seen her face in his life. Amédée, as a mark of respect, allowed Madame Davies to speak first.

"It appears Clara Campo is lying dead in the garden. Should we call the police?"

Maurel turned white and bellowed, "The police? I should think so! Come with me!"

The manager, followed in turn by the other three, rushed as quickly as he could down the staircase. Lola was now in a four-person race, and the homestretch was the service entrance at the back of the palace, leading to the gardens.

Once through it, this is where Hector Maurel, Madame Davies, Amédée, and Lola caught up with the drama. Maupassant was still at the scene. Alone.

"Where's your friend?" asked Lola.

The writer didn't want to betray Saunière by saying he'd fled in order to avoid recognition or involvement. As soon as he'd seen a cab on the bridge opening out onto the Croisette, he had muttered a vague excuse and scampered hell-for-leather to hail it down.

"He didn't feel well," Maupassant answered. "He felt it better to return to Antibes."

Lola hurriedly made the necessary introductions. Everyone immediately lined up in position according to the social hierarchy and their rank. This seemed to be of importance to them, particularly as the evening had taken such an abrupt and heartbreaking turn. Perhaps it was reassuring to fall back on formalities.

Maupassant was the leader of the group, speaking loudly and with authority. He was positioned closest to the body of poor Mademoiselle Clara Campo. The manager hung back, slightly to his side, agitated, nervous, peeking left to right, worrying that any one of the hotel guests might arrive at any moment.

Madame Davies positioned herself just behind Maurel, leaning forward, a hand in front of her mouth, sputtering, "It's her! It's Clara Campo, all right! Poor little thing! She smells of absinthe! How did she end up here? Goodness! I had no idea she drank!"

She seemed to take it as a given that if the chambermaid had ended up dead in the garden, then it was her own fault and nobody else's.

"She didn't drink!" said Lola.

Nobody seemed to notice that Amédée was having particular trouble with all this. He had walked off into the distance after having taken a long and hard look at the young girl's face. He was pale and without expression. Broken, he turned to face the sea, trying his best to hide his sorrow.

Only Lola hadn't found her place in this scene.

Her heart was racing, a whirlwind of emotions. Added to this immense sadness was a new sentiment—one of unexpected suspicion toward Amédée. *He knew her more intimately than he wants us to know,* she thought. *She was more than just a work acquaintance. He is incredibly troubled by this. Could it be that he has something to do with her death?*

But she, too, was trying to hide her deep pain. She was making a good job of it, having had practice since her childhood at masking her feelings. The effort was still arduous, however. She had fallen into her normal societal behavior when out in company—looking from one person to another, changing the tone of her voice depending on whom she was talking to. She had been speaking with Maupassant as she would a friend, and in lighter tones to the other two men, as she did with all members of the opposite sex.

Nobody, other than the learned writer, had made note of her personal turmoil.

However, she was now using a respectful tone with Madame Davies, who, in Lola's view, was the only person present with any kind of authority. And it was indeed the latter who decided what to do next.

"We need to move her away from prying eyes," she said.

"Yes. Perfect. You are right," said Maurel, panicking.

Madame Davies pointed at Maupassant. "You."

"But, madam, the evidence—" Maupassant started.

"Quickly, now. Quickly," she said.

Hesitating, Maupassant, the strongest of the three men present, sighed, then moved toward Clara, bent over, took her cold body into his arms, and lifted her up. Guided by Madame Davies, he carried her toward the hotel basement.

While everyone else followed Maupassant, Lola stayed in the fresh air for a few minutes longer, trying to pull herself together, to breathe deeply despite the tightness of her corset.

Her eyes were drawn to the dark, black waters of the Mediterranean and then the earth below her feet, where the corpse of her friend had lain just minutes earlier. She crouched down to study the bush, to examine the twigs, the nearby footprints, the grass and the way it had been moved, and the surrounding area. It was only once she had gathered her initial impressions that she followed the rest of the group inside. She didn't want to miss out on any human clues. She particularly wished to observe Amédée.

She noted they were using the same pathway to return to the hotel as the body had evidently taken upon leaving it. She looked at the marks on the ground, on the grass, and on the gravel, coming from the basement. The rest of the group followed the traces almost perfectly, but in the opposite direction.

She remembered the eloquent words Maupassant had used: *What if we were to make invalid something that could be used as evidence?* They were in the process of destroying all those traces on the ground. Perhaps they could be documented at a later date by the police if there were to be a substantive investigation.

7

WHEN NOTABLES CONFER

Once they were all back in the building, they made their way down the basement corridor with the designated doors and cupboards containing everything needed for the smooth running of the hotel. Madame Davies overtook Maupassant and stopped in front of the laundry room.

She got out a heavy trousseau of keys from her pocket and opened up the door. She stepped back to leave the doorway clear for Maupassant.

The room smelled of lavender, but soon enough, the malodorous vapors of absinthe invaded the space. In a corner, piles of white sheets lay across several ironing tables, waiting to be pressed. Maupassant spied one that wasn't too laden and placed Clara Campo's body upon it.

Lola rushed forward to the table and picked up the hand of her friend and clasped it in her own. With her other hand, she held Clara's cheek gently. A furtive tear fell onto the forehead of her dead friend. Lola noticed the state of her nails, the contortion of her fingers, and the tiny ink stain on her right hand.

Her eyes met Maupassant's. He had seen the stain too.

But in addition to what came naturally to Lola—the ability to observe, to scrutinize, and to commit to memory everything she saw—the ink stain opened the internal floodgates, bringing back diz-zying memories of school and sheer reverie.

She shivered, and a deluge of images assailed her mind. As she would later tell me, she was overwhelmed at this sudden burst of mem-ories. Had she been at her happiest back then? It was a period in her life that had been light, a period in which her parents had always smiled, where each of their gestures and every step they took had been full of promises and joys to come.

She reminisced, pondering the rare occasions she would go to school. Her parents needed her to help in their work, which meant she was often absent, and her results weren't as good as they might other-wise have been. More often than she should have had to, she was forced to wear the dunce's hat and sit in a corner of the classroom behind the nuns' pulpit at Saint-Thomas de Villeneuve. Her classmates reveled in mocking her.

Clara Campo had been a brilliant student, however. She'd always attained the best marks in every subject—perhaps because she'd never missed a single day of school. She was always pointed out by the teach-er as being the example to follow. She was given the solos in the choir and was always asked to make the speech when the mayor visited.

She'd made her mother proud. At that time, her mother wasn't yet drinking, and her father still lived with them. Madame Campo often held out a generous hand Lola's way, helping her through some of her more difficult moments.

When the law was passed enforcing secularity in schools, there followed a lack of qualified teachers, and so nuns were allowed to con-tinue to instruct in girls' schools. Lola's father had been a stubborn, hotheaded man with anarchical ideals, and she'd always heard talk against the church and religion at home. This is why she hadn't been keen on the sisters.

The contrast between herself and Clara had always been glaring, and yet they were inseparable and cherished one another like kin.

Lola could almost hear the voices of children singing, could almost smell the pots of ink and feel her skin crawl as the white chalk screeched against the blackboard, and yet the chattering of her friends grew more distant by the second. Next, she saw the image of the letter Clara had sent asking for help. A feeling of guilt invaded her, crushed her. Why hadn't she answered?

The voice of Maurel jerked her back to the present.

"Amédée!" he yelled, sounding distraught. "Take my velocipede and go and get Commissioner Valantin. You know where he lives, don't you?"

The concierge, like Lola, remained mute in contemplation as he stared down at the now-stiffening body of Clara. Upon hearing these words, he jolted into action and marched out of the door.

"How are you going to make sure nobody sees her when we have to take her out of the hotel?" asked Maupassant.

The manager and Madame Davies gawked at him in disbelief.

"That's not a problem," said Maurel. "We've had to evacuate enough dead bodies out of this hotel in our time. Unfortunately, a lot goes on behind the scenes here in Cannes. Many people die of consumption, as you know."

"That's true. I'd never really thought about it. I see sick people all the time. Gaunt folk walking along the Croisette. I never see funeral processions, though. I never hear death knells."

"You've just pointed out exactly what's so special about this place. Nobody comes to Cannes to die, monsieur. This is a taboo subject in all conversation. People come here to get better, to breathe good air, to catch some rays of sunshine, to walk on the sand, and to bathe in the warm waters. And if they should disappear, it means they've carried on with their journey toward Italy or been cured. The word *fatal* is never uttered in Cannes."

"And how do you go about maintaining such an illusion?"

"Every hotel is set up to deal with this situation, monsieur. We have staircases and hallways for this specific purpose, for sick people, and our guests never know of them. Our little Clara will most certainly be taken to the hospital via one of these secret passageways, or she'll be taken to her parents or perhaps directly to the church. The commissioner will decide."

"But this isn't a sick person we're talking about," said Lola.

The manager stared at her nastily, as if she were responsible for the fact that Clara wasn't merely sick.

"Quite right! This is a lot more complicated! Death by a chronic case of ethylism," he sneered.

"She didn't drink," repeated Lola adamantly.

"Let's bide our time and see what Valantin decides," said Maurel. "Perhaps she was ill after all."

All heads turned to face Clara. Under the stony, deathly pallor of the young girl, the suffering she had been through showed, and despite the frothy spittle pooled at the side of her mouth, her cheeks were fleshy and full, and it left no doubt of the good health she'd enjoyed prior to her untimely death. A hush filled the room, interrupted only by a sigh from Maurel.

Madame Davies started unbuttoning Clara's elegant boots so as not to soil the tablecloth any more than was necessary.

The scent of lavender had subsided and been overtaken by the pungent stench of the manager's cigar smoke, the fumes from the two oil lamps placed on the sideboard, and the light, almost acrid odor emanating from the corpse, all comingling with the powerful and bitter waves of absinthe. It hadn't dawned on any of them to open the windows.

The group had been settled awhile, in contemplation, when Amédée suddenly returned, his face flushed. He announced, "Monsieur Commissioner Valantin will soon be upon us. He has taken his phaeton to collect Dr. Buttura en route."

Without responding, the manager left the room. Maupassant didn't remain in his position either, choosing instead to walk in circles around the tables, examining the clean laundry, the ironing equipment, and the storage cupboards.

Madame Davies, now seated under the window, seemed lost in thought, likely reflecting on the work that lay ahead the following day and the fact that the lack of sleep would slow her down.

Lola never moved far from Clara's side. She could hardly tolerate looking at the face of her friend, the traces of saliva, the perplexed expression, the sickening pout. She'd noticed that her skin had been slowly marbling and darkening—becoming bruised in tone. She preferred to remember her as being fresh, soft, and youthful.

Amédée had found himself a place in the corner, away from the others, and didn't allow his eyes to leave Clara Campo, his face still feverish and his hands behind his back, fidgeting.

A carriage and horse could be heard pulling up outside, followed by voices piercing the nighttime stillness.

"I apologize for having woken you, Commissioner," said Maurel. "Given the particularities of this dramatic event, I preferred to alert you directly and not simply call upon the first policeman we found on the beat. And good evening to you, Doctor!"

"Good evening, Monsieur Maurel," answered Buttura.

"You acted correctly," asserted Commissioner Valantin, his voice gruff and broken. "Show us the way."

This short exchange was followed by the crunching sound of footsteps on gravel. Within a few minutes, they had arrived in the laundry room. The manager moved aside to let pass a dashingly well-attired man in his forties, muscular, with a handsome mustache and a clear tone to his complexion.

Maurel declared, "This is Commissioner Valantin. He has given new structure to the police system over the last four years, and he's seen off a lot of the rogues!"

The commissioner proudly curled his mustache with his fingertips while greeting the gathering with a nod.

Behind him stood an older man, with white hair crowning his head and sweeping his neck in luxurious waves. His gray mustache was long and hung down his chin dramatically, and he wore his sideburns in the fashionable Second Empire style. His eyes appeared soft and kind as they observed the body lying across the table.

"And this is our good doctor, Buttura. Renowned at the hospital for some time now and eminent author on a work on Cannes and its benefits to health," continued Maurel.

The doctor walked over to the dead girl as Maurel introduced the others in the room to the commissioner.

"Our general housekeeper, Madame Davies; our night concierge, Amédée Lambert, who had incidentally just started service when these people here burst in; and Mademoiselle Filomena, whom you know perhaps—"

"Hello, Filomena," said Buttura. "How are your parents?"

"It's *Lola* now," replied the young woman sharply to Maurel. "Hello there, Doctor. They are in good health, I thank you."

"Why Lola?" asked Maurel.

"I no longer wish to go by *Filomena*. I'm forging a new career as *Lola*. From now on, it's what I expect to be called."

The manager shrugged and finished his introductions as though Lola hadn't cut him off.

"And Monsieur . . ." He hesitated on the name. "Monsieur?"

"Of course! We haven't been properly introduced. Maupassant. Guy de Maupassant."

The manager blanched. "You're Maupassant? The journalist?"

"I wouldn't define myself as such. I am a writer. I don't only write newspaper articles," Maupassant started to explain. "But does my profession pose some sort of problem to you?"

The deathly paleness of the manager's skin took on a bright-pink hue. "Of course it does! You journalists are all the same! You spend your days searching the gutters for whatever stories will help sell your *penny dreadfuls*! I fear the worst of whatever story you'll be writing on this, monsieur! Just my luck! This was bound to happen to me in my hotel! And it was you who discovered the body! A bloody journalist!"

"Oh, stop with all the whining!" cried Lola. "You could at least try to be polite with Monsieur de Maupassant."

"You! You would do well to keep that mouth of yours closed!" he spat. "I only tolerate your presence here as a favor! It would not astonish me in the least to learn you have engineered all this on purpose to ruin me!"

Lola was about to reply quite colorfully when Maupassant touched her arm in an appeasing manner. He stepped in front of her and stated, "I understand your alarm, monsieur. Please believe that I will be loyal to you. Also understand that I am here this evening incognito, and so I'll be making no advertisement of my having been present."

The manager tossed a defiant look at him before turning to Valantin. "How do you wish to proceed? I'm concerned the hotel may receive bad publicity, and this could reflect poorly on our beautiful town!"

"Don't worry. Dr. Buttura will examine the girl, and we'll then be given authority to move the body. I think you should be able to get on with your lives as normal."

This didn't reassure the manager, but he stepped aside to let them do their work. He spied Amédée in the corner.

"Come on, Amédée, get back to the reception desk! Why are you hanging around here? Hurry, my man!"

Amédée slipped away despite seeming as if he wanted to stay.

The doctor lifted Clara's eyelids and took her pulse. He then pronounced the death and sucked in his breath, his face darkening.

"So you've called it, then? Is that it? Can we take her away?" asked the commissioner.

"Yes, yes, of course. Only one matter bothers me. I'm afraid this wasn't a death of natural causes. I won't easily be able to sign a burial permit."

The manager rolled his eyes in desperation.

"Come now, let's not panic here," said Valantin. "I'm sure a solution to this ghastly situation will be discovered soon enough. Please know that I am just as attached as you to the idea that the reputations of the good hotels of this town remain intact. Could you please send for someone to fetch a hospital car?"

With a halting voice, the manager asked Madame Davies to send Amédée off on his velocipede a second time, but on this occasion to see the nuns at the Hôpital de Saint-Dizier at the top of the Suquet.

The doctor approached Maupassant. "So, you're the famous writer, is that correct? I read one of your stories and will admit to having been very fond of it. My wife is simply enchanted by your fiction. She'd be absolutely delighted if you would sign a copy of one of your works for her. She read your serialized novel in *Gil Blas* and subscribed just so she didn't miss an episode! What gives us the honor of your presence here in Cannes, pray tell?"

"My mother is currently sojourning here. She is suffering from ill health."

"Nothing too serious, I hope?"

"She has poor nerves, and the beauty of the town and the surrounding countryside are soothing her somewhat."

"Does she take sea baths?"

"Yes! She also enjoys long walks on the hill."

Lola let out an exasperated sigh. Maupassant smiled. The manager and Valantin stared at her sternly, and Buttura inspected her with distinct surprise.

"Very well, very well. At what point are you going to stop with this mundane conversation?" she quizzed. "What about Clara Campo? Is she no longer a subject of interest?"

"Mademoiselle *Filomena* or *Lola*," said Valantin. "You are not yet transcribed on our great list of *wanton women*, but don't consider yourself unknown to our services. We have a file on you. I don't imagine that in your position, it would be advisable to talk to these gentlemen in so haughty a tone."

Lola moved away and took the chair that had previously been occupied by Madame Davies.

"Right. So we'll await the troops as if nothing has happened here. It's always advisable in such cases, have I got that right?" she said.

Maupassant smiled again, Valantin and Buttura ignored her, and Maurel held back from slapping her across the face. He sent daggers at her, and she stuck her tongue out at him.

As she sat and mulled things over, Lola's attention turned from Maurel, whom she considered to be nothing more than a cad, to her dear friend and what she must have endured. Those idyllic images of her childhood before the Franco-Prussian War were now replaced with the less flattering memories of the events that occurred following their schooldays.

Clara had worked in the Château du Suquet. They had continued to see each other, but when Lola had started her modeling work, her friend had made it more than clear that her own reputation would be at stake if she were to be seen in her company. She risked losing her position at the castle. She wanted to find a good husband. She wanted to start a family, and she had stated that the only thing she could really offer was her purity.

The fact of the matter was that Clara had tried to save Lola from what she felt would be her terrible fate: perdition. She thought that by blackmailing her—by threatening to no longer see her—she would help her quit this terrible existence. She was afraid Lola would fall and never be able to get back up again—the sicknesses she would have, the humiliations.

Some time had passed since this dispute of theirs, and they had not been in touch since.

How did Clara find this job as a chambermaid at the Hôtel Beau Rivage? Lola asked herself.

She knew it to be a particularly well-recognized placement. Her good manners must have played some role. The wages in the hotels along the seafront were more advantageous and boasted appreciable benefits. Simply having access to impeccable hygiene in order to perform the role correctly was a blessing. Hot water, bars of soap, lighting allowing one to read late into the evening, and so on.

There were also all the hats, ribbons, laces, gloves, and ranges of toiletries given to them by ladies who weren't to be seen in the same outfit twice. This could oftentimes represent a fortune. The fine leather boots that Clara was sporting were witness to this—for Lola knew her friend to be someone who didn't go in much for coquetry. She enjoyed reading and would most certainly have sold most objects acquired this way in order to buy more books.

The season was short in Cannes, and its inexorable end loomed in the not-so-distant future. Inevitably, the hotel guests would leave. This was another choice reason for working in hotels. The relationships built with these women didn't have the time to break down. They would disappear like migrating birds within a few short months, without having had the time to find arguments with which to reproach their servants.

She understood exactly why such a post had been so convenient for poor Clara. But why had she written the letter asking for advice? What had been so urgent? Could it be something to do with her death?

Gazing at her friend's body, Lola asked herself what had been the point of her impeccable behavior, her restraint, her education? Where had it got her in the end? Impecunious, but in full stride, her head full of plans . . . and then gone.

In this stifling room, Lola was conscious of how fragile she felt. Until this point, she had always made her way forward through life with confidence. A confidence due to her age, her strength, her health, her cheerful character, her hopes for a better life. She had felt invincible.

But now here lay the lifeless body of Clara Campo, her longstanding friend, and it dramatically brought back her sense of mortality. She felt as though she was suffocating and then realized she had been holding her breath.

The door opened gently. Madame Davies had returned from her mission.

"I woke up a valet. I needed him to take Amédée's place at the desk," she said. "But I didn't divulge anything. He has no idea why Amédée had to leave, and I asked Amédée not to say anything, even to the hospital sisters. He's just to say that Commissioner Valantin requests a stretcher and an ambulance here at the hotel. They'll think that someone has taken ill."

Nobody spoke. Madame Davies approached Lola, who shot to her feet and offered her the chair.

Taking in a sharp breath of the foul air, like a drowning person reaching the surface of the water, Lola looked around and met the eyes of Maupassant. He made a move toward her while the manager, Valantin, and Buttura discussed what was likely to happen over the coming hours.

"I get the impression that the poor advertisement that this body could bring upon the hotel is their only real concern," whispered Maupassant. "And not the cause of death."

"Yes," retorted Lola. "The investigation is certainly going to be a botched job."

"We'll simply have to wait and see what happens in the initial stages."

They could overhear snippets of the conversation between the three notables. The word *accident* recurred several times, as well as *reputation*, *honor*, and *discretion*.

Madame Davies, a little drawn back from the others, wasn't participating in the discussion, but she was worried.

The manager appeared furious and feverish and was talking ten to the dozen. The doctor responded to his words laconically and with a reassuring tone. The commissioner was doing the least talking. He simply observed the pair, almost mockingly, as if this fear of scandal didn't concern him in the slightest. He wasn't taking the time to inspect the body, either, or the location in which it had been found. And he had hardly even questioned the two people who'd had the misfortune to discover the girl.

After several minutes of forced decorum, openly pressed by Maurel, Commissioner Valantin walked toward the two witnesses and addressed Maupassant.

As Lola later explained to me, she didn't feel affronted by this. She already knew that her role in this drama would count for nothing.

"Monsieur, I have an official request to ask of you. We have decided for the moment to not alert the press. No conclusions have yet been drawn, and we don't want to put a spoke in the wheel, so to speak, of the investigation. I know that you write for several newspapers."

"Yes, that's right. Principally for *Le Gaulois*."

"That's it. Can I—without wanting to censor you, of course—ask you to act with the greatest discretion? That means not speaking a single word for the moment. Evidently, you will have exclusive rights to the story at a later date."

"I won't give you my word, but you can rest assured that I am a decent man."

Lola rolled her eyes. She felt such exasperation. "And me? Are you going to ask me to hold my tongue?" she cried out, showing that her best behavior was now at an end.

Maupassant grinned under his mustache, expecting the three men to be slightly embarrassed, but they simply glanced at Lola indifferently and returned to their conversation.

Madame Davies had been watching this scene unfold but was now contemplating her hands, her head lowered.

Embarrassed for Lola, Maupassant clicked his heels together, Prussian style. "Gentlemen, if it doesn't inconvenience you too much, we would like to retire. I currently reside at 1 Rue du Redan. And Mademoiselle is—"

"Your address should be enough, monsieur. Thank you kindly," interrupted the commissioner.

Just as they were about to leave, the door opened again, and two nurses stepped in with a stretcher, guided by Amédée.

The writer and the courtesan slipped away without looking back.

8

Home Sweet Home

In the hours that preceded their return, while Lola and Maupassant enjoyed reenacting scenes from *Fanfreluche*, which included eating the famous ortolans in the private dining rooms of the Hôtel Beau Rivage, I went to collect my large trunk and several smaller ones from my now-abandoned bedroom on Rue Châteaudun.

My bags were already packed. It wasn't because I had been certain to be taken on by Lola. No. It was all about the night before. You see, I'd decided to put an early end to the ups and downs that was my life, and my natural fastidiousness had led me to put my affairs in order before doing so. I had emptied my cupboards, packed my belongings, and arranged all my books and dresses. I had even written a letter for *her*. Thankfully, nobody was any the wiser, and my first step on the road to recovery, upon returning to my room with a conflicting but intense desire to live, would be to burn the missive.

Just as soon as I'd parked the landau in front of a horse trough, jumped down to the ground, and handed the reins to a little street urchin who was hanging around in front of the door so he could hitch the horse for a sou, my landlady assailed me.

"Isn't that the famous Filomena's carriage?" she spat out enviously and contemptuously in equal measure.

I made no immediate reply, but as I climbed the stairs to my bedroom, I announced in a firm voice, "Send two men up for my trunks, and make ready my request for payment. I'm leaving your establishment."

I heard her mutter, "About time. Not only are you as poor as a church mouse, but you reckon yourself to be a cut above. You'll wind up on your back like the rest of 'em! You reckon you're part of the upper crust, but you're not!"

I pretended I hadn't heard, and the whole business was done and dusted within the hour.

On the way back to Les Pavots, I made a detour to the fine food and wine merchants on Rue d'Antibes. With the money left to me after having paid my debts, I bought two bottles of sherry. I had so often passed that window and dreamed of buying something with which to get squiffy on those long, lonely nights. I also bought a pack of small cigars, the least expensive they had.

Once I'd arrived at Les Pavots, which I already considered home, Gustave helped me carry my luggage up to my nest under the rooftop, the ivory tower of the house. There was an unused, small room at the top of the stairs on the second floor into which Gustave placed my effects. I was afraid at first that this was where I'd be staying, but when I saw the space that was to be mine, up another floor still, I almost cried!

The room was so big—absolutely immense! The value of a woman having her own bedchamber can never be stated too often. This bedchamber had everything I needed to be content.

Some furniture had been placed there in a discarded fashion. It wasn't anywhere near as fetching as that on the second floor. They must have been Lola's first pieces, those she'd used when she'd left home.

There was a wardrobe with shelving for all my personal belongings, a three-drawer chest, and two occasional tables. On one stood a basin, mirror, and jug (which Rosalie was now filling with water), with a covered chamber pot partially hidden underneath. The second was larger and round and had three panels. There were strange stains upon it in a range of colors and a chair in front. *My very own desk*, I said to myself. *For me and me alone.* I immediately set out my writing equipment—my nibs, pens, ink wells, and books.

Gustave brought up some logs and nicely arranged them next to the fireplace in which a cheerful fire was already crackling.

The bed was narrow, in the shape of a boat, as was the fashion in Provence. It looked to be made of walnut. The sheets smelled of orange blossom, as did everything else in the house. On the pillow, Rosalie had placed a small embroidered cushion stuffed with lavender. A little brown woolen rug next to the bed would mean I could glide my slippers onto my feet in the morning without my toes getting cold on the hardwood flooring.

And to my great surprise, the small black cat with stunning white markings was fast asleep in the middle of the eiderdown.

Within a period of twenty-four hours, I'd gone from a profoundly chaotic and violent desperation to a bourgeois calm. This filled me with a sense of confidence.

This had been a most excellent welcome. A roof over my head, food in my belly . . . all in exchange for my services. Somewhere I could be alone with my thoughts, without having any personal obligations to a single soul. And I even had a cat! I was elated. Gustave wanted to chase the kitty out of the room, but I stopped him.

"This is Mademoiselle's cat," said Rosalie. "We got him to keep the mice population down, but he just watches them pass and doesn't lift a paw. He's a lazy little coward. The biggest creature he's ever caught is a fly. And he's even frightened of them!"

"What's his name?"

"Gracious! I couldn't tell you! Not the foggiest clue! Perhaps Mademoiselle has given him one, but I doubt it."

After they left, I spent some time arranging my belongings and then writing in my journal. Nothing could have woken the mog. He was so deep in slumber.

At around ten in the evening, I made my way down to the kitchen, where Rosalie welcomed me. I had one of my bottles of sherry in hand. It tends usually to be the case that governesses and the like are not well received in kitchens. It is not considered correct that they dine with the domestic staff, but I hoped—as had so far been the case with all the other usual formalities—that this rule, too, would not be respected. Perhaps it was a rule not even known to Rosalie and the others.

The cat had woken, followed me downstairs, and was rubbing around my ankles. Rosalie was busy knitting in front of the fireplace. I believe she, too, must have been a little restless.

"I left you some broth and a little chicken if you fancy it. And I've made some almond biscuits with sugared cream. Tell me your news. How have you settled in?"

"You're trying to get me in your pocket, aren't you?" I asked, placing my bottle down on the table.

She watched with satisfaction as I finished my supper. The cat was sitting by the range, and I gave him the chicken bones to finish up. We settled in front of the warming flames to eat the biscuits and enjoy a glass of sherry together. Rosalie appeared to appreciate the gesture. In addition to the glass I'd given her, she took the bottle and poured a big slug onto her biscuits with some of the cream. The cat spotted some droplets of the now-alcoholic cream on the floor and trotted over to lap them up.

"Incredible! A cat that likes sherry!" I said.

When I levered myself out of my chair to return to my room, he stumbled toward the back door leading to the garden. We burst out laughing.

"I reckon you've just gone and found the perfect name for him!" she said. "We'll call him Sherry. I'll tell Mademoiselle."

She wished me goodnight and gave me two bottles of paraffin oil.

"When someone reads a lot, like you, they need light. There's not enough oil in that top room, and that little lamp uses up paraffin quick! Here's a little stash for you. Should last a week. Don't use it all up in one night!"

I felt like Sherry, the cat who'd got the cream! I read lazily under the lamplight, a cigar in my left hand, and that's when I heard them return.

9

THE PACT

I heard them outside. Lola was seeking a quarrel with Maupassant, needing an outlet for her emotion, like a cat scratching at a tree. I could make out snippets of the conversation.

"And it doesn't bother you that the woman you're accompanying is treated with such negligence?"

He made no reply. He was possibly reflecting on the short life of Clara Campo. He'd never known her, of course, but she was taking up his thoughts all the same. He must have been trying to calculate the reasons as to how and why she had lost her life, and why a young woman would be out of her bedchamber in the first place at that time of night.

"Did you see how they're handling this?" continued Lola. "It's unbelievable. They're all built of the same mold, aren't they? The way they speak to me. Or don't speak to me, as is the case. The way they're going to deal with this investigation. It's written already. I know the outcome right now."

"I don't understand your point."

"Don't play innocent with me, Maupassant!"

"Innocent? I've been called many names, but I don't recall anyone calling me 'innocent' before today!"

"You know fine well that domestic staff count for nothing in their eyes. That's why it's of no consequence to them to discover what really happened this night!"

As I listened, I realized I was now one of them, these domestics whom nobody cared for. I belonged to that class, to those who counted so little.

"You could be right. But I *am* thinking about your friend. Her life is over. I don't know why this is having such a profound effect on me."

"I don't imagine there's any possible way you could comprehend. You've never understood what it feels like to be left behind. Rejected."

"Perhaps not, but I've known poverty."

She snickered, mockingly. "Yes, poverty until your father sends another lump sum, you mean! Anyway, you're a man. It's not the same. I think I'd rather have gone home with your friend Paul! That's what I think! I believe he'd have better understood. He seems like a true gentleman!"

Maupassant retorted, "Gentleman enough to flee! But you've no need to complain. Stop moaning. You have a roof over your head."

"Typical!" Suddenly softening, she said, "The carriage has been put away. I wonder if Miss Fletcher collected her belongings. She's probably asleep by now."

Their voices sounded more distant now, or weaker. They were whispering, possibly with the intention of not waking Rosalie. From the sound of their footsteps and the clacking of doors, I could tell they'd stepped inside and made a detour to the kitchen. There must have been champagne in the cold room, a small space in the back where Rosalie kept the vegetables, cheeses, and wines.

I tried to imagine what they were doing down there when I heard Maupassant exclaim, "Me? I didn't do . . ." He almost choked on his own giggles.

"Shhhh!"

They tiptoed up the stairs and into the mirrored room. I stood by the open door of my bedchamber, wondering whether or not to descend and join them. I'd been listening carefully, picturing what they were up to.

"Oh, it's divine to be back home!" she murmured. "I couldn't handle wearing this stifling underwear for a second longer! Those people back there! Especially that Davies woman. The only thing that worried her was who was going to do Clara's workload tomorrow!"

The deep voice of Maupassant resonated despite his efforts at whispering. He didn't know how to keep his voice down.

"Give me that bottle. This whole episode must have knocked the wind out of your sails. There are no words of consolation that can soothe when confronted with death."

"The worst part is, who will perform her last offices? She'll be all alone at the hospital, no doubt."

"Yes. When Flaubert died, I was the only one who stayed with him the night. I washed and dressed him and made him ready for visits, which there was no shortage of once news got out. I hope there are some friendly hands to help me when my final hour of need arises."

"How morbid you are."

"Right enough."

"And there's bound to be an autopsy for my poor Clara, don't you think?"

"Well, that can only be a good thing. It would mean they're not likely to treat the case so flippantly. That Valantin seems like a good fellow, doesn't he? Efficient?"

"Efficient when it comes to taking working girls to the hospital and having them screened for goodness knows what, that's for certain! But there wouldn't be so many of us girls out there working if we could earn an honest living."

I imagined Maupassant twirling his mustache. "That Englishwoman is already having an effect! Her ideas are rubbing off on you. Watch out! You'll be overtaking Louise Michel any day now. My word! An anarchist!"

"I cannot tolerate the idea of Clara being buried without anything being looked into, as if she'd died of a trifling cold or something. But what's troubling me the most . . . nay . . . tormenting me is . . . *me*! How selfish I have become! Any sadness I carry is borne of a sense of shame. I feel guilty that I didn't respond to her request for help. If I'd only known. *Che vergogna!* I'm not even capable of assisting an old friend! I could perhaps have done something to stop all this from happening!"

They'd abandoned their hushed tones, and their voices now boomed. No vehicles passed outside. A few barks from a neighboring dog could be heard in the distance and some loud drips coming from a rain barrel outside on the vegetable plot. Night was sovereign.

The noise of their conversation could do nothing but attract my curiosity. Who was this Clara? What were they saying about her?

Not able to follow, I stubbed out my cigar, slipped my dressing gown on over my nightdress, and crept down the stairs to spy on them more closely. The steps creaked under my weight, and there wasn't a chance I could hide my being there. They stopped talking. They had surely heard me.

"A ghost," Lola said, tittering nervously.

I pushed open the door and stepped into the room. It was easier to make my presence known than to be caught eavesdropping. They turned to face me, glasses in hand, their expressions tense. They were startled, but the fear then subsided into laughter.

"Whatever's the matter? Do I have something on my face?" I asked.

"No! Of course not!" Lola said.

Maupassant rushed to his feet. "Please, take a seat. Would you care to join us for a glass? We were expecting a ghost, and when we saw you . . ." It was nervous laughter. "Please, pay us no mind. Oh, if you only knew what we've been through tonight! We're a little on edge!"

I was soon seated next to them, a glass of golden bubbles in hand. They then explained the whole sorry tale. The writer had his back to the mirrors. As he recounted the night's events, it was as if he were reading one of his stories aloud.

When Lola interrupted, her account was more colorful, yet clumsier somehow. I watched as Maupassant uttered phrases as if he were impregnating his expressions with imagery, with raw emotion. At times, it was almost as if he doubted his own words, and at others, as though he were feeding off Lola's.

Lola looked so animated as she told the tale, but at the same time, she appeared furious every time she glanced at Maupassant. The two of them were so emotional to be speaking of the dead young girl. It took me a while to understand that this wasn't a story they had invented for amusement's sake, and it wasn't a story they'd been told by someone else on their evening out. I couldn't fathom what I'd heard.

"You have to do something!" I cried at last.

"What can we do?" Maupassant returned.

A smile slipped from Lola's lips as she lost herself in contemplation, watching the bubbles rise in her flute.

I clarified, "I'm outraged by what you're saying about the manager, Valantin, and the doctor, about their reactions to all this. Aren't you?"

"Of course I am!" he exclaimed.

"As it stands, I've nothing to do with any of this," I said. "I'm domestic staff now, aren't I? But I can't help thinking, 'What if it were me?' Well? Are you going to do something or do nothing? Are you going to leave this poor Clara to her sorry destiny without ever trying to discover the reason behind her death?"

Sulking now, Lola continued staring at her flute.

"I am saddened by the death of poor Clara, but I never knew the girl personally," said Maupassant. "Though, to the end, I'm seeking the truth just as much as you. I have a sense of curiosity that knows no bounds. This is how I was created." He turned toward Lola. "Come, Mademoiselle Lola, what do you want to do? Speak from your heart!"

Lola sighed and merely shook her head, and the more she refused to talk about the whys and wherefores of Clara Campo's death, the more Maupassant tried to convince her to join him in a parallel investigation that could run alongside the inquiry being conducted—or not conducted—by Valantin.

"You knew this girl well, Lola. That's correct?" I said.

"She was my best friend as a child, but events have separated us over the years. She couldn't accept that I'd given up on making an honest living. She rejected me, and I could never forgive her for it. She refused to understand what had happened to me. Why I do what I do. And . . . we lost touch. I won't forgive her."

"But . . . but . . . ," said Maupassant, shocked by what she'd just uttered. I too felt outraged by her newfound indifference.

"You have no idea what my life is like!" Lola suddenly cried. "I have more worries than this! I have to find myself a regular monthly sponsor. It's not a question of money, but my position is at stake. I can't have Valantin finding out that Eugène has left me. As soon as he knows I'm no longer under protection, he'll do everything in his power to put an end to me and my work. It would also be a perfect chance to get away from the crime scene and from sticking my nose into what happened this evening. I know him, and I know his methods. Hospital, asylum, prison, listed, carded. That's how it goes for women like me. Please, Guy. You have other preoccupations, do you not?"

So she'd moved on to calling him Guy now, had she? He glanced at me, unsure which approach would be best to take.

"I thought you were full of remorse, full of regret. You said she'd asked you . . . that her mother . . . ," he said.

Lola sipped her champagne as if she hadn't heard a word.

A noise from the window and a rustle coming from the curtains made us all jump half out of our skin. But it was just the cat. He'd climbed up the trellis and was now bouncing around the room like a wild animal. Lola sprang up and gave chase, trying to catch him.

"My cat!"

"You have a cat?" asked Maupassant. "Me too, but I left her up in Paris."

"I named him Délice, but everyone finds the name ridiculous."

"It is, for a cat," I said as an idea struck me. "But for your new nom de guerre, it would be perfect! Lola Delight!"

"Royal even," added Maupassant. "The name Lys is royal, and it sounds the same. I see you as Comtesse Deslys. It has a ring to it. What do you say to that?"

"Sold! Lola Deslys! I can work with that!"

Lola had picked up the cat and placed him on her lap. She was stroking him absentmindedly while he pawed at her sumptuous clothing and purred.

Silence engulfed us, the only sound the cat's purring, until Maupassant said, "It seems so strange that Valantin is ignoring everything that seems unnatural about Clara's death."

Then, as if she'd suddenly made a great decision, she said eagerly, "You noticed that too? And what about the odd-looking yellowish saliva around her mouth and chin?"

"Hold on!" I said as I darted to my feet and scuttled out of the room, the cat on my heels.

I hurried back with my ink pot and a small notebook of the type I often used to jot down my thoughts. Maupassant looked at me with a mocking smile.

"You have the tools of a writer!" he said.

"I'm going to write down everything you say in case anything is forgotten."

"That's not a bad idea," he said. "We might be able to glean some clues that way. Don't let us neglect any of the details, even if they seem trivial. Any fluid from the body is very important to note. Like the saliva you mentioned, Lola. We should try to get a sample."

"You saw it, didn't you, Maupassant? The frothy substance?"

"I did," he replied. "She must have been sick or coughed something up before she died. We'll have it analyzed by a chemistry laboratory and find out its composition."

"Perhaps a perfumer could do it, but we'd need access to the body to get a sample. Did you see how she looked? How she must have suffered? Her expression was far from natural."

"Yes, it was as if someone had ripped out her insides."

"Her hands were so tense, and her right one had a strange purplish ink stain. Did you see it? It's quite unusual for a chambermaid to write, isn't it? I can assure you that they hardly have the time for such things. Although, she did write to me, of course."

"And you said that Clara was an excellent pupil, did you not?" I asked.

"Yes, so she could indeed have been writing another letter or a diary entry—who knows?"

I quickly wrote a list of all their remarks.

"She also stank of absinthe, and yet, she was no drinker."

"Heavens above! I almost forgot!" cried Maupassant. From one of his large pockets, he pulled an empty bottle of Édouard Pernod Lunel. "I found this in the bushes near Clara's body while I was waiting for you."

I took the bottle and placed it next to my ink pot.

"I suggest we gather together everything we can—all the physical evidence along with what you both remember seeing. We'll need a box of some kind . . ."

Lola rose, climbed onto an armchair, and took down a hatbox from the top of the dresser, throwing the contents onto the floor. She handed it to me, and I placed the empty bottle of absinthe inside. As an additional surprise, Lola passed me a ribbon that she'd taken discreetly from Clara's hair.

"When did you swipe that?" asked Maupassant.

"When nobody was watching. I don't even know what made me do it! Perhaps to keep as a souvenir. Did you notice something else? Dirt on the toes of her new shoes. It looked as though they were really scuffed. As if she'd been dragged."

"Indeed! I followed the traces on the ground while you went back inside for help. They led me to the servants' quarters. On my way back, I noticed they stopped just a few steps away from the bush."

Suddenly worried, she asked me, "What are you actually writing? And why, Miss Fletcher?"

"This is how the detectives do things at Scotland Yard. Investigation notes should be taken down. No detail is too small."

"Qu'es aquò?" said Lola with a humorous touch to her voice.

"The British police," explained Maupassant. "It seems they have an excellent reputation."

"And they get the best results with this method? Better than our French bloodhounds? Better than the famous Vidocq? What is this really about, Miss Fletcher? Do you like playing detective? You should know full well that you, myself, and Guy . . . not one of us is capable of this. You do realize that, don't you?"

"I don't know about myself," said Maupassant, "but it is true that women don't possess incredible powers of deduction or logic as we men do."

I exchanged a look with Lola, horrified to witness that she allowed him to say this without so much as a minimal protest.

"I'm afraid I concur," she added. "We don't go much in for research, discovery, questioning . . . What do I know of any of that? But then nor do you! This is nothing to do with men or women but professional aptitude! We have no idea how to pursue this. Not one of us, I repeat."

Her words bothered me, but I couldn't put my finger on the exact reason why. I felt stung, frustrated. Deep down, it was as if I felt that finding out the truth of Clara's death would be the answer to all my problems. It would give a new meaning to my life, reestablish a sense of worth, and add balance to my fragile dignity. And yet there was something else in this desire of mine. It was as though I was trying to impress Lola in some way. I wanted to prove to her that I was more than capable. I wanted to show her that the confidence she had in me was justified and that she would not regret having taken me into her employ. But why would the opinion of a low-standing courtesan hold any gravity? Even though she was my new mistress, why should it matter so much to me?

Maupassant hesitated before saying, "There are several points of great interest to me here. If truth be told, I'm not as cynical as you might think, and I'm quite tickled by the idea of finding out what really happened. If they file the investigation away, we'll never have any answers. My Flaubert wouldn't have delayed another second—he'd have tried to discover whatever he could. This would have provided him with some excellent material for a good romance novel! But I'm afraid the three of us stand little chance of getting to the bottom of all this."

His words made me feel such indignation. I felt a force pushing me to defend my position.

"I am of the mind that even with three amateurs at the helm, with little method and no experience, we could gain more of an understanding and act more conscientiously than the police. Or am I mistaken?" I asked.

Maupassant, reflecting on the challenge ahead, replied, "Miss Fletcher is right. It's quite obvious that we should continue. We have a responsibility to this young lady. Come, Lola! You're not prepared to just let this drop! She was a real friend to you! Come now!"

"You think so?" asked Lola, lowering her head modestly. "No, what I said just now . . . I was right. I don't think we have the ability . . ."

As she spoke, she glanced at me from the corner of her eye, and I saw they were gleaming. There was something triumphant, mischievous, and satisfied in the look she gave me. That's when I understood that Maupassant and I had reacted exactly as she'd hoped. She had already decided what she wanted us to do back when she had realized that the investigation would be quietly forgotten, that her friend Clara was a nobody to the officials.

We were to work in tandem with the police, but without their knowing it. We were to shine a light on the untimely demise of her friend. Justice for Clara would prevail. We would avenge her death.

Lola had acted as though she were dragging her heels, but it was nothing but a wonderful act.

"I will be at your service as a secretary," I said. "I could categorize information and evidence for you and put my skills to work in any way I can."

"As for me," Maupassant added, "I always have everything one might need on my person. Also, I am considered to be a man with a good reputation. I can go out into society, particularly now that I'm enjoying more success as a novelist. And you, Lola, you have access to Clara's family and the domestic staff at the hotel."

"As you wish," said Lola. "I feel quite convinced now that this will work. We need to find out how and why this happened to my Clara. I want justice for her."

We clinked our glasses together to seal the deal. Lola eyed me and gave me a knowing smile. And yet there was a sense of indulgence in it. I could see how well she liked Maupassant. Something plucked at my heartstrings. Why did this hurt me so?

Had my sadness returned?

10

A CERTAIN PHILÉMON CARRÉ-LAMADON

A number of cockerels crowed that morning, and a faint light had already started to fall upon the town even before we had made it up to bed. At the Chapelle Saint-Nicolas, just behind the Hôtel Central, the clock struck nine. At the very same time, the outside bell rang loud and clear, waking me with a start.

I felt a sense of alarm and rushed out of my bed to the window to peek outside.

A round and red-faced man, stuffed tightly into his suit, which was dusty from his climb up the hill, was standing outside the front of the house at the gate. He looked as if he'd just stepped out of a Dickens novel. He had an impatient air about him as he wiped the sweat from his brow with a large handkerchief. He then rang the bell again. I heard Rosalie say, "I know! I know! I'm coming! Good Lord! It's not the end of the world if I take a few seconds . . ."

I leaned out across the sill to see if Lola had made an appearance at her own window, but it wasn't the case. I returned inside and slipped on my robe. I was going to do the job for which I was being paid. I scurried downstairs to meet this impetuous fellow so as to ensure he wouldn't disturb Lola.

As Rosalie was making her way across the front garden, she turned back to peer at the house and caught a glimpse of me in my robe standing by the front door.

"Where should I put this gentleman? Should I make him wait in the dining room, mademoiselle? Or in my kitchen?"

"Ask him to wait in the small bedroom," I said.

I meant the small box room that wasn't being used for anything, the one I'd been afraid would be my bedchamber. As Rosalie was guiding the visitor indoors, I scampered up to the second floor and placed two chairs into the room in question.

The gentleman entered and examined the chests in the corner, the odd pieces of furniture scattered here and there. He had an air of suspicion about him, as if something were about to jump out and bite. He sat on one of the chairs, dusting it down with his handkerchief before he did so.

"I won't be staying long," he said. "Are you Mademoiselle Giglio?"

"No, I'm her secretary, Mademoiselle Fletcher," I replied in a haughty tone, trying to keep my voice as superior-sounding as possible, although I was somewhat out of practice.

If he was troubled by my presence, he was doing everything in his power not to let it show.

"Patissot. I'm from the notarial offices, Blanchardon's. I have some documents here, and they need to be signed. Monsieur de Bréville's father had written a statement expressing his wish to end the allowance put in place by his son for the benefit of Mademoiselle Giglio."

"Yes, yes. Mademoiselle Giglio was forewarned of this in a letter sent yesterday."

"Certainly, but this needs to be made official today. Here are the papers to sign."

The door opened, and Lola, like a furious tornado and practically in a state of undress, rushed in and tore around the room, forcing the papers to fly into the air with a flourish.

"What in the name of . . . ? What are you doing here?"

The man stammered. "But . . . but . . ."

Lola's angry and theatrical entrance had successfully elicited the reaction I'd been seeking from him, only she'd managed it in mere seconds.

"Who do you think you are? You should get to your feet as soon as a lady enters a room. Don't you know how to behave?"

He shot up in haste, almost as if the chair had burned his rear. His deference was almost piteous to observe.

"Patissot, notary clerk at 7 Place des Îles, the offices of Blanchardon. Here to serve you, madam."

Lola calmed visibly. "Monsieur Patissot, I am very pleased to make your acquaintance. It seems as though you're having difficulty performing the task for which you were sent. I understand this, for who could possibly take pleasure in announcing this sort of matter to a lady? You're about to bring me to ruin, aren't you? I heard you from my bedchamber!"

I stood and stepped away from the chair so Lola could take a seat, which she did. She picked up some of the papers from next to her feet. Patissot remained standing, not quite knowing what to do with himself. I left the room to hunt down another chair for myself. When I returned, the three of us perched around one of my empty trunks, which we used as a table, spreading the papers out before us. He had regained some of his composure and spoke with courtesy.

"Madam, I'm afraid I do have very bad news for you. Monsieur de Bréville never put the house in your name, and due to the pressure put on him by his parents, he has just sold it."

"What? No! Sold Les Pavots? My house?" She rose to her feet. "Monsieur, I need your advice! How am I to counterattack? Is it even possible?"

"Alas, I'm afraid not, madam. Everything they've done is legal," he said, nodding toward the papers. "Your sole possibility is to take them to court, but I can in no way guarantee a victory, and the scandal would be unbearable. I think you would suffer more than they."

"To whom did they sell it?"

He leafed through the documents and announced, "A certain Monsieur Philémon Carré-Lamadon is the new proprietor."

"Philémon!" she gasped.

"Who is he?" I asked.

"He's a friend of Eugène. A real vulture."

She was annihilated. Wiped out. She had nothing to say. Patissot gave her the various papers. Hoping to justify my first day of gainful employment, in the full knowledge that it was probably my last, I took them from her and perused them before instructing Lola to sign everything. It was all in order. She had no recourse on this one. She signed.

I saw Patissot out. We hadn't even offered the poor fellow so much as a glass of water.

"You have brought no glad tidings with you today, monsieur," I said as we walked together down the stairwell. "This visit of yours has resulted in four people being turned out onto the street."

"It wasn't done willingly. But I must tell you one more thing, for I dare not broach the subject myself for fear of offending the lady's sensibilities. Monsieur Philémon Carré-Lamadon did not buy this house for himself, for he lives in a sumptuous villa in the Terrefial quarter. This is naught but a chalet to him. The idea is that he is to start up a new contract with Mademoiselle Giglio. She would have the same conditions and obligations as with Monsieur de Bréville fils. Do you understand my full meaning? If you were to try and persuade her to accept this offer—and if she is not too honorable a woman—she would at least get the opportunity to stay and reside within these four walls."

"She's part of the furniture, is she? Sold along with the house itself?"

"It's a bitter pill to swallow, I am aware of that. But her debts could be mounting. Bankruptcies are rife in this area. Shops are closing down on a daily basis on the Rue d'Antibes. These are upsetting times," he said. "Unfortunately, hers is not an isolated case."

"Your words are not very consoling," I said. "Goodbye, monsieur."

He saluted me with ceremony. As I slowly made my way back to Lola, I bumped into Rosalie in front of the door to the kitchen. I got the impression that she knew everything. She shook her head slowly and stepped into the back pantry, mumbling, "I'll bring you up some hot chocolate."

I couldn't immediately find Lola on the second floor. I checked every room before heading to her bedchamber. It was closed. I knocked lightly and entered. She had returned to bed and lay curled up in a ball under some lace sheets.

"What are you going to do?"

She considered me. She was lost, forlorn. "I don't know. I'm stuck. I must think things over."

"They could be trying to pull the wool over your eyes when they say they're unafraid of a legal trial. They would suffer just as much as you, believe me."

"No. They wouldn't. Patissot is right. My situation is barely tolerated by the law. I don't want to make any waves. You were right to make me sign those papers. When I had Bréville on my side, they couldn't make any moves against me. But I now find myself alone and with nobody to back me up. They'll put me on their famous lists, and I know it. I'll be forced to comply. I don't want to be on their list, Miss Fletcher. I don't want to spend the rest of my life as a known prostitute."

"How well do you know this Monsieur Carré-Lamadon?"

"Too well. He and Eugène studied together at the Stanislas school. That's where they put students whose parents don't want them to mix with the general populace."

"Yes, I remember the name Philémon . . ."

"That school! The place is full of aristocrats, as I'm sure you can well guess. But it doesn't stop them seeking out the company of members of the opposite sex. Philémon is a disgusting specimen. He was part of Eugène's little gang. We had some fun together, I will at least say that. Picnics, walks, boating, card games . . . Philémon would have a different mistress every time we saw him. His parents own three cotton mills in the north. He always had his eye on me, and he would try to sneak behind Eugène's back to get to me. I can't tell you the number of advances he made! Let me try to put it politely. There *were* some shenanigans—I must admit. Eugène knew nothing of it, of course. I could never have told him. He wouldn't have been able to tolerate the betrayal of his friend. And I can handle my own affairs, anyway!"

"It's strange that Eugène would sell this house to Philémon."

"Indeed. Do you think there's some sort of hidden agenda?"

I sighed. "I must tell you that Patissot told me of further news, and I now have the burdensome task of having to relay it to you. Please do not hold it against me."

"What's with all the precautions? Just tell me!"

"Philémon Carré-Lamadon is offering you the same arrangement as you had with Eugène. He will allow you to live in this house and will forward you the same sum of money each month. It will all remain as before."

"Really? Gosh! In exchange for what?"

My lack of a response caused her to flush pink.

"I see! Goodness! How practical of him! My bed's not even cold! I refuse to believe that Eugène would countenance this!"

I still had no words for her. She grimaced and stared over at her tapestry on the wall, lost in her thoughts, before turning her face into her pillow and sobbing.

"He can go to hell! I might be for sale, but it is I who chooses to whom I am sold! I hate people who are underhanded! I need to think of a way out of this. The solution will come to me as I dream. Imagine going to someone's house to tell them they're ruined! Try to envisage what it would be like if that were your job! I have other fish to fry, you know? I have to think about Clara!"

I left her wrapped up in bed and returned to my room under the eaves to take a smoke of my cigar before getting dressed. I only had two dresses. A black one and a white one. The black one was the only thing I could wear to work. I also had a sports outfit for walks and lawn tennis and a bathing suit.

I tidied my room and took down my chamber pot to empty. I didn't think Rosalie should have to do this for me. When I found myself without a father, without a mother, and without a fortune—the circumstances of which I would always keep hidden, if I could help it—and was forced to go out and find work, the hierarchy in my employer's house was complex. I had been taken in by friends of a distant cousin, and despite the special relationship I enjoyed with Lady Sarah, I have never seen domestic staff in the same light since. My prior prejudices were soon a distant memory. My time there was spent penniless and in shabby clothes, thus completing my social education. Domestic staff have a great many barriers in front of them, and well I knew it.

I met Rosalie in the hallway, and she handed me the promised hot chocolate. I climbed the stairs again with my cup in hand.

As I gave my feet a rest in my armchair facing the window, sipping the warm drink and taking a few pulls on my cigar, I set about thinking. What was to become of me? I'd only just arrived, unpacked, and now I would be obliged to take my leave? Impossible! Also, I was committed now to uncovering the truth behind the death of Clara Campo. Poor Clara! Today's events had eclipsed her terrible fate.

Where would I go, anyway? After all, Lola had already given me an advance on my salary. I'd used it to pay my landlady, a few debts, and to buy my sherry, of course. It would mean I'd have to stay a while longer, at least until I could work off what wage I'd received.

Life was teaching me a new lesson here. I'd decided to live it to its fullest, to savor daily events, to accept to live without Lady Sarah and all the complications that that entailed.

I then went down to the second floor with the intention of straightening out the box room that now doubled as our office. I pushed my empty trunks against the far wall, creating an improvised shelving area. I set up a table and chairs in front of them and arranged some sheets of paper on top of it. In plain sight, right in the middle, I put the hatbox containing what little evidence we had and the notes I'd made during the discussions the night before. That was the start of the investigation right there. I set about writing down my adventures thus far.

Several hours later, Lola's sleepy voice traveled through the house just as the bell rang at the Chapelle Saint-Nicolas, signaling midday.

"Rosalie!" she called. "Can I have some of your excellent chocolate with an omelet, please?"

I heard her drag a piece of furniture across the floorboards.

I walked to her room and opened the door. She had moved one of the tables over to the big open window leading out to the balcony. Without turning to me, she said, "Is that you? Have you seen the weather out there? And this panorama?"

I moved toward her. "Do you mean the station and the smoke from the trains?"

She turned and smiled. "Is that a demonstration of English humor?"

The affectation in her voice that was so often there had disappeared. I was now getting a glimpse of the real Lola. Her frivolity must have been something she used only in the presence of men. We smiled at each other. There was a sense of understanding between us.

Rosalie entered the room with a large tray. On it was a dish of cold ratatouille, a cured ham, a wild mushroom omelet, and several slices of thick black bread—all this to be enjoyed with a steaming jug full-to-brimming with hot chocolate. At this exact moment, the cat made an appearance.

"You can smell ham a mile away, can't you? You'll never believe me, but this cat is such a greedy little guts, he even eats bread!" Lola said.

"He had a drink of Miss Fletcher's sherry last night!" exclaimed Rosalie. "He trundled off looking quite tipsy!"

I joined Lola at the table. She had begun to eat almost as soon as the tray had been put down. She waited for Rosalie to leave the room before saying, "Right! We're going to have to start from scratch. I'm no young chicken, as you can see."

Her remark made me chortle.

"I'll get straight to my point here. I'm not going to be able to keep you on. Nor Rosalie. Nor the car. Nothing."

A coldness struck me, and I shivered as I pictured myself walking the streets alone, dragging my trunks behind me. A sorry sight. There was bound to be wind and rain. There always was in scenes such as this. There was a novel in it, I was sure. I thought of Philémon's proposition. If she accepted it, all our skins would be saved. I, Rosalie, Gustave, and Lola would all be fine.

"If you would allow me, you said yesterday that you would have to find a protector. You were of course speaking of a gentleman with whom you would have . . . relations . . . which would then permit you to retain the house, your allowance, and so on. Am I correct?"

"Yes, why are we talking about this again?" she asked innocently.

She knew exactly where I was coming from, but she wasn't going to make it an easy task. It looked as though she had every intention of shooting the messenger. I felt embarrassed, but went ahead nonetheless.

"Well, I am baffled as to why you are not accepting Philémon's offer."

She stared as I turned a bright scarlet. I'd reacted selfishly. I'd presumed that if one had to sell one's charms to get ahead in life—and why not call a spade a spade—why would one care to whom? All cats are gray in the dark. And yet I could see that, for Lola, dealing with Philémon was as low as it got. She had a shred of dignity left, didn't she?

It was like something straight out of a Maupassant novel. He'd have enjoyed hearing it, but I doubted she trusted him enough to tell him.

"Let me explain," she said.

"No, please don't feel as though you are obliged. Forgive me."

"I insist, Miss Gabriella the Honorable Fletcher Lady of Ramsey, or whatever your name is. I sleep with men for money, but that shouldn't mean I belong to them. I like to choose who I go to bed with. And I hate owing people."

"I understand," I acknowledged.

"No, you don't. And there's really no need to pretend. You cannot possibly understand any of this. Did I ever have a choice? If I hadn't decided to become a courtesan, I would have ended up working in a laundry, a factory, or as a maid. When you're as poor as I was, you have to find a way out. Could I have dealt in stocks and shares? Speculated on the markets? With what? My looks are my luck in life, and so I have had to use them to my advantage. What's wrong with that? Is that not enough for you already? Do you think I should lower myself further by having dealings with Philémon?"

I regretted having spoken without thinking the matter through properly. I had been pushed by my pragmatic nature.

"I shouldn't have—"

"And I still have great affection for Eugène, although he has done little to deserve it. It's such an immoral act to try to set me up in a house . . . with his best friend, no less! This house was a haven for the love we shared. The mere idea should cause him shame. It would be degrading for me. I'm not an object. That's how I feel. You can consider the subject closed."

"I regret even suggesting it."

"I live by my instincts. I allow myself to be loved without tenderness, but it disgusts me. My work gives me little pleasure. I feel indifferent toward my visitors. But I was madly enamored with Eugène. My heart opened to him."

"I must admit to feeling afraid. I thought I had found in this house a place to rebuild my life, and now—"

"When I come to think of it," Lola said maliciously, "why don't you try it for yourself?"

I turned my head away in exasperation. There was no need to provoke me so. Why was she playing with me thus?

"There is a market for sapphic love. It's even considered fashionable these days. I know a café with a billiards table on the Rue Teissière. It's very confidential, but one day a week, there's a day when men aren't allowed in."

I knew it was only innocent mocking, but I felt embarrassed by her words all the same. I must have looked stunned. She laughed.

We heard some steps in the front hallway below. Rosalie was climbing the staircase, but she wasn't alone. She opened the door with a single, fast movement and grimaced before crying out, "I've been doing a lot of announcing of guests recently, haven't I? Here's Monsieur Philémon. He wants to see you, mademoiselle."

Lola glanced at me, obviously petrified.

We caught sight of Philémon just as he was about to enter Lola's lounge. He had a caustic smile on his lips, stretching his mustache almost up to his temples. His eyes shone greedily. He spied Lola through the door and licked his lips as if she were a crusty brioche ready to devour. He was young, impeccably dressed, sure of himself, a man of undoubtable fortune and used to success. He was wearing what all fashionable young men wore in spa towns—he appeared every part the English sportsman. He was attired in trousers with a stunning wide check pattern, supple ankle boots with short spats, and a long light-colored coat made of fine wool with a small velour collar in a warm chocolate brown. Only his topper was classic, but even that boasted two colors.

He looked pleasant enough, but to the well-trained eye, his ferocious appetite to dominate was clear. As soon as he entered the room, he threw his cane onto the nearest chair and marched over to greet her, shaking her hand with avarice.

"My dear!"

Lola immediately looked like the "little wife." Perhaps it was her natural demeanor in such circumstances. She allowed him to take her by the arm and lead her farther into the room. She placed herself down on the couch in a semireclined position and invited her guest to take one of the armchairs.

"My dear Philémon! How thoughtful of you to come here to console me."

He blinked several times. She resumed, "Have you heard what that swine of a man Eugène has done to me? He's playing the patriot! He's gone over to the war in Madagascar! I didn't even know he knew such a country existed. I certainly didn't!"

"Come, Filo, he's a hero! One cannot remain angry with a hero for long! Don't blame him so!"

"A real hero is someone who stays with his family and takes good care of them."

Philémon smiled, taking advantage of the situation. He twirled his mustache as if letting something unsaid remain in the air.

"Oh, I know what you're thinking—I'm not his family. I'm a nobody to him. I'm just a little frivolity on the side, a strumpet, a girl he no longer wishes to see or be seen with. Am I right? I'm sure he's told you the whole story. I can't convey to you how low spirited I am."

A few tears fell down her cheek. Philémon removed a large handkerchief from his pocket and held it out to her. His face, particularly his mouth, showed how agitated he was. I felt a little troubled at having witnessed the scene without invitation and so withdrew back into our new office room and stuck my head in my notes in case either of them should be watching me. I left the door open. But neither of them paid me any mind. I still had quite a good view of the goings-on.

"Don't cry," said Philémon. "It's a waste of time and energy. What can I do to help?"

She wiped her eyes and glanced at him in supplication. "Oh, there's a lot you could do to help me, Philémon. Everything, in fact!"

"Very well. Let's both lay our cards on the table. You must know by now that I am the new proprietor of this . . ." The fact that his sentence remained unfinished sounded almost threatening.

She sighed and cried some more. "Yes, I realize that. Eugène explained everything to me. Yet he knew that . . . Well, I fancy he thought it for the best. He didn't want to . . ."

Coldly and with incredible presumption, he said, "You know the arrangement, don't you? You've been told of my generous offer? Will you accept it?"

Lola stood and glided toward the window. Her voice was charged with emotion.

"I'm hardly in a position to be able to refuse you—but I will. I loved him, Philémon, and you know that better than anyone. I was faithful every step of the way. I know it sounds ridiculous to say that, given my profession, but I was a wife to him. We knew one another from such a young age! You remember the picnics we would go on to the islands when you were at Stanislas."

Philémon was visibly upset. He could sense he was heading into some difficulty. He must have taken it for granted that Lola would be an easy, submissive little woman. And yet he wasn't exactly imposing his new status particularly forcefully.

He whispered bitterly, "Eugène led me to believe that . . ."

"Yes, yes, I know. I even accepted as much myself when it was first proposed, but I now realize I am brokenhearted. I need time, Phil. You understand that, don't you?"

"Time . . . if that's all this is, then yes, you shall have some time. You must think me the devil himself!" The frustration could be heard in his voice, despite his reassuring words.

"I knew it! I was so sure of it! You're such a gentleman!"

I could hear a huge sense of relief as she spoke.

She threw herself into his arms and started weeping yet again. She pushed him back and stated, "I'm so very unhappy! I didn't want to make a spectacle of myself. The weeping woman and all that nonsense. You are a jubilant soul, Phil! And this is a very cheerless house. It's as if it's all being erased, wiped out without a trace, just like Lamartine said!"

She threw me a glance and winked. I was unsettled in that I felt overwhelmed. Almost scared. She was clearly so used to manipulating men, but in this case, she had been lessened, lowered. The way she was living her life was being managed by someone other than herself. This Philémon was paralyzing her.

He spoke dryly. "Filo, you know that we're negotiating here, don't you? This is a business arrangement. You must promise to accept."

She must have been raging on the inside, but she simply tapped her foot gently and rhythmically on the floorboards.

"No. I have made no promises, Philémon. I don't want to feel like a prisoner in my own home. Please don't spoil everything now. Your words sound sour."

He made a sweeping motion with his arm. "Fi, forget what I said. I know you have promised me nothing."

He stepped over to her, took her by the wrist, and pushed it back as he leaned in close to her face. He spoke directly, and the undertone hinted of danger. "I want you, and there's no more to it. And I'm a man who gets what he wants."

"Let me go, Phil. You're hurting me."

He stepped back and took a deep breath. "I'm not the kind of person who accepts being duped, Filo! I only bought this house because you live in it, and because you were supposed to be all wrapped up inside like a gift! I wanted us to find an easy arrangement, and I thought . . . Well, it is of no consequence what I thought. That was premature of me, and I can see that now. Nevertheless, these are my conditions. I hope and expect that you will honor your part of the contract as stipulated."

"Yes, yes, everyone understands. Anything else?"

Philémon's eyes turned a shade darker. His lips moved to form the shape of an unconvincingly seductive smile.

"You can pay rent."

"What? You expect me to pay rent? How? You know that Eugène's parents have put an end to my allowance, and it wasn't even enough in the first place."

"I know, Filo. But if you think about it, my offer is fair and honest. You'll soon come to realize this. I'm offering you the same way of life, the same house, the same allowance, and a love ten times stronger than what you had with Eugène. Eugène was a goose. He betrayed you, plain and simple. There'll be none of that with me, I can assure you. You'll want for nothing as long as you're with me, and you're not going to find a similar offer any time soon! But while I await your answer on the matter, you can pay me rent. There you go. Settled. I will send my lawyer to you, and you can draw up a tenant's agreement together."

"I'm shocked at how harsh you are being with me, Phil. Honestly! But . . . I accept. I'll pay you every last sou and on the dot! Just give me some time to pick myself up."

He moved closer to her again and whispered in her ear, "You can have all the time you need. I have but one desire and that's your contentment. You know that much is true."

She moved back, shaking a little. "How are you going to set the rent? What will the price be?"

"One thousand francs per month. This is a pleasant house, and the neighborhood is much sought after. You have a station here, and

Eugène sold it to me above market value because of the hidden jewel inside!"

Lola looked as though she were suffocating, and she made no attempt to hide her consternation. "A thousand? But . . . Phil . . . How can I . . ."

"A thousand francs is a reasonable ask for a residence such as this."

"It's exorbitant. That's the word you mean to use. You're bleeding me dry."

"My darling, I am your devoted friend. Come on, Filo . . ."

"You should know, Phil, I no longer wish to go by the name of Filo."

This news left Philémon looking quite bewildered. "Is that so? A new whim?"

"If you wish. My new name is *Lola Deslys*. Eugène leaving me has made me a new woman."

He smiled, or rather smirked. "I see."

"Adieu, Philémon! Leave me to my misery!"

Philémon left the room and could be heard skipping down the stairwell, whistling "L'Amant d'Amanda." Minutes later, his distant voice called from down the street, saying, "I adore you, Lola Deslys! You're the spiciest woman in Cannes!"

I wondered what to do and say as I walked into the lounge and approached the divan. She thrust herself up abruptly, pushed past me, picked up a plate from the luncheon tray, and threw it against the wall. The next thing we heard was the voice of Rosalie.

"Breaking the crockery won't solve anything!"

"Maybe not," said Lola, "but I feel a whole lot better!" She hovered next to me, sulking, arms by her sides; then she scoffed bitterly as she sat. "I have to find the money to pay this rent. I will not give him the satisfaction of seeing me in the street."

"You're right. But what possibilities lie within your means?"

"As I said to Maupassant yesterday, I don't need a man to protect me. I just need the money to trickle in steadily."

"What about Clara? Are we continuing with the investigation?" I asked.

She jumped to her feet. "I have to warn her mother. I hope the police aren't with her already."

Lola stepped into her spacious wardrobe by her bedchamber door and beckoned me to follow her. She pulled out a brown dress in a coarse tweed and slipped it on without bothering with a corset.

"Could you help me untangle my hair?"

She had long, thick curls. It was certainly a magnificent head of hair but very difficult to tame. I wasn't as gentle as I might have been, and she cried out as I tried in vain to discipline her unruly mane into a wide plait, which I then tied to the top of her head in a tight bun.

The scent of her hair and the feel of the wild but silky strands in my hands caused a shiver to run down my spine. It was accompanied by a troubling emotion. I shook my head to chase the feeling away. She placed a dull gray hat on top of the bun and fixed it with some pins. She started putting on fine woolen gloves, but slipped them off after a moment's hesitation.

I looked perplexed at her choice of attire and its lack of style.

"When I go back home, I prefer not to be recognized. I like to dress like anyone else. And if I intend to gather a few clues while I'm there, I have to be able to show that I haven't changed. Which is actually true. I haven't. I wonder if Maupassant has found out anything else?"

She slipped her hands into her basin and rinsed her face and mouth, spitting the used water back into the bowl and then pouring it all out of the lounge window.

"Where do the Campo family live?"

"On the Mont Chevalier, just a couple of doors down from my family. She has only one parent left—her mother. Her father died at sea five years ago. Her two youngest sisters are still in school. There are new laws now. Her mother won't be allowed to send them to work, and I'm sure she doesn't have enough to feed them well. There's an older boy. He works at the glassmaker's."

She tottered off down the stairs, not even bothering to dab on any rouge.

I watched from the balcony as she turned onto the Boulevard de la Foncière and then to a cinder pathway on the right.

The quickest way up to the Suquet was to follow the railway track, climb up to the top, and then turn onto the Rue des Suisses. She knew the way.

11

LOLA FORAGES FOR CLUES

As Lola arrived at Clara's family home, the old gossips were out in force on their doorsteps.

"Why! It's little Giglio! How's life treating you?"

She waved as she slipped inside. The front door was below ground level, and the street-side barred windows let in little light. It was such a gloomy place. The only room in the Campo dwelling was empty. Not even a chair. Clara's mother had more than likely hocked what few pieces of furniture she had to buy a couple of bottles of spirits, or perhaps the bailiffs had taken everything. As far as Lola could remember, the place had been a lot bigger and warmer, but it had all shrunk somehow.

Her throat tightened as she beheld what had become of the Campos' abode. Her dear friend's mother had been such a generous soul, and Lola was so grateful for the help she'd received from her in the past. It was difficult to see this now.

In a far corner of the room lay a large straw palliasse and a chamber pot that hadn't been emptied for some time—this explained the acrid smell in the room. There were some clothes in rags hanging up on nails, with more scattered around the room here and there. Odd bits of dirty crockery lay strewn on the ground, and an empty bottle stood on a fruit box that seemed to be serving as a table in the middle of the room. Clara's mother was sitting on the floor near the box. Lola was finding it hard to breathe with the stench of eau-de-vie that pervaded the air. The smell was certainly coming from Madame Campo, and added to it were other odors from within the room itself—the general smell of waste and filth.

"Is that you, Filomena?" she asked, her voice slurring. "Have you come to see Clara? She doesn't live here anymore, you know? She stays at the hotel where she works."

"I know," said Lola, desperately sad that she would have to tell Clara's mother. "Let me help you and make you more comfortable."

She helped Madame Campo to her feet, removed the dirty glass from her hand, and took her to the palliasse. She decided that the first thing to do would be to go to the top of the street and collect some fresh water from the fountain.

Madame Campo watched her, dazed, coughing intermittently. The hacking and wheezing was clearly leaving her feeling exhausted.

Lola cleaned and arranged the small living space, washed up the pots, and swept the floor as best she could. She spotted a pile of Clara's books by the wall, but couldn't bring herself to put them in order, despite them lying in disarray. She couldn't even touch them. The books had been Clara's life. Her treasures.

She walked back up the street and emptied the chamber pot out into the communal cesspit and rinsed it out in the fountain. It was only after performing these tasks that she felt able to talk to Clara's mother. She had put it off long enough. She now needed to tell her the sad news. She was afraid that the police might arrive at any moment and deliver the message before she'd had the courage to explain the whole sorry tale.

Once she had returned to the apartment, she squatted down gently next to Madame Campo on the straw mattress and took her by the shoulders. She whispered in her ear, not quite knowing how to phrase what she needed to say.

"It's Clara, Mother Campo."

"What about Clara?"

"She had an accident at work. She fell."

The mother stumbled to her feet, looking distraught. Another coughing fit ensued.

"She's fallen? Where is she? Is she hurt? Does she need my help? I want to see her. Did they take her to the hospital? Where in God's name will I get the money to pay the hospital?"

She was muddled, unable to fathom whether to go to her daughter's aid immediately or work out how she would deal with the expense of it all. It was too confusing for her.

"No, it's of no use, Madame Campo. It's too late."

"It's too late?" She stopped speaking. The cough stopped too. A sense of calm fell over the two of them. She stared at Lola vacantly. "How so?"

"She's no longer with us, Madame Campo. She's gone."

"Where did she go?"

"She's gone! It means she's dead!" shouted Lola brusquely, not knowing how to force Madame Campo to accept the reality of it.

Nothing. The older woman could not find the words. She fell back on the mattress in a slump and into the arms of Lola. She was blind drunk. Stupefied. Unable to believe what she was hearing. She didn't cry. She didn't speak. The news had hit home, but it was as if the magnitude of it was only slowly registering. She eyed the room, noticing how her affairs had been rearranged and cleaned, including the palliasse on which they were sitting, which she usually shared with her two youngest children.

She finally broke her silence. "How will I feed the little ones? What will they eat?"

She looked sick. Drained of every ounce of energy. Lola could not handle seeing her in such a pitiful state. She didn't know how to respond, and in trying to rid the atmosphere of such desperate sadness, she questioned her, without thinking—through sheer nervousness.

"What about your eldest, Giuseppe? Isn't he working with the glassmaker now?"

"He went off with one of those girls who sells her wares door to door. They both like to be on the move and travel about. He sends money on occasion, true enough, but it's never much."

"How did Clara get the position at the Hôtel Beau Rivage?"

"It was through Amédée, the night concierge."

Lola stored this information away. "She wasn't working for the Hiberts?"

"No. They moved. They rent their château out to the *faïencerie*, and they didn't take her with them. Last summer, Amédée saw her out on the Rue des Suisses and remembered she'd been up at the château with the Hiberts for some time. He asked her if she'd like to work at the Hôtel Beau Rivage for the season. She started in October. Everything was going so well! Especially at Christmas! She laughed! She sang! She was overjoyed! My little girl! Thank goodness she met Amédée! Such a great boy! We might have died without him. We had that many debts."

"You still do your sewing work, though, don't you?"

Madame Campo lowered her eyes. "Clara was right. She would tell me off that I didn't always complete my orders and I sometimes worked badly. She said I was nothing but a drunk. It's true enough that if I don't give someone their sewing back when they ask for it, nobody will trust me with their things! I saw her as nothing but an ingrate! But it's not true! She was right. And then the sadness! Why did it have to fall upon her? My little one! Why so dismayed? Just when it all seemed to be going well for her."

"What are you saying? What sadness?"

Another cough beset with phlegm escaped from her throat. Lola noticed some blood on Madame Campo's sleeve as she wiped her mouth and put her hands to her face.

"So much melancholy! She didn't want to go back to work when she came up here to visit. My poor little thing! We women get ourselves into such states! And I would shout at her and blame her!"

Without fully understanding what she was alluding to, Lola spoke in a consolatory voice, trying to calm her. "That's just how it goes. It's life, and there's nothing that can be done about it. We argue and then regret it later when it's too late."

The words were banal. They fell flat, and she felt stupid.

"I told her to go and see you, to ask your advice. She wouldn't listen. You would have known what to do!"

Lola felt her face grow warm with the burden of responsibility. She dare not tell Clara's mother that she had been sent a letter and had neglected to answer it. They exchanged a look. Lola's was guilty. Madame Campo's was distraught. The tension broke, and the tears came pouring out of the mother's eyes. True sobbing.

"It was only thanks to her that we even managed to eat this winter! What will we do? How can we possibly manage now? She always brought us home bread and gave me money too! My little girl. What will I do without her? She was the one I confided in. We made so many plans together. I can't go on without her."

Lola tried to get Madame Campo to lie down comfortably, though her sole thought was to get out of there, to flee as far as possible from the sense of guilt she was feeling. Without a word, she fled, and as she left, she spotted some hawkers out on the street, girls she knew from her past.

"Madame Campo is in there. You must help her. Her daughter Clara is dead. An accident. She fell and hit her head. That's it. She's gone."

Lola sped down the street so as not to hear the outpourings of grief from the young sellers. Disorientated, she felt the need for some sort of comfort. She turned back and made her way to her own childhood home without clearly deciding to do so. It was an automatic reaction. She didn't often visit her family. She was always afraid of getting into yet another dispute with her father. She stepped inside the small building. A modest structure. Her family lived on the fifth and topmost floor in a long and narrow room with a window looking out westward onto the street.

From time to time, before the Prussian war and the injuries he'd received in battle, Lola's father would work as a fisherman. On even rarer occasions, he would lend a hand on some of the hotel construction sites for some cash in hand on the black. That must have been how he'd managed to tile the floor of the main room. The tiles were all different in color and size, and the result was odd-looking to say the least. But at least it was clean.

There were a few sticks of furniture around the place that Lola's parents had brought with them from her grandmother's house in Italy. A wooden bed, a sideboard, a table with two chairs, and a couple of stools. Sometimes, these pieces would find their way to the pawnbrokers, but they usually managed to get them back at a later date.

Upon entering, Lola saw her mother, Agata, standing at the table, ironing. Her hair was pulled back into neat plaits twisted into a perfect bun at the nape of her neck. She was always so meticulously dressed. The starchy vapors and the heat were making her sweat, but she still appeared as neat and tidy as ever.

The inside of the room looked well cared for despite signs of her work all over the place. The brass boards for the humid clothing, the woolen cloth protectors, the bars of starch, the candle ends for waxing, and the large bowls of clear water were much in evidence.

Lola's mother was proud of her dexterity. She had an excellent reputation for laundry and worked for some of the grandest houses in town. The only reproach one could make about her work was that she sometimes left collars a little too rigid through the overuse of her stiffening agents. Competition was fierce, and in order to retain customers, she would often charge a sou or two less than her rivals. She herself had a keen sense of what it meant to be well dressed, and despite a face that was often high of color due to the heat from the flat irons, she never had a button undone or a thread out of place. Her dresses were always perfectly hemmed, never a mend unmended.

The humidity meant that fleas and lice were rife throughout the apartment. The water wasn't pure, and the smell attracted them. Her bed linen was washed very irregularly. The straw mattresses were rarely changed, and the air was always damp. But the family was used to it. They had been tenants for many years and had no intention of leaving any time soon.

She glanced over to one of the mattresses and saw that her twelve-year-old brother, Mario, was taking a nap, his face partially hidden by the covers.

"Filomena!" her mother cried. "It's you! My, my! How thin you've grown! Come! You must eat a little something. Do you want a coffee?" asked Agata, scrambling to welcome her.

She placed down her iron on an openwork metal stand that was already holding two more. She picked up a *cafetière* that may have been hanging around for quite a while and reheated several times over and poured some of the thick black brew into a pewter tin.

She stepped over to the sideboard and cut a thick slice of bread from a crusty loaf and set Lola at the table. In the skillet over the hearth, some tomato sauce was bubbling. She went to add a few spoons to the bread.

"Mama, I've already eaten enough today! Stop acting as if I'm half-starved! Here, I brought you some soap," she said, pulling a bar of her homemade soap from her pocket where she always kept some. Her mother held it up to her nose, breathed in, and sighed in ecstasy.

"How marvelous! Oh! It smells as good as ever! My neighbors will be so jealous!"

"And Papa? Where is he?"

Agata frowned. She picked up one of her implements and set about ironing again. "He's with Bergeron. And do you know what they're doing? They're playing dice. That game eats up everything I earn. I wonder how we manage to put food on the table."

"He goes too far. He should be helping you."

"You know he's been like this since his accident. And I'd rather he went there. I can't stand him when he's at home getting under my feet and blaspheming all day long! It's as if he expects to grow a new leg! Shouldn't there have been some sort of invalid pension by now? He's a sour man. He blames the whole world for what happened to him. That's why he's always hanging around with those anarchists, chewing the cud! You did the right thing leaving! Just at the right time too!"

"Honestly, Mama, you're a saint. I can't begin to imagine how you've handled all this."

"I see him as he was before the war. I just close off my ears whenever he speaks. There's a lot worse out there, you know."

"Yes, I know."

"He's never beaten me."

"If you're content with the way matters stand . . ."

"Have you just come here to hand me a bar of soap and criticize your father?"

"No, I came to tell Madame Campo that Clara . . ." Lola looked down at her shoes, trying to find the right words.

"What about Clara?"

Lola sighed and looked up, meeting her mother's eyes. "She died last night."

"What? No! I don't believe you!"

"It's true. I was the one who found her."

"*Miseria!* What will her mother do now? She drinks so much she can't even hold a needle straight. And she still has the little ones to feed! Where did you find Clara?"

"She was on the ground, lying in the gardens of the Hôtel Beau Rivage. She worked there, you know?"

"Yes. She would bring food home to her mother. Money, too, I reckon! She got that job through Amédée. Do you know him?"

"I've met him once."

"He really took a fancy to her. I believe he wanted to ask for her hand. He certainly gave her the chase, but she wasn't having any of it."

"How do you know all this?"

"She told me herself! She didn't want to speak to her own mother about it. I don't think she dared. She used to tell me a fair amount."

"So she rejected Amédée?"

"Yes, she found him to be old and not all that handsome. Poor *piccolina*! Did they call out a doctor?"

"Yes, old Buttura. He pronounced her death."

"He's a good man. He's like us."

"Like us how?"

"He's Italian! He understands better! He's a man of courage! I didn't always have to pay him when you were sick when you were babies. I even found a couple of coins left on the table once, so I could buy the medicine you needed."

Lola didn't respond. Her mother, too, stopped talking. She put the iron back into the live coals and sat awhile, waiting for it to reheat.

Eventually, she asked, "What about you and your lovers? That rich man's son? When is he thinking of marrying you?"

"Soon, Mama, soon! Do you need any help? Would you like me to give you some money?"

"Of course not! Your sisters are doing well for themselves now that they're married women. There's only your father, Mario, and me left at home now. I can manage. We don't need a lot."

"That's what you would say! So typical! And why isn't Mario going to school? You know it's the law now, Mama?"

"He goes to help the baker, Russo. He came back with this bread today! That's how he gets paid!"

Lola looked down at her slice of bread. It wasn't even fresh. Her little brother was working for day-old bread! It was a disgrace.

Lola felt a rapid sense of suffocation come upon her. She could no longer tolerate the odor, her mother's voice, the confined space. For the second time that morning, she fled.

As she stepped out into the street and over the sewage-filled gutters, she lifted her head to look at her mother, who was leaning out of the window. She waved, and Agata blew her a kiss in return.

Seized with emotion following her visits, Lola realized that she had learned something important. Amédée knew Clara well. Not only was she indebted to him because he'd got her a place at the hotel, but he'd been in love with her, and she'd turned him down. Lola couldn't wait to get home and note this in their new Scotland Yard file.

She stopped in front of a young farmhand standing out on the street, selling milk drawn straight from a goat, and bought a cup. The taste of the fresh milk was strong and bitter. She felt it give her the energy she needed before giving a franc to the child and moving on her way. He stared at her in marvel. Returning to her childhood roots had forced upon her a certain anxiety and made her witness something she had forgotten for some time: poverty.

Although lost in thought, she was still aware of her surroundings enough to avoid the puddles of waste and to keep her distance from the mules and horses tied up on the pavements. If you were the type not to pay attention, a kick from one of these beasts could certainly take you by surprise.

As she walked, she thought of Eugène. Since being with him, she'd no longer offered her services, but she now recognized she'd been wrong not to do so. She'd believed herself to be in love. That she no longer had any need to sell herself. She had been mistaken. Never again would she be taken in by the pretty words of a liar. Three years. Three years they'd been in love. Was that the natural time limit for such an experience?

Before she met Eugène, she had been a regular at a *café-bastringue* in the center of the town. It had often helped her to make ends meet. It wasn't far from the Rue de la Rampe and only a stone's throw from the market. It had been run by a certain Alexandra. She was a crafty woman, but Lola tended to get on well with her. Patrons would sing and dance in her café, play billiards or use some of the private rooms out back for clandestine card games. Upstairs were private bedrooms that could be used for . . . well, what Lola would use them for. Alexandra always allowed girls to go up there and work. It was undeclared income for all involved. Lola used to go there frequently. It was a somewhat grim picture.

As it wasn't that far a walk, she decided to go and meet the new proprietor. Alexandra had sold up not long before. There were things Lola thought she could learn by talking to him. She grilled him for some time and managed to glean some interesting pieces of information. Madame Alexandra now had a new boutique—of a very particular kind—on the Rue du Bivouac. It was a place for secret rendezvous. He didn't wish to tell her any more than that, and Lola had to buy a few glasses of absinthe for some of the poorer girls in there to get them to give her the details.

What Lola would later tell me simply took my breath away.

Officially, it was a newspaper house, selling books, postcards, maps of Cannes, and tourist guides. Several lounge areas allowed customers to read the works before making a purchase. On the second floor was a reading room where one could enjoy English-style tea and biscuits. A few discreet bedrooms were to be found hidden to the sides, with curtained doors. A little delicate gallantry was known to take place within, when the curtains were closed, with little chance of being uncovered by someone one might know. It was known as a rendezvous house. No explanations needed, and none given. It was said that some of the most famous women in Cannes would show themselves there regularly. Actresses, singers, women famous for lying on their backs . . . but also members of the bourgeoisie and the world of fashion. The latter would tend to arrive incognito. And there were those who felt the need to find solace due to the lack of interest shown to them by their husbands. Or they had the desire to be showered in gifts such as fine perfumes and jewelry beyond what their husbands could afford.

Three years of being madly in love had clearly left Lola behind the times. It seemed Madame Alexandra had come some way since Lola had last been in contact with her.

She left the *bistroquet* and once again considered her dilemma. Should she go home to live with her mother? Or accept Philémon's proposition? Philémon. What a self-satisfied cad! He knew how close she'd been to Eugène, how involved her heart had been! This was beyond her forces! The thought of him was simply enraging! But then she remembered what it had been like to be hungry when she had worked in the perfumery. And when she had spent nights in the arms of Jules and his friends before meeting Eugène. Had she come this far to become a plaything? An object to be exchanged among bored men? She felt sick at the thought of Eugène's betrayal. No. He and Philémon would be too contented with themselves if she allowed herself to be treated this way.

It was time she took back the reins and took her fate into her own hands. She couldn't just be tossed around in the wind with no idea of her final destination. What if she were to keep the house? Could she really pay such an exorbitant rent? She'd been through worse than this. Much worse!

She made up her mind. She would refuse Philémon and find the money for the rent. Sou by sou.

The car was already paid up for the month ahead. That was one less thing to worry about. And she could always return it if she found herself in too much difficulty.

She would go and see Madame Alexandra and come to some sort of arrangement. The future suddenly appeared a little less daunting.

12

A Prince Goes Incognito

Although I was in my bedchamber, I heard Lola return. She made no attempts to hide it as she stomped around, singing boisterously and slamming doors behind her. After a quarter of an hour, I heard, "Miss Fletcher! Come down! We have work to do!"

I quickly glided down the stairs and, when I saw her, noted that she'd changed and put on her fancy clothes: a flouncy pink-and-violet dress with masses of ribbons, flowers, and bows covering every inch of its surface.

She was hovering over the phonograph, slotting in a cylinder that had been lying close by. The song was a modern piece. As it played, she sang along loudly and with confidence.

> *Mignonne, quand le soir descendra sur la terre,*
> *la la la . . .*
> *Nous irons écouter la chanson des blés d'or . . .*
> *Aimons sous les rameaux superbes . . .*
> *la la la . . .*
> *Car la nature aura toujours . . .*
> *la la la . . .*
> *Et des roses pour nos amours . . .*

On the armchair sat an extravagant, gaily colored hat, just waiting to be propped onto her thick head of hair. She'd put on her war paint too—bright-pink rouge on her cheeks, black kohl-colored eyes, and red lipstick.

After relaying all that had happened with Madame Campo, which I noted in our book, she said, "There are a few details that need ironing out. I've decided to fight for this house, but I'm not yet in a position to do so. I must let Rosalie and Gustave know what is happening, and you must help me in this task. Stay close to me." She paused before adding, "This will be the last thing I ask of you. You can pack your belongings after this. I apologize profoundly."

She felt responsible for them and felt a deep shame at being unable to keep them in her employ. She worried less for my outcome, considering I was a woman of privilege, having benefited from a good education, being well dressed, and having access to other resources.

"Oh dear . . . ," I finally managed to say. Deep down I had expected Lola to accept Philémon's offer. I could hardly think of what to say.

"There's nothing left in the coffers. I can no longer hold to my commitments and pay you appropriately. We don't know each other sufficiently well for us to come to another arrangement, whatever that might entail."

"I-I'm so embarrassed," I protested. "My trunks and clothes are all here. I have no idea what to do with myself. You were right when you guessed that my situation was untenable before arriving here. Could you please think on it awhile longer? I have nowhere to go."

"I don't want to put you out on the street, Miss Fletcher! But please be under no illusions here. I have thought about this quite thoroughly. You will have to go. I'm sorry, but I know you will be better for it in the end."

She shouted, as was her usual fashion, "Rosalie! I need you up here! And tell Gustave to join us!"

The scene was an eye-opener. What a difference between how she was dealing with us all and the way Lady Sarah had said her goodbyes to me. Lola was having trouble expressing herself, her voice so altered by the emotion of it, wavering on the brink of tears. She tried to explain what her official situation now was. There was no way she could afford to pay any of our salaries. Eugène had lied to her, and the house had never been in her name. She now had rent to pay to Philémon if she were to stay.

Rosalie muttered, "Too much faith in people . . ."

Gustave cut her off. "There's no need to wear yourself out with all this talk, Filo. We understand. We're not idiots! We've followed every episode: Bréville, his parents, Maupassant, the notary . . . We hoped that . . . Well, never mind. It's through no wrongdoing of yours. We know that."

"I'm staying," said Rosalie. "Where would I go, anyway, huh? You're bound to bounce back and land on your feet again. And I hardly think you'd manage very well without me."

"But, Rosalie, I can't! I cannot pay your—"

"I'm free to make my own decisions, aren't I? This is what I propose: I stay here, and you feed and house me. I don't want it to be for the long term, but I'm convinced you'll be set up straight soon enough. And when you're ready, you can pay me what you owe me then. Is that not a grand plan? It would be as if I were giving you credit of sorts."

"But I can't accept—"

I interrupted, "It's a very good idea. I think we should make a written agreement and that the credit is given with interest. Rosalie doesn't do charity, but on the contrary, she makes investments. And she's betting on you."

Lola appeared delighted at the idea of putting it all in writing. She threw herself into Rosalie's arms and wiped away her tears at the same time. I could never get over how often French women could turn on the waterworks. Or was it something unique to the women of the Midi region of France?

Gustave looked embarrassed, shifting his weight from one foot to the other.

He explained that he had a family he had to keep, and he wouldn't be able to work for free, even with the promise of a salary at a later date.

"Of course," said Lola. "I'll write you the most beautiful letter of reference so you can find work without so much as a day's delay! And I owe you notice. I will pay you as soon as possible. I will write it all down. The same for you, Rosalie. Miss Fletcher? Could you help me with this, please?"

I went into our new office and took a seat. I found my very best pen and set about writing a beautiful reference for Gustave Planchon, the man of all trades. Gustave hid his desire to cry quite well, but I could see the emotion in his eyes. All three of them were moved.

"I'm going to seek out a position right away. I'll be back in the week to collect my belongings."

"Before you go, could you please help Miss Fletcher bring down her things? You'll drive her wherever she wants to go and then bring back the car? You'll be free to leave afterward."

As she said this, she turned her head away. Gustave nodded and went outside to fix the horse to the cart.

Startled, and suddenly desperate, I said, "Couldn't I be your official driver until you find a replacement? Until things get a little better for you? Under the same arrangement as Rosalie?"

"You know I'm in no position to keep you on. It'd be best if you returned from whence you came as soon as was possible."

I was taken aback by her words. Back to where I had come from? If only she knew!

And yet I knew she understood something of it, for despite her young age, she had certainly met with the greatest of misery in her life. I was clearly a burden to her. I couldn't stay. I had to pack up my clothes and papers and go. What I feared most was the demon inside me . . . the one who'd spoken to me that night on the pier just off the Croisette. I didn't wish to show her how upset I was, so I climbed the stairs up to my attic room and made a start on packing my bags and trunks.

A little time passed, and the heavy footsteps of Gustave on my stairwell let me know that he was coming up to help carry my affairs down to the carriage.

"Do you want me to drive you someplace?" he asked. "As soon as I'm done with you, I'll be off myself."

As we stood outside, I took a final glance at the facade of the building that housed the lonely Lola Deslys. Such a pity. I had felt very much at home there. I helped Gustave with the last of my bags and stepped up into the carriage. I heard the front door open up behind me and turned to see Lola, complete with gloves and hat, walking out into the garden. She was off on her excursion to buy foodstuffs and provisions.

With an unreasoned impulse, I shouted, "Would you like me to accompany you to town? It's almost as though your staff uses your vehicle more than you! It's ludicrous! Just this last time?"

She scrutinized me with a hint of pity in her eyes. I had been so insistent, she dared not refuse.

"Indeed!" she finally said. "I need to start parading around the place a little. It's right that I be seen. Let's go. Gustave, you're free to take your leave now. I wish you all the very best. You deserve it so."

After the final goodbyes were said and a last embrace from the man who had worked there for years, Gustave walked off at a brisk pace toward the Boulevard de la Foncière, his bag over his shoulder. I moved into the driver's seat of the cab. Lola climbed up front next to me, under the pretext that she had a little counsel to bestow upon me. Receiving advice as to how to drive at my age, from a child of twenty-one, was a strange thought indeed, but I felt merry. I allowed her to think that my sudden gaiety was all to do with the fact that I was about to be driving the horse, but the truth was that I was contented to be spending a few more moments with her.

"Oh, you're smiling!" she said. "I'll never comprehend what a woman of your position would be doing in a house such as mine. You could have very well lost your reputation."

I got the feeling she wanted me to confess something, some sort of proof that she could trust me. I was so absorbed by the thought of driving that I was unable to respond. As I thought of Lady Sarah, my color heightened. What might she have said to her—to our—friends and acquaintances?

"What's the horse's name?"

"Oh, it's a little nickname. Gaza. He was given to me by Eugène on the day our mayor was elected."

Recognizing the bemused look on my face, she went on to clarify:

"Gaza. Gazagnaire. The mayor's name. Do you understand? He's a wonderful mayor. He moved the brothel behind Cercle Nautique, which means it's not far from the theater. It's very advantageous for us girls."

After a few seconds, I changed the subject and said, "And Clara Campo? Our agreement? We made a pact, did we not? With Maupassant?"

She didn't respond, and I felt walled in by the lack of words.

We had just turned out from the small driveway and onto the street that would take us to the station and past the majestic gates of the Hôtel Central, when a stunning victoria loomed in front of us, trying to overtake us. Its roof was piled high with luggage. Gaza whinnied in fear. It looked as though they were heading for the hotel. It seemed as if a collision would be inevitable, but I managed to gain control of the horse. For a few seconds, the frightened horses on the victoria bucked up, leaving both carriages immobilized. The upholstered cushions on the driver's seat were hanging over the sides of the victoria due to the weight of the driver, a bearded man in his forties with a stout frame. His eyes glided over me before coming to a standstill as he beheld Lola. He looked excited as he gazed upon her, blinking uncontrollably. He was dressed head to foot in tweed, and although a little worse for wear, he could have passed as a member of the English upper class. There was something in the way he held his head, the way his clothes fitted as if tailored to him. I found him intriguing. I remembered just then that I had seen him somewhere before. He'd been present at a grand dinner at Lady Sarah's London residence.

Lola turned her head delicately toward the horizon, her cheeks glowing a little. And then, because she was so very attracted to the idea of seduction no matter what the circumstances, she allowed her eyes to meet his, a gentle smile escaping from her lips. The man returned the smile, undressing her with his eyes, and then peered behind us to the house. Once the horses had settled, he cracked his whip and forced them to continue, removing his hat slightly from the top of his head by way of salutation.

"I left that one awestruck," said Lola, quite obviously enchanted by him. "He'll be back, that's for certain! That's the advantage of living steps away from the palace and the station, you know. You get to bump into people like that!"

"But . . . but . . . do you know who that was?"

"Of course, miss! Why so flustered? It was the Prince of Wales! I knew he'd be coming. It said as much in the newspaper. I think he's trying to keep a low profile. He came in on the train from Paris—on the quiet, you know? Come, miss. Let's not tarry any further. I have things to do."

Her sense of aplomb left me feeling aghast. I said nothing.

Lola gave me directions as we drove. I was glad because I had no place in mind for myself and my bags. She chose the strangest of routes. The problem was, she didn't have much of an idea as to where she was going. We meandered down the Rue du Bivouac, the Rue Hermann, followed by the Rue Saint-Honoré, the Rue de la Vapeur and then onto the Place des Îles. She was looking for something and getting more and more annoyed that she couldn't find it.

"They said the Rue du Bivouac! Oh, where is it?"

Out of the blue, right in the middle of the Place du Châtaignier, just on the corner of the Rue du Bivouac, she screamed out, "Reading rooms! Here it is! Honestly! I can't handle it when people give you the wrong directions to a place! Drop me here, and then you take yourself off. You don't have to hang around for me. Come back in a half hour. I won't be any longer than that!"

I felt quite proud to be sitting up so high on the driver's seat despite the astonished and gently mocking stares of passersby. I had on my boater hat and knew I looked quite the spectacle in my short dress and flat boots.

I watched as Lola walked into the establishment and started leafing through a few books, not really reading, but more than likely admiring the illustrations.

The decision had been made by the proprietor to mix what might be known as "good" literature with some of the more popular and "saucier" best sellers and periodicals. This explained why I could spy a few copies of Maupassant's "La Maison Tellier," next to *Les Fleurs du Mal* by Baudelaire. There was also a reproduction of the stunning Manet painting *Nana*, with copies of the latest Émile Zola title just in front. And Flaubert's *Madame Bovary*. There were postcards of Degas prints and several books by Armand Silvestre and Paul de Kock. A large part of the window space was given to English writers. Thomas Hardy shared space with Wilkie Collins. It couldn't have been more appealing or more eclectic.

Although much of the floor space inside seemed to be taken up by women, a few men also pushed open the double swing doors at the front of the building and stepped inside to peruse the books. I saw Lola talking to the teller before climbing the elegant spiral staircase.

I inspected my pocket watch. It was always around this time that the parcels were dropped off at the post office next to the town hall. I spotted the driver of the mail car coming from the Rue de la Vapeur at the end of the street. Maupassant had told us that he was often back and fore from the post office, sending or receiving the latest version of whatever novel was next to be published. I decided to go and see if he was there.

I made my way slowly down the length of the Allée de la Marine and in front of the town hall. I was slowed down at one point at the crossroads by a number of vehicles all seeming to be making deliveries at the same time. I almost missed him. I saw him leaving the telegram office, looking hurried, a parcel under his arm. He was rubbing at his eyes as if dazzled. Yet the sun was nowhere to be seen. He didn't spot me immediately, and when I stopped the landau just in front of him to allow him to cross, he raised his arm in thanks absentmindedly. He recognized me upon a second glance and laughed heartily.

"Miss Fletcher! How fetching you look! Have you got a new position? You're a driver now?"

"That's right! I'm Mademoiselle Deslys's new horsewoman!" I called out.

Several people turned their heads my way to get a look at who was doing all the shouting.

"How original! And what brings you to this neck of the woods?"

"I came to seek you out! Jump up! Let me accompany you!"

"With pleasure!" He climbed up to my side. "I live on the Rue du Redan. I came to collect the latest draft of my book."

"I'd adore it if I were your first reader! If you would allow it?"

"No, no . . . it's all a big secret for now. You'll see why. So, what's the news with you?"

"Gosh! So much has changed since we last spoke, but I don't think it my job to tell you—"

Slightly annoyed, he cut me off. "In that case, don't!"

"Have you got any further ahead on the Clara case?" I asked.

"Indeed. I passed by the morgue, as a matter of fact. Buttura has requested that her burial be postponed. There are several ways to preserve a body in this day and age, but our doctor friend has been inspired by the works of Dr. Lacassagne's institute. They're all amateurs down here, of course, but this man appears to do a handsome job. I think they'll be able to stop decomposition in its tracks. Or at least for the time they need to thoroughly analyze the corpse."

"I'm amazed to hear all this! What is the method, exactly?"

"It all started up in Lyon. Lacassagne used liquids that are able to conserve things in their natural state—liquid phenic acid, arsenous acid, combined with heavy quantities of glycerin and methylic alcohol. Ice water also works wonders, but it has to be replaced very frequently. The doctor didn't want to damage the stomach in any way, as it's important to know exactly how much she had had to drink. And so, he is unable to inject this mixture into her. He can only use it on the outside. It could destroy any results he gets if used internally."

"I think I've had enough of the grim details now. You're quite incorrigible!"

He snorted with laughter. "So . . . your turn now! Do you have any news of Clara?"

"Oh, of course! Mademoiselle Deslys went up to the Suquet and managed to glean two or three pieces of information that could be of vital significance! Come over to the house to see us, and I'll let you read through my notes."

He rubbed his eyes again. They looked red and sore, as if he'd just survived a sandstorm.

"Is there something wrong? You appear to be suffering," I said.

"It's nothing. A trifling matter. I inherited an illness from my mother. We have very fragile eyes, and sometimes I can't even keep them open. They're quite sensitive to the light. Ocular paralysis, it's called. It can give me quite shocking migraines!"

"How dreadful!"

"Quite! The eye is so important! The eye is where one finds the window to the soul! Did you know that? Yet in mine, one sees nothing more than suffering. When a full attack overcomes me, I have to lie down and take a few sniffs of ether. And I take a daily dose of sodium salicylate! God help me should I forget! My heart beats so fast when I take my ether that I can feel it, almost hear it, throughout my entire body. It's quite deafening."

"Do you need any assistance? Would you like me to go to the apothecary for you and purchase a remedy? Cornflower? Should I call a doctor?"

"No. I'm quite fine. I have everything I need. I'm very lucky that François takes care of me so well. I have suction cups. He places them on my skin for me. He really is very good. The only difficulty is that when the pain from the headaches gets to be too much, I'm obliged to increase the laudanum dosage. It means I lose concentration when it comes to editing my texts." He howled with laughter. "If my writings are a little wobbly in recent times, this is the reason!"

"False modesty doesn't suit you."

He moved in closer to me, his body touching mine. "You really are quite magnetic, Miss Fletcher. You know that, I'm sure. Please don't abuse my heart too much!"

I shifted away from him slightly, smiling.

As we drove the length of the pebbled beach, we pulled into sight of the lavender fields blowing in the wind on the seafront just before the Rue du Redan. He jumped down from the carriage, grasping the parcel in his hand.

"I don't wish to trouble you with my worries. They are but few when we compare them with the sorry ending poor Clara had to suffer, are they not? We should rejoice in being alive. And thank you so much for this ride. It's always so agreeable to travel in such style and comfort! I hope, now that you know where I reside, you will come and pay me a courtesy visit? François will absolutely adore you! I must introduce the two of you."

And he left me in a fevered hurry.

I took some time to drive down the length of the Quai Saint-Pierre, admiring the naval vessels unloading their cargoes next to the bright pleasure yachts, before returning to park up outside the reading rooms.

I awaited Lola, perched high on my driver's seat, holding the reins with one hand and a cigarillo with the other.

As soon as Lola arrived, I knew she was in a much better mood than she had been. She looked like a cat licking her whiskers after devouring an entire jug of cream. Her step was light as she left the building. I watched as she scanned the area around us; then she hopped up onto the seat next to me and proceeded to tell me all about her visit.

13

MADAME ALEXANDRA

She had spoken to the teller in the bookshop on the first floor—a conversation full of double entendres—before making her way up to the second floor, where she was able to witness for herself what truth existed beyond the rumors.

In a large, resplendent lounge full of armchairs, divans, and stylish tables reclined young women, dressed in their finest, drinking tea in the company of men of all ages. Some were sitting alone, leafing through reviews and savoring sweet delicacies.

Lola felt immediately as though she were too visible, her clothes too colorful and flamboyant for such a place. She wondered whether she had made a mistake as to what sort of establishment this was. But when she saw a gentleman rise from a table, leaving a group of friends behind, shortly followed by a young woman dressed in the latest fashions, both of them heading down the same small corridor, she knew she was indeed in the right place. She picked up a book and engineered herself into a seated position at a small table, almost falling to one side as she sunk down into the sumptuous ottoman.

A young and stylish man approached her and served her a pot of tea along with a small pink dish full of biscuits and a jug of cream. A tall woman with a tight blonde bun covered with a fashionable black widow's veil made her way across the room toward Lola. It was a few seconds before she recognized her as being Madame Alexandra herself. She looked nothing like Lola remembered. She had lost the neglected and vulgar appearance she once bore, and it had been replaced by something much more respectable, almost austere.

"Madame Alexandra! Don't you recognize me? It's me, Filo! I used to come and see you at the Chat Rouge with de Bréville and Stan's group! Don't you remember? What's happened? You're in widow's mourning dress?"

Madame Alexandra burst out laughing and slapped Lola on her shoulder.

"Filo! Of course, I remember you, my little sweetheart! What a sight! Whatever happened to you? How you've changed! What a shape on you! He's feeding you well, that Eugène! You are absolutely magnificent!"

Lola quickly explained how she had entered into a dispute with Eugène and what a catastrophic situation she now found herself in.

"It was all my own fault, of course," she said. "I made the mistake of believing him, and I shouldn't have."

"There's a lesson learned!" Madame Alexandra cried out. "You've been taught that we all have to pay for our mistakes in this grim little world of ours."

She went on to explain to Lola how business worked in her new establishment and how much it was appreciated, even by the local security forces. It seemed the place was very well thought of because the services offered there were kept so discreet.

Lola made no secret she was in the market for a new suitor for the following winter season. In the meantime, however, she was hoping to meet someone from Cannes, someone who would likely be staying in town that summer. Someone long term would be the absolute jackpot.

"Do you need an advance, my dear? Shall we draw up a contract?" asked Madame Alexandra.

With a nod from Lola, she took Lola to a small office, where she opened a large registry book and noted down "one thousand francs."

"I'm going by a different name now," said Lola. "Could you write Lola Deslys? I've started a whole new life."

Madame Alexandra wrote this down in the most beautiful hand-writing Lola had ever seen. She then opened up a safety deposit box hidden in the corner and took out a coffer full of gold coins.

"Understand that I'll expect to see you here at least two days a week for the next month. That should be enough to reimburse me."

"I'd like to know in advance who my . . . special friends will be. And if I don't find them to my liking, am I allowed to refuse?"

"That's fine with me. When I can, I'll send you notes when some-one wants to meet with you here. Will that do? If you feel so inclined, you can come here more often. If I hear of anyone wishing to start up a lasting companionship with a girl, I will let you know of it. But please, no more parakeet colors when you come here. It's better for us all if nobody makes a spectacle of themselves. Showing off the merchandise in such a manner has long since seen its day.

"We're looking for a higher class of girl here. Understated. That's what it's all about. All aboveboard and correct. We give men the il-lusion of seduction. Simple banal adultery and nothing more. Next time you come here, please use the door behind the building. There are some overzealous members of the police force out front who don't know that their bosses are friends of mine."

Lola, grateful to Madame Alexandra for the advance, skipped to-ward the spiral staircase despite being bound to her in writing for the foreseeable future.

On her way back down, she crossed paths with a dashing man in his forties, a virile-looking gentleman, tall and well built, who took a step to the side of the stairs to allow her to pass. He appeared to have dressed himself with care, in a city suit of carefully woven alpaca and a patterned waistcoat in cashmere, all in pastel orange and light-mauve tones. His top hat shone in an impeccably fine black goatskin, and a genuine topaz glistened atop his cane. She smiled at him reflexively, knowing it was a good habit to get into given her new mode of employment. He stared at her fixedly as if the mere sight of her provoked revulsion. What she had first interpreted as courtesy was clearly, in fact, disdain.

What a boor, she thought with indignation as her smile dropped. *If he's afraid of contagion, this is hardly the place to be.*

He turned his head, making no response, and continued his way up the stairs to the second floor.

14

ICE CREAM AT THE GRAND CAFÉ

As Lola's tale came to an end, she stepped off the front of the carriage and returned to the passenger's seat behind me. She spread out her skirts, layers, flouncy laces, and ribbons and half lay back across the bench.

"Go down the Boulevard de la Croisette in front of the Beau Rivage, the Gonnet, the Grand Hôtel, and the Cercle Nautique. In fact, let's go as far as the carriage will allow. Once the roads become too stony, we'll turn around and make for the Allée de la Marine and the Quai Saint-Pierre. Go as slowly as the horse will walk. I need to be seen and admired. The time is now. It's *passeggiata*, as my mother would say. I need the men of this town to know that my heart is for the taking." She tittered giddily. "We need to get the message across to as many of our acquaintances as possible, both old and new."

"Understood," I said.

And I obeyed her to the letter. The Boulevard de la Croisette flowed like a river under the light of a dusky sky. A happy crowd walked alongside a slower set of people, bent over, huddled together, edging along in pain and glancing up at the better-dressed and more-handsome folk in either envy or indifference. Life and death rubbing against each other cheek by cheek. Those who had come to town to celebrate what it was to be alive were intermingled with those who had come to end their days in the sunshine, grasping on to a final hope. The whole scene vibrated with a thousand dazzling lights: beautifully varnished shoes upon which the dusty roadside seemed to have no tarnishing effect, the shiny black hats, the women in stunning jewels that glittered and glistened from inside their carriages, the bright white teeth beneath reddened, smiling lips.

Our vehicle is what made us stand out from the crowd. We slowed down. A successful move, for heads in top hats turned to stare at us, and this was indeed our aim. The women however, turned their faces away. Every few minutes or so, Lola would wave at the crowds as if she were Queen Victoria herself. She would shriek exaggeratedly, making requests of me to stop every now and again so she could exchange greetings with friends.

As we traveled farther down the coastal road, I spotted Philémon. I made a sign to Lola. She asked that I hasten a little and turn down an adjacent side street. We just managed to escape him, but her demeanor darkened.

"I don't know whether or not he saw us," she said quietly, a worried tone to her whisper. She brushed her skirts with her hands as if to rid herself of such cares. "Let us continue our parade. I'm not going to allow him to get in my way."

When we reached the town hall, she made me slow down and pointed out the commissioner, who was exiting the building via the front door in the company of Maurel, the manager at the Beau Rivage. She caught their eye, and we carried on with our exhibition. The hustle and bustle on the street below slowed down somewhat as people looked up to admire us as we passed. They craned their necks to witness the nervousness of the horse, the splendor of the carriage, the gorgeous colorful silks in which Lola was so pleasantly attired, and the horseman's— or horsewoman's in my case—unusual outfit.

We heard a number of oohs and aahs as they marveled at such a sight. This was the first time I'd ever experienced anything like it. We were the center attraction. Until that moment, I'd never really paid much attention to how business played out on the Croisette. We were not the only ones to be showing ourselves in such a manner. It seemed it was quite the done thing. Vehicles of all descriptions, all containing brightly dressed women, were shamelessly flaunting their wares up and down the boulevard. Each carriage was being driven slowly and each stopped in turn to receive salutations from men on foot. When Lola would ask that I stop the carriage, I could hear her brief conversations—such shallow subjects and all full of innuendo. It took us over an hour to reach the Grand Café, on the Allées.

Just as we were upon it, she shouted, "Stop! I feel like an ice cream, don't you? Drop me here, go and find a place to leave the carriage, and then come and join me, please."

"But . . ."

"But what? Cat got your tongue?"

"We're alone! They'll never let us in unaccompanied."

"We'll sit out on the terrace. We don't need men that much, do we?"

I positioned the carriage and horse a few steps away from the café and attached the beast to a ring on the side of the road. The long promenade that is the Allées, just opposite the Pantiero, was very busy at this hour. The music kiosk was playing its fanfare, and the cafés were serving drinks and ices. Surrounding the tables on the terrace that boarded onto the pavement sat gentlemen in dark suits. Unfortunately, it wasn't easy being served in this type of place unless you had a gentleman on your arm. We would have had no difficulty getting into one of the larger tearooms in the center of town, but Lola had decided that she wanted to be seen by men and that this was where the men were.

Men of all statuses frequented this establishment. The bourgeoisie were seated alongside shopkeepers, foreigners, rich business tycoons, aristocracy . . . they were all there, reading newspapers, talking politics, or exchanging gossip.

As I went to meet her, I felt very much ill at ease. She had found a table on the very edge of the terrace next to the Allées. The waiter hesitated as he went to take her order. I was afraid he would chase me away, believing me to be undesirable company, but I knew I couldn't abandon her there. I moved toward her, pulled up a chair, and sat beside her. Strangely, I had quite the opposite effect on the waiter than I'd presumed. He seemed somewhat reassured by my presence. My masculine outfit and hat must have made him feel I was at least dressed the part. We were the only women without male company.

On the Allées were two women, in their carriage, eating ice creams that their driver had been out to purchase for them. That was as much as was tolerated.

We ordered bergamot sorbet with *marasquin*, and as we waited, she continued to tell me of her encounter with Madame Alexandra. Her explanations as to what she'd signed herself up for struck me as being direct, to say the least. I was flabbergasted at the contradictory feelings her words aroused in me. My moral education meant I was initially suspicious of her—suspicious, in fact, of anyone so easily able to sell their body to survive. Yet I also felt her actions had been just and couldn't help thinking that thanks to her endeavors, better times now lay ahead of us. It hadn't taken long for me to change my opinion on the matter! The thousand-franc loan, I believed, was not only a good omen, but perhaps a trap of some kind. I reasoned she'd been a little naive on the subject.

"You know why she gave you that money, don't you?"

"Because she's not all there!" she mocked.

My expression must have betrayed my consternation, and she yelled, "You should see your face! No! Of course, I know why! I'm not as silly as I look! She has me hook, line, and sinker! She knows I can't go elsewhere for work now! I belong to her for the moment. At least until I've returned the money to her."

She laughed disdainfully and explained it was of no importance to her. She cared not whether she was given the money prior to or following her "activities"—as long as she was permitted to spend it of her own free will.

"As long as I'm a single lady without a husband, I should do as I please with my fortune. Is that not the law? Am I not fortunate? And as Rosalie would say, they're not exactly queuing up to marry me, are they?"

I got the impression that I was so tightly wound to her destiny, to what would become of her, that I had to find a better way for her to make ends meet.

She pointed out a young girl, unwashed, barefoot, in simple country dress typical of the region, who was walking along the street with an enormous hatbox in her arms. The box was almost bigger than she was.

"That's how I started out in life," said Lola. "And that's why Clara could never understand some of the choices I made. She was protected—up there behind the thick castle walls. I know she worked hard, but she was protected all the same, and I was out on the streets."

She smiled as she spoke. I wanted to take her hand in mine, to stroke it lovingly. I wanted to protect her.

She beckoned the child over to our table. "What's your name, princess?"

"Magali."

"Would you like an ice cream?"

Without waiting for the girl to respond, Lola lifted her arm to get the attention of one of the serving staff.

"Do you like chocolate?"

Magali nodded, and Lola ordered her a small carton that she could take away with her.

The little child was delighted and skipped off into the street with the pot of ice cream balanced on top of the hatbox.

"When I was her age, doing what she does, I used to take great joy in walking up and down the streets around here, watching all the beautiful ladies. Nobody ever offered me an ice cream, of course. What I was fond of more than anything else was going inside the big villas. The varnished furniture, the huge bouquets of flowers, the maids dressed up like queens, the floors so shiny you could see your face in them. Perhaps had I never seen such marvels, the idea would never have crossed my mind to go and make myself useful to Madame Camoux."

"And why did you stop . . . that kind of work?"

She peered off into the distance pensively, her face then turning impassive.

"You're a curious one, aren't you? I did it for as long as I could. One day too many, Miss Fletcher. Little girls shouldn't be sent in and out of great houses like that without protection. They're so shiny, these places. They're like ice. I learned one day that all good things come to an end. That's all there is to it."

She tittered a little, but something sounded hurt in her voice. Something bitter. I wondered what could have happened to her for her to still be suffering to this day.

We were an unusual sight, sitting there in the fresh and dry springlike sunshine. In addition to the Grand Café clientele who could not stop themselves from covertly staring at us from the corners of their eyes, passersby were also gawking at us despite themselves.

Farther up the street, I spotted a woman walking slowly toward us. She was in company, joined by a small group of people. My heart pounded in my chest. I recognized her immediately. The shape of her was forever imprinted on my memory. Lady Sarah! I stiffened, my breath caught in my throat. I hoped above all else that she wouldn't see me. Not now. Not here. Not with Lola Deslys! I felt the color drain from my skin as I turned my head to Lola, trying to give the impression that I was engrossed in her words, but not hearing a one.

My world turned upside down as this most elegant of women passed in front of the terrace slowly. By her side walked her nurse and, running ahead, her two children—Harriet and Oscar. They spotted me and started running toward the table, but their nurse, whom I'd never seen before, called them back before they could approach too closely. Lady Sarah slowed down her step and turned her head in our direction. I was petrified. I held her gaze, my eyes unable to move. It took her no longer than a second to get a good idea of the scene before her: Lola and me, unaccompanied women sitting happily at a table, enjoying ices—with Lola talking loudly and passionately about something or other.

Several expressions played across her features. Amazement, disbelief at seeing me with Lola, followed by scorn and a feeling of . . . could it have been resentment? Jealousy? Or was it simply my imagination? After staring at me fixedly, she turned her head and moved on. She didn't quicken her step, she simply walked away. From a deathly pale pallor, my complexion suddenly burned, as if on fire. I was thankful that Lola appeared to have noticed nothing of the incident.

Could Lady Sarah really have been jealous? I must have been dreaming. From what I knew of her, perhaps her strong sense of propriety had been awakened in seeing me with another. My running into her like that had to be seen as some kind of a sign. What might Lady Sarah be thinking? Did she believe that deathly stare of hers would create in me some degree of shame?

I decided I would have to insist—I had to fight to stay within the employ of Lola. There was nothing else to be done. I would manage it somehow.

I declared, "I beg of you, Lola. Don't reject me."

"Listen, Miss Fletcher," she said softly, in conciliation. "I have no means of paying you. But nor do I wish to throw you out into the street. You must leave, but do so at your own pace when you see fit. Would that be more agreeable to you?"

I had no desire to show it, but I truly felt as though I were drowning in relief, in happiness.

"You can do the same as Rosalie if you wish. Stay. But you deserve so much better than remaining with me without enumeration. You also risk losing your honor. This is an offer I'm putting to you, but only if you fail to find an alternative arrangement."

I no longer cared to hear the details of what she had to say. I had gained a few hours, a few days . . . perhaps longer. It was a joyous thought indeed. I would find out soon enough what the future entailed. It was clear to me that the perspective of staying in the presence of Lola was the principal reason for my joy.

Lady Sarah often had a foreknowledge of such things and must have sensed it. Had she guessed, just in watching me briefly, that I was smitten with Mademoiselle Lola Deslys, the courtesan? Had she known before even I knew? I felt somewhat at peace. As we went on with our discussion, I noted that my melancholy and worried state had completely deserted me.

A long lull in the conversation followed as we both reflected on what we had discussed and decided. Suddenly, Lola took my hand, and I flinched.

"Look! It's Amédée! Don't turn around! I know the man he's talking to! A nasty old devil! I can't for the life of me remember where I've seen that ogre of a man before. I wonder whether I remember his face from back in the days before Eugène."

"That Amédée is dubious of character, is he not?"

Amédée was gesticulating wildly at the man he was speaking with before stamping off at a brisk pace without further ado.

A fellow customer seated next to us finished twirling a newspaper around its wooden stick.

"May I?" asked Lola.

He handed over the rolled-up paper courteously, but still regarded her with an air of suspicion. She smiled widely at him, showing all her teeth, looking at him boldly . . . so boldly, in fact, that her insistent glare led her to winking at him, which caused him to titter. He arose, waved at us both elegantly, and hastened away. She passed me the newspaper.

"Read it to me . . ."

I skimmed the main titles.

"There's no more talk of the death at La Païva?"

"Not that I can see. Do you wish me to read the advertisements too? At least two out of five pages are advertisements alone!"

She grimaced with disinterest as I screamed out, an epiphany coming to me, "An advertisement!"

"What in the heavens is the matter with you?"

"I have an idea! We need to cover this town in your image! We need to have a portrait made . . . you in the most beautiful surroundings, boasting the most promising of smiles . . . with your name in the corner. We can launch your career! Like that of a young actress!"

"Do you mean put it in the papers? Or upon a postcard?"

"A postcard? That's an even better idea! Bravo! A wonderful thought! I was imagining little visiting cards, but a postcard is a much better option! Very good! We can sell them on newspaper stands near the station! We'll make the printing costs back easily! Now, there's a way to spend a thousand francs wisely!"

"But what about the rent? I was counting on this money to cover the first month."

"Don't worry about that now!"

I felt so sure of myself. All I wanted to do at that very moment was to return home and set about working without hesitation. This was my real job: managing the career of Mademoiselle Lola Deslys!

"You want to dictate our every move, don't you, Miss Fletcher?"

I smiled.

On the way home, she asked me to drop her off with the photographer, Numa Blanc. Once Lola got an idea into her head, she was unable to wait more than a minute or two to see it through.

15

THE DREAMS OF AN ORPHAN

The next day, as morning broke, after having dressed myself and arranged my room, I descended the stairs to speak with Rosalie.

I didn't try to convince her to help me transform the house into the sort of residence of which we wouldn't be ashamed when receiving visitors, for I didn't want to embarrass her. Instead, I simply exposed the fact that we were now part of a common enterprise in which we all had a role to play. I highlighted my own participation in the work that lay ahead of us, but pointed out that Lola was to be the key to it all. She would desperately need our assistance. The house had to be the jewel in her crown. An homage to her image. The most perfect of settings.

"In other words, we're mixing apples with oranges here. Is that what you're hinting at?" Rosalie asked.

"Yes. Quite literally. It's all a little mixed up here. We need to get organized."

Rosalie appeared upset. She just sat there, as still as a millpond. So I set about the work alone. I walked around the house, collecting dirty dishes and cups. Rosalie sulked. When I returned to the kitchen and began cleaning them in the sink, she stood.

"Leave it. Go back to that study you've made for yourself and . . . do what you do."

Despite my protestations, she refused to allow me to continue cleaning.

"They'd steal the bread from your mouth, these Englishwomen, despite their airs and graces," she muttered to herself as she set about washing the dishes noisily.

I went upstairs and took my place at my desk to deliberate on the best way to run the house and to manage the accounts in the most inventive way I could.

The clattering from the kitchen woke Lola.

"Ah! About time! Your room needs airing!" shouted Rosalie.

Lola stood in the doorway to my office and frowned at me sleepily, "*Ouh là!* What's got into her today?"

"I can hear you, you know?" cried Rosalie. "Come on down to the kitchen! I have coffee brewing for you!"

Lola puffed out her cheeks and slumped down the stairs, saying, "Come, Miss Fletcher! Have you seen the sunshine out there today?"

We sat outside under the pergola with a large bowl of coffee each. I was enjoying the peace, my face turned up to the warm February sunshine.

Sherry had jumped up onto the table and was slurping the pot of cream that Lola had poured out onto a saucer for him.

Every few minutes, a local would pass and wave at us, or we'd spot a luxurious carriage pulling up in front of the majestic gates of the Hôtel Central and all the fracas that went with it.

Lower down the hill, the station welcomed noisy smoking locomotives. We were lucky there were so many fruit trees in the area to clean our air.

Just as on my first visit here, nuns and small groups of their charges were walking up and down the hill. Dressed in black, some of the orphans looked in the poorest of health. They were morose and thin, their complexions so pale. One peeked over to our table, her eyes feeding greedily on our now-breakfast-laden table. She loitered a little and studied the breads and jams out in front of us and looked at the lazy way in which we sat reclined on our chairs. The appearance of two fairies couldn't have astounded her more. She stuck her little nose in the air, taking in the marvelous odor of the freshly ground coffee.

Lola turned her head to look at me and said, "I hate seeing them walking up and down the street. I could cry for them. I'm fortunate in that my schedule means I rarely run into them."

Lola lingered awhile until the group of orphans was some distance away before standing up and rushing inside, not a touch of joy remaining on her face.

I cleared the table and followed her.

The rooms upstairs were gleaming! Rosalie had cleaned, scrubbed, waxed . . . the place shone like a diamond! It smelled of coal-tar soap.

I took Lola into the study and explained how I envisaged keeping the accounts from then on. I had prepared columns labeled "Money In" and "Money Out": rent, housekeeping, groceries, toiletries, and so on. There wasn't much in the "Money In" column as of yet, just the thousand francs from Madame Alexandra and a few notes from Bréville's father. Of course, the amount represented more than ten months' wages for a typical worker, but it amounted to what Lola would have to earn each month just to cover the rent. We would have to diversify our means of earning money. Lola sounded enthusiastic at first, but the numbers and lists quickly bored her, and she offered me a game of cards. I sighed.

"I hate card games," I said. "I associate them with too many bad memories. All those endless games of rummy I had to endure with the most boring of people."

Lola let my words hang in the air and then said, "I wonder how much Clara earned as a chambermaid?"

"I know you have a lot playing on your mind right now, but I doubt the salary of a chambermaid would make a dent in what you owe. What about your soaps? I find the fragrances you use particularly lovely. So suave and sophisticated. Could you make a living out of them? More and more women are taking care of their personal hygiene and appearance these days, don't you think?"

"You're right! And I forgot to tell you that I also make a range of body oils and creams. I started when I was very young. I used to *borrow* the essences from the perfumery. Many of the people I worked with did the same."

"The sole worry is, you have to work your way out of private sales and into making it in greater quantities. You could teach me how to do it, and I could help you. I enjoy bringing money in. Rosalie too! What do you think of that? We could all get involved."

"The soaps are a good idea. It could help us out of this tight spot."

"For now, I believe you should entrust me with the thousand francs. It'll mean you won't lose them or spend them unwisely."

"We've already spent them, in effect, with your printing idea," said Lola, her mouth pursed.

"Yes! Exactly!"

She held out her reticule to me, and I slipped it inside a coffer I'd found in the pantry and placed on one of the shelves. This would now serve as our vault. I attempted to explain to her how I'd organized the accounting ledger, the columns, dates, rates, practices . . . and the preferences of gentlemen. It could all be of immense use to us.

Lola mocked me and my deep-seated need to have everything in writing. That reminded me of the status of our investigation. I took out our notes on Clara and started to write down the story of her past from the details Lola had given me: the people she'd known, her family, her friends, her bosses—current and former—her work colleagues. Lola described what she thought might have been the events leading to her death.

"She was asleep in the hotel. We should go and take a look at her room there. The marks on the ground led to the servant quarters and then stopped dead in front of the bush. We know that much already."

Lola sketched a quick picture of Clara, and we stuck it in the middle of the book using a little flour and water. We didn't have very much to boast about in the way of clues. Those that would have been the most use to us were on the body itself. The damaged boot, the spittle around her lips, the ink on her finger.

We created a list of principal witnesses. Amédée was in prime position alongside Madame Davies and Madame Campo. Other than these three, the list looked pretty bare. And they were only witnesses to her character. There was nobody on the list who could have attested to any of the facts. Because nobody had any idea of what had happened. Nobody had seen anything. Nobody had heard anything. It was surprising, but that was how it was. How were we supposed to fare better than the police?

The atmosphere in the study was discouraging, to say the least. We had little in the way of energy that morning.

"I wonder where Maupassant has got to," asked Lola.

"Let's hope he knows a little more than us," I said. "I met with him yesterday, and he told me he had a lot of work to do on the draft of his latest novel. Corrections, I believe. He talked of terrible headaches, and his eyes were sore. But he did speak with the doctor and with Valantin."

"We'll soon see," said Lola, optimism rising in her voice. "I'll get in touch with my old friend at the perfumery to see if she can sneak out a little more orange-blossom essence for me."

She changed into a brown flannel dress. It wasn't quite as sober as the one she'd worn to visit her childhood home, but it was a definite change from her usual style. It at least had a few flowers on it and a couple of caramel-colored ribbons. The outfit was finished off with a velvet hat with rust-colored petals and a moss jacket that was cinched in at the waist. Still no gloves.

She went down to the kitchen and took a small drawstring canvas bag from one of the cupboards and slipped in a loaf of finely sliced bread, a leg of ham, a large dish towel, some wine goblets in earthenware, and a carafe of wine.

16

ANTOINETTE, THÉRÉSINE, AND PALMYRE

As Lola would later tell me, it took her at least ten minutes to reach the Rue Hermann. She crossed over the railway line just as the Paris train was setting off for Nice. She had to run to avoid the black smoke and made it to the other side of the walkway coughing.

At the perfumery, the huge windows let in so much sunlight that they gave almost a cathedral effect to the factory. As she entered the great hall, she saw at least thirty workers sitting on benches in front of huge basins of fresh flowers.

The whole scene was the same as when she'd worked there years earlier, before meeting the photographer, Numa Blanc. It was here that she'd learned the perfume-making process, and it was here she'd made the decision to always be sure she smelled delicious.

She spotted her friend Antoinette and waved to her. She took her food and drink out of her bag and shared it with her friend as they exchanged pleasantries and then delved deeper into conversation: Lola's need to make products to sell, the whole story of her lover and his abandoning of her.

"Could you help me with the essences?"

"Yes. That bastard Joseph always leaves a little early on Wednesdays, and the man who stands in for him never checks us on the way out.

He's a timid piece. Whenever he comes anywhere near us, he colors up like a virgin! I can surely slip a few bottles up my skirts."

"That would be incredible. Let me know how much you want for it."

With a rustle of fabric, a young girl around the age of fifteen, dressed in a blue-and-white smock, came and stretched out on the bench in front of them. It was Thérésine, a friend of Antoinette. From the pocket of her apron, she removed a small tin box full of rolled-up cigarettes and a few matches.

"Oh! I know you from somewhere!" Thérésine said. "I saw you in your carriage yesterday on La Marine. You were beautiful! I was out making an emergency delivery. Starched lace it was. The dress you were wearing was out of this world! My friends and I talked of nothing else all evening, I tell you! We were so proud! You're known to us, you know! You're one of us, aren't you? That's a rare thing. Gives me hope, it does."

"Hope?" Lola looked in Thérésine's eyes. "Don't envy me, my dear. I'm not in the most amusing of professions, let me assure you. You always run the risk of arrest, and you have to leave your old life behind. Forever. Most people no longer wish to have any kind of contact with me."

Thérésine didn't seem convinced. "And what about washing and ironing with toxic vapors? And being on your feet all day with no relief for our aches and pains—you don't reckon that's hard, do you? And I won't even mention the wages!"

"Yes, well, at least you make an honest living," said Lola as she packed up her things.

After leaving the perfumery, she decided to make her way to the Rue Bossu, with the intention of taking a look around poor Clara's room. Her idea was to sneak in through the service entrance. It was the same door they'd used to remove Clara's body from the building. Perhaps Lola would be able to glean a little more information?

The service entrance at the Hôtel Beau Rivage was hidden between a couple of delivery carts and several horses attached to iron rings. Lola entered without being questioned by a soul and, without hesitation, took the staircase leading to the cellars rather than the corridor to the kitchens.

She found herself in the same maze of laundry stations and service rooms that they'd been in just early yesterday morning. She looked for a way to reach the sleeping quarters. She finally came across two corridors each with a door showing illustrations—one of a woman in a long dress and wide-brimmed hat, the other of a man in top hat and tails.

She appreciated the effort they'd gone into to distinguish the two, although she'd never met servants quite so well dressed in reality. She wondered for an instant whether the doors might be locked, but they weren't. She pushed down on the handle, and the door to the female quarters opened with ease. She stepped inside and closed it quietly behind her.

Each door was labeled with a family name. She continued down the corridor until she reached the door marked "Campo and Audoin." Again, the door opened easily, and she walked into Clara's chamber with a mixture of anticipation, fear, guilt, and sadness. She remained still for a moment, trying in vain to slow down her breathing.

She knew she had to work quickly. She had no intention of being caught. The staff at the hotel would be busy until late at night, but she knew that servants would sometimes take breaks, and she didn't want to be found out by the other chambermaid who shared Clara's room. Perhaps she came down here during the day to rest her weary legs.

The room was small and poorly furnished. A little wood burner stood in the center, separating two beds and two minute bedside tables. The ensemble was perfectly symmetrical, with a wardrobe on either wall and a chair at the end of each bed.

One of the beds had been made up, the linen firmly tucked in. On the bedside table next to it lay a large bowl of water in which several pieces of undergarments were soaking. Apart from the last detail, the room looked reasonably well maintained. A basket could be seen under the far-side bed, with trinkets and several sweet papers. Suspended on the wall above one of the tables was a cross etched with the date of Easter the year before.

Lola had the thought that it must have been de rigueur to keep a well-maintained chamber. Either that or they were regularly inspected by the housekeeper.

She spotted a framed photo on one of the bedside tables and approached it. She recognized it immediately. It was a photo of Clara and her family that had been taken the day of her communion. Her father had still been alive, standing in the middle, surrounded by his wife and progeny.

That had been her side of the room, then. That was where she'd spent her last nights. Where she'd dreamed, smiled, or cried in the evenings. Lola studied the personal belongings of her dear friend. Next to her empty washbasin and the photo was a candle stuck to a holder, an oil lamp, and several small bottles of liquid. She sniffed them. They were full of paraffin.

Even without the family portrait, she would have known that this was her friend's space, as there were dozens of books stuffed down the side of the bed. Among them was *Contes de la Bécasse* by Maupassant.

As she flicked through it, a postcard fell out and glided across the floor. Lola picked it up. It was a scenic picture depicting the Swiss countryside. On the back, it read, *"Le Rubli, Canton de Vaud, Suisse."* Nobody had written on it. Lola quickly stuffed it into her bag next to the empty glasses and carafe.

Clara had pinned up a small collection of fans to the wall just above her bed. They were beautiful—bright silk, Japanese in style, with mother-of-pearl handles.

"These are a little beyond your means, my darling . . . ," whispered Lola. "And I don't believe this is the sort of gift Amédée would buy for you either."

She pulled one gently from the wall, but it slipped from her hand and fell beneath the bed. She leaned down to search for it. From this position, she could see a screwed-up handkerchief next to the chamber pot. She picked it up and noticed a yellow crusty substance on it. She popped that into her bag also.

She continued her search of the room, rummaging through every drawer, even the roommate's. At the very bottom of the last drawer, she found a bottle of Édouard Pernod Lunel absinthe hidden between two shirts.

"So the roommate is the drinker . . ."

She heard echoing footsteps coming down the hallway outside. Lola panicked. A uniformed chambermaid followed by Madame Davies burst through the door, where they found Lola, crouched down on the floor, going through a wicker basket under Clara's bed.

They almost jumped half out of their skins when they saw her.

"But . . . but . . . who are you? What are you doing here?" asked the girl.

"You're the young woman who found Clara in the garden!" said Madame Davies in her pronounced accent. "What are you doing here, Mademoiselle . . . errrr . . . Lola?"

So she had clearly not forgotten a thing from the last night, as she'd remembered Lola's new nom de guerre. She must have been paying attention to Lola and the others and everything they'd said.

"Clara's mother asked me to collect her things," she said, unfazed.

"Well, this is a cavalier way of going about it, is it not? You would have done well to advise me of it. It is forbidden to come down here unless I am informed. Even for those who live here, let alone people from outside the service!"

"Yet all the doors were open."

"We have had no need until today to keep doors locked down here. There's nothing to steal by all accounts!"

"Your behavior is quite shocking," said the chambermaid. "This is my room."

"And you are?"

"Palmyre Audoin. I shared this room with Clara."

Palmyre Audoin's voice had an instant calming effect on Lola.

"Please excuse me my intrusion." She sat down on Clara's bed. "This business has left me all of a quandary. Clara was my best friend. I didn't think it through. I just came down here. Would you allow me to take her things?"

"You can pack them all up, but then you must return to Clara's mother and get something in writing."

"Well, she doesn't know how to write."

"In that case, she must make an appearance here in person."

"She never leaves the Suquet. She worries about how she should dress. She doesn't want to go anywhere near the Croisette. I'll write a message and get her to sign it. Would that do?"

"I just need a document of some sort that removes the responsibility from me."

"The police have already been in here, I dare to guess?"

"The police? Here? No, child! What would be their business here? You know full well that Clara was found out in the garden."

Yes, but she was dragged out there, and that means she could have died in here, thought Lola without expressing as much aloud.

She turned to face Palmyre. "Where were you on Saturday night?"

"It was my day off. I was at home with my family in Cannet."

"And how many days off do you usually get?"

"One a month. On my days off I usually leave at around seven in the evening. My brother comes in his cart to pick me up. I sleep the night at my parents' home and come back here very late the following evening."

"I find your questions are a little intruding," said Madame Davies. "What is it you're looking to find out here?"

"I have no fear in telling you. I don't believe Clara's death was an accident. I believe her death was provoked by someone, and I want to find out who and why."

The two women stared at each other, Palmyre openmouthed.

"Can you tell me what you know of Clara? About her life? What was she up to? Perhaps what you know might help me."

Palmyre was clearly burning with the desire to speak, but she glanced at Madame Davies, a look of concern on her face. It was the older woman who finally broke the silence.

"I knew Clara only a very little. It was her first season here with us, whereas Palmyre has been with us for three years. Clara was a secretive girl. It was difficult to determine her character. She didn't really get involved with the other members of staff. She had something of a pretentious side about her, or it could be that she was just a little aloof."

Lola could understand what she was saying. She had known Clara so well. At school, everyone believed she put on airs, but it was down to her superior intelligence. She would often freeze up in front of her school chums because she had simply no idea what to say to them. Her friends weren't interested in books.

Shops, ribbons, boys . . . but she wasn't captivated by any of those trivialities. She wanted to speak with others about the characters in the books she would devour, but there was nobody with whom she could share such things. And so, day by day, she became more distant from others, from reality. And she was considered a show-off by her peers.

"As the season started out, I believed her to be an amiable young girl, a smiling creature. There was nothing not to like. I mean, she was cold at first, but it was nothing to worry about. But then it was as if she were taken over by a madness of sorts. She would sing without end. She was gay at all hours, and none of us recognized her! But still she shared nothing with us."

"And when did all this start?"

"I believe it was around the Christmas holidays."

"Did you notice that too?" Lola asked Palmyre.

"Everyone noticed! One night we talked. We spoke of what we believed fate had in store for us. She confided in me that she'd delight in nothing more than spending her life sitting in a rocking chair reading novels. I told her that my deepest desire was to marry my cousin, Rémy. He is promised to me. But I have nobody to dower me. That's why I save everything I earn—"

Lola cut her off, having heard enough of the secrets of Palmyre Audoin. "What of Clara? How did she intend on making this idea of hers come true?"

"That's what I asked her! It was naught but a silly dream. But she was insistent. She got angry with me. She said she wouldn't always be a chambermaid. If only wishes came true. Because in her case, she was on the right path. She had a solid future ahead of her. That dream of hers could so easily have become her reality." After a few moments' restraint, she added, "Yes, it was around about Christmas."

"And how well do you know Amédée, the concierge?"

"We all know him."

"Is he a jealous man? Violent even?"

"Violent? I don't know. Why would you ask such a question?"

Out of nowhere an irritated Maurel bounded into the room. "What in the Lord's name is this circus? Madame Davies! I asked that you clear Mademoiselle Campo's effects so that we could put a new girl in here! I hope you're not going to be all day about it?" He threw Lola a furious look. "And you! What are you doing here?"

"I came to collect Clara's things. I'm sure this will be of some convenience to you, if you want to free up her half of the room."

"Be quick about it! What were the three of you speaking of in here? I smell a conspiracy in the air. I hope you're not here to stick your nose in where it's not wanted, Filo . . . Lola! Is that clear? Clara is dead and well you know it. I realize the pain you must be feeling, but you won't find any answers here. It was an accident. These things happen every day, unfortunately. You shouldn't be in here rooting around! Is that something you can comprehend?"

"There's been no rooting around! I'm doing a service for Madame Campo, and that is all there is to it."

"What is it you're seeking, exactly? Are you wanting to cause trouble for us all? You're fortunate that Valantin didn't pick you up yesterday!" He turned to face Palmyre. "What has she been asking you about Campo, huh? What is it she wishes to know?"

Audoin trembled in fear upon hearing her boss's ferocious voice. She shriveled up in front of our eyes.

"She asked me where I was on Saturday night and what I knew about Clara."

"And me? Are you going to ask me what I know about Clara?"

Lola shook her head. *I certainly don't want to know what you thought of Clara*, she said to herself, blocking her ears mentally and protecting herself against whatever was about to come out of Maurel's mouth.

"Well, I'll tell you. Clara was an easy girl. There you go. Just like all the girls from up on the Suquet! Was she a friend of yours? I imagine you made a real pair!"

He left the room with a proud gait, snickering. Lola had been right to not pay him much mind.

She walked home with Clara's belongings, a little less light on her feet than earlier, overcome by a great many worries.

17

A Promising Advertisement

I saw Lola arrive. I descended the stairs and walked outside to meet her and took her bag off her shoulder as soon as we'd greeted. She certainly looked as though she needed to be relieved of the weight.

She smiled as soon as she saw me, and this simple welcome warmed me from the inside out.

"So, how did your meeting go with your friend at the perfumery?"

"I'll tell you everything. I went to visit Clara's bedchamber too. I even managed to bring back a few souvenirs!"

Despite her tiredness, she remained animated and lively as she told her tale. She recounted the entire exchange she'd had with Antoinette the perfumer, little Thérésine the laundry girl, Palmyre Audoin, and Madame Davies.

"And that Maurel is a nightmare of a man!" she cried. "He can't see any farther than his nose. How selfish! Poor Palmyre was trembling in front of him. He wasn't speaking to her, he was barking. And he even suggested that Clara was some sort of working girl! Clara! No doubt because he tried to have his way with her and she refused him! That wouldn't surprise me in the least. It wasn't easy to get round Clara! And she was right to be the way she was. She was deserving of real passion.

A kind and gentle fellow. That Maurel! What a swine! He wasn't always like that, you know. I wonder what has made him so."

"His responsibilities?" I suggested. "The fact that he has more money now? Or more debts? Is he irritated by life in general? Has his wife gone elsewhere?"

She sighed. "No, he's not married."

I continued to wonder aloud. "Perhaps he's our man! That would explain his desire to quash everything, to bury the incident."

"Could be! But I would be swayed more by the idea of Amédée. Maurel is a cold-blooded animal. Nothing interests him other than his career!"

We had settled into the kitchen. She wanted to teach both Rosalie and me a lesson in soap making. She had enough essence from her stock to prepare two dozen or so soaps. She had never made such a big batch before, but the work we did together was amusing and allowed her to find the level of energy that had been lacking.

I made a proposal. "We should find some elegant little bags to present them in. A little luxury case of some kind would add value to them and mean that we could increase the price."

"What about my Calais handkerchiefs? I have a ton of them!"

"Are they embroidered?"

"No."

"I think we should add some initials to them. It would be like a brand. *L* and *D* intertwined."

Rosalie went to fetch the sewing threads, and we set about this arduous task. Lola and Rosalie were very bad embroiderers. They knew how to sew, but had been used to mending and the like.

I gave them a lesson in how to sew the perfect monogram. After half an hour, we had decorated five handkerchiefs with lace in a pale rose color and stunning arabesque embroidery. With the help of a few ribbons of the same shade, we had created the most beautiful sachets.

Later, Lola announced she was heading to the baths to negotiate a new deal for our soaps. She changed into a springtime dress, put a remarkable floral hat on, and placed our soaps into a basket, which she held out to me at arm's length.

"We'll have to take these soaps as they are. They're not really dry yet. Never mind! Come with me! I want to introduce you to people. It means you can complete the transactions with them in the future. We'll start out down at the baths on the Rue Montaigne, because I already know them there. If we manage to persuade them, I believe we'll stand a better chance with others."

Our negotiations failed. They appreciated the offer but admitted they would have to postpone a larger order. They took but three bars. I felt disappointed, but not so for Lola. At least, she wasn't showing it if it were indeed the case. But I was starting to know her well, and I could detect anxiety in her voice that she was doing her best to cover up with false joy.

As we left the baths, she held my arm in familiarity. "My grandmother always said, 'Money must come in every day, even if it's just a few centimes. If money doesn't come in one day, you've taken a step back too far!' I don't think they wanted to say anything, but I believe they were quite charmed by our product! A soft and creamy soap that smells this good! Who could resist such a thing? You'll see, Miss Fletcher! This is going to be a triumph!"

"It's going to be a storming success!"

As we passed the food store on the corner of the Boulevard de la Foncière, she slipped inside, and before I could protest, she'd bought a bag of brioches. She'd spent the money we'd just earned.

As we walked upward, I tried to explain that we would be unable to save a centime if we carried on like that, and we wouldn't be able to raise the rent to pay Philémon. She shivered, and knowing she'd been given a telling off, she chuckled forcefully.

Back at the villa, a delivery boy was awaiting us. He'd come with the postcards of Lola. There was a small, empty space along the bottom for whoever purchased the card to write a few words.

Lola clapped, every trace of her fatigue now gone. It had to be said that the cards were a pretty sight. She had a naughty expression, the look of a thousand promises, and her hairstyle was half-undone, giving the impression of pure abandon. Her mouth was in a half smile, almost mocking, and the décolleté was deep, drawing the eye in . . .

The lettering was cursive, on a diagonal slant and in a golden relief print. The whole picture was charm itself. A promising advertisement if ever I'd seen one. This had certainly made up for the soap debacle.

Lola laughed gaily and started spreading the postcards out onto every surface of the house: tables, armchairs, fire mantels . . .

"Rosalie! Come and see this!"

Every one of us exclaimed that the card looked to be a real gem, but we also noted that the design itself might have been a touch exaggerated. But Lola's joy was contagious!

"These cards will bring us a fortune! You'll see! Philémon Carré-Lamadon had better watch out!"

Lola and I set about writing the address of Madame Alexandra's reading room on the back of the cards so that those who chose to take one could meet with the flesh-and-bone version of the model.

As soon as Lola retired to her bedchamber, I took out the notes we were keeping on Clara Campo and wrote down everything that Lola had managed to discover that day. Her conversations with Palmyre Audoin, Madame Davies, and Maurel and her description of Clara's room. Between the pages of the book, I slipped the postcard depicting the Swiss countryside and into the hatbox went the fan and soiled handkerchief.

Later that evening, around ten o'clock, as I ascended the stairs, I spotted Lola leaving her room, although I thought she'd been asleep for some time. She wore her bright-red evening dress. In fact, she had on the full works—a tiara, gloves, a silk stole . . . her outfit was complete.

"I'm going to the restaurant next to the theater. I want to speak with Maupassant. I'm sure he'll be watching a play there tonight. He said as much. I'm going to tell him of my little visit today and Palmyre Audoin, and I'll see if I can get myself invited into one of the private dining rooms. The restaurant manager usually gives me one of the swankier tables. He knows I can get his punters drinking. He might even give me a commission. I need to start picking up a few of my old habits again. With any luck, I'll bump into Cortelazzo. I will be specific with him this time. I'll tell him I want to be one of his chorus girls."

A strange pained feeling entered my body as it dawned on me that she wanted to meet with Maupassant again. But that was no business of mine.

"I don't want you going alone on foot," I said. "I'll take you in the carriage."

She accepted, but made it more than clear that she wouldn't have me waiting for her. She wished for me to go straight to bed upon returning to the house, as there was the risk that she might return home with company.

18

A Fugitive from the Sacré-Cœur

Lola joined a table of friends and a few of the town's bourgeoisie who were out and about eating and drinking to their hearts' content. Among them were two passing winterers who had come to town to negotiate with these businessmen, for some of them were the richest men in town. They were as different from one another in comportment as they were in dress. One of them was attired in the brightest of colors with a flamboyant shirt and a silk tie. His mustache was smooth, and he talked with panache. He was most certainly a ladies' man. The other had a shy countenance, and his apparel was sober, dark—he could well have been a man of the church. He couldn't take his deep-blue eyes with their long, dark lashes off Lola.

The theater manager walked over to the table to greet the Cannois tradesmen. He waved at Lola indifferently.

She did, however, manage to hand him one of her cards, which he placed in his pocket absentmindedly before moving on.

The others at the table were curious as to what she'd given him, eager to look at the portrait themselves. She handed out her cards to the impatient ensemble. Each of them looked at the card and then at Lola with a little more interest than before. In the voices of the other women around the table, Lola noted a hint of jealousy. This more than persuaded her that the postcards had been an excellent idea. She succeeded in convincing the waiter that she could leave a few of the cards on the bar.

Not a single man she was with was free that evening. She didn't want to run the risk of putting too much pressure upon them, but she did fix a few appointments over the coming days at Madame Alexandra's rooms with the shy blue-eyed man.

When she heard applause from the building next door, she knew the play was finished and went to meet the spectators as they left the theater and flooded into the foyer, hoping to meet with someone of interest.

This was one of the most dangerous moments of such an evening, as there was a high risk she'd be spotted by an officer and her details would be taken down. This meant that her game—a game of seduction—had to be played as gently as possible. What a complete paradox!

She was starting to feel a little bored by the time Maupassant finally left the theater. He appeared enchanted to see her again, and when he learned she was alone, he suggested he might walk her home.

His mind was elsewhere, however. He appeared absent and concerned.

She told him of her visit with Madame Campo and her trip to see Clara's room at the hotel.

"I'm thoroughly ashamed of myself. I'm afraid I've neglected to uphold my part of the bargain!" he cried. "I promise you this will be remedied by tomorrow. I'll get my spats on and go and mix with some of the hotel's clients. I need to find out what floor Clara worked on and who her clients were in the days leading up to her death. Then I'll go and spend some time with them and ask the necessary questions."

As Lola opened the gate, a caterwauling pierced the stillness of the night.

"It's Sherry! Sherry!" Lola called the cat. "I'll take him up with me."

But as she called his name, there was no sign of him, and yet he usually came the first time.

Lola crept around to the shadowy part of the gardens behind the house and walked down the steps to the cellars. Guided by the sound of purring that was getting louder and louder, she spotted an opaque mass that looked a lot like a pile of clothes and the shining bright eyes of Sherry, phosphorescent in the darkness.

But there was another sound, a muffled cry, louder than the purring.

"What is that?" exclaimed Maupassant. "That's not Sherry! There's something else down there!"

Lola leaned into the stairwell to try to get a closer peek while Maupassant lit a match from his pocket. In the ethereal light, they saw the small tar-stained face of a child who appeared to be around ten, curled up on the ground, her face ravaged by fear. She was gripping on to Sherry. They could tell she was a girl not really by her face, but because she was wearing a baggy dress rather than trousers. She had two long plaits down her back.

As soon as she realized she'd been spotted, she attempted to run, still holding the cat close to her chest. But Maupassant was quicker. He managed to grab a piece of her clothing as she fled, and a struggle ensued. He received some scratches to his face, but he got the little girl under control within seconds.

The cat had jumped out of her arms and was now watching the scene with interest.

Maupassant picked up the little girl and carried her back to the main door of the house and inside. They went upstairs into the lounge, and Maupassant was as careful as ever to turn his back to the mirrors in order to avoid his reflection. Lola woke up Rosalie, who, in turn, opened the door to my stairwell and shouted up for me before lighting the gas lamps in the rooms. Maupassant, in better light now, saw how filthy the little girl was. He had already guessed as much by her smell.

He set her down onto an armchair and looked to be concerned for himself above anything else.

"Where have you come from, little one?" asked Rosalie, ever practical in nature.

I intervened at this point, hoping to encourage her to speak. "Your mother must be worried, mustn't she?"

"Let's take the child back to her mother," said Maupassant, eager to please me.

As soon as his words were spoken, the little girl threw herself to the floor and sobbed. "No!"

She hurried behind the divan. Lola asked us to delay a moment and then whispered something to Rosalie, who left the room quietly. A few minutes later, Rosalie returned with some leftover lamb stew in a thyme sauce. The steam wafted into the air, a real tantalizing treat for the nostrils.

Lola grabbed the dish and crouched down. The child crawled over to her and took the spoon that was being held out.

"What's your name?" Lola asked softly.

With her mouth full of food, she looked up and managed to splutter, "Anna."

"How pretty! I'm so jealous! I would much rather have been called Anna than Lola!"

The little girl smiled and carried on eating. Her tears had now dried, but she was shivering despite the warm temperature of the room.

"This little dove has a fever," said Rosalie. "She's very ill. We must fetch a doctor."

Maupassant shivered. He looked worried. He was afraid of illness. He felt himself to be fragile, like his mother . . .

"Consumption?" he asked, anxiety in his voice.

"I don't want to die," said Anna. "Like Adèle."

"Who's Adèle?" asked Maupassant.

"My best friend. She died this morning. I don't want to die."

"Where did you come from?" asked Lola.

She scrutinized Lola and stated, "From the Sacré-Cœur. But I don't want to go back. I won't go."

"What's this Sacré-Cœur?" asked Maupassant. "A church?"

"No, it's the orphanage. It's not far from here," I said. "Are you from the orphanage, child?"

"We're all going to die there. That's why I ran away. I don't want to end up like the others."

"What others?" asked Maupassant. "You said it was your friend Adèle who died! Singular!"

"Yes, this morning. But she wasn't the first. Jeanne says the orphanage is evil. We're all going to die."

Maupassant turned toward us. "We need to let Buttura know. He lives on my route home. I'll tell him to come over. He might come during the night, or tomorrow morning at the latest. Or just take her back to the orphanage."

Anna watched him, her eyes begging for help.

"Out of the question. I'm not taking her back to the orphanage now. She can spend the night here, and after the doctor has examined her, we'll think about what to do next," said Lola.

"She can't sleep here in this state," reasoned Rosalie. "I'll heat up some water and set up the big tub, and we'll wash her."

Maupassant left the house in a hurry, and the rest of us gathered in the kitchen.

Sherry followed our every move. He'd fulfilled his mission. He'd warned us of the presence of this intrusion onto our territory.

Rosalie put the little girl's clothes to boil over the fire while I scrubbed her with some of the gorgeous soap we'd made earlier that day.

"You live a quiet life here, don't you, Mademoiselle Lola?" I said ironically.

Lola winked at me as she shampooed the little one's hair and passed a comb through to remove the lice.

The cleansing process took over an hour. We dosed her in lavender oil as another means to get rid of the crawly creatures. Sherry had run away in fear. He didn't appreciate the smell all that much.

Rosalie had prepared a makeshift bed on the sofa, slipped one of Lola's nightgowns over Anna's head and arms, and covered her with a sheet. As soon as we placed her upon it, she was away, fast asleep.

19

THE AUTOPSY

When Dr. Buttura paid a call the following morning at nine, everyone in the house was awake and dressed except Lola.

Rosalie had taken an old skirt of Lola's and tried to fashion a dress of sorts out of it. The little one could hardly stand. She was so weak. The bowl of milk we'd given her, along with a slice of bread and butter, hadn't done enough to perk her up. She was shivering and sweating simultaneously.

She finished her breakfast down in the kitchen, and as soon as the last morsel passed her lips, Rosalie picked her up and carried her back to bed.

When we heard the bell ring on the gate, Rosalie shuffled outside to meet the doctor, and I climbed the stairs to wake Lola, taking her red kimono with me.

Once inside, the doctor leaned over the little girl and listened to her breathing for what seemed like forever. He peered down at her, worried. He stuck his rubber stethoscope onto her chest and tapped her knees a couple of times with a small wooden hammer.

He didn't look pleased at all.

"Monsieur de Maupassant tells me that this young girl comes from the nearby orphanage. Do you know that to be true?"

"That's what she told us. Why?" I asked.

Buttura appeared to be disturbed to hear this. "We've had to deal with a number of deaths there this winter. Unfortunately, I'm unable to go inside in order to perform a full inspection. Dr. Gimbert is in charge of epidemics, but he has also been denied access. Madame de Valton, the general manager of the place, will not allow any of us entry."

"Does she have the right to do that?" I asked.

"She hasn't formally stopped us, but she always finds a good reason to cancel every appointment we make. It's very odd."

"Have you done any autopsies? Do you know what these children died of?"

Buttura looked down, shamefaced.

"The truth of the matter is that no autopsy has ever been requested. These children are orphans. They are simply considered to be ordinary deaths. Banal diseases. Fevers."

I gave Lola a knowing look. We were thinking the same thing. *It was exactly as such for Clara.*

Buttura noticed the way we'd glanced at one another. He must have felt at fault, because he protested, "If we performed an autopsy on every corpse in Cannes, with all the cases of consumption, typhus, apoplexy, and dysentery, we'd need an army of doctors here! And that's not counting those who die of old age, nervous fatigue, bloodletting—"

"Yes, but there are a number of cases here, all in the one place," I said.

He reacted as if suddenly relieved, as if we were on his side. "You're right! But I'll go on the attack this time with Madame de Valton. I'll make sure she lets me into the orphanage. The state of this child here will allow me to be insistent without coming across as discourteous. I will say that I have been sent by local government officers to inspect these establishments. It's true that they are registered charities and receive a great many subsidies from a great many places. The government will want to know what's happening."

"Does that mean you'll take Anna with you? Does she really have to go back there?" asked Lola.

"Yes, I'm afraid it's where she belongs."

Lola moved away from us, walking slowly to the window, her back turned on the room. I imagined she didn't much like the idea of sending the little one home. I expected her to put up more of a fight than this.

"They often walk past my house when they're out exercising," she said, her voice distant. "How sorrowful it is to see them in their little black smocks. They're all so thin. I can't stand children being locked away. What is it they're supposed to be guilty of?"

Buttura looked across to her with compassion, but his eyes were glazed over somewhat. It wasn't Lola he was thinking of, but the little ones he'd visited on occasion in the past.

"They're guilty of striking fear into the hearts of local officials," he said in sadness. "They represent a risk. They could end up on the street as thieves, common criminals, or prostitutes. It's as if the state has decided to imprison them in advance."

"I don't understand why Anna was dressed so shabbily yesterday. Why doesn't she have a black dress like the others?"

"She must have been in her nightdress. The black uniforms are reserved for outings. Inside the home itself, the girls wear much less presentable attire. But if her clothes were really in such a terrible state, it must mean that her sponsor, whoever pays for her to be in the home, is late with what they owe."

"And she was covered in lice!"

"That's exactly the reason I need to get into the place," gulped the doctor.

"What if we were to keep her here until her health has improved?" I asked him.

"I'm afraid I doubt very much you'd receive the authorization. Never would an orphan be allowed to reside at the house of a lady who lived . . . by her charms. Please excuse me, Mademoiselle Lola, but that's just the truth of it."

Lola made no response. I don't believe she'd even been listening. I asked if Buttura would care to join us for a cup of tea or a glass of sherry, and he accepted joyfully.

As he sipped his drink, he declared, "If an orphaned child wishes to become a valid citizen at the age of one and twenty, it costs a fair fortune! Did you know that?"

Lola turned to face him. "How much do they have to pay?"

"Well, you see, the nuns will only raise them until the age of twelve. Their schooling is finished by then. They have to stay at the orphanage, though, for they are not free to leave until they come of age."

"And so how do they occupy themselves for nine years?" I asked.

"They have to work, I suppose, and to pay their board, they give over their entire wage to the orphanage." He pressed on over our gasps. "I feel exactly the same as you. This custom is quite shocking! Especially as their board is paid for upon entry. They all have sponsors. If they don't have someone who is prepared to pay their way, they don't get a place. They never have anything saved or put away for them for when they leave. I fully understand your indignation!"

"Here's how we'll solve this problem," I said. "Mademoiselle Lola is suffering a shortage of finances at this given moment—"

But the doctor interrupted me. "If it is of any consolation, she is far from alone in that. Read the *Échos de Cannes*! You'll see nothing but family after family going bankrupt. Their worldly goods are more often than not sold at auction."

"It can be of consolation to know you're not wallowing in the mud alone," said Lola, smiling a little. "By the way, do you have any news of my friend Clara? Has Valantin advanced in his investigation?"

"From what I know of it, there will be no investigation. Well, no official investigation, in any case."

The doctor lowered his voice and leaned in toward Lola, close to her ear. Was it the effect of the sherry or something else? He was about to betray a confidence of some kind, I could tell. Was it because Anna was fast asleep, clean, and comfortable in her soft sheets? Did he trust us because we'd taken such good care of her? Was it because we had shared in his disgust at how the orphans were being treated? It certainly seemed as though he was about to open up, in any case.

He spoke in hushed tones, with an air of conspiracy. "Yesterday, I completed an autopsy on Clara without having received an order to do so. I couldn't sleep because of it. I think I discovered some things that will be of interest to you. I feel as if I can confess this. I sense you are of a good nature and that you had a genuine tenderness for the girl. I believe you'll perhaps make better use of these results than Valantin."

Lola gave him an encouraging smile.

"Her heart was atrophied. But I don't know much else on the subject. I could see that she'd drunk some kind of liquid that had attacked her mucus membranes. I sent a sample to the laboratory in Lyon for analysis. The lab is run by a friend of mine, Lacassagne. We'll soon find out what there is to know."

"Do you mean that you fear she may have been poisoned by someone?"

"No! I said nothing of the sort! And why by someone? She could very well have poisoned herself. I never come to hasty conclusions. Never. I gather the facts and then leave it to the police to find the answers."

A heavy stillness filled the room, interrupted only occasionally by the labored breathing of Anna. Buttura stared nervously at his empty sherry glass. He opened his mouth as if to say something further, but hesitated before finally spluttering out, "And that's not all. She was in an interesting . . . errrr . . . condition . . ."

"Clara? No! Not possible!" declared Lola categorically.

"I'm afraid so. She was sufficiently advanced as to leave no doubt."

I placed my hand on Lola's arm. She was overcome by this revelation. She shoved me away and shuffled back over to the window. I heard her murmur, "So that was what it was! She was with child! And I didn't answer her letter."

She wrung her hands together, wiped away at her tears furiously, her eyes meeting those of the doctor once more. "Do you believe she . . . did something to herself?"

The doctor and I said nothing, both of us clearly fearful of breaking the silence. Lola did it for us. She sobbed, "But why didn't she speak of it to me in person? If she killed herself . . ."

"I suppose it is not possible to say anything at this stage," said the doctor. "You're right, of course. I admit to it being my initial thought, but as I told you, I forbid myself any kind of speculation. But she was certainly with child, and her heart showed every sign of having suffered an attack due to a toxic substance. A poison from the digitalis family or something that looked very much like it. That's all I can say on the subject for the moment."

"Do you believe she might have wanted to end her life?" I asked. "Such a woeful tale! A woman that young! That beautiful!"

"There really is nothing we can judge correctly at this stage. We know nothing of the circumstances. I'm so sorry."

"Now I understand why she truly appeared as though she had suffered," said Lola listlessly. "The agony she must have borne . . ."

The doctor placed his glass on the mantelpiece and absorbed the quietness around him pensively.

"Will they be returning the body to the family any time soon?" Lola asked.

"Indeed. I was hoping to speak with you about that. I have asked that they use the same methods as practiced in the morgue in Lyon. That means chemicals are injected into the body to preserve it, and the remains are kept on ice. Valantin wants me to sign the paperwork so that her body can be buried as soon as possible. However, I would prefer to wait for the analytical results, and that will take time. Please let Madame Campo know that her daughter will be with us for a while."

Lola agreed to this and then took the doctor to one side and whispered, "Doctor, as you can see, this little girl is in no fit state to be moved. I appreciate that I won't be given the right to keep her. And I agree! I can't see myself managing too well with a child under my feet. Also, as my friend Miss Fletcher underlined, I don't have the financial means to pay the nuns or make a donation of any kind. But I simply do not have the heart to send her back there with that fever of hers. What would you advise I do?"

"Mademoiselle, we have to tread delicately." The doctor turned to face me. "Madam, would you be so kind as to accompany me to the orphanage? If Mademoiselle Lola comes with me, I'm afraid she won't be able to hide—excuse me, mademoiselle—her true intentions. You, however, give off a certain level of education and thus come across as reassuring. Am I mistaken?"

I lowered my head, feeling my skin burn. This "education" of mine always gave me away. It also revealed my social decline.

"So, here's my proposal. I will introduce Miss Fletcher and recommend she take care of the girl. You can explain your wish to help get her on the mend over the coming days. You'll say she saved your cat or something like that, and you wish to thank her. That would sound perfectly reasonable coming from an Englishwoman. The sisters will calculate how much they might gain from this. You can ask them for a monthly estimation, explaining that you'd be thrilled to take her on as a chambermaid, or at least train her up as one, but that you have no idea how much time that might entail."

"You have a good heart, Doctor," said Lola, shaking his hand. "Let's start out like that and see where it gets us. I believe once the child has regained her strength, she may be able to tackle life at the orphanage once again. She'll be that much stronger."

"Please don't thank me! It's because of this sorry event that I'll hopefully be able to make my way through the doors of that pitiful establishment! That Madame de Valton will hardly be able to hold me back now! And this was all down to this little escape artist!"

"Her name's Anna."

"In any case, whatever happens inside those walls will no longer be allowed to stay there. I'm sure the presence of Miss Fletcher will force them to change their behavior."

Our visit to the orphanage took place much as the doctor had imagined it would. He asked to see the mother superior and detailed that the reason behind his visit was Anna and what had happened to her. And so he was left to carry out an inspection. He asked that I follow him as he worked.

After having walked through the most at-risk areas—the infirmary, the basement kitchens, and around the septic tanks outside—the doctor started to manifest signs of his anger.

He asked that he be allowed to make use of the offices in order to start preparing his notes. Before beginning this endeavor, he demanded that the nuns draw up a contract that would give me the authority to keep Anna with me until some improvements had been made on the site according to his report.

"But we cannot simply leave . . . this is contrary to . . . ," said one of the nuns.

"If each of the minors in here were to be given permission to stay awhile in the homes of charitable souls like Miss Fletcher, we could avoid any future loss of life," he said. "At this present moment, you are in no position to refuse this woman. The work you are obliged to do here is quite urgent."

"What work? We cannot possibly raise the funds to start—"

"You must raise the funds. You have patrons, do you not? One word to the duchesse de Vallombrosa or the comtesse de Caserte from me and it is done, let me assure you."

The mother superior turned a violent puce. "It's just that . . ." She didn't finish her sentence.

I was given a number of documents to sign and a complete file on the girl, the daughter of two peasant farmers, Janette and Pierre Martin. The sheets included notes on her past and a full list of expenses that I would have to pay to the orphanage were I to sponsor her and the amount they would wish to receive should I intend on keeping her at my home. I quickly scanned the papers and noticed that her real name wasn't Anna, but Anahita. It is very often the case that a name that finds itself out of the ordinary is quickly adapted to one that is more familiar to the common tongue.

And the name Anahita was far from ordinary. I'd never heard one quite like it. Was it of Italian origin? Spanish? Or a Gypsy name perhaps? It seemed quite strange to me that Cannois farmers would give such an exotic name to a child. I decided it had to be a local name in the patois of the region. Something Provençal that I'd not yet come across.

I left the courageous Dr. Buttura to his discussions with the nuns as to why they were so reticent to help improve the environment in which these poor girls lived.

Upon returning home, the smell of lavender coming from the second floor was so strong it was staggering. Rosalie had clearly aired the whole house and used lavender oil to disinfect the floors and surfaces.

The little girl was sitting down, a slight smile on her lips, and paying particular attention to every move made by Lola, who was dressed in the most spectacular fitted dress in a vibrant burgundy silk. She had stained her lips blood-red and pinned a hat to her head with several violet silk flowers pushed into her hair.

"Are you on your way out?" I asked.

"Yes. A messenger boy has just been here. He gave me a note from my friend down at the reading rooms," she said in a secretive tone, winking at me and nodding over to Anna.

"I'll drive you," I said.

"Perfect. It wouldn't look good to arrive with dust on my dress. But you need not wait for me while I attend to my business there. You can dip into our funds and take some of what we have left to go and buy a decent outfit for the little lady. She can't go around dressed like that!"

I used a ribbon to take the child's measurements. I measured the length from her neck to ankle, her feet, her arms, and around her little waist.

I then went outside to prepare the carriage.

As I lifted Lola into her seat, I heard her talking to the cat. He'd leaped up to the second-floor balcony and was watching us as we left, Lola waving at him gaily.

I didn't ask Lola any indiscreet questions regarding her meeting with Madame Alexandra, but I knew she would be seeing a man there.

Lola asked me to make a detour along the Quai Saint-Pierre and the Allée de la Marine before dropping her off in front of the building.

While she did what she did best, I went to Hélène's on the Rue de la Foux to find what we needed for Anna.

As we were approaching the end of the season, her prices had been reduced, and I managed to obtain two dresses for the price of one. I also had enough to purchase a woolen cape, three underskirts, two night-shirts, some stockings, and a pair of flat walking boots in leather—a lot like those I was wearing.

The dresses were a dark purple, almost to the point of being black. The cape was in a lovely midnight blue. The ensemble struck me as being both somber and in very good taste. This meant that the nuns couldn't feign shock when she returned to the orphanage wearing her new clothes.

As I maneuvered the carriage onto the crossroads on the Rue Notre Dame and the Rue Bossu, I could already see Lola waiting for me. She was looking through the reading room windows, pretending to be interested in the piles of books in the display.

As soon as I pulled up beside her, she hopped up into the carriage, wearing a huge smile and shaking a velvet pouch full of coins.

20

THAT DÉJÀ-VU FEELING

Upon arriving, Lola was introduced to Harold, an English winterer who was passing through Cannes for a few days to visit with some friends.

She posed as a widow—at Madame Alexandra's instruction—as this put the client at ease. After having shared a pot of tea together in the lounge and exchanging a few pleasantries—with some difficulty not being of the same mother tongue—they made for one of the bedrooms, a charming suite decorated in a decidedly bold fashion. Hunting scenes bedecked the walls. There were no lewd or unchaste engravings to be found, as was usually the style in a place such as this.

Lola kept herself from taking the initiative and allowed the gentleman to make the first move. They lay down on the satin sheets and stroked one another through their clothing. Lola did her best to give off a prudish air. It wasn't all that hard, for it had been some time since she'd had relations with Eugène, and she did feel ever so slightly embarrassed.

Estimating that enough time had been spent on the preliminaries, Harold lifted himself up from the bed and took off his trousers, shirt, and underclothes. He wasn't the most talkative of fellows. Lola took her opportunity to remove her dress and placed it gently over the back of a chair so as not to crease it.

In her underskirt and corset, she reclined on her back across several pillows. He had a toned body and typically British features. His skin was deathly pale with dozens of freckles spotted over his forearms. As soon as he'd stripped, a wild look came across his face. He jumped toward her.

When Lola started breathing more forcefully, making the sort of noises that would lead a partner to believe she was enjoying herself, it brought the activity to a swift conclusion, both sighing in relief.

Lola was delighted that it had all taken so little of her time. He collapsed onto her. She kissed him on the neck and whispered, "Darling."

But he didn't appear to appreciate her softness. Harold was a reserved man and would more than likely have preferred the company of a young woman much like him in character. She lay prone on the bed, telling herself, at the very least, she would allow him to initiate his own departure. She wouldn't rush him.

She wanted more than anything to make a good impression, though she knew he wouldn't become a regular if he were to leave town soon. But he probably had friends with whom he might speak of his good fortune in finding her. From the very moment they'd entered the room, the entire act had lasted no more than ten minutes.

After a decent interval, he got up and dressed himself. Before leaving, he thanked her, which she found to be incongruous. Lola had enough time to fully wash herself and dress before leaving the room.

She would go on to explain to me at a much later date that as she'd glanced back at the bed, she'd noticed something shining between the folds of the sheets, just below the wrinkled pillows.

She'd smoothed out the folds and picked up an earring. It was an old piece—a pendant form in heavy gold with several stones and a huge droplet diamond at the end. She'd bit into the metal and felt the resistance against her teeth then rubbed the diamond against the window, feeling the glass bend under the pressure. This was a jewel of some value. She'd felt this almost intuitively and had had that déjà-vu feeling about it, as she was sure she'd seen this earring somewhere before.

She'd slipped the earring into her pocket and resolved to ponder on it later. There was not a chance she'd return it to Madame Alexandra, but she'd also thought there was no way of making any money from it without drawing attention to herself or being accused of theft. She'd known she'd have to keep quiet about it for the moment.

As far as reentering the goings-on at Madame Alexandra's, this first meeting hadn't been as bad as she'd anticipated. By the time she joined me in the carriage, the event was almost entirely forgotten to her.

Well, everything except the earring.

21

CHERCHEZ LA FEMME!

Just as I was tying up the landau in front of the gates, we met with Philémon Carré-Lamadon on his way back on foot from the Hôtel Central, swinging his cane with vigor as he trotted along the street.

His face lit up as soon as he spotted Lola climbing down from the carriage. He approached her, displaying his deference with the widest of smiles, as I entered the house and climbed up to the second floor to spy on them from the window.

"Lola! I've been trying to find you for the past few days, but you've been on the move, it would appear! You've been impossible to track down. I've passed by the villa several times. When I noted your absence yet again earlier, I decided to go down to the hotel and play a game or two of billiards. I was joined by my friend, the duc de Luynes, who is sojourning here in Cannes for a week or so. Did you know that Wales is in town?"

"No, I had no idea!" tittered Lola innocently. "You do make me laugh so! Maupassant yearns for nothing more than to knock those who call him Wales! As if you're on familiar terms with him!"

But her mocking had no effect on Philémon. Humor rarely touched him. It slid off him, in fact—water off a duck's back.

"And I suppose you're on more-than-familiar terms with Maupassant?" he questioned sternly. "He's quite the brazen young man, isn't he? I would be careful of him if I were you."

"Tell me, for what reason did you need so desperately to see me?" cooed Lola.

"I believe you know the reason, my beauty! I'm awaiting an answer from you!"

"I gave you one, unless I am much mistaken."

"I still live in hope that you may change your mind. I have an inkling that you'll do so soon."

"Perhaps!"

Lola's attitude made me feel anguished. What game was she playing with him? I'd been made to believe that she was intent on refusing his offers and was dedicated to finding a way to pay the rent without him.

It irritated me to see her flirt with him so. I felt it to be a dangerous game. She was overestimating herself.

More than anything, I was furious with my own attitude. I felt pangs of jealousy that I was unable to master. I had no rights over what happened to her, her choices, or which of her *cherubs* she chose to entertain. After all, she'd just come away from one such cherub, and I was sure she'd thoroughly entertained him! Would I have to be like an ostrich? Sticking my head in the sand so that such things would not upset me?

The mannered display that Lola was putting on, contrasted with the pressing posture of Philémon, left me feeling nothing short of exasperated. He was acting like she was his property. He was so sure of what was his. Sure of the end results of this game they both played. Sure of his rights over her.

"Don't you dare tell me that my offer isn't in the very least tempting! I'm not like Eugène, you know. I would take you out! I would show you to the whole world! You would have the use of the house and the carriage all year round! You know I'm only ever here in winter! There's not a single cost that wouldn't be covered!"

"You are a generous man, Phil. I know that. But you must comprehend that my heart remains broken. I cannot simply carry on as if nothing has happened. I am making every effort, let me assure you, but it isn't as simple as that."

"The devil it is! You know me, my dear. You know I always get what I want. All it demands is patience. But I fear my patience has its limits."

He followed her beyond the gate and into the garden. He briefly took the time to scan the surrounding area before pushing her up against the trunk of a nearby tree. My heart was pounding. I couldn't find the courage to intervene. I couldn't see Lola's face clearly from my position, but she must have been taken aback by this unanticipated violence.

His tone hardened. "Let's desist with the toying now. You know very well you have no choice here."

"You're no bully boy, Phil! You said as much yourself!"

"And I thought you were much more pragmatic than this, Lola. You disappoint me. Truly," he said, grimacing nastily. "I'm reaching the end of my tether now. Forget these caprices you enjoy so much."

Lola tried to slip free, pretending that she had taken the whole scene as some sort of farcical joke.

"This isn't droll, Phil. Please, let me go!"

"I believe it's high time you showed me a little respect and pay off some of those debts you're accumulating. What do you think?"

He lifted her skirts and pulled her up against him.

I felt my blood freeze. I took a step back, creeping like a scared animal. I picked up a fine porcelain basin, not fully understanding what I was about to do. I returned to the balcony, closed my eyes, and threw the basin in what I believed to be his direction. When I heard the ceramic smashing, I hurried back inside so as not to be seen.

He let out a furious scream. "Good God! What in the . . ."

Footsteps. The gate slamming shut.

I risked a quick glance before leaving the room. He was scampering back down the hill toward the station, rubbing his forehead ferociously.

Lola retreated to the safety of the house and walked slowly upstairs and into the sitting room. She threw herself down heavily and removed her gloves and hat, which she placed on her lap.

I sensed her anxiety. I had retreated to the office and was sitting at my desk, from where I could see her every move. I was pretending to write in my notebook, but if she'd studied me more carefully she would have seen how my hand trembled. Sherry jumped onto her knees, purring. Lola caressed him, but I could read her like a book. She was doubting herself. I asked her if everything was fine.

"Not really, Miss Fletcher! All this effort we've been going through to pick up a few coins here and there, and this whole time Philémon has known he holds me captive. I wonder why I'm delaying. Why don't I just capitulate and do what he wants of me?"

"Oh, mademoiselle, please! You have already come to the conclusion that you cannot accept such a proposition or tolerate such a horror of a man! He's offering nothing more than a mercantile transaction as if you were mere chattel. Don't you find that a revolting suggestion?"

She looked at me, the irony shining from her eyes.

"Gosh, Miss Fletcher! You speak so passionately for an Englishwoman! Believe me, there are matters a lot more revolting on this earth than what Philémon is offering. Yes. It's a transaction in which I am the victim. Or the duped party. Or the object. You call it what you will. But there is something flattering in what he asks of me." She shook her head. "I know what my problem is. My weakness. I'm far too proud. Why is it I can't give in to him? It will be the end of me, this fierce self-regard of mine. My mother has always said as much. And I must admit that I was hoping for so much more with that soap idea of yours. But how are we to find the money to pay the rent? My engagements down at Madame Alexandra's will simply not suffice. And I must reimburse her first, of course. I'll never manage it. I won't be able to bring in enough. You should recognize my dilemma, for it is you who keeps the accounts!"

"It certainly is, but—"

"You must realize that a protector such as Philémon could bestow upon me a generous monthly allowance! Surely you would welcome this! Am I not right?"

"Yes," I acknowledged, disheartened.

"And the money would be nothing to him! He can't wait to take me out and show me off. I would add to his fortune, no doubt! And all I'd have to do is close my eyes from time to time and tolerate his . . . ways."

"If you say it like that . . . ," I said, ready to accept her decision.

"No! Three times no! You know how obstinate I am! I won't do it. It's an impossible solution! I'll say it again—*no!*"

I set about pretending to write again so she wouldn't see my smile of satisfaction. She shot up quickly, the indignant meows of Sherry almost waking Anna, who was still sleeping on the sofa. She threw her gloves and hat onto the sideboard, pulled off her short coat, which she hung over the back of the chair, and helped herself to a large glass of wine from a decanter.

I saw her rummage through her skirt pockets and remove something that shone in the dappling sunlight. Was it a necklace? She started opening the drawers of the sideboard, searching for I knew not what. She finally happened upon a small wooden box, which she pulled out triumphantly and opened, and placed the secret treasure inside. Was it a gift from her visit with her gentleman friend?

We heard the front door open down below, though there hadn't been a knock. She shot across to the window.

"It's Maupassant! At last! He's been avoiding the little one, I fear!"

She brushed her skirt down quickly, flattening the lace, and said without meeting my eye, "I think I'll deduct the price of that basin from your remuneration. It was Gien porcelain, my dear."

I smiled as she let out a little gasp. "Quick! We must hurry! Cover up the mirrors! We don't want Maupassant having another hysterical moment, do we?"

The voices of Rosalie and Maupassant drifted up the stairs. They were both speaking at the same time. I flew out from my small office into the main room with a sheet from Rosalie's laundry basket and covered the mirrors to the best of my ability.

Rosalie sounded as though she were elated, giggling even. She was promising something or other, but I couldn't quite catch the words.

They climbed the stairs, and we heard a gentle knock at the door. Maupassant entered the room.

With a finger on her lip and her other hand held out to greet him, Lola skipped over and invited him in. She pointed to Anna on the sofa and beckoned him to come and join me in the makeshift office. No sooner had he taken a seat on a small basket chair than Sherry was perched on his lap. Maupassant scratched the cat's back and spoke softly. Sherry was quite satisfied with the warm welcome received from Maupassant and hopped up onto his shoulder and then onto a shelf before setting about cleaning himself.

Lola remained standing, pacing the room like a circus lion trapped in its cage.

"So, this is where you work?" he asked, giving the room the cursory examination. "It's certainly original."

"It's better than nothing," I said sulkily.

"So?" he asked. "Buttura came by, is that correct? And the girl is sick? What's going on exactly?"

"You cannot even begin to imagine the things we learned from that fine doctor!" exclaimed Lola. "Tell him, Miss Fletcher! I insist!"

I attempted to resume what we had been told regarding the deaths of the young girls that winter at the orphanage and how it had been nigh on impossible for the good doctor to gain entry to the building. I also divulged what we had discovered of Clara and the state of her health at the time of her death. I explained that the autopsy had been carried out despite there having been no formal request from the police.

However, I was unable to finish most of my phrases. Lola interrupted me incessantly. She punctuated most of what I said with enthusiastic cries, indignant shakes of the head, and detailed precisions when it came to the more shocking passages.

"Can you believe all this?" she exclaimed.

Maupassant didn't reply for quite some time. Finally, he spoke. "Ladies, we find ourselves confronted with what is known as an inverse enigma. And given your characters, I am only half-surprised by this," he announced in an amused fashion.

I felt anguished upon hearing these words. "What is your meaning, monsieur?"

"Well, let me paraphrase Dumas père. At least, he was the first in a very long line who used this expression, *'Cherchez la femme,'* that behind every crime is a woman. Seek out the woman, and you'll find the root cause of that crime."

"Yet another turn of phrase that shows how unjust people's attitudes are toward the gentler sex," I shouted. "Every time a problem presents itself, one only must utter this phrase, and everyone giggles in agreement! As if it were a universal truth! I don't know where you're going with this, anyway. In this case, let me remind you that the woman is dead!"

"So let us reverse it. Behind every crime is a man. Look for the man, and you'll find the root cause of that crime. *Cherchez l'homme!* You have said that she was with child. Let us find the man who seduced her. Because the way that Lola speaks of her young friend, it can only have been thus! She must have been persuaded by some vile man! What do you think of that? There is a chance that whatever villain seduced and impregnated Clara had a direct link with her death. Although we don't know why for the moment, of course. But there's a chance all the same."

Lola agreed wholeheartedly with the idea of finding this man.

"Let us take note of any member of the opposite sex that was close to Clara in any way," said Maupassant.

"Amédée!" I cried out triumphantly. "Amédée lusted after her. Perhaps he couldn't control his impulses and forced her . . ."

"Who else do we know?" said Lola. "Let's have their names."

Maupassant dictated as I wrote them down in a column of my notebook.

"Well, there's Amédée, and the hotel manager, Maurel, of course. Sometimes men can have certain 'rights' over their female employees. It could be a case of that. There might be a male servant who worked alongside her too. What about her clients? We're going to need to get our hands on a list of all the male guests staying at the hotel when she became pregnant."

"But it could well have been a total stranger," Lola said. "Perhaps there was an incident with a complete unknown. Or even someone who had coveted her for a while. Didn't you say she worked at the *faïencerie* and that she detested it? Perhaps the boss there had taken a fancy to her? Made advances? It might even have been a colleague? Perhaps this man wanted to see her again, and he got what he wanted in the end?"

I sighed. "The list is getting too long now. We'll never whittle it down."

"Let us try to uncover the names of the guests at the Beau Rivage at around the time she must have become pregnant," Maupassant said. "Do you know when that might have been? Do you know the exact dates?"

"December," said Lola. "It must have been December. It's coming back to me now. Everyone who knew Clara agrees that she was very joyous and gay toward the end of December. She was singing without end, and what was once a timid character became a joyful one."

"Who says this?" I asked.

"The girl who shared her bedchamber. Though it runs contrary to the idea that she was the victim of abuse," Lola added.

"It certainly adds to the whole mystery. *Cherchez l'homme.* If we find him, we could be well on our way to getting some answers. It may have been a case of passion—pure and simple love," Maupassant conjectured.

Lola whispered to herself sadly, "What sort of man could have helped Clara Campo leave that faux reserve of hers behind? How could he have made her lose herself so much that she was prepared to give herself to him? Who is the father of the child she carried?"

Maupassant rose in a swift movement. "I know that you are unlikely to be able to come with me, and I won't force you to, but I intend to go and see Valantin. I believe it important that he is aware of our thoughts on this. You never know. Perhaps he needs us."

"Valantin? You must be out of your mind! I'm certain that the case is done and dusted as far as he is concerned!" exclaimed Lola.

"You are probably right, but I feel it wise to make sure of it. And it could be that our contribution would help him in furthering his search. I hope so, at least."

"I will come with you," Lola said. "I want to be kept abreast of events. You won't keep me away!"

"And you, Miss Fletcher?"

"I'll drive! I wouldn't miss an opportunity to go out and about in the same car as Guy de Maupassant and Mademoiselle Lola Deslys! What a parade it will be!"

Downstairs, Lola gave Rosalie the instruction to stay close to Anna during our absence.

Maupassant joined me outside in preparing the horse and carriage, although I didn't need his help, of course, or I would never have asked him, at least.

I peered back at the house to watch for Lola. A young boy had appeared from nowhere and was banging on the front door. He was warmly attired, but his clothes were ragged and torn and had certainly seen better days. Lola opened the door.

"Mario? What are you doing here? How is mother?"

I understood then that Mario was her little brother. Mario shrugged.

"Rosalie, please have a look through some of Eugène's things and give Mario what clothes remain, particularly any shoes. You'll do that, won't you? My mother can fix the sizing, and she'll sell anything she doesn't think is suitable. She'll earn a sou or two there."

"Where's your cat?" he asked.

"He's upstairs with Anna."

"Who's Anna?"

"She's an orphan girl who isn't well, and she's staying with me until she feels better. Why aren't you in school? Didn't you hear what I said to Mama about this?"

Mario shrugged again and stepped inside.

"Rosalie, could you make him something to eat?"

"Rosalie, could you do this? Rosalie, could you do that? This house would collapse to the ground if it weren't for me!"

Later, in the cab, as soon as we saw the town hall, I stopped the carriage and dropped them off within a short walking distance of the police station. The two of them walked briskly toward the main entrance and almost collided with the commissioner as they neared the door. Valantin was heading toward a closed carriage and dashed past them. The driver was awaiting him, tapping his foot nervously as the horses whinnied.

Maupassant followed Valantin and grabbed him by the arm just as he was about to climb up into the vehicle.

"We need to speak with you about the death of Clara Campo."

"It was more than just a death!" Valantin scoffed. "You mean murder! Someone was responsible for her death! I'm on my way right now to arrest a suspect! Would you like to witness an arrest? Come on! Climb aboard, writer! Up! Perhaps you might stop interfering with your far-fetched stories and come and see what the police look like in action! Resounding it will be!"

He'd invited Maupassant to join him, but had completely ignored Lola. In fact, she must have been invisible as far as he was concerned, because he hadn't even acknowledged her presence. This didn't stop her from hopping up into the carriage with the two men.

"So it is all resolved!" huffed the commissioner once they'd settled down onto the seat.

"Already?" asked Maupassant in disbelief.

"Yes! We don't hang about! What do you know of it, in any case?" he asked, sounding interested. "Are you here to tell me something I don't already know?"

"Clara Campo was with child."

"Yes, I am aware of it. We discovered this in the autopsy report I'd asked Buttura to compile."

Lola shoved Maupassant in the ribs with her elbow. The expression on Maupassant's face didn't change in the slightest. Valantin, seated on the bench opposite, looked at Lola suspiciously.

"What ever is the matter?" he asked her. "Why did you elbow him just then?"

"Me?" Lola retorted innocently.

"Here's what I make of this banal little story," explained Valantin with satisfaction. "Young Clara had been quite depressed of late. She kept her complaints to herself. She had more than certainly had to tolerate the advances of Amédée, the porter. They possibly had a liaison of sorts. He might even have abused her, for all we know. The wait was too much for him. Rather than accept her rebuttals, he killed her."

"But even so," Maupassant said, "you're quick to reach a conclusion, are you not? Your judgment, once made, cannot be revised. Are you fixed on the idea of it having been the concierge?"

"Yes, I am! And I know how to make men speak! I'll get it out of the oaf, I assure you. I'm sure he has only one thing on his mind. A confession. He'll want to relieve himself of the burden. I have to tie this all up as quickly as I may! The whole affair is quite transparent to my eyes! Good Lord! How pleased I am to have unraveled this mystery. And an additional advantage is that it concerned domestic staff and domestic staff alone! This means the hotel will suffer little scandal from the affair. Its reputation will remain gladly intact. I won't make a mention of where the body was found in my report, and I'm counting on you in terms of the utmost discretion. It won't be of any interest to the gossipmongers within the upper classes of Cannes. Rumors are only of any value to them if there are crowned heads involved," he concluded.

"You can say that again!" joked Maupassant.

All this time, I was following behind at a slow pace, keeping my distance but with the police vehicle in sight. They stopped on the Croisette, just beyond the bridge. All three of them descended, and Valantin led the way to the hotel through the side entrance just a short walk away.

I parked the carriage and stayed in my seat. I was starting to feel somewhat tired and listless but knew I dare not leave the vehicle unattended. Yet I had no clue as to how long they would be in there.

Fortunately, my small box of cigars was in one pocket and a few matches in the other. I leaned forward and inhaled deeply on my smoke. I watched the stunning reflections of the light on the water. And the people around me . . . well, they watched me.

22

AN ARREST

They found Amédée Lambert in his bedchamber in the men's quarters.

Valantin didn't bother to knock. He opened the door forcefully and bounded into the room. He was followed by a support team of security agents who'd made their way to the hotel separately. They maneuvered themselves into position on either side of him. Maupassant and Lola held back, observing everything.

Amédée had taken off his uniform and dressed himself in his more casual evening attire. He was lying back on his bed with a small frame in his hands. It looked as though he had been crying. There was no apparent response to Valantin's intrusion, and this calmed the police commissioner somewhat. He positioned himself on a straight-backed chair after having taken the frame from Amédée's hands.

He wasn't surprised to see it was a photo of Clara. But Valantin showed no expression and started interrogating Amédée immediately.

"We need to take a statement from you, monsieur. It's crucial. Within this hotel, it would seem you were the closest friend to Clara Campo."

"The closest?" he asked, sounding troubled. "No, I don't believe so."

"You got her the position, did you not?"

"Is that forbidden?"

"Of course not, but we're just hoping to establish the facts about Clara Campo. We need to examine what she went through before her tragic demise so we can close the case as quickly as possible. Her family is waiting to bury her, and we want to give them the permission to do just that. What can you tell us about her final night?"

"Nothing. She finished her work at nine in the evening, and I started mine at around eleven."

"So in the two hours that you were both off duty that night, did you see her or talk to her at all?"

"No. At about half past eight, I went down to the kitchens, and the chef cooked me up a plate. As is often the case with the boys there, I ended up having a political discussion with Prosper, one of the porters. And then, realizing the time, I changed into my uniform and went about my duty."

"So you could have seen her when your shift began, couldn't you? Did she come out of her room at all?"

"No, I don't believe she came out of her room."

"Right. Did you perhaps notice anything suspicious that night? A movement? A noise?"

After a lull of a few seconds where he looked to be searching his memory, he replied, "Nothing. Not a single sound, monsieur. Nothing out of the ordinary at all. It was a quiet night."

"There weren't any new members of staff starting? Anything like that?"

Amédée played the same game. Silence. Nothing. He simply reflected. However, he looked anguished. He hesitated and then said, breathlessly, "There was nobody."

"You know that we're going to verify whether or not you were in the kitchen, don't you?"

"Oh! I'm such a half-wit! I've made a mistake! It was the night before that I dined in the kitchen! I remember now that I was feeling a little queasy that night. I'd been having stomachaches all day. The truth is that I didn't leave my room at all that evening. Not until I started work, of course."

Valantin turned to one side and whispered something in one of the security agents' ears. The whole scene erupted. The two police officers threw themselves on top of Amédée, screaming at the top of their lungs. Amédée tried to fight them off, but the commissioner hollered, "You're going directly to the station, Lambert! I don't like being taken down the garden path like this! You have no alibi for that night! You'll be more inclined to speak with me once you've spent a night in one of our cells."

With his wrists in cuffs, Amédée was dragged outside toward the service entrance, his head lowered onto his chest.

"What are you going to do with him?" asked Maupassant.

"Our first stop is the town hall basement. We have some rooms there. I'll question him. When he's admitted what went on, I'll charge him. We'll get to the bottom of this, never fear!"

A police carriage was waiting for them behind the hotel. I hadn't moved from the landau. I was still sitting patiently. When Maupassant and Lola exited the hotel, they found me and explained all that had just taken place.

"I'm not convinced," said Maupassant. "You both must come and partake of refreshments with me at the Grand Hôtel. Come!"

"You're quite insolent, Maupassant! We don't take orders from you!" I cried.

"Oh, you must always do as a writer asks, even if his behavior is irritable to you. Come, Miss Fletcher, I'll have none of this!"

"No. Not this time. I am covered in dust, and I smell of horse manure. I would prefer that the whole of Cannes thought me a horseman. I enjoy hiding behind this Gaza of yours, Lola. I cannot conceive of anything worse than walking among all the guests at the hotel, wearing these clothes! No! It's out of the question!"

"Leave her! Let her hide herself away! Come on! We can go on foot! Miss Fletcher, you go home and make sure all is well with little Anna. We can walk home."

I was a little vexed they didn't want me to drive them to the hotel, so I followed closely behind them as they trotted along the promenade and watched as they spoke with wild gestures. Lola's excitement was due to the idea of a trip to the Grand Hôtel with a man as well known about town as Maupassant.

As they disappeared into the majestic building, swallowed up by the huge entranceway, I picked up speed and made my way back to Les Pavots.

As for Lola, as soon as she stepped inside, her demeanor changed immediately, her mental disposition equally.

For it was time to advertise her name. To the chagrin of Maupassant, she started placing her postcard everywhere she could—on tables, stands, the front desk, and every available flat surface—giving wide smiles to all those who observed her. With every one of Maupassant's friends they crossed, to whom he felt obliged to introduce her, she would place in their hands her miniature portrait.

Maupassant became more and more annoyed by her behavior and forced her to take a seat at a table.

"I brought you here so that we might talk about Amédée and our mutual observations. I cannot fathom that following the scene we just witnessed back there that you can be in such a frivolous mood! A man was arrested! His life is on the line! Does that have no effect upon you?"

"Do you believe the two of us might change the law? From my position, if I can imagine a way in which I might act, I will do just that! But for the moment, I must be allowed to reflect upon it in my own manner."

"I don't feel as though Amédée has the right profile to be a killer," Maupassant continued.

"What about that lie he told?"

"He's a liar. That much is evident. But I ask myself why? He is a gentle-natured man. I don't think he could harm a cat!"

"I should hope not!" exclaimed Lola. "Well then. Have you finished? I am absolutely in agreement with your deductions. Why don't you invite that painter over there to come and join our table?"

"Not until you've given me your thoughts on this. I insist! I'm confused by everything we've seen today, and I would appreciate a sensible discussion! It appears as though the whole matter is done and dusted as far as you're concerned."

"And if I do so, do you promise you'll invite some of your acquaintances over?"

"I promise."

"Amédée, like you said, can't have done anything to hurt Clara. He treasured her. He was immensely devoted to her, but he did not blame her for her rejections of him. He knew she was a cut above him. However, it didn't stop him attempting to woo her regularly or prevent him from asking for her hand."

"But why would he lie?"

"It's clear enough! He's lying for two reasons. The first is because he doesn't wish us to uncover the truth about where he was on the night in question. He wasn't where he says he was. But that doesn't necessarily implicate him in Clara's death."

"And what's the second point?"

"He saw something, but he doubts what he saw."

"How could he possibly have seen anything if he wasn't even present?"

"That's what we need to understand. We need to delve further."

"And how do you know all this, might I ask?"

Lola wanted to explain from whence came her certitudes, but as I would go on to understand, she had great difficulty describing her gift to others, this intuition of hers. I imagine she was afraid she would be mocked. As far back as she could remember, she'd felt she could sense the emotions of others. She sometimes made errors in judgment, but that was when she failed to allow her heart to speak to her. She was flustered as she tried explaining this to Maupassant.

"It's as transparent as glass, my dear!" she finally said. "I looked, I observed, I dissected, just as your friend Flaubert taught you to do!"

Maupassant invited several of his friends over to meet with Lola, but he left her little time in their company. As soon as she'd finished the last sip of her lemon tisane, he stood, took her by the arms, and propelled her out onto the street.

"What's bitten you?" she protested.

"I cannot tolerate the idea of an innocent man being held under lock and key. We need to go and tell Valantin what we know!"

"Police always want hard evidence. You're getting anxious and agitated for no good reason. If you want to help Amédée, we simply must discover where he was that night. That's all there is to it!"

"And how are we to come by such information?"

"We're going back to the Beau Rivage. Palmyre Audoin, the girl who shared the bedchamber with Clara, started to tell me about Amédée. But if Maurel sees me, I'm finished! He has made it very clear that I am not welcome there. He doesn't want me meddling in his affairs, he said. It was fine when we were with the commissioner, but not alone."

Lola guided him through the back streets that lay behind the extravagant villas that bordered the Croisette.

As they approached the Rue Bossu, she spotted a familiar face making her way toward the back entrance of the hotel.

"It's her! Look! It's Palmyre!" Lola waved her arms and bellowed, "Palmyre! Palmyre!"

The young girl turned around, astounded at hearing her name being shouted from across the street. She recognized Lola and walked over to her.

"What on earth is happening? I can't be seen with you, you know? Maurel wouldn't take too kindly to that!" She smelled of absinthe.

"Come, then," said Lola. "Let us walk somewhere else. We'll get away from here."

"No! I'm late enough as it is! I went on an errand for a guest. I had to pick up some jewelry from Siegl's, and it wasn't ready. He made me late! I must get back inside the hotel and hand it over. It's for a baron, and he said he needed it before dinner."

Lola and Maupassant both understood she'd used the excuse of the errand to take some time for herself and that she must have stopped by a bar for a tipple. Maupassant leaned in toward her.

"Mademoiselle," he said with a charming smile. "Allow me to introduce myself, as it would appear Mademoiselle Lola has forgotten her manners. Guy de Maupassant, writer by trade."

He bowed, took her hand, and kissed it gently. Palmyre pulled it back harshly, a confused look on her face.

"I think I know the name. Clara had one of your books. She would sometimes read to me."

"I do hope you enjoyed my stories."

"They were a little . . . outrageous . . . at times," she said, her cheeks suffused with color.

"The reason I'm in the company of this young mademoiselle is because we discovered the body of Claro Campo."

"Yes, I know that."

"We would like to learn a little more of what happened that night. What *really* happened."

"Is it because you want to write about it? There's no way I can help you. If Maurel learns of it, I'll be dismissed on the spot."

"Palmyre," said Lola. "I know you want the truth of the death of Clara to be uncovered as much as we do. Is that not true? She was a dear friend, was she not?"

"Gracious. It's not that . . ." Her mood appeared to darken. "They treat us as if we were nothing here. They don't care about the truth. The only thing of significance in their eyes is that all scandal be avoided. So I'll do what I can to help you, but we must be quick about it. Ask me precise questions, and I'll do my best."

"Yes," said Maupassant. "So, to my first question: Do you know where Amédée was on the evening of Clara's murder?"

"Of course! Everyone knows this! Amédée is a card player. He must have gone to his favorite bar. He likes to do the rounds, playing all sorts of games."

"But," Maupassant interjected, "I do believe that activity is quite illegal here in Cannes."

Both women looked up at him incredulously and then continued their discourse.

"Do you know where he liked to play?"

"The Rat Noir. It's a cabaret bar."

"Of course! I know it well! And I've just remembered something! The other day I saw Amédée! He was speaking with the owner of that bar! Roussel! I didn't recognize him at the time, but I'm quite certain of it now!"

"What is this Rat Noir place?" asked Maupassant.

"A real hellhole. I used to go there back at the beginning of my relationship with Eugène. The card games are all clandestine, of course. They have a few bedchambers up on the second floor."

"I see! Interesting!"

"Do you have any other questions?" asked Palmyre, fretfully. "I have to go . . ."

"Have you told Lola everything you know about Clara? Her state of mind? She was content, is that right?"

"She was happy over the Christmas period. That much is true. But it wasn't so in more recent weeks. She was very unhappy, even to the point of being quite nasty at times. When I spoke with her, she looked at me with hate, and it scared me so."

"Hate?" asked Lola. "Come now! That's rather unlikely! I can't conceive of Clara being hateful!"

"And yet, she was. She was angry on a permanent basis. She was biting everyone's heads off! We were all walking on eggshells!"

"And what did she say about her future? She gave the impression of feeling bold and certain about it. Is that right?

"Yes," she laughed bitterly. "She wasn't even recognizable."

And on these words, Palmyre galloped off toward the hotel and slipped into the servants' entrance.

"Well, that fits nicely with what Valantin said," concluded Maupassant.

"This has been such an exhausting day for me," said Lola. "I want to go home and find out how things are with the girl. It will be simply sublime to spend an evening lazing around."

"Allow me to accompany you home."

On the way back, Maupassant said, "At least now we know the reason Amédée was lying."

"Yes, and why he didn't give us an alibi either. But now he knows he stands accused of murder . . . well, he's not so stupid as to get himself caught up in all that. He'll tell the truth."

23

EFFERVESCENCE

Everyone slept with great difficulty that night—woken intermittently by the screams of Anna reverberating around the house.

She no longer had a fever, but was suffering from nightmares. We all got up to comfort her. She told us of a fire burning the whole house down. She'd tried to run, but the flames caught up with her. She called out the name of Janette. Aunt Janette.

Rosalie, Lola, and I remained by her side, but it was the sweet voice of Rosalie singing a lullaby that finally allowed her to feel some peace.

Once she'd fallen back to sleep, Lola wanted us to go through the file we'd been given by the orphanage. Until that point, we hadn't had the time to do so. I'd had a quick glance through it on the day I'd signed to take her into custody.

We weren't surprised to read that there had been a fire.

She'd been no older than seven when she lived on a farm in the Camplong district. Her parents, Janette and Pierre Martin, had died in the blaze that had ravaged their home. Everything they owned was gone in a flash. They left a great many debts behind them, and the plot of land on which the farm had stood sold for enough money to pay for lodgings for the first year for Anahite at the Sacré-Cœur.

Her name had been shorted to Anna quite naturally. It was probable that her parents had also done so when she'd lived with them.

Janette was the name of her mother, not her aunt. Why had she cried out "Aunt Janette"? It was possible that the little one's memories of her previous life were confused.

"What about the name Anahita?" asked Lola.

"Isn't it a name from around these parts?"

"Not to my knowledge."

Maupassant arrived shortly after sunrise, just as we were sitting down to an early breakfast. He poured himself a coffee. It was such a mild morning that we had decided to take our victuals out in the garden. Anna was feeling much better. Rosalie had helped her get up, wash, and dress.

She had eaten with the maid in a small courtyard adjoining the kitchen and was now playing nearby under the orange and lemon trees. The cat joined in, running through the daisies on the lawn. Maupassant told us of his meeting at the city hall. He'd been there to deliver his corrected drafts and had taken the opportunity to visit with Valantin.

"Amédée was freed this morning," he explained. "He admitted where he was that night before going on to work his shift. His alibi has been confirmed by several individuals, including the patron at his favorite drinking den."

"Ouch," said Lola. "He must have been dismissed from his position by now!"

"I don't know for sure, but I suspect as much," Maupassant said with a nod. "I've been thinking about something else as well. I know how I can get ahold of all the haute monde in one place at one time. Tonight there's a huge ball at the Cercle Nautique. Anyone who's anyone will be there!"

"I'm sure I'm not invited, am I?" asked Lola, frowning, but with a glimmer of hope in her voice.

"Indeed. Only those of 'good stock' will be granted entry," said Maupassant. "But I was thinking of you, Miss Fletcher. You could certainly join me. I know you're without a great fortune, but you're a young woman of the English nobility, no less. They won't refuse you."

I sneered, for I still had my pride. "A joke, I presume? A servant at the Cercle Nautique?"

Lola rolled her eyes. "Stop it with your false modesty! It doesn't suit you!"

"For the sake of our investigation," said Maupassant, "I insist! And I can guarantee I won't be having a marvelous time of it either! I hate balls as a rule. Crowds exasperate me! The jolliness of it all is something I find appalling."

"How you exaggerate!" said Lola.

"I tell the truth!" he insisted. "And I'm also very much afraid of running into a certain businessman I met last year. I led him to believe I could sell him the Île Sainte-Marguerite! What a farce!"

I felt committed to the cause, but unsettled. "I don't have the right clothes! I'm a governess or a maid or whatever I am!"

"More jokes! Your clothes are much better tailored than mine without even mentioning the quality of the fabric! I wear prêt-à-porter!"

I was desperate to play more of a role in the investigation. And there was the added hope of seeing Lady Sarah, of course.

I felt overjoyed in my anticipation. The mere thought of seeing old friends again had me brimming with excitement. They had all rejected me so easily from their circles! They thought it the end for me! It would be so shocking for them to see that I was still in the game and getting on with life quite shamelessly. My habitual reserve gave way to a desire for sulfurous provocation.

Maupassant had succeeded in convincing me.

"It won't just be stiff aristocrats and the wily bourgeoisie," he continued. "What I revel in at these events are the people who come in their droves to be in the presence of greatness. The false counts, the freeloaders, the fallen women—they'll do anything in their powers to be introduced and invited, and they try so hard to hide their attempts. They're all nobles, each one with a title! Or spies working for the consulate! They all swear to these facts, of course! The tricksters! I love them. I luxuriate in watching them. I delight in conversing with such people. It's quite comical, the absurdity of it all!"

"There's no need to tell me! I know that world well enough! But you said not five minutes ago that it bored you half to death!"

"Never mind that. Will you join me?"

"Yes, I accept."

Clearly not one to sulk, Lola clapped excitedly. "Excuse me, my dear, but we have quite a lot on our plates now! We have to turn your dress into something more becoming of a high-society ball. It is true that you do look like a widow or someone in mourning."

She stood and moved to the house, where even from outside I could hear her running around like a whirlwind, with Anna hot on her heels. As Maupassant made to depart, I recognized that I felt quite triumphant.

"I will pick you up at nine," he said. "Please leave the horse and carriage here this once. We can get a cab."

Lola and Anna came back to join me on the pergola after a short time, and we watched him leave. Just as he was out of view, I caught sight of a second gentleman making his way toward the front gate. He was dressed smartly, if not a little stiffly, in a top hat and tails. He had come from the Hôtel Central. He was just about to ring the bell when he caught sight of us. He leaned in toward the bars on the gate and shouted, "A message for Mademoiselle Deslys? Am I at the right address?"

"Give it to the little one! It'll be fine!" said Lola, smiling.

Shocked by such familiarity, he held out the envelope to Anna, who skipped back to us with it grasped in her little fingers. The man didn't move away, but he remained where he was, turning his head from side to side, pretending to admire the surroundings. Lola ripped open the envelope, read what was inside, and smiled at me dreamily.

"Do you have a response, mademoiselle?" shouted the messenger.

Lola sprang to her feet and leaned back onto the pergola. "Certainly! My answer is: Why not? But make sure you wink when you say it!"

The man clicked his heels, gave a quick salute, and hiked back down the hill, his cane clicking on the sidewalk.

Lola showed me the card. It was from the Prince of Wales. The crest, the coat of arms, the crown, and everything. He had invited Lola to a secret meeting the following day. In his suite, no less! And he'd signed it Bertie. He also suggested she wear widow's garb and a long, thick veil.

"About time! I thought he'd forgotten me!" was the response from our unflappable Lola, who slipped the card inside her pocket.

The afternoon that followed was rather tiresome for a woman who is not a lover of frills and trinkets. But Lola could hardly stop herself. She covered my black silk dress in pink and green ribbons. She found a matching pair of gloves for me, adorned in identical frippery. There was a lot of pink, and I felt more than a little ridiculous.

Anna waltzed back and fore between us and around the room in circles, looking through drawers and chests. It certainly appeared that she was over the worst of her illness!

Sherry played with all the leftover adornments on the floor, and Rosalie came into the room to voice her opinion from time to time.

Toward the end of the afternoon, the door flew open in a flurry. It wasn't Rosalie this time, but Mario who burst into the room, looking proud of himself. He was wearing the most stunning flannel jacket, trousers and braces, and a sturdy pair of gaiters. All were a few sizes too big for him. It looked like he was dressed as a dandy. Or a parody of one. Anna looked at him admiringly.

"What are you doing here?" asked Lola. "What about school?"

"School is no more! They've closed so they can prepare the Easter parade!" boasted Mario.

"Stop with the fibs! Seeing as you're here, you can help Rosalie."

"Can I go down with him?" cried Anna.

Lola gave them both the nod, and the children raced downstairs happily.

It was then decided that I needed some added frills on my dress with a train of lace that trailed along the floor behind me as I walked, with a silk hook that I was to hold on my little finger, lifting the train and thus making walking easier. It had been a long time since I'd last danced, and I hoped more than anything not to be ridiculed for my efforts, although I might not even be asked!

Lola's excitement for all the satin and ribbons and lace was starting to wear thin, but I no longer had the strength to protest. I even allowed her to rub some rouge onto my cheeks and lips.

By the time Maupassant came to collect me, I looked like a porcelain doll in the window of a toy shop: frills and flounces and all things feminine.

Lola had lent me a small pink beaded reticule. It was so small, in fact, that it served no purpose. I could hardly breathe for she'd pulled my corset that tight. The hat I normally wore had been replaced with feathers and flowers stuck to one side of my head, pinned into my hair and dangling over my left ear.

My walking shoes had been removed, and instead I wore an uncomfortable pair of patent heels in a deep claret shade with taffeta bows. They were far too small for me.

To finish off the look was a heavy necklace with imitation diamonds. How cumbersome it felt around my neck! A lace fan dangling from my wrist completed my constraint. In summary, I felt clumsy, ridiculous, and ungainly.

As soon as he laid eyes on me, Maupassant burst out laughing. He helped me up into the cab—thankfully, as I fear I would have been unable to do so alone!

"You're done up like a circus horse, aren't you?"

"And that's exactly where we're going! The circus!" I said, smiling at my own joke.

24

THE BALL AT THE CERCLE NAUTIQUE

Despite being out of sorts due to my attire, the evening ahead was of importance to me. It was the first time in a long time that I was to find myself among my peers—those who had condemned me and watched as I'd taken a downward spiral into hell.

Just as we were about to depart, Lola darted out to give us a couple of last-minute recommendations. We had to try our hardest to obtain information from the likes of dukes and duchesses, as it was unlikely that she'd be allowed to exercise her talents in circles such as theirs any time soon, and if they were staying at the Beau Rivage, they may know something of Clara. We were to make a mental note of all details.

As we walked through the grand foyer, we were forced to blink to allow our eyes to become accustomed to the light, for the Cercle Nautique had electricity! How modern!

The sheer magnificence of the great ballroom was a sight to behold. The immense crystal chandeliers lit the whole room like something magical—something beyond all imagination. There wasn't a dark corner or a shadow to be found. The elegant guests were flooded with light. Such luxurious luminosity reflected the worldly men and women it shone upon. Extravagance and affluence at every turn.

The great room was fit to bursting. I hadn't seen a crowd like this in some time. The noise was incredible.

The guests chattered and moved from group to group, allowing themselves to be admired. It was a genuine display, each person desperate to show off their fortune and their beauty.

The men were all dressed in their finest black suits and bow ties—a uniform of sorts. But they had to have something to distinguish them from the others—their most treasured possessions, of course—the women on their arms. The whole scene played out as if it had been written. Some of Europe's most influential men showing off their power to one another.

The wives, daughters, and mothers were exhibited in all their opulence. A vast array of sumptuous silks, fine feathers, divine perfumes, and glistening jewels that sparkled brilliantly under the incredible new-fangled lighting.

And it was just then that the truth dawned upon me. The contrast between where I found myself and where these people were was staggering. I had nothing in common with them. I wasn't a wife, a daughter, or a mother. I wasn't even a protégé of the illustrious name of Clarence any longer. I was a nothing. The social circles present in this room were so far removed from my own.

The enchanting and dizzying ambiance stunned me! I clung desperately to Maupassant's arm, and amazed by my impromptu abandon, he threw out his chest with bravado.

After being formally presented to the duc and duchesse de Vallombrosa, who were hosting the event, we were thrown into the lion's den. A group of pretty women caught Maupassant's eye. I knew some of them, the English contingent, at least, so I walked in their direction, ready to introduce my partner.

Several of the women recognized me and turned their heads so they would not have to greet me. I stepped back, separating myself from Maupassant, and took a glass of champagne from a passing foot-man. I needed some Dutch courage.

The dancing started within no time at all. As Maupassant passed from group to group, he would occasionally look in my direction. He seemed to be talking at some length with the gentlemen present. He beckoned me over, inviting me to converse with the guests, to gossip and chatter.

I didn't venture in his direction. I watched as he made his way to the smoking room—where I would so dearly have welcomed an invita-tion, but women weren't allowed—and imagined him being a lot more at ease in there. I'm sure there were many pieces of saucy information passed from gentleman to gentleman in that lounge—enough to set tongues wagging all over Cannes.

Maupassant was well known for his salacious tales, and as he later told me, his fellow smokers usually begged him to tell one. But strange-ly, he felt his audience was more than a little distracted. There was something or someone else on their minds. Those around him started pressing him more intently, and the question on everyone's lips was, "And what of that young woman we saw you with in town the other day at the theater?"

"She was in a carriage. That woman on the street."

"Lola Deslys and those cards she leaves everywhere. Who is she? Tell us, monsieur!"

Appreciating the irony of the situation, Maupassant, in bril-liant form, boasted of Lola's merits in the boudoir, as if he knew her intimately.

"But," he finally said, enjoying their titillated expressions, "let's get back to talking of maids and chambers, chambers and maids! Surely you must all have a few naughty tales to tell me! Something I can use for one of my books? Come on! Any dalliances with servant girls? Maybe a fanciful night in one of the local hotels? Anyone staying at the Beau Rivage? There are some beauties there!"

"That's the hotel I stay in over winter!" exclaimed Baron la Coste, a sickly looking young man, clearly suffering from consumption. "And now that you mention it, monsieur, I admit to having heard of something quite recently. Something that happened on the Swiss floor in January."

"What is this 'Swiss floor'? That's a strange expression."

"Oh yes! Maurel, the manager of the hotel, thought it a good idea for the enjoyment of all guests that they be roomed near families of the same origins. He wanted people to be able to meet more easily, for them to feel more at home. Of course, it's not always followed to the letter. Guests are often mixed and matched. For example, I'm Breton, but I found myself housed up on the Swiss floor."

"He has some fine ides, that Maurel. And so? How was life with the Swiss?"

"Oh, there's not much to say!" said the young baron. "I'm afraid it might disappoint. One night, as I was making my way downstairs to dinner, I heard something. Voices out of nowhere. I couldn't tell where they were coming from, but a door swiftly opened in front of me, and a young chambermaid came rushing out in floods of tears. She was agitated beyond belief. She looked at me aghast and made a run for the service stairs."

Maupassant listened with interest. "So far, you do not disappoint, my good man. Quite the contrary. A scene such as this evokes powerful imagery in the mind's eye. Why, it could fill a novel in and of itself!"

La Coste was delighted to hear this.

The other gentlemen stepped away one by one, becoming bored with such a simple story. For them, there were tales of property scandals afoot that were of far greater interest.

"Can you describe this young woman?"

The baron shifted on his feet in agitation, somewhat ill at ease. "I don't boast the same talent as you, Maupassant. What can I say? She was what I'd call insignificant. Light-brown hair, perhaps chestnut, of medium height, neither plump nor thin, not particularly amiable-looking, I would say."

"Well, she was crying, for pity's sake."

"Yes, her face was red and full of emotion."

"And her clothes? She was dressed in the typical uniform of a maid, I would imagine?"

"Yes," answered la Coste, a touch of pity in his voice.

"Anything else of note?"

"Yes, now that you mention it. I remember she had ink on her finger, and I found it quite odd. Why would a chambermaid be writing anything down?"

"Indeed. I cannot believe it," said Maupassant excitedly. "In fact, they usually have very white hands or perhaps fingers that are slightly reddened from all the menial tasks they do. They're not known as scribes! And can you remember from which room she came?"

The young man motioned for Maupassant to follow him to the double doors separating the smoking room from the great hall, where he pointed out a couple whispering on a green velvet courting bench.

"There they are. The young girl came from their room, unless I'm much mistaken. I remember seeing them exit that suite on another occasion. It was room three two seven. Do you wish me to introduce you? I could say you're a neighboring guest?"

"No, no, we won't disturb them for the sake of some idle rumor." Maupassant smiled. "It might appear inappropriate."

He found me just as I'd decided to join a group of young women dressed in white. They looked much more approachable than all the others in the room. There was something attractive in their demeanor. They were giggling and mocking some of the dancers out on the floor.

As I neared, they looked petrified. It was as if they'd seen a ghost. I let them alone, choosing to turn on my heel and forget about befriending them. Their reaction baffled me.

But it wasn't me they'd seen. With two guards on either side of him, there stood the Prince of Wales directly behind me. He was dressed in the most gleamingly beautiful military uniform I'd ever seen—a red coat, white trousers, gold medals, and cords. And you'll never conceive of the next part—he asked me to dance!

"Miss Fletcher," he said, holding out his hand just as the first few chords of Offenbach's "Valse des Rayons" played from the orchestra. I lowered my head and nodded.

Wales! Wales himself! Or Bertie to those who know him intimately, of course.

I curtseyed clumsily and placed my right hand onto his. He must have noticed that I was trembling slightly, for I was so very taken aback by this unforeseen and intimidating proposal. He pulled me through the scintillating crowd of dance partners. Of course, the very first subject we discussed was Lola Deslys.

And so the tone was set.

For the six minutes or so that the music played, it was question upon question on the subject of my dear friend Lola. I did manage to ask him how he'd known my name and who I was.

"The empire boasts the world's largest intelligence service, my dear. I know every truth there is to know about you. A little less on our friend, however. She certainly strives to cover her tracks. Indeed, one might be led to believe she has something to hide."

"I'll leave you to uncover her little secrets."

His cheeks blazed red, but I don't believe it was a question of timidity. I imagined it more likely that what I'd said had evoked a sordid image of some kind in his infamously licentious imagination.

I had great difficulty tolerating our tête-à-tête. I felt confused, and my head spun from the thousands of different sounds around me. We were besieged. Almost every eye in the room was upon us as people whispered and pointed. The gossips would have much to keep them amused for some time. Wales was known as a bon viveur, and I wondered whether all the attention I was in receipt of would be of some service to me or would bury me completely.

This was one of the most prestigious events on the calendar, and Wales must have been the most in-vogue man in town. Surely this would help my plight. I ruminated on it, and as Wales escorted me to the side of the room, I caught sight of Maupassant, his face astounded.

The voices around me subsided, telling me my moments of glory were over. The prince left me where he'd found me, bowed, and meandered through the crowd with his bodyguards in tow.

And out of nowhere, all those women of good families, who, prior to this, had wanted nothing to do with me, were now upon me, seeking my company and singling me out for questioning.

"Do you know the prince?"

"A little."

"And are you here with Guy de Maupassant? I simply adore his work."

"I very much doubt you've read any of it," I said cuttingly.

The girls paled, embarrassed.

One continued, "I thought I saw you in the most gorgeous landau on the Croisette. Was that you?"

"Indeed, it was!"

"Come, Miss Fletcher! You must tell us everything! You know that your young friend is the only person talked of in town these days. Her portraits are to be found everywhere, and even the *Échos de Cannes* made mention of them this morning! What a splendid way to get tongues wagging! Is she an actress?"

And so I learned that Lola had made the news and was the talk of Cannes! I made a mental note to get a copy. A newsprint tidbit like this would tickle the whole household!

More and more young girls, evidently tantalized by any revelations that might be made, continued to flock toward me, their faces simultaneously horrified, scandalized, and delighted.

"Tell us about her! Come along! Don't keep it all to yourself!"

I looked around. I had no intention of provoking anger among the chaperones. And yet the situation was quite enchanting. Lola, without even knowing of it, was very much the belle of the ball. She had become a fashionable figure, and it had all happened quicker than we might ever have hoped. It was all thanks to the magic of the print press and the singularity of this town, where notorious rumors spread like wildfire. If I were to speak more on the subject, it would be like introducing the devil himself. These girls were innocent, protected. Dare I do it? I savored the subversion of it all.

"You haven't yet told me your name," I said to one girl.

"Of course! Where's my head?" sighed the young girl. "I'm Lorna Wylve, the daughter of the Duke of Brent."

She went on to present me to her friends and acquaintances, all the progeny of lords and barons, of course. After we'd all been formally introduced, I let go with reckless abandon. It felt so joyous.

"In fact, Lola Deslys is a great friend. She's an actress, and she started her career at the Folies Bergère, where she was a known crowd-pleaser, but thought to be too young."

It was all balderdash. I improvised as I spoke.

"She's continuing her career here in Cannes. She's made the decision that she wishes to remain here."

A great number of oohs and aahs punctuated my words. I knew they wanted the more prurient details.

"Does she have many lovers?"

"Decorum and propriety forbid me from revealing the number. A young man stands ruined already because of her. It happened last year. And at the moment, a second young gentleman, who set her up in a most comfortable villa on the hill, is desperate because she will have no more of him. He has left for war quite bereft. An elegant means of suicide, some would say."

Throughout our exchange, I tried to pry information from them as much as they did from me. I wanted to know if they'd heard any whispers of any recent unusual goings-on within their circles.

"Indeed! There is much hearsay afoot," cried the young countess. "Of course, all of us try to maintain a certain distance from any scandals, for we don't wish to be contaminated. But we have eyes and ears! In my hotel alone—"

"Which is . . . ?" I interrupted.

"The Beau Rivage."

As soon as she pronounced those words, my attentiveness doubled. Noises had been heard around Christmastime that there'd been an incident with a young chambermaid, but they knew none of the details. I noted all of this before the conversation returned to Lola. I took the opportunity to tell them of the perfumery and her soaps.

"She even has a soap bearing her name, you know? And the smell is quite intoxicating!"

Without warning, I heard a deep and velvety voice mingling with those of the giggly young ingénue, but I hadn't noticed anyone else approach.

"And what is your role exactly, Miss Fletcher?"

Lady Sarah!

Was she prepared to brave what people might say? How had she dared to even approach me? How long had she been listening in on the discussion?

"She's a dear friend of hers!" explained the young leader of the group.

"Really? A dear friend! Miss Fletcher?"

I couldn't find my voice. This game was no longer amusing. As she gazed upon me, I lost every ounce of confidence I'd had. Her eyes looked me up and down. I sensed how ridiculous she must have thought I was with my faux necklace, voluptuous feathers, and colored ribbons.

I searched in vain for a witty comeback, but I had none. I wanted to tell her how the Lolas of this world often reveal themselves to be far superior in soul than certain so-called ladies. But the words didn't come.

My eyes searched the crowd for solace. I was on the brink of tears. The music stopped, and the couples separated with smiles and delighted expressions.

The young slips of girls encircling me had no idea of the drama unfolding before them and went on to make comments on the evening's menus, the known actresses in the room, and the famous courtesans of Paris who were thought to be landing in Cannes any day.

I spotted Maupassant standing not far from me. I must have appeared lost and bewildered, because the look on his face was one of deep concern. The orchestra recommenced with a Brahms waltz.

Within seconds, Maupassant materialized by my side with charming allure. He smiled wryly and said to Lady Sarah, "Please forgive the intrusion. I feel my manners must be excused, for I am about to deprive you of the company of Miss Fletcher. I have long since promised her this dance!"

The gathered throng covered their mouths, giggling, their cheeks turning pink, whereas Lady Sarah stared at him, livid at the imposition. He swept me away in his arms and held me close against his chest. I was so grateful at his having rescued me that I allowed him the liberty of this improper closeness.

I danced with complete abandon. I felt as if we were alone in the room, as though I'd truly escaped. Maupassant watched me hungrily. As the dance came to an end, I hoped to meet Lady Sarah's gaze from the safety of his arms, but she had disappeared.

"Let us leave now," I said breathlessly.

He followed me, not saying a word. As we settled into our cab, he asked, "Who was that woman?"

I made no response, but sought out my cigars, which lay crushed inside Lola's small, pearly purse.

25

LOLA AT THE RAT NOIR

As soon as we'd left for the ball, Lola had slipped into the dull brown dress she usually wore whenever she went into the old town. She didn't wish to draw any attention to herself that night. She'd also decided not to wear a corset. Comfort was key. A discreet hat with a small veil completed her look. She would pass quite unnoticed.

She picked up her purse and disappeared off into the somber streets.

There was no possible way she would be recognized as the glowing creature who had brought that splendid display of color to the Croisette the other day in her outrageously spectacular carriage.

She didn't want the police on her tail. Raids were very common in all the bars and cafés that stayed open into the night. The bar district reminded her of her darker days, just before she'd met Eugène.

If I had been aware that she'd meant to expose herself this way with a view to furthering our investigation, I would have done everything in my power to dissuade her. And she must have known it, for she hadn't uttered a word of her plans to me.

She had often walked these streets. Not literally. No. That sort of business had always taken place indoors. The taverns and cafés would welcome Lola, for she was so young and so pretty, and above all else, she knew how to behave with decorum.

She worked on commission. She would collect glasses and get the clients drinking, and the tips she earned would nicely supplement what she managed to bring home as a model. She would on occasion, if she'd had enough to drink, allow herself to be taken upstairs with a generous bourgeois or two.

It wasn't a period of her life she was particularly proud of, or one she was fond of remembering. Her precarious situation and the fragility of her circumstances meant that she was ever afraid of tomorrow. She'd felt forced to accept the company of men she found unattractive or boorish, and she'd felt sick to her stomach when it came to the act itself, for what was sometimes asked of her was risky in nature. She partook of carnal "pleasures" with dangerous, perverse, and unhealthy partners.

The fear of the police and of the violence of some of her meetings meant she lived in continual anguish. It was impossible at that time for her to find a genuine lover. Everything she did made her feel ill.

She knew the joy that could be had in making love. She had no difficulty with the act itself. She found it to be a natural behavior and enjoyed the gifts and financial aid that came with it. She was young. She had little means of income other than this. It was advantageous from the outset.

She always tried to find something pleasing or engaging in a partner. She always endeavored to find an element of choice in what she did, but in the worst of times, it was not always the case.

That evening, without anyone's knowledge, she'd taken it upon herself to go to the Rat Noir to seek out whatever she could on Amédée and his character. She went there despite her trepidation, despite the feeling of being drawn too closely into her past—a past that was both far away from and too uncomfortably close to what her life had become.

As she entered the cabaret bar, the mere smell of the place was enough to bring about a barrage of memories. The gaudy colors, the smoke, and the bitter odors of absinthe, rice powder, and sweat almost made her gag.

A few women were propping up the bar at one end of the room, their heads close together, whispering their secrets—no doubt the woes of their love lives, their financial toils, their petty jealousies, and the mean streaks or brutalities met in the men who supported them. They were languid in appearance, weary and slightly drunk. A few men were trying to entangle themselves in their hushed discussion, and like them, they drank glass after glass of stale beer. Every now and again, one of them would speak using the foulest of language. Liquids of every color stood in glasses strewn haphazardly across the tabletops. Some of the customers were busy playing cards while others meandered aimlessly throughout the room or watched over the piano player in the corner.

Roussel, the proprietor, recognized Lola as soon as he saw her. He was small in stature, unwashed, and gave off a convivial air. But his eyes were small, piercing, and calculating and denied the constant smile he bore on his lips.

"My beauty! Have you come to help me? What about your lover? What became of him?"

From his tone, she quickly understood that the whole world knew already that she had been dumped unceremoniously and had been left in the most vulnerable of situations.

She responded crisply, "Eugène is quite well! He had some business to tend to and so has gone to stay with his parents for a few days."

She intended to leave him with the impression that nothing was definitive and that she and Eugène would most likely find one another again.

"Tell me, do you know Amédée Lambert?"

The proprietor gave a cursory glance to a group of men at the back of the room.

"What do you want with Lambert? I don't want to get involved with you and your sweethearts. No, it's not for me! Or is it something to do with what became of Campo? It's got nothing to do with him, let me tell you! He was with me when she had her little accident."

As Lola followed his gaze, she caught sight of Amédée slumped over a table at the other side of the bar.

She went to move away, but Roussel placed a proprietorial hand on her forearm. In a soft voice, he mumbled, "What are you up to, pretty one? If you're joining anyone at any of these tables, it's to work. Do you follow? You know the ropes down here. You'll get a percentage of every drink drunk, and I don't need any thanks. I don't go in for that sort of thing."

Lola felt a knot form in her stomach. She was so angered by his words. He had just dredged up her past and spoken to her as if nothing had changed between back then and now. When would people stop thinking of her like that? At what point would she make her way out of the slump of a life she'd once led? She pulled her arm away from his harsh grip and walked with confidence toward Amédée, coming up behind him.

His back was arched over the table. He lifted his head to take a slurp from his glass of absinthe. There weren't a great many empty glasses on the table, which told Lola that he must have been drinking somewhere else beforehand and that he hadn't been there long.

"Boo!" she whispered into his neck.

He jumped up in shock. "Huh? What? What is it?"

"It isn't anything at all! It's me! Lola! Clara's friend!"

He looked bewildered and then started to whimper. Lola's display had attracted the attention of a bourgeois man drinking beer, surrounded by middle-aged men and much-younger-looking women. There were four glasses on the table in front of him. So this was his fourth round. He'd be quite inebriated by now.

The man's face bore a blond mustache and freckles, and he wore smart checked trousers. At first glance, Lola believed him to be English or Scottish. Belgian, even! It was quite possible. He levered himself out of his chair, glass in hand, and made his way over to Lola. He bent down to whisper in her ear, removing his top hat as he did so.

"Would you permit me to join you?"

He had a strong English accent. So she'd been right. Why would there be an Englishman in a drinking den like this?

"Only if you swap the beer for champagne and you offer my friend here a glass too," Lola replied coquettishly.

She knew he was the ideal target when it came to getting a customer to spend some money, and it would also allow her to spend a little time with Amédée before Roussel would insist she move on. But the women who'd been enjoying his company thus far were not about to let Lola collect their spoils. She heard curses and protestations from their side of the room.

Roussel, who hadn't yet taken his eyes off Lola, quickly came to understand what was happening and knew it would be in his interest to allow it. Not a single woman in the place had thus far managed to persuade the Englishman to stop drinking his beers in favor of a more expensive refreshment. But here was the fresh-faced Lola, and he'd gone and bought a bottle of champagne within minutes. This wasn't the sort of thing that happened every day!

He stomped over to the girls and shooed them away to other tables to try their ways on other unsuspecting men.

The man in the checked trousers pulled out a chair for her and another for himself, and they installed themselves on either side of Amédée.

"You're a real gem! What are you doing in a decaying little hole like this place?" he said.

"My friend here has a broken heart, and I've come to console him," she explained, pointing to Amédée. "And what about you? Surely your wife is at the Cercle Nautique this evening. Shouldn't you be with her?"

He chuckled giddily. "A wonderful deduction! How in the devil's name did you guess that I'm supposed to be at that ball tonight?"

"It's simple, my dear. You are dressed rather brilliantly, and there is only one event in town where you would be required to wear trousers quite like those!"

A waiter brought over the bottle of champagne and three flutes. Lola helped herself and swallowed it down in a single gulp just after clinking her glass against that of the Englishman. She nodded at Amédée, who was looking at them but could hardly have seen them properly though his tears. Every couple of seconds, he sniffed and wiped his nose on his sleeve.

"Come now, Amédée, you mustn't allow yourself to get into such a state."

She forced him to finish his absinthe while she took his glass of champagne and drank it for him. The three unlikely companions were on their second bottle of the good stuff before Amédée spoke. Lola needed to make sure she caught every word coming from his mouth. But at the same time, she needed to keep the Englishman at a distance without boring him so much that he failed to order more drinks. Amédée explained that he'd lost his job.

"When I think that she wouldn't even have been working there if it weren't for me! If only I'd known! I would have given anything to marry that girl!"

"Yes, her mother told me of that."

"I asked her so many times, but she would have none of me. She begged me not to pursue her. She felt me too old. The hussy!"

"No! Why would you say a thing like that? Clara wasn't like that, and well you know it! Please don't speak of her that way!"

"Really?" he screamed ferociously. "What about her great secret? What was that, you might ask? The beautiful and chaste Clara? So reserved! So superior! Such a little prude! She wasn't the Mother Mary! What about the kid? Did it appear out of nowhere?"

"One can fall with child for any number of reasons! It by no means should lead us to the conclusion that she was immoral! How do you know she wasn't abused? How do you know she wasn't deeply enamored with someone and let herself go in a moment of weakness?"

The Englishman was following the altercation with immense interest and had shifted his chair to the other side of the table so he was near enough to allow his hand to graze Lola's thigh. She allowed him to leave it there, knowing it would excite him enough to stay at the table. Whenever she leaned in a little closer to Amédée, the Englishman would lean in closer to her, his mustache touching her hair, his nose on her neck, his lips getting closer and closer to her décolleté. He moaned lightly.

"You're right!" lamented Amédée. "She doesn't deserve me to foul her name thus. If she was still here, I'd take her as my wife. I'd even claim the child as my own. She was a part of my soul, that girl."

"Come, Amédée, get ahold of yourself. Tell me, did you notice anything amiss with her lately? Had she met with anyone new that you know of?"

He took out a large handkerchief from his top pocket and blew his nose loudly. The Englishman moved back hastily, a grimace on his face.

Amédée looked deep in thought and then said, "She spoke about a Swiss family that had come to stay in the hotel just before Christmas. There was something about them . . . The man was a savant of some kind. He was publishing a book about the gardens of the Riviera. They were nobles, the comte and comtesse d'Orcel de Montejoux. I found out about them, you see? Because I was jealous! But then she just stopped talking about them."

"How many in the family are staying at the hotel?"

"Three. The father, the mother, and their seventeen-year-old son. I remember the father's name. It was Charles."

"Are they still in Cannes?"

"The parents are, yes, but the son had come only for a short time to spend the holiday with them. He lives in Gstaad and returned home." He then stared at Lola in disbelief. "You don't believe . . . No! Charles d'Orcel? The comte? You don't believe she went to his bed, do you? Of course! You're right!"

"I didn't utter a word!"

"It's true! It's him! He's the father! That disgusting old bastard! A real pretty boy! Always dressed up to the nines as if he's about to go out wenching like a man half his age! In his gaudy jackets! Perfumed and powdered like a dandy! The swine! That wretch of a man!"

Lola left him to express his anger and bitterness. She felt that he'd started down this path of rage and wouldn't be turning back any time soon. She busied herself by taking some glasses back to the bar to earn some commission. The Englishman followed her every step, insistent, heavy-handed, sticking to her like glue. At one point, he started pulling her by the elbow, trying to convince her to join him upstairs.

"Let me go!" she hollered. "Do you want to create a scandal?"

But the Englishman was far too drunk by this point to care about the attention he was drawing from onlookers.

"But you made me believe . . ."

"I did nothing of the sort! I never make promises of that kind! *I* choose with whom I go upstairs!"

"Come on, Lola," said Roussel. "You're not exactly what we'd call a saint! Take it as the compliment it was meant to be! At least do something to shut the rowdy fool up!"

"I don't do that these days, Roussel! Didn't you know? Keep up, my old friend!"

A young student, likely hoping to receive a reward in kind or perhaps just hoping to get involved in a bar brawl, stepped in at this point.

"Can't you see that she wants nothing to do with you?"

The Englishman hadn't yet let go of Lola and was continuing to try to push her toward the staircase. The student grabbed hold of the nearest glass of champagne and threw the golden bubbly liquid into the Englishman's face. The man let go of Lola and grabbed the young student by the collar. A free-for-all was about to ensue.

Lola took her chance to make a run for it. She had to leave what little money she'd earned from her commissions behind. Just as she was about to step out onto the street, two police officers, dressed in civilian attire, grabbed her by the shoulders and marched her roughly to their patrol vehicle parked a little farther down the street.

Behind her she heard whistles, screams, glasses smashing . . . The police whistle blew, more officers joined in the fray . . . and most of the people in the Rat Noir were taken into custody. As they arrived at the *commissariat* on the Rue Macé and she was taken into one of the large holding cells, Lola noted the mixed crowd inside. This was her worst nightmare. Only now it had become her reality. She was about to be incarcerated, made to line up with the other girls, and paraded in front of a doctor. She might even end up listed, declared, obliged to submit herself to this outrageous custom of naming and shaming known prostitutes.

The police passed from time to time and removed people from the cell who they believed had been unduly arrested. This meant the bourgeoisie, the Englishman, the student, Roussel . . . Little by little the space emptied.

After some time, she realized that the only people left were women much like herself. Everything she was worried about when she'd gone out to the cabaret bar that night had come to pass. The only thing she could do was try to talk her way out of the situation before becoming trapped like a rat in a cage. She called an officer over, with the idea of showing him the note given to her by the Prince of Wales. It was signed, "Bertie." Surely it might give her a way out.

"Why are we being held like this?" she asked.

"You're waiting for the doctor. He'll be here tomorrow."

"Tomorrow? But that's just not possible! I can't stay here until tomorrow!"

"And why is that? Mademoiselle has an important meeting, does she?"

"I do!"

The policeman burst into a fit of laughter.

"Instead of howling like a buffoon, you'd do well to watch yourself. I could have you dismissed for this. Go and get Valantin. I'll only deal with him."

"And you expect me to go and wake him in the middle of the night, do you?"

"Do as I say and go and fetch him. And be quick about it!"

The man tried to give off a proud air, but the aplomb in Lola's steady confidence had sent a shadow of worry across his face. He walked over to a fellow officer, and Lola watched as he muttered something in a low voice.

They removed her from the cell and put her in an office, which they proceeded to lock. She stayed in there with the first police officer she'd spoken to. They were alone.

"You see this register here? It's where we note any arrests made, but it's just for us. That means I'll write all the goings-on of tonight, or at least those in which you were involved, in pencil. It's your lucky day. I'm not going to wake the boss, but I'm not in the mood for any mistakes tonight. They make no bones of sacking people in this place. The whole town is packed full of rich folk who cite the law and know all their rights. They dictate the policing services here!"

He wrote down her name, her address, and the place and time of her arrest. He also wrote the reason for them having taken her into custody: suspected harlotry.

"You can go now, but you'll have to be here in the morning to explain to Valantin about all of this."

Lola wasn't sure that Valantin, who'd been wanting to get his hooks into her for months, would allow her to get away so easily. She wanted the whole episode finished with before returning home.

"I'd prefer any traces of tonight to be erased now, if that's possible."

The officer snorted again. "That's what you'd prefer, is it? Well, there'll be a price to pay for that, my dear. And do you know what *I'd* prefer?"

She'd missed her chance to show him the card from Bertie. It had long gone. The man's eyes were on fire as he grabbed her by the hair and pushed her down to her knees.

She would recall to me the painful details of what happened next some time later. As she spoke to me, her eyes glistened with tears, and her chin trembled. She forced out a smile as she told me that the only thing she thought about at that moment was how much she regretted not having picked up her money from Roussel.

Lola sprinted home, her face streaked from crying, bereft with humiliation.

When she realized we weren't home from the ball, she quickly undressed and took herself off to bed. She made as little noise as possible so as not to wake Anna, who was sleeping soundly in her spot on the sofa.

She was deep in slumber when the cab dropped us off at the gate and woke her with a start. She walked over to the window and observed the horses and the driver perched high on top of the cab below the faint light of the lantern. The horseman held it up as Maupassant and I made our way carefully from the carriage to the side of the street.

Maupassant held me tightly and chattered loudly. He was doing his best to woo me again, and I persevered in doing my best to put him off.

26

A Swiss Comte

I tried my hardest to convince Maupassant to go home. He had sent the cab away and was insisting that I grant him entry into the villa so we could enjoy a final glass together. He said he needed the strength for the walk home. He followed me inside and up to the second floor.

Lola, in a state of undress, surprised us on the stairwell just as I was wondering how I was going to get Maupassant up to my little room without waking her.

"Miss Fletcher, could you go downstairs and see if we have any champagne left? Bring up three glasses, if you would, and then come and join us in our new office."

I obeyed her gladly, relieved of the fact that I would no longer have to deal with Maupassant alone.

I heard her whisper to him, "And you! You make a little less noise, if you will! I don't want you waking the girl. Tread carefully! Come and tell me everything!"

As I walked back upstairs with the bottle and glasses, I felt a certain excitement at the prospect of recounting the evening to Lola. It was that very night the idea hit me that I could write in great detail, perhaps even novel-length detail, what it was we had all lived through and learned since the death of Clara.

Everything there was to say about the dead chambermaid, Lola, Maupassant—I could write of this terrible death and pay homage to her through this investigation. I could give back Lola, through the gift of a book, her place in this world and society, the place she had so sadly neglected to take . . . and then lost. I could describe this pretentious society in which I had grown up, these people I knew so well.

I had been writing an intimate journal for a great many years, and perhaps now was the time to move on to something new, to other sorts of writing. A novella? A biography? I didn't yet know what form my text would take, but I was looking forward to giving it further thought.

My meeting with Maupassant might have given me the impetus to explore this desire. Of course, I'd never be able to write in French. My mastery of the language was insufficient. And I also did not wish for either Lola or Maupassant to know anything of my attempts at literature.

I feared their rejection, their reaction, their mocking of me. This meant I would write in English. If they happened upon my work, they'd be unlikely to read it in a foreign tongue.

"So?" asked Lola as I entered the room, interrupting my thoughts.

"It was somewhat edifying," I reported as I sat, taking the time to choose a quill and open up our notebook to the right page. I readied myself to write down everything we had to say on the subject of young Clara. "And I was quite the observer! It wasn't my first night at the Cercle Nautique, but never before have I felt quite as disengaged. I am no longer a member of their world, but this isn't a deprivation by any means. It's liberating! How I hate the receptions, balls, concerts, and the like that this society so enjoys."

"Well, while you played at being introspective at your high-society ball, I got hold of some firsthand information, I'll have you know!"

"And how's that?" I asked, worried. "I thought you'd spent the evening here with Anna. Did you go out, or has someone been to the house?"

Just then, I remembered seeing her scraggy brown dress hanging over the back of a chair in the living room.

"You went to the Suquet, didn't you?" I said.

"Yes! And what of it?"

"Did you go and see your mother?"

"No! What could I have possibly learned from my mother? I went to the Rat Noir for some information on Amédée Lambert."

"You're so stubborn! You know how dangerous it is up there! The police are always performing raids at that time of night!"

"I know what I'm doing," she said crisply.

The bravado in her voice was in stark contrast to the trembling of her hands, and I noticed a red rim around her eyes.

"What happened tonight?" I asked, alarmed.

"Oh! What do you want to know of it? You're not my priest! Not my mother! It's a good thing I took it upon myself to go, for I met with Lambert himself, and I learned a whole host of interesting details!"

She sulked.

"Oh, really? And so did I!" said Maupassant.

"And I," I joined in.

Each of us wanted to be the first to speak, and Lola and Maupassant shouted out at almost the exact same time, "A Swiss comte!"

We laughed at the coincidence and each took it in turn to describe the details we'd managed to glean from all the rumors uncovered that evening. Lola had the full name and description of each member of the family. Maupassant had found out the room number in which they were staying at the hotel. As for me . . . well, I hadn't got such enticing information, but I was able to confirm that talk of the family was rife among the young women at the ball.

"It's all rather vague, but as the family is a hot topic of conversation, I believe there must be something in it," I said.

"If you had only seen Miss Fletcher!" enthused Maupassant. "She had a whole circle of ladies around her! A darling little group of English virgins desperate to marry!"

"Is that so?"

"In fact, one of the reasons they were hanging on my every word was very much down to you, Lola," I confirmed. "In a mere few days, you have become the person most talked of throughout the entire town of Cannes! Your portraits! And our trips in the landau! I fear we're quite the sensation!"

"I can corroborate that," said Maupassant. "Every single gentleman I spoke to wanted to know who you were."

"It's the ultimate absurdity," said Lola. "I'm not allowed anywhere near these young women, and yet all they want to know about is me!"

"It gets even better! Miss Fletcher danced with . . . *Wales!*"

He pronounced the word with affectation, imitating the typical man about Cannes who wanted to give the impression of being on intimate terms with the British royal family.

"Yes," I retorted, "life can be strange at times! What success we've had! It really was all thanks to you, Mademoiselle Lola! The only reason he recognized me wasn't because I'd once met him at Lord Clarence's in England, but that he'd seen me by your side. He had the intelligence services trace me! Or so he said! He wanted to know everything there is to know about you! What an evening! And I can't stop thinking about their mannerisms! What fun it was to observe them so!"

"You see!" cried Maupassant. "You're just like me! You watch people! Can you believe the number of kings and princes and dukes all sharing the same piece of flooring? And they're all such cretins!"

The pair of us giggled.

However, Lola protested. She looked upset. "I'm afraid I cannot agree with you. I find them much of use, these kings you speak of. I'm delighted there are so many of them in Cannes. Future kings too! Like Bertie!"

"But you know that most of them belong to the royal families of countries and kingdoms that no longer exist! They're just old titles!"

"I don't care! I wish I were a part of their world! How I would revel in such an easy existence. You jest, the both of you, but you know not of what you speak! Those who are excluded understand exactly what it is!"

Maupassant and I felt a little ashamed at having saddened her so, but the desire to continue to laugh was quite overwhelming.

"You'll see! I'll be up there with them one day! All those kings of yours will be forced to salute me! They'll respect me! I'll have them eating out of my hand! And I'll show their queens a thing or two at the same time!"

"You'll do anything it takes to climb the social ladder! I believe I might give you a little nickname, Lola!"

"A nickname?"

"Belle Amie!" And he guffawed.

I laughed along, but I failed to appreciate the joke.

"Why that name?" asked Lola in irritation.

"Oh, you'll be fully aware of my meaning in a few months. But in all honesty, you are a kind young woman. A generous creature. You're really nothing like him at all. But despite this, I believe I'll still call you *Belle Amie* anyway. It's also the name I'll give to the next boat I acquire."

"You are intolerable when it comes to secrets and mysteries, Maupassant! Keep your puzzles to yourself! We have enough matters to untangle for the sake of poor Clara!"

"Speaking of enigmas," said Maupassant, "here's another. A true lady, an English lady, took it upon herself to importune our Miss Fletcher here. I don't know her name, but I'm sure Miss Fletcher can tell us everything."

I shot him a panicked look, feeling suddenly sober.

"What's this all about?" asked Lola.

"The lady wouldn't leave her alone!" insisted Maupassant. "I found the way she circled around our friend here quite indelicate!"

He was trying to add a little humor, but it was leaden to say the least. Lola sensed how uncomfortable he was making me.

"I don't think jesting with my dear companion in this manner will help you advance any in this little guessing game of yours," she said, trying to add some frivolity to the scene, which only served to accentuate my unease.

"I have my way of doing things," Maupassant joked. He knew he was getting nowhere and looked angered.

"Enough of all this! Come and sit a little closer to me," she whispered, trying to distract him, but doing so in an exaggerated fashion so it might pass for a joke if he refused.

I wonder if she still thinks of me? I thought, feeling a flutter in my chest.

"She didn't know how to rid herself of that woman!" Maupassant insisted, continuing with his schoolboy humor. "Isn't that right, Miss Fletcher?"

I felt disturbed by all the mockery, whispered my excuses, and retired to my room.

27

ENCOUNTERS

It was the most startling happenstance that the following day, after having hung around for over an hour, Maupassant should encounter Comte d'Orcel on the Croisette just after breakfast.

The latter was just leaving the hotel and making his way to the naval base on foot. He proved to be a tall man, with a toned torso and a virile, sporty appearance. His somber suit in black and white was tailored perfectly and looked to have been cut in the most expensive fabric. His overcoat was made of a fine ivory silk, which Maupassant, in envy, later described to be most elegant. He wore a watch that gleamed in the morning sun with a thousand diamonds and a silk tie of the most divine and deepest midnight blue.

Maupassant looked upon him in immense admiration and dared to initiate a dialogue, asking if he were not the famous naturalist and author of the botanical guide he'd heard so much about.

Flattered, d'Orcel acquiesced and engaged in a discussion with Maupassant on the subject. Maupassant was lucky in this respect, as he had a good, solid knowledge of the field thanks to his brother, Hervé, a great plant enthusiast and the sort of man who dreamed of horticulture, greenhouses, and cut flowers on an industrial scale. Maupassant used this as a pretext and suggested to d'Orcel that they together examine the fruit of their reciprocal research.

Their mutual enthusiasm for the topic ensued around a glass of beer at the Grand Café. They also exchanged ideas on the winter season in Cannes, hotel life, family, offspring . . .

Maupassant hoped to interrogate his interlocutor without his knowing it. Feeling adulated, d'Orcel talked quite freely, but Maupassant soon noted that any subject upon which he hoped to gain d'Orcel's confidence was met with discrete avoidance. This was particularly the case when Maupassant mentioned the service staff at the hotel. The comte eluded the subject with clever address.

"Do you know what? My wife admires your work so! She's also something of a poet herself! She tries her best, in any case."

"Oh! Poetry! Is there anything more noble?" Maupassant said with an irony that d'Orcel didn't catch. "Has she been published?"

The comte's face brightened. "No! But what an enchanting thought! Would you accept an invitation to come and take tea with us at our hotel? I would very much relish the chance to introduce you to Andréa. How she would adore to speak of literature with a genius such as yourself!"

Maupassant didn't know whether to rejoice in the fact that he had achieved his ends in that he could now take a look at the famous d'Orcel suite or to lament at the thought of what dreadful form of entertainment might await him with this man's wife. The very thought of having to show wild enthusiasm upon hearing the pretentious scrawlings of a high-society woman who thought herself a poet was beyond his strength.

Upon entering the apartment, that which the young chambermaid had left so fretfully, it took him no time to befriend Andréa d'Orcel de Montejoux.

He listened patiently to her as she read her poetry aloud, and he feigned to marvel at its quality, the sensitiveness of her quill, and the modesty of her sentiments. In turn, the comtesse incessantly repeated her take on his stories and novellas.

He was now not only on familiar terms with Charles, but was fast establishing a relationship based on pure flattery with the man's wife. This amused him somewhat.

Just after tea was served, Maupassant spoke of a pain in his thigh that had come about following a long walk that very morning. He insisted that he felt very uncomfortable having sat for too long and that taking a turn about the room would be most refreshing.

As he strolled in a wide circle around the suite, he noted the collections of books, the decorative piece of art, and the flowers. Andréa smiled, so enticed she was by Maupassant's presence.

He looked at a framed photograph upon which appeared the comte and comtesse alongside a scowling adolescent with a pimpled complexion.

"Your son, I presume?"

"Yes! That's Maxime! Our pride and joy!"

"And is it here that you write, my dear? Do you use this very bureau?" asked Maupassant as she cooed with enthusiasm.

He made a move to pick up the quill from the ink pot. As he pulled it out awkwardly, the ink ran onto the tip of his finger. He immediately thought of showing the stain to Lola upon returning to the villa. Perhaps this was where Clara had obtained a very similar mark upon her skin on the day of her death. It could be. The comtesse got to her feet quickly.

"Careful! That ink is a menace! It's quite tenacious! I have it sent for from Italy. I find the violet shade inspires me! I am highly meticulous in nature, and I fear accidents such as the one that has just befallen you, my friend. I always write wearing a painter's smock that I bought from the same supplier from whom I purchase my ink. I never work on my poetry without first slipping it on over my clothes. Oh, if you could only see me dressed thus! I'm the most abominable sight!"

"Please allow me to doubt that very much, madam."

"And do you write every day, monsieur?"

"I try. I tend to initiate my work very early in the morning, and when I feel like I've squeezed myself dry, I choose to take a stroll outside to explore my environment."

"That's such a wonderful way to go about it," said the comte. "Expending energy in a physical manner is indispensable following a copious amount of intellectual effort, I find."

"And you, perhaps as a couple," asked Maupassant, "do you have ways of distracting yourselves following an episode of writing?"

"We have just discovered lawn tennis, and I must admit we are quite the enthusiasts," said Andréa. "But we have only just started learning, you understand, and we dare not, as yet, play against any of our friends. We know people who have been enjoying the game for a lot longer than we."

"Lawn tennis? Why! I am so very fond of it! I must say that I have progressed immensely since meeting my friend Gabriella. She has even won trophies, you know? Perhaps I might introduce you to her? I'm sure she'd be glad to help you improve your game. And I believe she's a baroness or something. Her father was the Baron of Rump Steak or some place in England that sounds like that. I have great difficulty in English."

They snickered heartily at my expense. As Maupassant left, Andréa pressed upon him several sheets of paper bearing her work. He took them with a smile.

While Maupassant was being entertained by the comte and comtesse at the Hôtel Beau Rivage, Lola was preparing herself back home. As requested, she did her very best to look the mournful window, and she did it fabulously in black taffeta and lace. She made her way to the Hôtel Central, covered head to toe in a transparent black veil.

The rendezvous took place in a secret suite on a floor that had been completely reserved for Bertie. The meeting with the prince, the future king of England, was completed with satisfaction for both parties involved.

It had been fruitful and hurried, leaving Lola the time to follow up with a visit to Madame Alexandra's. She left the hotel and sauntered over to the reading rooms. As soon as Alexandra saw her, she congratulated her on her well-thought-out attire.

"Widows' weeds! What a fabulous notion! Well done, Lola! That's moral adultery! Exactly what most of our gentlemen are seeking! Keep to that color! It suits you well!"

Lola screwed up her face in disagreement. "No, no, this was for Bertie. My color is bright carmine red."

"Indeed, it is! Red gets the blood pumping! But don't be adding all your nets and frills! It's the illusion of seduction we have going on here!"

Following her discussions with Alexandra, she made the decision to renew her wardrobe somewhat. She needed some fabric that was a little less flamboyant than her usual choices. The draper in town had some of the finest silks in the South. He was to be found on the Rue Macé, and there wasn't an item in his shop that wasn't both chic and original.

On her way there, she met with her friend Antoinette from the perfumery, who was walking with Thérésine, the laundry girl. They'd finished their day's work and were taking a stroll before heading to their respective homes.

They stopped to talk awhile. Thérésine wanted a closer look at Lola's dress. The ribbons, flowers, fabrics, boots, gloves, and hat. She wanted to discuss every detail. She was quite shocked to see so many delicate finishing touches all in black.

"It's quite exceptional for me to be dressed like this, you know? It's really not my color. I want every last thing I'm wearing to be red! A deep shade, though . . . something somber. I feel it's so much more mysterious. It'll be my ensign! Everyone will know me by it!"

Thérésine clapped her hands together, enchanted to hear Lola speak. "What a wonderful thought! A deep red wouldn't show any ink or bloodstains, either!"

The mention of ink stains caught Lola's attention. "Do you meet with a lot of ink stains in the laundry?"

"A fair few. Particularly gentlemen's shirts, clerks' clothing, and so on. We have our ways of removing them, of course! If you dip the fabric in milk and leave it for an hour before adding white vinegar and flour, it'll disappear. But we got a dress in the other day from someone staying at the Beau Rivage, and it was in a terrible state. There was a dark-purple ink stain on it, and we couldn't get it to shift. I don't know where she'd buy a shade of ink like that. I've never seen the like. What a state!"

"Do you know who she was?"

"No idea. It was in the hotel laundry basket—that's all I know of it. We're not supposed to know what belongs to who."

As Lola and her friends parted company, she wondered if the stain on the dress might be the same shade of ink as that on the finger of her dear departed friend.

It was only that evening that we were able to gather our thoughts together into our little notebook. The elements we'd gleaned were rich in content. We believed that the ink on Maupassant's skin was the exact same shade as what we'd been looking for. Our plan of action was really taking shape.

The next step was that I'd soon be giving lawn-tennis lessons to the comte and comtesse d'Orcel. That would be quite something! Once they were away from their suite and in my hands, Lola and Maupassant would go and search through their belongings and attempt to discover something more. The only part that concerned me—and it concerned me greatly—was my total incapacity to give anyone a lesson in lawn tennis. I'd never taken well to the sport. I wasn't the best when it came to competitive games against an adversary. Swimming, riding, activities practiced solo were more my forte.

I protested, but Maupassant brushed every one of my arguments away with a dismissive sweep of his hand.

"Come now, Miss Fletcher! Everyone knows that all the English know how to play lawn tennis. You must know what you're doing! You'll certainly know more than the d'Orcels! Leave your modesty behind, my girl!"

And so, I readied myself.

28

Paul Antoine Isnard de la Motte

Anna was well on the mend. She was still rake thin, but she no longer had a fever. She had a little more color to her face and was slowly but surely regaining her strength. The nightmares she had about the fire were still regular in occurrence. Mario would often stop by the house to watch over her. He would take her for a turn in the garden or surrounding fields.

We all understood that one day Anna would have to return to the orphanage and the sisters. But Buttura's report on the Sacré-Cœur was taking an age.

He passed by the house to give us a summary of the situation after visiting the orphanage that morning with Dr. Gimbert, the specialist in epidemics. The report they were writing was severe. They were demanding that a great number of changes be made to the building itself and the care of the children. They found that the orphans were going hungry too often, that they were forbidden to play outdoors and were kept locked inside the building or let out to play in an indoor courtyard. The high interior walls meant that they never saw daylight. The dorm bunkers were found to be dirty and overcrowded, with locked windows, meaning the air was never changed. The mattresses were full of lice and hardly ever changed or turned.

The orphans only washed three times a year. And never a bath! Just a strip wash! And this in a spa town!

The duchesse de Vallombrosa had been informed of this scandalous situation. A meeting had been called immediately with the express intention of uncovering why these orphans were living in such horrendous conditions despite all the money raised and given by the patrons and patronesses.

The duchesse used her influence to force the resignation of the treasurer, Madame de Grandmanche. It had been her wish, acting against the advice of the mother superior, to use the money collected for purposes other than the improvement and upkeep of the property. It turned out that she'd placed all the money in a bank. Her claim was that she thought she was doing the right thing. She fully believed that she could add to the capital by placing all the funds in an account. And then the financial crisis hit hard, and she tried her utmost to hide the fact that what monies were in there had vanished like melting snow.

But there was something else about the whole affair that worried Buttura deeply. There was a great resemblance between the deaths of the orphans and that of Clara. Yet at a glance, it would appear they had nothing in common.

The repairs highlighted in the report would soon have to commence. This would mean that Anna would have to stay where she was for some time. The fewer boarders *in situ*, the better. It was urgent that as many as possible be placed with foster families. It was suggested that they move the majority of the infants to homes in the countryside.

As they left, Buttura quickly mentioned that he had not as yet received the results from Lacassagne's lab concerning the Clara Campo case, but that he remained very proud of the improvised system he'd put in place to preserve the body.

Our mood was low after he left, so we turned our minds to other matters.

We set about making some more of Lola's soap. Anna and I enjoyed keeping ourselves busy by putting the little tablets to dry in the sun outside the kitchen door. Sherry watched us from on top of one of the kitchen cupboards. He was interested in the flurries of movement to and from the outside courtyard and the steam rising from our boiling pans.

Lola couldn't settle into the activity, for she was preoccupied with the delay in the results from Clara's autopsy.

"We can't delay much longer," she said. "How are we supposed to accelerate in this study of ours?"

We heard the outside bell tinkle in the distance, followed by a shout from Rosalie. She hobbled into the kitchen, out of breath.

"It's a client! Errrr . . . a guest! Should I bring him in here?" She plodded back out of the kitchen without waiting for a reply.

Lola went out into the hallway, leaving the door open. The man introduced himself as Paul Antoine Mottet, a salesman from Saint-Raphaël, a toiletries company. He was with Mario, whom he'd met on his climb up to Les Pavots.

He was a tall, big-boned fellow with blond hair and blue eyes. His thin mustache had been oiled into submission, and his powdered skin smelled delicate and soft, even from the kitchen! His mouth appeared full and sensual. He had babies' lips—bright pink and in the most beautiful shape of a heart. There was a mouth that looked like it enjoyed the finer things in life!

He was dressed most shockingly in the brightest shade of lapis-lazuli blue! His three-piece suit had been tailored in the most gorgeous velvet, with a mauve satin lining. Over the top of it, he wore a fine wool overcoat with a fur collar. His tie—a satin scarf knotted around his neck—matched the lining of his suit. His cream-colored ivory cane was mottled with turquoise.

The whole outfit was exuberant and subtly aggressive. He gave off the air of being quite nonchalant, but I could see his mannerisms were rehearsed. His slow gestures were calculated, a means to provoke whomever he was talking to into giving him their full attention.

I walked from the kitchen to join them. He bent forward to kiss my hand, and I was overwhelmed to notice how carefully he paid attention to me. He knew me. He knew everything about me. He saw it in me as soon as he'd laid eyes on me. We were cut from the same cloth, he and I. We were a separate species, mistrusted, set apart from the tribe—that of the well-to-do and the well-heeled. They wanted to see the likes of him and me disappear from their world. And yet we persisted in existing, in rising from the ashes, in blossoming. There were people like us in every generation, and it had been the case for centuries.

Rosalie called the young ones. They bounded over to her excitedly, and she took them outside to check on the soaps. After a moment's silence, Lola invited her guest into the kitchen and had him sit on one of the stools around the table. The wood was a little damp.

"So, you're interested in our soaps? Who told you about them? Have you come to place an order?"

"I've been informed of the very distinctive smell," he said. "They're handmade? I can see you're making them here in your kitchen. You don't have a workshop?"

I decided to intervene at this point—a more professional tone was needed. I was hoping above all else that this impromptu meeting would result in an order and that we'd be able to pay the damn rent at last!

"Not yet. You should consider yourself to be sitting in something of a research lab. Mademoiselle is our creative mind. She has a particular fondness for citrus fruits, just like the princess of Nerola! But we are also currently working with rose and violet. As you may have seen on your way in, the gardens here are full of blossoms!"

"I'm such a fan of what I smell in here! Such sweet perfume!" he exclaimed in a high voice, almost as if he were mocking me. He went on to declare with emphasis, "'The perfume of the soul . . .'"

I helped him finish the quote, "'. . . is remembrance.' Do you enjoy Madame Sand's work?"

He lost his slightly mocking expression and became animated at the idea of discussing Madame Sand's novels. We talked for some time before concluding how outrageous it was that she'd had to adopt a masculine pseudonym in order to receive the right to publish her works.

An exchange that was expected to be about Lola and her soaps had turned into a heated discussion about authors' rights and literature in general. Lola looked on incredulously. We discussed writers we esteemed, and I could hardly stop myself from gushing.

I spoke with such confidence and was so at ease within myself that I could barely hold my thoughts in. I expressed how fond I was of George Sand's writing and her liberty in expressing her inclination toward both sexes when it came to matters of a more . . . loving nature.

"Well!" Lola exclaimed. "I believe the ice is truly broken now, don't you? Let's go up to the lounge and enjoy a few bubbles! What do you say to that?"

She took off her gloves and abandoned them in a large basin, and we followed in her wake. As we left the kitchen, she shouted out to Rosalie, "Can you get a bottle of fizz and give it to the little one to bring up, please?"

As we settled into our seats, Lola positioned herself closer to our young guest and said, "Come then, monsieur! While we wait to be watered, tell us what you know! You didn't really come here to purchase my soaps, did you?"

"B-but . . . ," Paul Antoine Mottet stuttered. "What has got into you, pray?"

I smiled. "Watch out! She's quite formidable when she gets going!"

"In what sense?"

"You can't hide much from her. She has a gift! Divination! I'm inclined to believe she already knows a great deal about you! So you may as well tell her everything, or she'll only find out by herself!"

"Ha! Indeed! What could she possibly know?"

"I know that you're from a good family. A great one, no doubt! Perhaps a family in industry or prosperous merchants, at the very least. The signs are quite transparent to me. You squander the money given to you by your parents with your friends, and you live a boisterous lifestyle. But this isn't difficult at all—anyone could make an educated guess."

"Evidently! It's my ring, isn't it? Is that what gave it away?" he said, sounding delighted. "I'm rather proud of it! It's what's known as a pinky ring. They're all the rage in England. They're worn by . . . unmarried men and women. I wear the exact same model as Oscar Wilde!" Paul Antoine stared at me, a coy expression on his face. "And there are places, certain reading rooms, for example, where unmarried people like me can hold secret meetings with like-minded people . . . in total discretion, you understand."

I noticed the extravagant ring on the smallest finger of his left hand. It was a finely embossed piece with a large diamond in the shape of a cat's head. An odd design, indeed! It must have been worth a significant amount of money and was truly remarkable.

"That's partly it," said Lola. "But it's your motivations that tell me the most about you. You've come here, to my humble home, with a mouth full of lies . . ."

Mottet jumped up in surprise. Anna and Mario stepped into the room with a bottle of the best and three glasses. Their arrival gave us all a short break and distracted us somewhat from the words Lola had just uttered. I uncorked the champagne—Mottet refused to do so with a precious wave of his hand—and Lola told the children to return to the kitchen and continue to help Rosalie.

"But I want you to do the soaps with us, not Rosalie! Please!" cried Anna.

"Are you answering me back, young lady? I believe your education at the Sacré-Cœur leaves much to be desired!" said Lola, brushing her away.

As soon as the door was closed behind them, Lola picked up exactly where she'd left off. "Yes! You want to learn of my soaps, but it's a little more than that, is it not? I fancy there's a whole lot more you're here to learn."

"What have you heard of me?"

"You're not just a salesman, are you? You don't look anything like a merchant! You want to know how I make my soaps! And if you're here to rob me of my secrets, you've come a long way for nothing!"

"Oh! *Zut!* There's no point hiding the truth! You're right! That was a sorry tale I told! I'm glad I've been found out! Yes! I gave you a false name! I'm not Mottet . . ."

"I know. You're Isnard de la Motte!" she said triumphantly.

"How . . . how did you know my name?"

He knew he'd been unmasked and looked willing to recount the truth to us, but Lola stopped him. "Please, allow me. You hail from the exceedingly wealthy Grasse family, the Isnard de la Motte clan, and you've come to steal my recipe."

He nodded, resigned. "It's an exquisite smell."

"But why not make me an offer? You're rich! Wouldn't that be a more fitting plan?"

"Yes, I agree, but I believed your price might be more than I would care to bargain for. And why pay when you can obtain something free of charge? Well, that's what my family had me believe. I must say I don't share their thoughts or strategies. Really, I don't! Damn it! I couldn't care less about this frightful family enterprise! They are a foul lot, my kin! A patriarchy I cannot escape! My grandfather . . . oh, if you only knew! He wants to see me married to my cousin Marthe before the year is out! He wants me sitting behind a desk, verifying the logbooks and the like. A nightmare on every conceivable level! I have so much more to be doing with my time!"

"And what would that be? Enlighten me!" Lola said with a smirk. "Do you write, perhaps? Compose? Paint? Garden?" She looked over to me, pleased at her own humor.

He appeared confused, as if reflecting on what she'd said, but not wishing to show the effect her sarcasm had had on him.

"I want to live life like a lion and not like an accountant. I can't tolerate them, with their calculations, economies, placements, and their infatuation with property and monies."

"And so, pray tell, how do you live like a lion?"

"I make my way through my fortune and the allowances given to me by my dear father, and whether authorized or clandestine, I play in luxurious casinos and in infamous clubs and bars. I fritter it all away!"

"Lionlike indeed!" mocked Lola.

The discussion advanced on an array of subjects. We were slowly getting to know one another. Paul Antoine had by no means seduced us, but we did feel somewhat at ease in his company. Lola tapped her forehead dramatically.

"Actually, now I come to think of it . . . Do you have access to the laboratories at your perfumery?"

"Of course I do! I own the place! Well, I expect to inherit the place, at the very least!"

"In that case, you will, no doubt, have access to means of chemical analysis in this lab of yours?"

Paul Antoine was of a curious nature, and his interest was piqued at this abrupt turn in the discussion.

"How would you feel about performing a service of sorts? As a favor to me?"

"Why not? If you would only explain what it would entail?"

"Miss Fletcher, go and fetch what we need from our box of tricks!"

I left the room and returned hurriedly with Clara Campo's lace handkerchief, which was now stained with her yellowed saliva. I held it out to Paul Antoine, who took it gently in his fingertips, a grimace of distaste on his face.

"It's simple enough! I would ask that you analyze this dry substance you see here."

The shock on his face was a sight to see.

Lola added, "You'll know everything soon enough, I promise. All I can tell you for the moment is that an official investigation is underway, but it's taking too long to satisfy me!"

He rolled up the fabric and stuffed it into his trouser pocket. "Understood."

At the doorway, a deep clearing of the throat gave the three of us quite a fright.

"Guy!" exclaimed Lola. "You're in and out of here all the time these days! We're not a shop, you know! How did you sneak in?"

"I have the deepest respect for Rosalie, that's all. I know she hates presenting people, so I made my own way up. And I can see you're having quite the party without me!"

Paul Antoine stood, looking embarrassed. He took on a provocative countenance, bowing to us all ostentatiously.

"I have delighted in your company, and I hope to meet again with you very shortly. Monsieur," said Paul Antoine, nodding to Maupassant, and before we'd even had the opportunity to introduce the two men, he disappeared.

Maupassant circled the room in a convoluted fashion so as to avoid seeing himself in the mirrors and didn't even waste any of his precious time asking who our guest had been.

"Come, come, Miss Fletcher! Do hurry! Go and get dressed! You should be in your tennis clothes! You have a meeting at the Renshaw

Club on the Route de Fréjus. And take your time! Make them sweat! We need to take a good long look around those rooms of theirs!"

He'd organized the lesson at the best courts in town and the farthest away from the Beau Rivage. He and Lola could make the most of the time they were given to go through the d'Orcel apartment with a fine-tooth comb.

I felt a sense of fear for my friends, but the two of them were as giddy as children at Christmas and appeared more than ready to take on the challenge. I dressed in a short flannel dress and butter-colored leather shoes, without bothering to put on a corset. I picked up my racket and balls, made my way outside, and readied Gaza.

29

A Perilous Search

As I made my way through town, following a small road that paralleled the railway line, my two friends hurried to the Beau Rivage.

As soon as they arrived, Lola set about distracting the porter who was seeing guests in and out of the building. She had him fascinated from the outset, asking him of news of friends who worked there, confusing him with a host of names and asking a thousand and one questions of no consequence. Out of nowhere, she had the wonderful idea of feigning unconsciousness and dropped to the floor.

He rushed to her aid and requested the help of those around them. He managed to lift her and carry her over to the nearest armchair, leaving Maupassant just enough time to slip behind the desk and grab one of the two keys hanging from the hook marked "327."

There were several men standing in worried poses around Lola, offering what help they could, but they moved out of the way politely to allow Maupassant to step past them. Lola opened her eyes and yawned noisily, thanking the gentlemen with a confused smile.

After having made sure she was quite well, each of them went about their business, vaguely disappointed that the drama was over.

"You need to keep a watch out down here while I go up to their suite and take a look around."

"That's out of the question. I am far less known than you. You would be taking much too great a risk if you were to be caught. That's the trouble with being a famous man in these parts, Maupassant! I'll go up, and you stay here as my lookout."

With such insistence from Lola, Maupassant felt obliged to do as she'd said. "Don't fret, Lola. I'll keep an excellent lookout! You don't risk a thing with me!"

"If you happen to see one of the d'Orcels return, you must keep them entertained."

"Understood! I'll set fire to the entire first floor if I have to!"

Lola quickly climbed the main staircase and gently opened the door to the suite with the pilfered key, being careful not to make a sound.

Once inside, she took a systematic approach to her search and did everything with the utmost care, ensuring she left no trace of her having been there. She opened up drawers, files, and books. She turned the mattress to see what might be concealed underneath and rifled through piles of shirts, under cushions, and behind sofas.

She noted that the ink, just as Maupassant had observed, was indeed the exact same hue as that which had stained her young friend's finger. She placed some on her own skin to verify.

She made her way to the bathroom. On a marble table, she closely examined a display of medicinal potions, pomades, dental powders, and a small flask half-full of a glistening liquid. She had no idea what it might be. There was a handwritten label upon it. She reflected on how elegant a hand it was. *Nerium oleander.*

She lifted the cork and took a light sniff, but the liquid was odorless. She decided to take it and slipped it into her clutch bag. *I'm sure we can find a way of getting it back in here once we've taken a closer look at it,* she told herself.

In the grand reception area downstairs, Maupassant was sitting quietly, pretending to read a newspaper so he could discreetly keep track of who was leaving and entering the building. But luck was not on his side that day. A group of young women, young admirers of his, spotted him, and before he knew it, he was surrounded by adoring female fans asking him every question under the sun.

They were simply enchanted to find him there and thought nothing of invading his personal space to quiz him. The exclamations, the spicy remarks, the forced laughter, and the frivolity caught Maupassant off guard. He didn't know where to concentrate his efforts: on these young, pretty girls or on the front door of the hotel and on protecting Lola.

And it only took a minute. One of the ladies invited him to a soi-rée, and he was so engrossed in his answer that he missed the hurried entrance of Comte Charles d'Orcel de Montejoux. By the time his eyes were drawn back to the main hall and the task at hand, he'd missed the comte making his way to the hydraulic elevator.

Up in the suite, Lola was once again leaning over the bureau with the famous ink pot. She was attempting to read and commit to memory the fancy writings left there by the comtesse. She also noted a hardback folder containing several notes and bills. She rifled through them with speed. There were a number of receipts for jewels, toiletries, trinkets, and the like. It would seem that the comtesse's favorite jeweler when she sojourned in Cannes was the famous Siegl's.

The poetry written by the comtesse was hard to follow, and the many pages of botanical findings even more so. All the papers were in such disarray. She was deep in thought as she tried to decipher the virtues of several medicinal plants recently studied by the comte when she heard the key in the lock.

Before d'Orcel had had the time to push the door open, Lola dived behind a large trunk that was positioned against the wall by the side of the fireplace with its lid open. She had an excellent view of the entire room from where she was crouched and could see the comte clearly.

He was a tall man, much taller than she'd envisaged he might be. He must have been well over six feet. This was something that

Maupassant had forgotten to tell them in his account of his meeting with them. She had no idea what the comtesse looked like either. He looked to be a heavy man too. His light-gray trousers were fit to bursting. Lola couldn't tell whether he was a well-built, muscular type or whether he'd had one too many fine dinners.

He walked over to the desk and put several objects, including his keys, on top of some of the papers before opening a drawer. Lola's hands were trembling and her teeth chattering with the adrenaline coursing through her veins. She folded her body in on itself, imagining she were a mouse trying to make herself small enough to fit through a hole in the skirting boards. What in the world had become of Maupassant keeping watch?

D'Orcel left the main room and entered the bathroom. She could hear him running water. The bedroom door was to her left, and she knew there was another exit back out to the corridor through there. It would mean having to run a yard or so without being discovered. She took her chance and scampered to the bedroom, quickly hiding behind the door.

She could still hear him walking in and out of the bathroom. What was he doing? She braved a sneaky peek through the gap in the door and saw him taking his clothes off. *Why is he getting undressed? Why isn't he playing tennis? Have they not even started yet?* She looked around the room and, spotting the large wardrobe, started to panic that his tennis clothes were more than likely kept in the bedroom!

She heard his footsteps nearing. She couldn't come up with a plan, so she made a run for it toward the bed, lifting her skirts and ripping open her bodice to reveal her deep cleavage.

She tried her very hardest to place herself in the most fetching of positions, but it was hard to do so when she was having such difficulty breathing. The fear was overwhelming.

He stepped into the room, wearing nothing but a blue-and-white underslip and an open shirt exposing his big belly. Surprisingly enough, he didn't notice her immediately. *Well, that's certainly not muscle,* Lola thought.

He hurried toward the wardrobe, and it was only after a few steps that he noted the new arrival on his bed. His head moved forward as he considered her in disbelief, with an expression of total incomprehension. Taking advantage of his stupor, Lola was the first to speak, using the voice of a street girl with a heavy Cannois accent.

"Where have you been, my sweet pea! I've been expecting you! Come, my little chick!"

He didn't move, failing to understand the situation but keeping his calm with an indifferent, icy expression.

"Who are you?"

"I can be anyone you want for the next hour. Come, don't worry yourself," said Lola, anxious about the closed-off reaction she was getting from him.

"But what are you doing here?"

Lola lifted herself up and approached him. *Is he timid or dangerous?* she wondered. Despite her internal turmoil, she gave him a promising smile. She took his hand and placed it on her breast as she rubbed herself against him, not taking her eyes from his. But he stepped back as if she'd burned him. *Hell! How am I going to get out of this now?*

"Why are you so scared of me? I don't bite! Make the most of what life has to offer you, my little coconut . . ."

"Who do you believe I am? Is this some sort of trap?"

"Oh! My friend! You are a careful one, aren't you? There's nothing fishy going on here! Your friend Renardet sent me . . ."

"Is this some sort of farce? I don't know anyone by the name of Renardet!"

"You do! Come on! I'm your birthday present!'

"It is not my birthday," he said between gritted teeth, furiously, as if the simple fact of having to speak to a girl such as Lola was already far beyond his capabilities.

"No? Well! Isn't he a case! Did I get the wrong room? This is indeed two two seven, is it not?"

He pushed her forcefully, and she fell into the corner of the bedside table, hurting her thigh.

"Ouch! That is too much, monsieur! I'm going to have a bruise there now! It's not my fault if Renardet is playing a trick on you!"

"You are a liar! Why are you here? Speak, girl!"

"You must calm yourself, monsieur!"

So livid was he by her reply that he struck her across her face, causing her to fall to the floor with a thud. He pulled her up by her hair and threw her back down onto the bed. He shoved his hands between her breasts and under her skirts, searching violently for anything that could have been hidden on her person.

"What have you stolen? Who are you working for?"

She had thankfully left the vial of liquid in her bag behind the trunk in the main room near the door. She tried to resist him with every ounce of strength she had, but she was so small in stature compared with him. She spat in his face, hitting his eyes, which blinded him for just a second, but enough time for her to get to her feet.

He grabbed her by the waist, but she spun around on her heels, and as quick as a cat, she bit him on the wrist, forcing him to let her go. Instead of fleeing, she went in for the attack, scratching with her bare nails on his chest until she saw blood.

Incredulous, he looked down at the marks. He was so taken aback at what he saw that it gave Lola the time she needed to scamper from the room into the lounge, pick up her bag, and make a run for the exit. As soon as she stepped outside, she had the forethought to use her key to lock him in.

He has a key to get out, but it'll take him a few minutes to find it, and he'll have to dress himself before leaving!

As she hurled herself down the staircase, she couldn't help thinking that the comte's reaction to her having been in his room was far from typical. He was so angered, so aggressive, and the way he had treated her had been nothing short of abominable. His behavior had been that of a guilty man. In the past, she'd had to make a run for it on several occasions from aggressors of his type, but never had she met such hostility or rage before.

I know this man. I am certain I have seen him somewhere. But where?

She stopped on the second floor to try to compose herself somewhat. D'Orcel had indeed ravaged her, and she looked a sorry sight to behold. She did the best she could and took in a deep breath before descending the wide staircase down to the first floor. She knew people would be watching, and she made an enormous effort to act as though she deserved to be admired.

The lights lifted her complexion and allowed her eyes to shine. Her heavy breathing meant her chest was rising and falling dramatically, and all eyes would be drawn to that part of her anatomy. She took each step slowly, allowing people to stare. Making her presence so obvious was, she thought, the best way not to draw attention to her. She exposed herself fully to all who would look, making it seem the most natural thing in the world that she would be there.

Maupassant watched along with everyone else and laughed at her actions, not at all grasping their significance. She crossed the entrance hall at a brisk pace, not catching his eye, and he understood he had to follow her. She hurried even more once outside, and after crossing the gardens, hailed one of the cabs circling outside the main gate.

Maupassant climbed in behind her.

"The lawn-tennis club on the Route de Fréjus," she said. "Miss Fletcher must be having kittens! She's there on her own with the comtesse, and she has no way of letting us know!"

"What?" asked Maupassant, unsettled.

She stuck her nose up against the back window. "There he is!"

Comte d'Orcel de Montejoux, looking livid and out of breath, dressed in a massive overcoat, more than likely hiding the disarray of his dress underneath, was out on the street. He had just left the gardens of the hotel, looking frantically around, before stepping up into a cab that had just dropped off some guests.

"What is it?" asked Maupassant, frowning, his mouth agape. "What is that old devil up to? My God! I didn't see him in the hotel! Did he see you?"

"He must have slipped by your excellent surveillance! Thank you for that! And yes, we had an encounter! I'm telling you now, he certainly has something on his conscience, that one!"

"Oh, my poor friend! I'm so sorry! I really was on top of it back there! I don't know how I missed him! I'll never forgive myself!"

"You should indeed be sorry for it, Maupassant! I feared for my life! He attacked me!"

He laughed heartily. "If truth be told, I'm sure I wouldn't have enjoyed being in his place! I bet you put up quite the fight!"

"There's nothing amusing about it."

"But if he knew of our presence—or your presence, at least—why didn't he follow you?"

"When I left him, he was still in his undergarments. Maybe he's on his way now for his meeting with Miss Fletcher."

Maupassant told the driver to pick up the pace to the Renshaw lawn-tennis club. They wanted to warn me of recent events with d'Orcel and pick me up as quickly as possible. Maupassant then turned to Lola in concern.

"Don't move." He took out a small bottle from his pocket and poured the liquid inside it onto a handkerchief. "Where does it hurt? Come, let me clean you up a little. I always carry *Calendula officinalis* about my person."

She smiled, moved by his concern. "Yes! I forgot that you were a man of the county! You always come prepared!"

"Indeed, I do!" He dabbed the liquid on the bruises on Lola's face. "Hold this handkerchief on the areas it hurts the most. Gosh! What happened to you?"

As she recounted the details of her encounter, the gaunt horse trotted as fast as the driver could force him. They asked the driver to stop not far from the courts and descended rapidly. After paying him, they scampered into some nearby laurel bushes and squatted down to hide.

Between the thick branches of the shrubbery, they spied two female figures finishing up a game. It was, of course, the comtesse and myself.

I had been playing with her for some time and wondering why the comte had not yet made an appearance. I was worried for Lola and Maupassant. Had the comte gone to the hotel? They must not have been able to fulfill their mission, in that case.

Although they had taken pains to hide, I had watched from the corner of my eye as they climbed down from the cab and hid behind the bushes. I would have given anything for them not to bear witness to my appalling tennis playing. I massacred every single shot. I was clumsy and heavy-handed throughout play. As Maupassant had reminded me, I was fortunate in that I knew ever so slightly more about the game than the comtesse—which was a refreshing situation to find myself in! I remained anxious, however, that she would uncover the truth and know she was being duped.

At the end of the game, the comtesse walked over to the net to shake my hand, as is common practice, and we ambled over to some tables laid out in the shade to catch our breath. A young girl was selling freshly squeezed orange juice from a cart. I forced myself not to look over to my friends in the bushes for fear of the comtesse following my gaze.

I savored my drink and positioned myself next to Andréa d'Orcel and wondered when I'd be able to join my friends. I could hardly make my exit at that point, for the comtesse was asking me a dozen questions on my background and genealogy.

After I responded to the best of my ability, she placed her glass on the table and shook my hand again.

There was a cab stationed by the side of the far court, which she made her way toward. She climbed aboard, and something struck me as she did so . . . There was something odd in the behavior of the horseman. I couldn't quite put my finger on it. He was dressed in an overcoat that was far too big for him, and his hat was covering half of his face. I thought for a moment that it might be Amédée, but I put the ridiculous notion to the back of my mind. I lingered awhile until the cab had disappeared over the horizon before I went to join my friends.

"Well? What are you doing here?"

Maupassant squeezed my hands in an exaggerated fashion. "Lola got into trouble. I was supposed to be looking out for her, but the shark slipped my nets! What a total farce!"

"I have no clue what Maupassant was playing at! He couldn't see farther than the tip of his nose!"

"Yes, I wasn't much help. All I know is that d'Orcel is running late to this meeting."

"Running late? I should say so! I managed to play a couple of pawns, though! I was boasting to the comtesse about the benefits of aquatic gymnastics, and now I have a further meeting with her in a few days at the Bottin bathhouse! If I befriend her, she may well take me into her confidence and tell me some private details of her husband. What do you think to that?"

"Well played, Miss Fletcher!" exclaimed Maupassant.

"But!" I cried, tormented to see the bruise forming under Lola's eye. "What on earth? *My God!* We must get you to the hospital!"

"We'll do no such thing, Miss Fletcher. I thought you were made of sterner stuff! Keep your head! It's nothing! Believe me, I've seen worse!"

Maupassant clapped. "Come, both of you, let me invite you to take a pâtisserie with me at Rumpelmayer's! You like hot chocolate, do you not?"

"On a day like today, who could refuse?" I said.

30

RUMPELMAYER

Lola and Maupassant climbed into the back of the carriage, and I sat up front in my driver's seat as we drove to Rumpelmayer's. I stationed the carriage adjacent to the Cercle Nautique. They waited for me while I made sure Gaza was securely attached, and then we walked the short distance to the famous tea room.

The wind was up, and the strong gusts helped us pick up our pace as we scurried inside. The immense room sparkled in the stunning lights. It was a genuine treat for the eyes.

Lola ordered a dark hot chocolate, but as I declared I'd rather take a pot of tea, Maupassant felt obliged to follow suit. I watched as he looked on longingly at Lola's hot chocolate and felt pity for him. As a way of consoling himself, he requested to see the pastry trolley. The waiter brought it over to us, and we feasted our eyes on meringues, ganaches, pralines, and poires belle Hélène, the famous dessert invented by Escoffier.

"We should take something back for the bambinos and Rosalie," said Lola. "Next time we come here, we must bring Anna."

"Tell me what happened to you back there! You still haven't said a word to me!" I said.

As she devoured her cake, she told me everything that had befallen her in the company of the dreadful d'Orcel. Maupassant, having already heard it all, kept to himself and appeared lost in his thoughts.

Suddenly, he said, "It's him! It has to be him!"

"Despite his aggressive nature and odd behavior, I don't believe him to be an assassin," declared Lola.

"In that case, what kind of man do you believe he is? He must have seduced Clara Campo, for she was with child! It's certain in my view. Didn't we say, *'Cherchez l'homme'*? Well, here he is! What other sign do you want?"

"He might have killed her accidentally. He may have wanted her to rid herself of the child and given her a poison in order to do so, and that may well have provoked her death," I said.

"Don't forget that the police said the very same thing about Amédée."

"Well, we're not talking of the police this time," said Maupassant. "This is us!"

"Oh, *Boudiou*! I almost forgot! Look!" Lola took out her small clutch and the bottle of shiny liquid. She placed it in the middle of the table among the plates of cakes and pastries.

We were hooked, fascinated by what such a substance might be.

"I'm sure I've seen something like this before," I said, "but I can't recall where."

"How can we tell whether or not it is a poison and what type of poison it might be? I sniffed it, but it didn't smell of anything!"

"Are you quite mad? That's beyond dangerous!"

"Why don't you ask your brother?" I asked Maupassant. "He knows a lot about plants and the like, does he not? You told us as much!"

"Hervé has gone off to the mountains. I won't be able to get ahold of him any time soon. Let us take a sample of it and put it in a sachet for analysis. We'll find someone to help us, sure enough."

"So we're saying the comte murdered Clara?" I said. "But we're a long way off being able to prove such a claim."

"It's impossible to say anything about his guilt until we have sufficient evidence. And we don't. All we have is supposition," said Lola.

A hoarse voice interrupted us, and all three of us jumped, startled by the intrusion. It was the director of the theater on the Rue d'Antibes, Cortelazzo. He greeted us with ostentation.

"Maupassant! Why, I have been seeking you out most everywhere! I would so adore to adapt and stage one of your novellas! I know that my most humble little theater does not deserve such an honor, but I know a most excellent playwright who would gladly put pen to paper to rework your hand."

Lola pulled down her bodice a little, revealing a hint of cleavage, and started with her eyelash-batting routine. It didn't look as wonderful as usual due to the black-and-blue ring around her eye that had spread down to her cheek.

"You know that here in Cannes, throughout the winter months, we have spectators of such quality! Our audiences could rival any of those in Paris!" the director continued.

"What is this game you're playing? Everyone knows your theater is snubbed by anyone of note! You have trouble filling your seats with the local bourgeoisie!" Maupassant snorted.

"You are very ill-informed, monsieur. My theater is often full, and there is quite the cultural mix, let me tell you!"

"Yes! Only when you put on one of your charity nights! You are notorious for it!"

The director screwed up his mouth and looked at us each in turn, scrutinizing our faces. He recognized Lola, it seemed.

"And you, child, are you still hoping to appear on the stage?"

"Listen, Cortelazzo, let me make you an offer, and quite the bargain it is too," said Maupassant out of nowhere. "I cannot allow you to stage any of my work, but I will write a piece in the newspaper touting the benefits of your establishment. It will appear in a national, no less! *Le Gaulois*, for example."

The director gave him a look somewhere between courtesy and wariness. "*Le Gaulois* . . . In exchange for what?"

"You'll take this *child*, as you so kindly put it, Lola Deslys being her actual name, and you'll have her sing and dance in your chorus line at least once a week."

"You are harsh, monsieur!" said Cortelazzo, as his eyes undressed Lola, studying her shape, the beauty of her hair, teeth, shoulders . . .

Lola gasped with uninhibited joy.

"Let's get straight to the point. I can only give my actresses fifty to sixty francs a month. My actors don't earn much more than that. What my staff chooses to do in their time away from the stage is of no concern of mine. I have seven thousand francs a month to find for the rent. Can you conceive of that? If I need to get a little extra from those in my employ . . . well . . . That's all I have to say on the matter."

"I don't believe the particularities of the situation will bother Mademoiselle all that much, and nor do you embarrass her with your frankness."

Lola nodded with enthusiasm. "As you are putting all your cards on the table and we are trusting each other, let me show my hand. I need a window of sorts. I need somewhere to display what I have to offer. So, your theater . . . ," she said.

"*Dites plutôt mon bordel,* as the famous line goes!" cried Cortelazzo, overjoyed at having been fully understood.

He was clearly referring to his theater being primarily a whorehouse. The whole exchange I found to be sordid. It was akin to witnessing two horse traders attempting to bargain for a filly, except that Maupassant only had Lola's very best interests at heart.

But I uncovered a reality that I had never before encountered, and it appeared to shock nobody at the table but me. They all found it more than natural that actresses and singers would be quite unable to survive if it weren't for the fact that they also sold their bodies. As I thought upon this sorry state, I realized it must have been the case, too, for factory workers, for many people who worked menial jobs . . . and from a very young age at that.

And this business of theirs was far from easy to live. These young women would so often confuse love with their arrangements. They would be housed in an apartment paid for by the sons of rich families, much like what had occurred between Lola and Eugène.

Only the most naive among them must have thought that such relations would ever end in marriage. All they could really hope for is that they wouldn't find themselves with child.

Cortelazzo carried on speaking to Maupassant, using the third person to refer to Lola as if she weren't even present.

"She will have to supply her own costumes and jewelry, and the jewelry must be real, of course, if she wishes to benefit from a resounding image and stand out from the crowd. And make sure she rarely wears the same outfit twice. Publicity is all down to her."

"That sounds perfect. Do you have anything on the near horizon?" Maupassant asked.

"We're having a magic-themed night on Saturday. It is to be organized by the duchesse de Polignac. The benefits are intended to help an orphanage. Rehearsals are on Thursday and Friday. I'll see where we can put her. She'll either sing or dance. Not both for now. But whatever happens, she won't have the starring role, so don't go hoping! She is a perfect stranger to me. I don't even know if she can sing in key or move any better than a turkey!"

As soon as Cortelazzo left, Lola couldn't stop herself from clapping excitedly.

"This is an official job! They won't be able to card me now!"

Lola and Maupassant discussed the matter at length and came to an agreement on what clothes she should wear in order to attract the right sort of gentleman.

"It will be your night, Lola! It's up to you to show yourself off to your very best advantage! I know the duchesse! You can rest in the knowledge that some of the richest men on the Riviera will quite literally be at your feet on Saturday night! We must ensure you're noticed!"

"Oh, you can count on me," said Lola. "It's quite the rare thing that I go unnoticed."

"What about jewelry? He said it had to be real. Do you have anything?" I asked.

"Miss Fletcher, you're going to have to take her to a jeweler. You can explain the situation to them, and perhaps they'll lend you a piece or give you credit? Choose something special. We need to create a certain style. I want everyone in the place, even those seated in the back row, to know that she's dripping in diamonds. She must look like a rich woman to be picked up by a rich man!"

"I don't know why he insisted on real jewels," I said.

"It's quite obvious," explained Lola. "These buffoons of men want to pay for luxury or they gain no glory from their conquests. It's the only way we can get them to foot the bill. The more money I look like I have, the more they'll pay."

On that note, and after having agreed that we needed to obtain more information on d'Orcel, Maupassant rose, bowed, and went to join a group of friends he'd spied on the far side of the room.

"Seeing as we need something real and something of value, why don't we go to Siegl's?" asked Lola.

I must have looked confused, for she further explained, "It's where the d'Orcels go!"

And so I accompanied her to Siegl's on foot. As we walked, I asked that she stop a moment to give me time to find my cigarillos and light one.

"No! You'll have time for that later," she replied nonchalantly. This annoyed me deeply.

At the end of the street, as we turned the corner to arrive at the jeweler's, we thought we saw the figure of the comtesse d'Orcel leaving the boutique. She was still dressed in her lawn-tennis clothes, with a charcoal-colored fur cape loosely wrapped around her shoulders and a veiled hat masking her face from indiscreet eyes. She looked left to right, as if watching out for someone about to arrive.

I wouldn't be able to tell you whether or not she recognized us, but she glided off in the opposite direction, leaving us to enter the store without having to hide our presence from her. I managed to negotiate some credit with Siegl's so that Lola would look more than ravishing for her debut performance at the theater, as was expected of her.

Lola was fully uninterested in the bargaining process and did not help me in any conceivable way.

She spent her time distracting the salesmen behind the counter, hindering them from being able to concentrate fully on their work and building around her a veritable court of admirers. She chatted to them freely and with charm, speaking of the latest snippets of Cannois gossip. With the bruising on her face appearing to change hue by the second, she captivated them through her simpering tones and gestures.

I wondered where she was going with these dealings as I heard her talking of cultivated women in financial difficulty. Was she inventing it all as she was going along?

But without her even having to ask, one of the men talked of a woman who had just left the premises after selling a stunning set of jewels that had belonged to her family for generations. She had asked for ten thousand francs for them, and she had also requested they make a replica set, which she would collect several days hence.

So that was why the comtesse hadn't wanted to be recognized! But for what reason did she require such a vast sum of money? Had she informed her husband of the sale? Probably not.

As we walked back to our landau, I noted that several passersby were looking worried, upset, and agitated. I spotted an old friend of sorts, an English piano teacher, leaving a florist shop in a state of genuine distress. I stopped to ask if he may be in need of assistance. He told us, his voice shaking, that a terrible rumor was rapidly making its way throughout town. He didn't know the extent of its truth or falsehood. One of the young brothers of the Prince of Wales, the Duke of Albany, had fallen down the stairs at the Cercle Nautique! He had been in horrid pain! Bleeding for hours!

Something patriotic in me felt saddened by this news, despite my general distaste toward the British aristocracy. I had met Prince Leopold and his wife, Helene, once in London, and they came across as being the most amiable of people. He had been the same age as I. It went to show that you can meet with the darkest of destinies no matter where and to whom you were born. It was common knowledge, despite denials, that he had a hereditary disease from which many members of the royal household suffered. Their blood was unable to coagulate correctly, and several of Queen Victoria's children had been born with the affliction.

It felt strange to me that he should have fallen and suffered so dreadfully in almost the same spot upon which I had danced with his brother. It made me feel closer to the event. I chose not to elaborate on these feelings in front of Lola, for she made no response to my old friend, which told me in no uncertain terms that she was not at all interested in the subject.

As soon as we arrived home, she wanted to take a bath. This was a caprice of sorts and didn't seem like her usual attitude. I quickly came to comprehend that her intentions were to rid herself of the filth she felt upon her body following her ghastly encounter with d'Orcel.

Rosalie rubbed soap all over her body, occasionally rinsing it off her smooth pink skin with water from the can. I turned away, embarrassed by the whole scene, wondering why I needed to be there in the first place, and so I walked out of the room and went to join Anna.

The house felt odd. A melancholy atmosphere invaded every corner.

Lola entered the room sometime after, covered in a blanket. She should have been overjoyed with her new position at the theater, but she appeared to be obsessed with this dreadful memory weighing down on her very soul and couldn't rid herself of it. It was such a contrast to the show she'd put on in front of Cortelazzo. She started mixing a potion from a range of ingredients found in drawers and boxes—a thick green liquid.

"Can I help you with that?" I asked.

I removed the bowl from her as she stopped and stared into the room vacantly, and I stirred it with vigor into a soft paste.

"What's in it?"

"Clay, butter, camphor, lavender oil, and a few drops of *Helichrysum*."

"What's *Helichrysum*?"

"It's the essence of beaten women! For cuts and bruises! Everyone knows that! Or at least, we all know it where I'm from!"

She was still trembling slightly as she made her way to bed with the pot in her hand, ready to rub it into the most painful spots.

31

DEMONS

Lola's screams woke me in the middle of the night.

She must have been having the most terrible nightmare. With Lola and Anna finding no peace as they slept, this home had quickly become a place of troubled sleep. Was I the only person there dreaming happily?

I flew down the stairs and into her room. She was burning up, her bedclothes soaked in sweat. I took a cloth from her bedside table, dipped it in cold water, and dabbed at her forehead.

"Pass me that flask, Miss Fletcher."

With unsteady fingers, she pointed to a crystal bottle containing a blood-red liquid. On the label it read: "Laudanum Tincture—Medicinal Prescription."

She grabbed it from me, removed the cork, and took two large gulps before sighing and falling back down onto her pillow in relief.

"Come sit here with me," she uttered weakly.

I lay down beside her and felt quite literally embraced by the heat emanating from her body. She was mumbling words without making any sense. I thought it must have been a continuation of her nightmare or perhaps even a hallucination. Or was it the effects of the liquid she'd just consumed? The words I caught were spoken in a kind of morose reverie.

"There, there," I told her. "It's all over now."

"No, no, it'll never be over. Never . . . ," she said.

"Of what do you speak, Lola? This is naught but a nightmare!"

"It's not a nightmare. You don't know. You couldn't know. He's here. He follows me every place I go."

Her desperation touched me deeply, and I felt wholly compassionate toward her. She was delirious. I made attempts to calm her by taking her in my arms. But little by little, I felt I was losing control of the situation.

The closeness of her body, the heat and her softness had woken in me a troubling desire that had started to overwhelm me. It felt like the torments of hell itself.

It was Lady Sarah who had given me the opportunity to discover my body, as never before had I desired a person with such intensity. And yet I had been so afraid. And I was afraid now. This state I found myself in was out of place. Shocking even! Here was a woman who needed my support and my consolation—not to be prey to my wants. She was vulnerable, shaken, and she wanted only one thing from me: that I take hold of her hand and help her through the night.

"What is it, Lola?"

"Him, him . . ." Her voice was rising sharply. She started to become breathless, struggling to take in air. "I can't breathe. He's stopping me. He's pushing down on me. I can't do anything. He's stronger than me. I'm scared . . ."

This was a violent turn she was having. I jumped out of the bed and hurried to fetch more water. I also decided the room needed more light and put a match to all the oil lamps.

Walking across the cold tile floor was just what I needed. I felt the hardness under my feet, and the sensation pulled me from the snare of my emotions. She thrust herself up, haggard-looking, and watched me move, seeming to fully awaken simultaneously.

I fetched the glass of water and returned. The bright room seemed to have soothed her. She appeared much more at ease.

"Is that you, Miss Fletcher? But . . . what are you doing there?"

I put my hand to her head. The fever was no more. "You were having a nightmare."

"Oh! I believe not!" She fell back onto the bed again. "It wasn't a nightmare, in truth. It's something that really happened to me when I was a child. And from time to time, it comes back to me. Come closer . . ."

I was torn between the idea of experiencing once again the delicious feeling of forbidden desire and that of wishing to distance myself from this most uncomfortable situation, but nothing could be refused of Mademoiselle Lola Deslys, could it?

"Keep the lamps burning, though!"

And so, I climbed back into bed with her—this time under the sheets, trying my hardest not to touch her skin with mine. She felt for my hand and found it. I moved my body as far away as I could, still maintaining this link between us.

"I was but twelve years old when I delivered for Madame Camoux, the milliner . . ."

The words just flowed from her mouth. It was almost as if she were talking in her sleep. It felt like she was suffering an oppressive, evil night terror from which she might never awake.

"I really liked Madame Camoux. They lived on the Rue du Port, near the Allée de la Marine. She's Bénédicte's mother. I'll have to introduce you to Bénédicte."

"Who is she?"

"She's my milk sister. My mother was her wet nurse for over two years. I would very often go and play with her. We don't really ever see one another these days. I think that would be . . . inconvenient on her part. Well, I don't care if that's how she feels about me. I was never very fond of her. She's a devious piece."

"Devious?"

"Yes! She was so often up to no good, but would arrange it so she never got the blame. I always fell for it! She got married and lives quite a way off nowadays, right at the end of the Croisette. Her husband is a notary and invested in property. But her mother is still making hats."

"And how did you find yourself working for her?"

"From the age of ten, I would help my mother with her laundering work, but it got so it was too much for me. I used to burn myself a lot, and I felt inadequate because the iron was far too heavy for my skinny little arms. So when Madame Camoux came for me one day because she was missing one of her little street helpers, I couldn't have been happier. I was so pleased. I felt a freedom I hadn't known before. I used to run around the streets in every direction! I would deliver up on the hill or down on the Croisette . . . or to the shops in the town. It meant I could move . . . I could explore. I had an immense responsibility on my shoulders because there was so much money involved. It was simply marvelous! And to top it all off, I had to wear a little uniform of sorts. It was simple country attire, really, a plain dress—but with a little floral bonnet with ribbons and a shawl. I looked just like little Magali, who we saw outside the ice cream parlor! Oh, and the hats I delivered! They were simply sublime! Sometimes, the boxes were bigger than me! I remember how they would press so hard against my bony hips, and I'd have bruises there that never went away!"

A playful smile crossed her lips.

"But I didn't mind. The whole experience was wonderful! I remember wanting to learn so much of the fashions! I wished for nothing more than to become a milliner myself one day."

I had no idea where she was going with this, for I had little experience of such things. I felt that she simply wanted to fall back to sleep but needed to chase the ghosts away first. She didn't want to fall back into the abyss from which she had awoken.

"Well, there was nobody in the villa that day. It was such a big place. But there were no masters and no servants. I called out to them. I had a hat to deliver, and I had to get the money for it and be on my way. But what was I supposed to do if there was nobody home? I called and called. After some time, a man came from around the back of the house and let me in. I gave him the hat. He shoved me hard, and I stumbled to the floor. I had no idea why. I hadn't done him any harm. Was he a madman? His voice became cold and monotonous.

"I tried to grasp his hand so he could help me to my feet, but he kneeled down and placed his hand on my breast. I felt leaden down, unable to catch my breath. I knew that something strange and even dangerous was about to happen . . . or already was happening. He picked me up and took me to a servant's room, where he lay me out on the bed and lifted my skirts. I hid my face with my hands. I felt heat in my belly, and I thought I was going to be sick.

"He placed himself on top of me. His husky voice muttered something in my ear. He was so heavy. I felt something between my thighs. I started to shout, to try to fight him. He grabbed the top of my dress and it ripped. I cried because it was ruined. What would I tell Madame Camoux? He panted like an animal. I scratched him and kicked him as best I could and with all the energy I could muster, but he gave me a single heavy punch to the face, and I was gone.

"I gained consciousness a good while after that. I felt something cold and wet between my legs and pain in my stomach. He had left me with my blood running down my thighs. He hadn't given me the money for the hat. Like a fool, that was the only thing I could think about. I was going to be blamed for this. Should I go and try to find the hat? Should I make my way back to the boutique without the money? How was I going to explain the rip in my dress?"

"What did you do?" I asked quietly, interrupting the tense atmosphere that had built up through the telling of this tragic tale. I wanted so much to bring her back to the present moment.

She let go of my hand. "I set fire to the house."

"What? How?"

"Yes. It was the only idea I had, the only reason that would explain my ruined clothing and the state I was in to Madame Camoux. I took a newspaper I found lying on a sideboard, and I set it alight using the flame from a lamp. I torched several pairs of curtains down in one of the salons on the first floor, hoping that the whole house would soon be ablaze. I rubbed my hands in some ashes in the grate of the fireplace and swept them across my face and clothing. I stumbled to the scullery and quickly washed between my legs before running down the street and crying out, *'Fire!'* as loudly as I could. I must have been at least a quarter of an hour in that house, and that man didn't show himself to me again. But I now had a good enough reason as to why I no longer had the hat or the money."

"Nobody ever learned of what this man did?"

"When I got back, I was so overcome I spoke of it with Bénédicte, who I trusted, but she didn't want to believe me. She told her mother, and Madame Camoux sent me back home, saying that I'd stolen money from her. I never dared speak of this episode to another living soul. The laddermen from the firehouse gave me a medal for bravery! For sounding the alarm. I never discovered the identity of this man."

She turned her back to me, and an absence of speech ensued.

The aggression she must have suffered by the hands of the comte had brought forth these shocking memories. There was nothing I could do to help her. I couldn't save her from it or make the ordeal any easier to live with.

I heard her breathing become more regular in rhythm. She had fallen asleep. As for me, slumber was an impossibility. After a little over an hour, I left her bed to return to my own. As I walked through the main room, I noticed Sherry asleep on an armchair and picked him up to take him with me to my chamber, for I needed the company.

I had been a comfort to Lola, and now I needed a comforter of my own.

The next day, it was as if Lola had forgotten everything we'd spoken of the night before. There was a bottle of Mariani wine on the breakfast table.

"I won't offer you any," she said to me. "It's a tonic. I doubt you're in need of it. It's to counteract the effects of my sleeping pills. I take them when I have an episode. I believe I'd be drowsy all day long if it weren't for my little Mariani tonic in the mornings." The label read, "Mariani Tonic Wine with Peruvian Coco."

And so I had just discovered that Lola Deslys was a frequent user of a range of narcotics. And to that, I would have to add the abundant use, even overuse, of champagne.

Her one saving grace was that she disliked the taste of absinthe, which she linked to her drunkard father and her terrible memories of him.

32

ENCHANTMENT

On Saturday, the house was filled with an effervescent atmosphere that left us unable to concern ourselves with petty and mundane worries of the future.

Lola showered us with song in preparation for her first night treading the boards. The bruising on her face had turned to a yellowish and paler hue.

Anna was going from strength to strength. There were rumors afoot that there had been an outbreak of cholera in Marseille and on the other side of the Estérel coast, and so Dr. Buttura had recommended that she stay with us a little while longer. He knew that we had a certain level of hygiene in place and that our septic pit conformed to all regulations. It had been well positioned and was the correct distance from our small vegetable garden, in accordance with local government conformities.

In any case, Lola never even mentioned the subject of Anna's departure. She told us that our situation was more than precarious and that we could be asked to up and move to a new house at a moment's notice, especially as we hadn't raised the money yet to pay the rent.

There would be a rehearsal before her big event. We were all readying ourselves, and it had been decided that I would accompany

Lola to the theater and act as her secretary at the end of the show. She was certain there would be a great many requests for meetings with her.

"That's how these things work, Miss Fletcher. They'll come to you, and they'll bargain. With my postcards and the odd review here and there, I believe we'll be able to pay our debts to Philémon. You'll have to take a note of all my rendezvous: the times, dates, everything. And don't forget to take down their names and titles. And if you can manage to get them talking, it might be a good idea to try to find out their tastes and perhaps try to uncover how great or small their fortune is. That might help us establish an appropriate tariff.

"You should favor the older gentlemen. They tend to be less tiring between the sheets, and they're as rich as Crassus! And if there are any journalists working for well-established chronicles, they can have a taster session free of charge in exchange for a good written piece about me. Come along! I have complete and utter faith in you!"

Lola dressed herself with care in her *dame de cœur* dress—fine voile and transparent silk muslins in tones of pale pink and forest green, a change from her signature red, skimming her body from the shoulders to the ankles, leaving little to the imagination. Under her dress, she wore her beaded bodice tight, forcing her breasts upward into a plunging décolleté.

From her upper thighs downward, the fabric was covered in a heart print, with slits in the fabric, showing off her legs. Her wavy hair was left down, and we covered it in a cascade of pinned fabric roses. We added a large garland of flowers from the garden, which she held around her arms and shoulders, so it formed the shape of an enormous heart. She looked like a water lily pond! Or a huge creamy meringue cake! She gave one the immense desire of wanting to throw oneself into the forest of flowers covering her head and body, of collapsing onto a feather bed with her and drowning in her voluptuous curves.

Just as Cortelazzo had said, the show itself was set to be enchanting. The love story was a divine tale, and the songs within it were magical, indeed!

Lola offered to sing a song that had been famous for over a century. The song was written by a certain Claris de Florian and was called "Romance Nouvelle." It was considered to be a little old fashioned, but she knew it would do the trick. The reason behind her choice was the lyrics: *"Plaisir d'amour"*... And what a sight to behold as she sang them! She emphasized the word *plaisir* with a suggestive look in her eyes, her tongue licking her lips, and her lusty smile spreading across her face slowly.

When Cortelazzo had heard her piece in rehearsals as she sang, "The pleasure of love lasts but a moment . . . ," he weighed in with his opinion on the piece. "This is a little over the top. You're forcing this song too much."

He turned to the stage director to ask his view on the matter. He gave his verdict easily. "Yes, she can't sing, but those legs and that mouth of hers make that irrelevant. Put her up at the front. Center stage. Right in the spotlight! We'll do it at the end of the second act."

At home, but an hour before the show, Lola finished applying her cosmetics and the final touches to her outfit under the admiring gaze of the little one. Rosalie gave Anna a glass of milk before helping Lola on with her stockings. The face powder she wore was outrageously heavy. I suppose it had to be the case if she were to conceal the yellow marks under her eye.

As she lolled in the back of the landau, I gave her a thick sheepskin blanket to place over her knees, for I feared she might freeze. Rosalie and Anna waved at us from the balcony as I gave Gaza the signal to depart. It was at this precise moment that Sherry decided to jump into the back of the carriage and onto Lola's lap.

Anna laughed giddily, delighted at such a spectacle. "He wants to go dancing with you!" she cried out.

"What a naughty boy!" Lola joked.

"Why not take him with us, mademoiselle?" I suggested. "I feel he'll make a huge success of you!"

And that is how Sherry became a part of her act. Not only that night, but on many occasions in the future, and he was delighted with his involvement.

As she sang, he moved from her arms to her shoulders, kissed her face, seemed to fall only to be caught by her, rubbing himself against her chest, and nuzzling into her neck. His tail appeared to move to the rhythm of the piano, although this was but an illusion.

Even the women in the audience appeared delighted by the duo. Lola's clumsiness, the wrong steps, and flat notes among the other scantily clad chorus girls were soon forgotten when people witnessed the moves she made with her cat. What was sure was that she and she alone gleaned all the attention from the crowd. The principal actress was furious, but once Lola was on stage with the cat, there was no in-tervention to be made. They could hardly stop the show!

In the middle of her song toward the end of the production, Sherry's paw got caught up in the strap of her bodice, pulling it down to reveal her naked breast, which was then illuminated by the shining beading of the bodice under the stage lights. She threw her head back triumphantly. It was clear for all to see that she had painted her nipple the same color as her mouth. This caused a wave of outrage throughout the entire room. Ladies hid their shamed faces behind their veils. One young girl fainted. The gentlemen coughed and smoothed down their mustaches.

Up near the rafters, in the cheap seats, a voice could be heard shouting, "You go for it, Lola!" It was Thérésine, the laundry girl.

Lola knew she had gone too far and slipped backstage, feigning confusion. After the show, as Lola had foreseen, a number of men made their way behind the stage to talk to the actresses, dancers, and singers. The girls were lined up, waiting to receive whatever offers they may. We were among them. Sherry was being passed around from girl to girl, but once he'd tired of this, he jumped back into the arms of Lola and refused to move another inch.

Officially, I was there to help her change her clothing, but I took our large black notebook, and under the glaring eyes of the other girls, angered to see such a plan in action, I noted the times and dates given to me by gentlemen wanting to spend some alone moments with Mademoiselle Lola.

As she patted and played with Sherry, Lola managed to touch the hand of everyone who came to have their names marked in the book. In my view, they all got a little too close for comfort to her as they admired the results of the ripped corset still half-hanging from her shoulder. I managed to stave away a number of men, using the most courteous of pretexts, whom I found to be too old, or overly libidinous, despite Lola's prior recommendations.

Those that successfully penetrated my selection were those who tended to be younger in appearance or those who were quite clearly full of admiration for her. I asked to see their cards, as she had suggested, insinuating that it was easier that way for me to copy their names into our book, but it also gave me the chance to see if they had a title and to estimate what kind of sum they might be worth. I looked, too, at the state of their hats and clothing and what profession, if any, was marked on the card. It gave me an idea of who had a fortune and who didn't have a sou to their name.

Lola and I also exchanged smiles or slight frowns. This process allowed us to separate the wheat from the chaff.

I took a portrait of Lola and wrote the time and date of the rendezvous for each gentleman, alongside the prewritten address at Madame Alexandra's establishment.

There had certainly been some hefty investment into our enterprise: photography, printing, costumes, jewelry, and flowers, and it looked like we'd see a return as a result of this very first night! And once we'd made our money back, we could perhaps start thinking about the rent payments. Out of a total of twelve requests, I had accepted five. This would more than cover our expenses.

Back at the house, the most appetizing smell of roast chicken flowed throughout the first floor. Anna had laid the table upstairs and was impatiently awaiting our return. Lola looked upon her tenderly and then cried out, "Well, well! Off to bed with you, little girl! You're not in the slightest bit reasonable, are you? Look at the hour!"

Anna gave her a kiss on her hand and scarpered off downstairs with Sherry to a new room that had been prepared for her next to the kitchens.

"So?" asked Rosalie.

Lola smiled wearily as she sunk down into one of the armchairs.

"The first appearance of Lola Deslys on the Cannois stage was an immense success," I declared. "And I may now predict that our coffers will soon be brimming!"

Rosalie let out a triumphant shout. "I was so sure of it!" she said. "Very well! I'll leave the two of you to it! I'm falling asleep on my feet here!"

As Lola settled down farther into her seat, she picked up a newspaper that was lying on the floor. She flicked through it, staring mostly at the illustrations rather than reading the text. She exclaimed in a fit of energy, "My Lord! That's it!"

As I leaned forward to take a look at what she was seeing, I saw the portrait of the Grand Duchess Maria Alexandrovna, wife of Alfred, Duke of Edinburgh, Duke of Kent, and Count of Ulster. I found it to be more than a little banal.

"Why on earth are you shouting like that? Do you know her?"

Her eyes glazed over, and no response came from her lips. I was about to move over to the table to enjoy the fare placed there by Rosalie when she moved to her feet and marched toward her bedchamber.

"I'm going to get changed, and then I'm going out again," she said, her voice with a mysterious tone I hadn't heard before. "They'll still be dining. I'm going to the restaurant at the theater."

This last phrase caused me to lose what little appetite I had. I stood in front of the table, unable to think of what to say next. I had no clue as to where this unexpected feeling of disappointment and sadness came from . . . but it was profound.

Lola reappeared dressed top to toe in bright violet, and I offered my assistance despite my ill feelings. "Would you like me to ready Gaza and come with you?"

"Certainly not! I'll go on foot, and I can return home in a cab! *Mangia, mangia, che ti fa bene!*" she sang with abandon.

Rosalie had gone to all that hard work for nothing. She disappeared in a wave of orange blossom, and I set about clearing the table miserably. There was no possible way I could eat a morsel.

33

The Day after the Festivities

Strangely, although the day that followed the amazing premiere should have seen me feeling positive, I felt torn. I listed Lola's meetings again in our book, taking care to print the names of the men and their preferences as agreed with her.

I fixed their cards to the pages with a needle and thread, so she would have a better idea of who was who. As I did so, this brought about in me a feeling that put me very much ill at ease. I came to comprehend this feeling with a rapid realization. It was jealousy. This time, I knew I would have difficulty hiding such a sentiment.

Lola was certainly a pretty girl, exciting, overtly sexual, but I felt so much more than mere physical attraction toward her. I felt undone by the emotion of it and strode upstairs to my bedchamber under the rooftop to shelter myself from the feeling.

I pressed my forehead against the window and mused on my emotions toward the woman who had held out her hand to me and given me a place of refuge. It would be impossible to declare my yearning for her. She would not appreciate it, and I didn't feel there would be a way to recover from it once such a declaration had been made.

I would need a fortune and respectability, both of which I had lost, if I were to say such a thing and hope to be still looked upon with grace afterward. She was such an enigma to me. Both greedy and ambitious, she masked her generosity as though it were a weakness or act of madness.

Yet although I had an idea of her aims in life, albeit an abstract one—riches, respect, honor in the future—I still had to face the facts. There was the rent to pay, people to support . . . a whole life to maintain.

I was prepared to lose ground. What fascinated me the most was how this woman and what she represented to me had simply swept away the years of my life spent with Lady Sarah.

I was so grateful to her for having unknowingly healed the pain in my heart and that the dreadful affliction that had been haunting me no longer invaded my very soul. And yet a quite separate form of bitterness had taken hold of me. Love in the shadows. A secret desire. I felt condemned to suffering this unrequited passion, living by her side without ever speaking a word of it. I would have to watch her laugh, sing, love, and take men to bed while feigning indifference. So be it.

Either that or I would have to choose to never set eyes on her again. My choice had already been made. In fact, it wasn't really a question that required answering.

The following morning, as I ventured downstairs a little later than was usual for me, they were all sitting at the table, ready to devour an impressive breakfast laid before them. Some large sheets had been draped over the mirrors. Lola had sent Rosalie and Anna out to buy foodstuffs from the *Escoffier* merchants, and she must have given them quite a detailed list.

The white tablecloth was covered in a vast array of exotic delicacies. Cold hors d'oeuvres of jellied fish, vol-au-vents with a rich sauce and rabbit liver with rolled sausage, creamed chestnuts, roast beef, boiled eggs and duck legs, oyster and gizzard salads, lobster, and brightly colored vegetable flans. The cheese and desserts board hadn't even been uncovered yet. As for drinks, we had a choice of lemonade, coffee, tea, or hot chocolate—a dessert in itself!

Maupassant was seated at the table with the children, who were eating a separate dish of brioche stuffed with sour cream and prawns.

The whole display rendered me speechless. I was cross with Lola for having spent so much money and so inconsiderately! I reprimanded her harshly.

"You're so right, Miss Fletcher," she uttered as she frowned and rolled her eyes at Anna, causing her to titter. "Mea culpa. I won't do it again."

"We'll never find the money to stay in this house if you throw it out of the window like this! We'll never eat it all! Do you want to see yourself out on the street? This afternoon, I'll give you a lesson in how to manage a household budget! Because this isn't the way!"

"Oh! You're such a spoilsport! Let me live a little and take this one chance to savor my success!"

"Come, Miss Fletcher," said Maupassant. "What are you trying to achieve here? A leopard never changes its spots! It's a futile endeavor! This is quite charming. Quite beautiful. Let this woman overcome you with her sweet melody. That should be enough for us all, don't you think?"

"Are you speaking of me?" asked Lola dreamily.

"She's like a little bird up on her branch! She's light and airy and as useless to the world as she is indispensable," he insisted.

"What has got into you today, Maupassant? I'm pleased by what you say of me! He's quite right, Miss Fletcher!"

"He's being condescending!" I retorted.

Maupassant guffawed. His manner had been slightly mocking, in my view. Lola jolted up and rushed to the other side of the table, where she put her arms around Maupassant's neck and placed a kiss on his cheek.

"Calm yourself, Miss Fletcher! What I like most about Guy is that he never judges me. He accepts me just the way I am. Anyway! Maupassant has expressed a desire to meet Madame Campo. I'm going to get dressed, and then we're off!"

Rosalie started to clear the table with Anna's help.

"I'll leave you some tea and a little bread and butter, because the rest of it isn't for you!" she said to me nastily.

"But, Rosalie! Surely you can see that Lola's digging her own grave here! She shouldn't be conducting herself thus!"

"All I can see is that everything rests on that poor girl's shoulders and that she has every right to enjoy herself from time to time!"

This retort made me feel slightly uneasy, as she wasn't being un-reasonable in what she said. I turned toward Maupassant as I sat down with force.

"First things first, have you at least managed to return that little bottle to the d'Orcels' bathroom?"

"Yes, my dear Miss Killjoy. Mission accomplished."

This disappointed me greatly, as I wished more than anything to find him at fault.

"I see. And why is it you're hoping to pay Madame Campo a visit?"

"It's a chance for me to be able to enter one of the poorer houses up on the Suquet. You know I come to Cannes to observe the upper class-es and the like, but I remain curious as to the other side of the coin."

I shrugged with indifference. He annoyed me so greatly with the way he researched his writings so.

"Come and join us at the port afterward. It would be my abso-lute delight to invite you to luncheon with us on the *Louisette*, if that should tempt you. You could bring the child. I'm certain the fresh air would do her no end of good."

"I want to come too," interjected Mario.

"You're going to school! If you don't, our mama will have a fine to pay!" shouted Lola.

I felt somewhat thrilled about the idea of a boat ride, but I did not want him to recognize my excitement. I acknowledged his offer through tight lips.

"We'll be there."

I had the time to attempt to make some adjustments to my mood while Lola and Maupassant went to call upon Madame Campo.

They found her on her straw mattress, snoring noisily, surrounded by piles of empty bottles. She had clearly drowned her sorrows the night before. The house was in a worse state than when Lola had first been there following the death of Clara, but this time, she had no intention of playing the housekeeper. Not in front of Maupassant.

She made a quick attempt, however, to clear some space so she could put some of the leftover food from their sumptuous breakfast upon it. The noise woke her.

As Lola spoke to the old lady, persuading her to eat something at the same time, Maupassant walked around the apartment, taking notes. There wasn't a thing he didn't notice. He strode up and down the room, studying every nook and cranny. Madame Campo clearly felt intimidated by the gentleman who had not yet spoken a word.

"Have you seen Clara?" asked Lola. "It's been a week."

"No! They won't let me see her! I don't know what the hell they're doing! It's not right to have to delay all this time before burying her."

She sniffled, tears rolling down her cheeks. But Lola suspected she hadn't even had the strength to make it all the way to the hospital. She must have been drinking in order to give herself some courage, as alcohol so often helps with that, but then not had the capacity to follow through with her plan.

Had she even forgotten that her daughter had died? Had she been in that much of a stupor?

With Lola's help, Madame Campo managed to finish the food put in front of her. Following the last bite, a coughing fit came upon her, scaring Maupassant, who maintained a safe distance. He took out a mentholated handkerchief from his pocket and held it to his nose.

"I'm going to go to the town hall and speak to someone there about your circumstances," said Lola. "I presume they'll send you some subsidies of some kind. But you know they're not too fond of drunks, do you not? Particularly women!"

Madame Campo rustled up a last bit of dignity and protested, "Oh, little girl! Who do you think you are? I don't need anyone! And who says that I drink? I'm not a drunk! *Capito?*"

She stood and pushed Lola toward the door before staring at Maupassant with fury, but not daring to lay a finger on him. He followed Lola outside, bowing his head slightly and leaving a few coins on the floor in his wake.

Lola was deeply concerned about their forced departure and upset at having behaved so clumsily. They walked with haste toward the port. As they descended a long flight of stairs, taking them down a side street, Maupassant shouted in triumph, "Yes! Yes!"

"What on earth?"

He smiled secretively and replied, "I'll keep it a mystery for the moment! All in good time!"

I was waiting for them, along with Anna, on the Quai Saint-Pierre just in front of the *Louisette*. Maupassant winked at us each in greeting and shouted out to the sailor, standing at the prow, preparing the departure, "Galice! Are you ready?"

The *Louisette*, prior to its renovation, had at one point been a large fishing boat, a whaler with a huge sail and an interior cabin allowing for storm protection.

Galice approached the boat from the quayside and helped us jump aboard.

"Where are we going?" Lola asked, taking a seat on a chair on the back deck and settling herself in for the ride.

34

THE CRUMPLED LETTER

Lola sat right in the middle of where most of the action would have taken place had this boat still been used for fishing. But the area now served as an outdoor lounge for diners.

"If it is convenient to you, we'll take the pleasure of going on a trip around the bay today," Galice said, "and you'll all have the opportunity to taste our famous *oursinade*, prepared by my François here."

There was a strong breeze as Galice sailed the boat between the Île Sainte-Marguerite and the Cannes Riviera, traveling the length of the island.

Galice turned toward the tip of the Croisette and threw the anchor offshore just as we were in sight of the La Réserve restaurant. It brought back particularly bad memories for me. The waves that came to die on the rocks there moved the boat back and fore in a gentle swaying motion.

François and Galice joined us for lunch, and the jokes, chatter, and tall tales came in droves. Lola told of her success at the theater and treated us all to her song—even little Anna joined in. I went to the starboard deck and borrowed Galice's binoculars. The view of the Île Sainte-Marguerite and the fort was stunning, with the bay shimmering in the sunlight.

The end of the meal was celebrated with the ever-present champagne before Galice prepared the sails and François cleared our plates and cutlery into large wicker baskets. Maupassant, with conspiratorial gestures, satisfied that what he was about to do couldn't fail to provoke, pulled out a crumpled piece of paper from his pocket.

"What do you have smuggled away there?" asked Lola.

"I found this ball of paper at the bottom of the mattress at Clara's mother's house. It was in a jar that looked to be full of kindling and bits of newspaper with which to light a fire."

"But why in the world would you pick up such a dirty-looking thing?"

"Don't you see? The color! It's the d'Orcels' ink, bought from Venice, if memory serves me well."

He flattened it out and read it aloud to the group.

"'I'll be there at the appointed hour. You know where.'"

So it was a letter. A meeting time and place had been given, but only the author of the missive and the final recipient can have known the exact details.

"No address at the top of the page, no names, no signature, no place marked, no date, no time," I said with disappointment.

"On the contrary! This is a precious document all the same," said Lola with a burst of energy, holding out her hand to take the paper. "We can glean so much from the quality of the paper, the handwriting, the ink, and perhaps other signs that we are not able to see with the naked eye."

"Yes! I've heard that every fingerprint is unique! I read an article on the subject just the other day!" I exclaimed with enthusiasm. "I'm quite convinced that one day we'll be able to find a way of distinguishing prints and identifying perpetrators of crime through them! It is much discussed at the moment. As it stands, only Bertillon's anthropometry method allows us to recognize a criminal for who he is."

Maupassant searched through his bag and pulled out a few leaves of paper containing the poetry of the Comtesse Andréa.

I stared at him wide-eyed.

"It is the same writing in the very same ink. There is no denying it. Indubitable!" he said.

"Why is there a letter from the comtesse at Clara's mother's abode?" asked Lola.

I felt a bitterness fall upon me and couldn't stop myself declaring, "You know very little of the legitimate wives of the upper classes! They will do anything and everything in their power to protect themselves and their own. You see the comtesse? Why did she sell that necklace? She's a devious type! It's all so cunning! She's done something! They are a plague upon us, and they do it all in the name of appearance!"

"Now, now!"

My voice broke as I continued, "The only matter of any concern to these women is their social position."

Maupassant observed me keenly.

"Why regard me in that way?" I said. "What have I said that you don't already know? I'm sure it's all quite banal to you!"

Lola and Maupassant appeared nervous despite their abrasive stares. I searched my pockets for my cigars.

"I wonder what you must have lived through to look so unkindly upon your own sex?" said Maupassant.

I took a puff of my cigar and exhaled in relief.

"Just leave me alone and go and exercise your dissecting talents somewhere else. You have no need to practice on me!"

I forced myself to laugh, but I know it sounded false. Lola helped me find my conversational feet again by asking me a barrage of questions.

"Do you believe Andréa had a secret meeting with someone? With who? It must have been Clara! Or another man and Clara got hold of the note?"

"Would she go to some man other than her husband?" I interjected.

"And if so, who is her lover? And what does it have to do with Clara? What was the letter doing at her mother's home?"

"Just a coincidence? Maybe she picked up some papers from the waste basket in their room to use on the fire?" I suggested.

"Or did she wish to blackmail the comte with whom she may well have had an affair? But then, why have this meeting with the comtesse and not the comte himself?"

"No! It was the comtesse who arranged the meeting!"

"Yes, but it might well have been a response to a suggestion initiated by Clara! In person!"

"Clara may have known that the comtesse had taken a lover?" said Maupassant, joining in the debate.

"I believe that Clara was blackmailing someone," said Lola. "It's as clear as day to me! It explains her change in mood from being a gay and joyful young thing to someone dark and determined. I am quite convinced of it. Clara climbed into the bedclothes of the wrong man and tried to blackmail him afterward."

"I very much doubt that," said Maupassant.

We finally docked at the old port. As soon as we'd stepped foot back onto dry land, Maupassant rushed off to meet an acquaintance. Lola took my arm on one side, and Anna held my hand on the other for the walk home. Grouped together as such, I felt like we were a little family, and I once again savored my new life as a fugitive.

As we approached our villa, Sherry was perched high up on an orange-blossom tree, awaiting our return. As Anna called him, he jumped down and lurched up into her arms.

"Don't forget who feeds you, cat! You ungrateful little beast! How the little one has stolen his heart! What about me?"

I smiled. Rosalie came to the door, brandishing a letter. I opened it.

"Philémon!"

"Oh! He's like my shadow, that one! Insatiable! The insolence of him!"

I read the words quickly and blanched.

"What is he saying?"

"It's finished. This time it's really over and done with! He's throwing in the towel! He's giving you notice!"

"What? We're to be out on the streets?"

"Yes. He explains his desire to sell the house. He says he's been patient for long enough now. He states that you must ready the house for any potential buyers to visit, and he's given you an ultimatum to decamp."

"The scoundrel! So it's war he wants!"

"He awaits an answer."

I felt sick with worry, and yet, the more I agonized, the more it seemed to boost Lola's spirits.

"There's no use in being alarmed!" she said. "This is all about money changing hands and nothing more. But the rent will no longer suffice. If I want to stay here, I will have to purchase the property. It simply entails a larger sum of money. That's all there is to it. We need to find two hundred thousand in cash . . . or see if a banker or bailiff will lend us such an amount. My goodness! It's not asking the impossible! You know that having to find a thousand a month or two hundred thousand in one go requires pretty much the same level of energy! Now I come to think of it! I'd completely forgotten! I am such a featherbrain at times! There is something I must purchase in town! I'm going now! I'll hurry!"

"But we were going to have a cup of tea . . ."

"How English! There can be nothing of greater urgency than a cup of tea!" Her giggles punctuated her speech.

"At least let Gaza and me come with you."

"No, it takes you too long to get her ready. By the time you've prepared the tea, I'll be home."

Irritated by her mysterious trip, I strode into the kitchen without saying a goodbye. But she'd forgotten me already.

Anna was playing out in the garden with Sherry when Lola returned around an hour later. As the weather was fairly mild for the season, we made the decision to partake of our refreshments outside, and Rosalie brought us the pot of tea to enjoy in the fresh air. My morale was decidedly low. It was as if everything was playing out in a vicious circle yet again.

"What is it?" asked Lola. "Pray tell what is wrong?"

"I cannot say. It is as if I've already been here before, as if we've already lived this exact moment. Have you ever felt like that?"

"Never! But I think I know your meaning! It's a feeling of being submerged by reality."

"That's right. As if . . . As if . . ."

"It reminds you of when your . . . lady friend . . . asked you to ready your departure."

She spoke in a low voice, softly and tenderly. Her gentle way with me brought tears to my eyes. My feelings were rising to the surface, and there was nothing in my power I could do to contain them.

"I went without even being able to see her one last time. I remember walking to the gate. I walked slowly and with a heavy tread, but nobody called out. There wasn't a single sound behind me. And yet she knew I was going."

"Was she perhaps watching you from a window?"

"No. She wasn't. I built up the courage to turn and peer back at the house, just before stepping through the gate, but there was nobody, not a movement from a single window. It was as if she'd already rid her mind of me."

"I'm sure she just felt unable to show you her feelings."

"I always lived in her shadow. I would watch her darting around hither and thither, arranging flowers for her magnificent bouquets, parading herself at dinner with friends and her husband." I found it so hard to speak, my voice turning raspy. "And after she got that anonymous letter . . . that was it. It was all over. She wouldn't have her fragile reputation put in peril."

"An anonymous letter? What was that all about?"

Her questioning forced me to put my chagrin to one side. I looked her in the eyes, my anger subsiding.

"Someone sent a letter to Fergus, implying certain things. Fergus, her—"

"Yes! I get your point, Miss Fletcher! The wronged husband!"

"Yes! We were caught, despite the precautions we'd taken. Our secret embraces, our efforts to make something light in this terrible word in which we live, so full of mundane and superficial frivolities! How delighted I had been simply to spend a few hours with her, playing a game of lawn tennis or taking a walk out in the Denham countryside. And I thought she felt the same way. How naive I was!"

"We can all be accused of that, Miss Fletcher! Just consider how much Eugène hurt me!"

With bitterness, I resumed what I was saying without taking her interruption into account. "I must have spoken a thousand sermons of love to that woman, but it meant nothing to her when faced with losing her rank in society."

"What did you do? Where did you go?"

"A dismal little boarding house in a dank and dark room. She used to steal money from her husband. He gave it to her for fresh flowers for their home. It was the only money she had access to, despite their considerable fortune and her dowry! She built up quite the nest egg this way. And she gave me some of it, if I promised to leave Cannes."

"But you didn't keep your promise?"

"No. But I made myself a promise. I swore I'd never seek her out. I gave her everything she wanted."

"Well, there seems little point digging up the past. I don't know why you're putting yourself through it all again with such thoughts.

We need to keep up our spirits now more than ever. You're such a glum soul, miss!"

The tone she employed gave me back my smile. It was just then that the downpour started. It came out of nowhere and beat down upon us without end, and with it came strong gusts of wind and forked lightning across the skies. Little Anna squeaked and scuttled for cover. Lola followed her indoors, but I took the time to put our cups and teapot onto the tray and take it all back into the kitchen.

Once I'd finished cleaning everything, I went upstairs to sit in front of the fire and warm my bones, picking up the newspaper that had been delivered that morning but had still been lying in the hallway. I breathed in heavily as I turned the pages noisily.

"Are you already seeking out new employment?" Lola asked.

"I fear I must," I mocked, with a grin on my face. "And so should you!"

"Indeed! Read me some of the latest news of this dearest town of ours, would you? It will help take our minds off of matters."

I gave her a résumé of the main stories.

There was a clay-pigeon shooting contest organized for the following Sunday, and the dates for the International Regatta were set to be announced later that week. I turned the page and let out a sharp scream. "Good grief! Amédée has been assassinated!"

"No!"

Lola snatched the paper from my hands and searched the page wildly. She read snippets aloud to me, "In a stolen cab . . . out by the Delpiano storage hangars . . . It's a new neighborhood under construction . . . over on the other side of the railway under the Route de Grasse!"

And the thunder outside continued to roll.

35

THE BOTTIN BATHS

I woke up early the next morning so I could have a sea bath in anticipation of my appointment with the comtesse d'Orcel.

The entire town looked clean following the rainstorm and glistened in the morning sunshine.

Our trip out to sea on the *Louisette* had given me back my sea legs. I felt an urge to be in the water. After all, we were on the Mediterranean, and even though it was winter, it had always been a habit of mine, when I'd lived in Ramsey, my native town, to take a bath in the sea in the summer and, on occasion, in more inclement weather.

I tried to persuade Lola to join me, but she would have none of it, citing an urgent matter to which she had to attend. And yet there was nothing in our book of note. I had no clue what her plans might be.

"You don't seem to be able to fathom this. I have to find the big catch now! This is no time to play the waiting game," she said.

"I'll ask around at the baths. Perhaps some of the ladies there know of a moneylender. After all, if we want to borrow money, it's better to frequent those places where people have it!"

I was hoping to take Anna along, but Rosalie opposed me, saying she still remained too fragile for such pursuits. But I believed I might stand more of a chance with a child by my side, and Lola agreed.

"Make sure you are taken on my credit note down at the baths. I have an account at Bottin's. You can also hire a suit and bath towels, you know?"

"Thank you. I have what I need. But that will be just perfect for the girl."

And so Anna and I left at a swift pace, with her jumping up in delight, carrying my tapestry bag with my bathing costume and bath linens.

When we arrived at the Bottin bathhouse on the Croisette, I noted several winterers throwing interested glances at some of the ladies undressing on the beach, readying themselves for a dip in the sea. The house offered pavilions on stilts with warm salt baths and perfumed waters, but for the most courageous among us, there was always the real sea! And how revitalizing it was, yet the skies were thick with clouds, and the sun had yet to show its face.

As we walked into the building, I met with Dr. Buttura, who was just leaving. He often visited the bathhouse to give demonstrations on good hygiene to those suffering with ill health. He was in a hurry, but he made the time to inform me, however, that he'd received the analytical results from Marseille and that they'd discovered something of an intriguing nature, which tied in very nicely with what he'd suspected all along. He wished to speak with us on the subject, but he was unsure of when he might be free to pay Lola a visit.

Luckily, Maupassant had always been present whenever the doctor had called upon us, for which he was grateful, for he was most afraid of what his wife might think of the idea of him having spent so much time in the home of Lola Deslys. He was sure that she would not appreciate the gossip that might follow. As it stood, he was uncertain he would be able to sign the burial permit, although he had been receiving some pressure from Valantin.

After his quick departure, I thought about what he had said, and I realized that Paul Antoine had not as yet presented us with the results of his research either. I was sure that all this would anger Lola greatly, for she hated not being in the know.

I looked around, and there was no sign of the comtesse yet. This suited me perfectly, as I felt preoccupied with what Lola might be doing. I wondered where she might be during my absence and whom she could be seeing.

Once dressed in my bathing costume, holding on to the shivering Anna's hand, I made my way slowly to the cold waters. Anna outright refused to venture any farther and contented herself with playing in the sand by the sea's edge.

"Well, just for today, and because you've been quite ill recently, I'm not going to force you to go into the cold water. But soon, later on in the year, when the sun starts to shine a little more, I intend to teach you to swim. A young woman must be able to boast some sporting accomplishments!"

Anna couldn't contain her giggles. "I'm not a gentlewoman, you know?"

"But of course you are!" I replied.

I remembered discussing the Pygmalion myth with an Irish art critic once, and I believed I saw in Anna a way to test the theories of which we'd spoken. His sincerely held belief was that any person on earth could acquire the mannerisms of high society, if only they were in receipt of a fitting education.

We heard a shout in the distance, and she turned her head to see from whence it came. It was Mario. He'd spied us from the Croisette and jumped down onto the sand to join us.

"Just in time," I said. "I'd like you to keep Anna company while I go for a dip. She'll tire a lot less easily with you around."

As the winterers looked on, gawping in astonishment, I walked into the water and set about swimming out to sea using the sidestroke taught to me as a child by my father in the waters of our incredible sea.

I was so pleased to find my body unwinding in the waves, feeling the purifying and toning effects of the ice-cold liquid on my skin.

As I returned to the shore, I saw Andréa d'Orcel. She'd arrived at last. She was sitting at the end of a small jetty, and after exchanging pleasantries, I suggested that in order to avoid the onset of pneumonia, she should attempt a few gymnastic movements to warm her body.

Her smile was forced, but she accepted my advice nonetheless and dropped into the water. She allowed me to manipulate her body quite freely and copied my every move. I could see that something was bothering her. I didn't know whether it was what I was asking her to do . . . or something else entirely. I tried to converse with her as best I could while keeping a watchful eye on the children, who were jumping around in the sand with glee. Anna caught my eye and came running over to the water's edge.

"Can I go back home with Mario, please?" she asked.

Mario appeared embarrassed. I guessed that his plans were to sneak into the kitchen back at Les Pavots and appropriate a couple of Rosalie's cakes. I felt quite distracted and so authorized them to leave. I was far too preoccupied with the comtesse to argue with them.

I asked her a few questions, remaining fairly skillful in the manner in which I posed them. Secretly, I cursed the fact that I was able to approach this woman and break through the class barrier but that there was no possible way someone like Lola could do the same. And yet she was so much cleverer than I in getting men and women alike to open up about their personal lives. I must have been underestimating myself, however, for within mere minutes, Andréa had more or less admitted to the presence of a lover in her life and that it was out of her means to resist the powerful passion of their torrid affair.

She moved forward, invading my personal space, and looked at me with signs of distress in her eyes. I asked if I could help alleviate her suffering any. I found her gushing and unexpected effusion a little too much to handle. Perhaps I was better at extracting secrets than I'd imagined.

However, something deep inside told me that this behavior from the comtesse was far from typical. I was obliged to recognize that what she was saying coincided with our thoughts on her. Did she know what we were up to? Maupassant had already declared that she must have had a lover.

At least this discovery might help explain what the crumpled letter was all about. But we still had no idea why it was found where it was, and I didn't have the slightest inkling as to what reaction I was supposed to be showing her. What she was saying left little to the imagination, and we hardly knew one another. I had to improvise.

"And why shouldn't you rejoice in this, comtesse?" I said. "True passion is such a rarity. We must seize upon it when chance invites us to do so. With our husbands, we enjoy a contract of sorts, an understanding. And we all know as much. As long as you act in goodness, why be so saddened by it all?"

"Indeed. It's just that the lie burdens me so. But that's not my principal concern. The truth of it is that my lover is leaving me. I am sure he has another *friend*. And I feel so desperate about it. I'm going to see him now."

Her voice was shaken. I felt I ought to comfort her and so placed my arm around her shoulders as we walked indoors to the dressing cabins. She held on to me, her body pressed against mine. I tried to express my discomfort as I noticed her piercing eyes upon my body. She was a strange creature, indeed. What did she want from me?

As I dressed, I decided I would follow her after we'd said our goodbyes and try to discover the identity of her lover. Or at the very least, uncover a little more of her secret life. I kept a respectable distance so that she wouldn't catch sight of me, praying to the skies above that she would perhaps not know me if she did see me, for we'd only ever met in tennis or bathing clothes up to this point.

She wore an emerald-green ensemble, simple in cut, with a dark hat and thick veil. For added security, I placed my boater in with my bathing suit and allowed my hair to flow about my shoulders naturally. I hoped that the humidity in the air wouldn't make it any more straw-like than it already was.

The route she took seemed quite illogical to me. She walked first over to the Allée de la Marine along the seafront route and then turned back on herself toward the Place des Îles, crossing the Rue Notre Dame. For an instant, I wondered whether or not she may have been heading to Madame Alexandra's. That would have been the height of absurdity. But no.

She passed the reading rooms and crossed the Gray et d'Albion gardens, cutting through the Rue Hermann, and headed to the theater on the Rue Châteaudun, where she took the overhead walkway.

This was almost our neck of the woods. She was moving out into open countryside. There were a handful of isolated villas and the Brun et Barbier perfumery standing alone in a field of orange blossom, laurel, jasmine plants, and olive trees. A few peasants were scurrying about their business. She turned left, and I began to believe she was indeed going to Les Pavots.

She took a wide circle along the Rue Lycklama before stopping in front of the entrance to the Sacré-Cœur orphanage that I had come to know so well. I lingered a moment. She took out a key and entered through the front door. It was certain she couldn't be meeting her lover in this dreadful place, unless he were a gardener . . . or a priest!

Once she'd closed the door behind her, I approached the building via an alleyway that ran behind the gardens. There were several windows that looked down onto the cellars beneath the lower rooms. In the distance, I could hear a choir of girls singing hymnals alongside hammering and the sawing of wood. It appeared that the repairs demanded by the doctor were taking place after all.

I tried to peek through the dark windows. What was I hoping to see? I thought back to the day that Buttura and I had inspected the building. There was a small office inside where one of the nuns kept medicines and tinctures and the like. Having seen Andréa saunter so easily into this building allowed me to view the whole affair from quite a different perspective. What if the substance Lola found in the bathroom of suite 327 was something to do with this place?

At the corner of the building, I saw three steps leading to a cellar door. As I walked down them, I felt a sharp blow to my head, and everything went black.

36

Rue du Redan

The truth of it was that Lola had deliberately not told me of her intentions, so as not to worry me. When I left for the Bottin baths, she headed over to the Delpiano warehouse to speak to the guardians there about what exactly had happened with Amédée and the stolen cab and how his body had been discovered. She knew that it was a family enterprise and that his corpse had been found not far from where the company was located.

The rain from the night before had made the terrain extremely muddy, particularly where the horses and carriages were stationed in front of the building. Planks of wood had been placed hither and thither to facilitate passage, especially that of the drivers, who were back and fore to town with their rich passengers on board. Lola lifted her skirts to her knees and jumped from plank to plank, unable to keep herself as free from mud as she would have liked.

So occupied was she in this that she paid little attention to her surroundings and became flustered when she heard a voice close by say, "Mademoiselle Giglio!"

She lifted her head to see Gustave Planchon. *Her* Gustave. He held out his hand to her.

"Gustave? What are you doing here?"

"I've come to pick up a victoria! I drive for Delpiano these days!"

"How chic! I feel so relieved to know how well situated you are! Are you happy here?"

"It didn't sit too well with me at first, but I feel good about it all now. The pay is as good as it gets! And there are tips, of course! Are you here for a cab? Where are Gaza and your landau?"

Lola looked around fleetingly to ensure nobody was listening. "No, Gustave," she whispered. "That's not what this is about. I'm here to find out more about Amédée Lambert's death. Did you know him?"

"What a sorry tale! Of course, I knew him! I saw him many times down at the cabaret bar. I don't really know what sort of nasty work he must have got himself caught up in, but I know he had gaming debts. Well, that's hardly surprising."

"And did he work here?"

"Not exactly. The boss gave him a little work to tide him over, as a favor to him, really. He just lost his job down at the hotel, you see? Poor lad! First his fiancée passes away with some terrible illness or other. Then he loses his job. Then he gets into all that money trouble, and now he's a goner! That's a dog's life if ever I heard of one!"

"Who was his fiancée?"

"He said he was engaged to some girl from up on the Suquet. Campo, I believe. A young thing about your age. What a woeful business."

"Did he drive a cab at night, then?"

Gustave lowered his voice to match that of Lola. "No, that's what was odd about it. The boss said the cab had been stolen, and he reported it missing. Can you imagine the trouble Amédée was about to find himself in? He'd run off with that cab! And why? Who knows? But I'm sure he was capable of it. He was a loyal man but not when it came to playing cards. He always went far too far with those games of his. Poor man. He was found in a field over yonder. That big building plot over there. Can you see it? They found him with a bullet hole in the middle of his forehead. Why do you want to know all this anyhow, mademoiselle?"

"Oh, my mother knows his mother," she lied. "She asked me to find out what happened. The authorities aren't giving anything away for the moment."

"I can believe that! The police came, and they searched through everything. I heard them talking to the boss. They haven't got anyone to point the finger at yet."

"Have they found the weapon, at least?"

"Not a trace."

"I'm going to go and take a look around. You never know! Good day to you, Gustave! Good health to you and your family!"

Lola, her skirts still lifted as high as she dared allow, made her way carefully over to the field in question. But as she left the area in front of the warehouse, there were fewer and fewer planks of wood underfoot, and before she knew it, she was almost ankle deep in black, sticky dirt.

She froze for a moment, immobile, getting a taste of the place and imagining Amédée lying there on the ground with a hole in his head. She could see some Italian workmen not far from the entrance to the field, hard at task.

After a while, she felt almost as if the surroundings were speaking to her. What had been invisible elements moments before now became more tangible to her. The tracks on the ground were the first thing she noticed.

The rain from the night before had washed most of the traces away, yet she could still see that a carriage had been past here, through the earth, not far from where a new building stood under construction. Lola could clearly make out the print of the wheels and the horseshoe markings. Unfortunately, too many other footprints were intermingled with these for her to glean anything of use from her discovery.

But she knew that, ordinarily, there should have been no carriage entering this field, for it was off the road. And so, it meant that the markings must have been made by Amédée and the stolen vehicle. But then how much passage must there have been after that? Those who had discovered his body, the workmen, police, the drivers who had come to collect the horse and carriage. A real crowd had been here, and so there was no single hope of any great evidence coming to light.

She walked over to the men to ask them some questions. The man who had found the body volunteered to tell her what he knew. She had seen his face before and was quite sure he was a friend of her uncle. She was also well aware that her family and most of their friends had cast her aside as soon as they had learned how she earned her living. He greeted her, shifting from one foot to another. He was polite, but his face barely hid his disgust toward her. Yet he answered her queries all the same.

He showed her the exact position the carriage had been found in and where the body had lain. Lola positioned herself where the cab had been and tried to envisage the scene as it would have looked. *So he was up in the cab, at the front. Someone spoke to him, and he must have jumped down from the carriage and turned just here . . . Amédée was face-to-face with his killer. The bullet hit him straight between the eyes, and he fell to the ground.*

Lola searched below her feet and behind where she'd been told the body had been discovered. She followed the imagined trajectory of the bullet. She then spotted the scaffolding up against the building under construction several meters from the scene of the crime. It was a mixture of wood and metal. Was there a chance that the bullet was lodged in the wood?

She rushed over to the frame and searched frantically. It would be high up on the frame if it was here. At least the height of a man . . .

She spied what looked like a dent in a "Danger" sign just above her head. It might have been caused by the impact of the bullet. It was round and smooth and looked something like a silver flower stuck in the middle of a rusty sea.

She lowered her head and examined the ground directly under it. A shiny object! What luck to have found it in all this mud! She took out a handkerchief from her pocket and kneeled down, now feeling completely indifferent toward the idea of trying not to ruin her clothing. She used her gloved hand to pick up the bullet and slipped it into her handkerchief. It was still covered in coagulated blood.

She shivered and trudged out of the bleak field as quickly as her muddied feet would carry her. She traversed the Forville market, lost in her thoughts, but noticed that the old town looked a lot cleaner for having been drenched the night before. Lola felt a sudden sensation of rage fill her very core.

She cut down the Route de Toulon and turned left onto the Rue du Redan and knocked on Maupassant's front door.

He had hired some rooms situated at number one, an apartment building without a concierge. This was the last building on the left-hand side of the street as one walked toward the sea. He was fortunate enough to have the most marvelous view of the square and the Boulevard Malakoff that ran the length of the coastline.

Rather than taking the long climb up the staircase, she shouted up to him, hoping he'd hear her through his window. After a few seconds, a head with a chef's hat atop it popped out of a window. It was François.

"What is it?" he moaned.

"Hello there, Monsieur François! Is Guy there?"

But there was nothing she could say or do to get past the barrier François put between anyone on the outside and his master. He would never allow an intrusion when Maupassant was writing.

Exasperated, Lola stormed off without speaking a word. Just then, Maupassant leaned over his balcony and shouted, "Mademoiselle Lola, don't kill him, I beg you! He is only performing his duty!"

He walked down the stairs and opened the door for her while the valet, feeling, I imagine, that he'd lost a small part of his dignity, hid in the kitchen.

"Come in, *Belle Amie*! I've told François to filter people whenever I'm working, and he does so with such tenacity! But my door will be forever open to you, of course." As he looked upon her in her soil-encrusted dress and filthy gloves, he exclaimed, "Where have you come from dressed like that? François will be quite cross with you if you get any of that on his carpets! He'll hate you for it! At least take off your boots."

Lola did as she was asked and tried to shake as much of the mud off her dress as she could. With her feet in mauve stockings and her skirts tucked up high into her belt, she entered the main room. On a desk in front of the window leading out to the balcony, she spied piles of papers, some of them spread out with scribbled ink drying, others full of crossings out.

"This is my new novel," said Maupassant, gathering the sheets together. "The latest annotations."

Lola swept this information to one side with indifference. She approached a side table and opened up the soiled handkerchief. The bullet, deformed due to its impact with the metal sign, made its appearance, blood and all. As they both moved closer to inspect it, Maupassant wrinkled his nose.

"What is that dreadful thing?"

Lola went ahead and described, with great passion, the fate that had befallen her friend.

"We cannot keep this for ourselves," Maupassant said. "This is evidence of vital importance!"

"Hush now! Do you actually still retain hope that the police will do anything with this?"

"Come, Lola! Valantin is perhaps a puritan, though certainly obsessed with women of your kind, but one thing can be said of him—he wants to maintain order in this town and will do so at any price. I believe him to be an honest fellow. If he obtains evidence of this kind, he will surely do something about it!"

"You are very naive yet pretend to know everything!" Lola spoke with much excitation. "The comte killed Amédée. That I am certain of! Amédée must have known something about him and tried to draw him into giving him money. I don't believe Amédée revealed the whole story, do you?"

"Yes, perhaps he kept some information to himself. And if we add to that his broken heart, his desire for vengeance, his having lost his job . . . it all adds up. If we believe the comte killed Clara, he could also have been Amédée's assassin. What have the police disclosed about Amédée's murder?"

"I confess I know little of it," Lola said, "but rumors abound that he was in a lot of debt. I think we should set a trap for him—for d'Orcel!"

"We're going after him again?"

"We searched his place, but came up with next to nothing! We need to go back!"

Maupassant made no response. Lola broke the silence that hung heavy in the air.

"I've got it! I'll disguise myself as a chambermaid at the Beau Rivage! I'll reenact how it was for Clara and what must have happened. I'll interpret her every move the day she told him she was with child and that he was the father."

"It will certainly provoke a panicked reaction from him, and he might very well betray himself."

"Miss Fletcher will want to join us. Come with me. She must be home from her bathing by now."

Maupassant glanced over at his badly arranged papers with regret as he put on an overcoat and his boater.

"We're off, François! Please excuse my friend for the mud she's left in the entrance hall."

Lola shrugged and picked up the bullet in the handkerchief before exiting the room.

They continued their tête-à-tête as they walked at a brisk pace. Maupassant seemed fully recovered from his migraines and pains behind his eyes.

"If we set up this snare of ours correctly, we're going to require some honest and reliable witnesses. I'll inform Valantin of our idea," he said.

"Out of the question! He'll scupper the whole thing! He won't play the game and well you know it! Just stop all this with your Valantin, would you?"

"He's not my Valantin!"

"But we do need the comtesse to be present. That's indispensable! She needs to take note of his reaction. Can you imagine what it must be like to be a woman when her husband's guilt is revealed to her?"

"We can't anticipate how either of them will react to this."

"I know that, but I believe the results will be spectacular and will give us what we need to confront d'Orcel. And if she isn't present at the scene, she'll never believe us, especially if he were to later retract."

"I must insist that we have someone of an official nature present. We don't want our account questioned if we uncover anything of significance."

"What about the housekeeper, Madame Davies?"

"The manager would be even better."

Lola grimaced, but admitted that this request was reasonable enough.

As they entered Les Pavots, Paul Antoine was just leaving. He explained that only Rosalie and the children were home.

"Paul Antoine," Lola said, "let me present to you the famous Guy de Maupassant."

Paul Antoine took a low bow.

Maupassant sniffed uncomfortably due to the strong odor of violets emanating from Paul Antoine's clothing, for he was used to a much more virile eau de cologne.

"I have the results you asked me to obtain and the handkerchief. Our chemist has written a report and asked me to be prudent when handling the evidence."

He held out a letter in front of his face and started to read, "Oh! Here it is! 'A salicin residue, oleandrine . . . Toxicological properties: very deleterious, a poison of the heart . . . Dangerous in all its forms: powder, infusion, decoction, inhalation . . . sometimes used in the treatment of smallpox.'"

"Nerium oleander," whispered Lola, thinking of the small flask of liquid.

"Yes! *Nerium oleander laurus rosa,*" declared Paul Antoine.

"Laurus rosa? My grandmother used to use that to poison rats!" said Lola.

"Yes, for it is much more violent than strychnine. There were traces of it in the dried saliva."

The brief lull that followed was interrupted by Lola. "But where is Miss Fletcher? She went to the baths, but she should have returned home by now."

She remained motionless for a few seconds, deep in thought. Paul Antoine looked to be on the brink of speaking while Maupassant held his hand against his forehead. His migraine must have returned.

"You, Paul Antoine," said Lola with exaggerated conviction. "You're going to help us! You have to do everything in your power to find Miss Fletcher. That's your mission."

Paul Antoine strode toward the front door and then spun on his heels. "I don't even know where to start!"

"The last we knew, she was at the bathhouse with the little one!"

"But I saw the little tykes playing at the back of the house earlier, near the kitchen door."

"Well, you need to start there, then. The little girl's name is Anna. She might have an idea as to what has become of Miss Fletcher. We can't delay, I'm afraid. Please find her and then bring her along to the Hôtel Beau Rivage. We'll be in the d'Orcel suite, room three two seven."

37

PRESSURE

After Lola changed into a clean dress and put on new boots and stockings, she and Maupassant made their way to the Beau Rivage.

"Are you concerned for Miss Fletcher and her well-being?" he asked.

"Not really. She likely spent longer at the baths than anticipated. But I do wish she were here for this d'Orcel encounter."

They slipped in through the service entrance, and while Maupassant stood watch, Lola went into the laundry room to steal a chambermaid's uniform. She picked one out of a basket full of soiled linen so that it would be less likely to be noticed as missing.

They climbed up the service stairs and forced open the door to the manager's office. He refused to have anything to do with their plan.

"It's simply out of the question! What makes you believe I could act against my own clientele in such a manner? I would forever lose my reputation and credibility. I am here to assure the comfort and protection of my guests, not to accuse them of God knows what with your fantastical defamation! I won't have anything to do with this masquerade!"

He ordered them back out of the door through which they'd crept. But something in the tone of Lola's voice caused him to pause for just that fraction of a second too long. He looked puzzled.

"Listen, Maurel," said Lola, seizing the opportunity. "There's no point doing your paragon-of-virtue speech with me. We both know too well the sort of activities you allow here. And I know enough about you to oblige you to help us in our quest for the truth. For once, why not act on what is genuinely moral? Good Lord! Be a man, would you?"

He responded with acrimony, trying his hardest to hide his fear. "You hush now, you dreadful bint! I will not allow this! D'Orcel is a man of integrity, and you are about to ridicule him! You won't be able to count on me for support when you need it! When I consider everything I've done for you!"

But Lola persisted. "I'm not speaking only of your suppers and your commissions with girls like me. I'm talking about the little cons you had in place when you worked at the Hôtel de l'Univers!"

His skin reddened as he turned his face away.

Maupassant was the next to speak. "You have everything to gain from this operation of ours. At the very worst, if these guests are as white as snow, you can simply allow them to stay here free of charge for some time and give them a big basket of candied chestnuts as a peace offering. But if this should all transpire as we hope, we'll learn that Charles d'Orcel murdered Clara Campo and Amédée Lambert, and you'll be a knight in shining armor! The man who helped catch the fox among his hens! And don't you fear! He'll have to endure such obloquy from his peers he'll be condemned outright."

Maurel groaned and shrugged. Against his better judgment and with intense apprehension, he whispered, "Come on, then. Let's do it. But I want you to promise to desist with this harassment once we have proven d'Orcel's innocence."

Lola tutted, furious at his half-hearted attempt to solve this matter once and for all.

As they made their way up further flights of stairs, Lola and Maupassant added the finishing touches to their plan. Lola would be the first to enter the suite, and she would do so alone.

As they stepped onto the floor, paying careful attention not to be seen by any other guests, they heard a rustling from around the corner. They looked to see what it was and noticed the comtesse in her emerald-green outfit open the door to their suite an inch and look inside. She then disappeared from sight, the door slamming behind her.

"That was the comtesse! Why was she being so cautious?" said Lola.

They waited a few moments before stepping out into the corridor in front of the suite. As Maupassant moved farther down the hallway, so as not to be seen by the occupants of the suite, Lola opened the door and simply walked straight in.

Andréa d'Orcel was sitting in the principal room in front of her bureau, as if she had been happily occupied for hours. Lola noted that she was perhaps slightly out of breath and guessed that she must have climbed the stairs. Some of the strands of her hair were out of place and had curled in the humid air. It was a sign that she had been to the baths and hadn't taken the time to restyle her coiffeur following her dip in the water. Lola supposed this was because there hadn't been a ladies' maid around to assist her. On the floor beside her lay a thick, dark veil.

Charles d'Orcel was sitting in an armchair, reading a newspaper. Without paying any attention to Andréa, Lola threw herself onto Charles, her head in his neck, the tears flowing out of nowhere. He jumped up with a fright, shocked to have been so easily taken off guard. In her chambermaid's uniform, d'Orcel didn't seem to recognize Lola as being the wanton woman he'd discovered in his room but days earlier.

She sobbed in such a dramatic fashion and with as much vigor as she could muster, crying out, "My darling! What am I to do? I am so lost! Your baby grows within me! What will we do? Please don't leave me all alone!" She turned then to the comtesse. "Madam! It is with no easy heart that I come here! It was not my wish to break up your peaceful home! Your reputations! But who else could I turn to other than the father of this child? Could you please take pity on me! I am but a poor girl!"

Andréa d'Orcel reared up, her skin pale, her lips tight with rage.

"Mademoiselle, a little decorum, if you will," the comtesse said. "You are lying. Do you expect me to believe you are a chambermaid? I have already seen you! You were dining at the table of the baron de la Roche in this very hotel! You're a professional! You are sullying my residence with your very presence here! Who has paid you for such a trick as this? Get out of here!"

Lola fell to her knees and grabbed at Andréa's skirts. "That's not true at all, Comtesse. I swear I'm telling the truth! The comte gave me this child. What will become of me? What will become of my baby?"

Lola continued in desperation to hold the scene together, because it certainly wasn't playing out as she'd imagined. The reaction from the comte was so strange. He seemed dumbfounded, stunned, and yet he wasn't panicking. It seemed he now recognized the prostitute who had "mistakenly" entered his room and who he had assumed was a thief.

"But . . . it's you! Why, madam, are you so insistent on harassing me thus? What have I ever done to you?"

The comtesse, who should have been the more taken aback by this situation, didn't seem perturbed at all. It was as if she had full control of the situation.

"You leave this instant, or I'll call the police." She freed herself from Lola's grasp and strode toward the door. "So be it. I can see you're not leaving, so I will go and fetch them myself."

As she opened the door she came face-to-face with Maupassant. He stepped into the room without invitation and without a single word of explanation. He closed the door carefully behind him and commenced with some improvisation of his own. His idea was to give the impression, initially at least, that he'd come to the comte's aid.

"Monsieur d'Orcel, the police found one of your cufflinks in Clara Campo's bedchamber. She was a maid up on this floor, and as I am sure you are aware, she was found dead in the hotel gardens."

"No! I have never heard such a thing! The little girl who cleaned our suite? She was here all winter!"

"Yes! You are about to be formally accused of killing this woman, whom you had impregnated, as was revealed by the autopsy."

The bafflement of Charles was mesmerizing to behold. He looked spectacularly out of his depth. There was no doubt from his behavior that here was a man who had not the foggiest clue what was happening. Andréa d'Orcel was now crimson in complexion. She shuddered with indignation and was just about to utter something when Lola got there first. "Seeing as not a one of you believes me, I'm going to the police myself. At least they will listen!"

The mention of the police pulled the comtesse to her senses. She was furiously angry and spoke to Lola as if she were naught but a common thief.

"Is it you behind this vile plot? Monsieur de Maupassant, can you not recognize this as complete nonsense? The little chambermaid was a thief! She must have stolen his cufflinks! That's why they found them among her things!"

"But, darling, of what do you speak?" asked Charles d'Orcel.

He turned to Maupassant and leaned in toward his ear, "Dear friend, I have no idea what all this is about! Am I honestly to be accused of having committed some sort of crime? Am I supposed to have conceived a child with both of these women? What is this tall tale? I haven't even misplaced any of my cufflinks!"

He fumbled around in a box of jewelry and pulled out several pairs of cufflinks with pearl settings along with some tie pins and sovereign rings. Maupassant looked into the comte's palm full of gold. He wrinkled his nose.

Is it really this big, soft man who had been so brutal to Lola? The man who had taken her spark away?

Lola noted that Maupassant had made exactly the same face in the company of Paul Antoine, and it was the smell of violets that had tickled his sensitive sense of smell. *That's it!* she thought. *The comte smells of violets.* This association of ideas drew her eyes to the hand of the comte. It was so fast, her eyes moving quicker than her thoughts. The pinky ring! She would recognize it anywhere—it had a large diamond in the shape of a cat's head. It was Paul Antoine's! She remembered seeing it so clearly just a few days earlier on the young perfumer's finger.

And now he was wearing it! The comte! But . . . but . . .

Lola froze. She stared at the comte in astonishment and yet remained motionless, petrified. D'Orcel observed her and panicked. He dropped all the jewelry in a flurry as if it were burning his hand. Maupassant, in turn, looked bewildered. He clearly had no idea what the atmosphere in the room was all about, only that d'Orcel and Lola couldn't take their eyes off one another.

The comte's face took on a fiercely dark aspect. He was paralyzed in fear and confusion. He placed the ringed hand up to his head. Was it shame he was feeling? Lola's gaze moved from his hand to his eyes and back again. She had a feeling she had indeed seen the ring when she'd been on her search of the suite. But she couldn't for the life of her remember where she'd seen it.

She walked forward, not taking her eyes from his. He surreptitiously tried to remove the ring from his smallest finger. As Lola was so much shorter than he in stature, her nose only came up to the knot in his tie. And it was thanks to the detail on this preciously knotted mauve-and-orange scarf that the image came to her. *A man on a stairwell.*

Madame Alexandra's. That's where it had been.

She'd thought she'd seen him somewhere before when he'd struck her, but she hadn't realized it was the same man she'd seen at Madame Alexandra's. What had Paul Antoine said about the meetings he had at the reading rooms and elsewhere? That these types of venues were useful for those with special tastes?

So let us add up what we know, Lola said to herself. *He is wearing Paul Antoine's ring, and he has discreet meetings at Madame Alexandra's.* The comte knew she had guessed his secret. He lowered his head, ashamed, mortified. *I didn't recognize him! I was too blinded by my theory! What a fool of a girl I am!* she thought. *He goes to the reading room to meet with young men, and one of them must be Paul Antoine!*

"I believe we've made a mistake," cried Lola to Maupassant. "It can't be the comte. Because he's . . ."

The comte turned and fell down into his armchair, crushed by the truth that was about to be revealed, his forehead in his hands. She paused as she searched for her words. "He's not . . . attracted to . . . women . . ."

She glanced at Andréa d'Orcel, who, in turn, looked to her husband with hatred in her eyes, allowing herself to fall down to her chair in front of her bureau.

"Why couldn't you have been more discreet about it?" she hissed at him through her teeth.

So she's known for some time. Everyone waited with bated breath for what would follow. Out of nowhere, Lola asked Charles d'Orcel if he was in possession of a firearm.

"Yes. I have a Devisme revolver given to me by my father."

He sprang up and moved toward the bureau.

"Don't move any farther!" shouted Maupassant. "Tell me where it is, and that will suffice!"

"In the bottom left-hand drawer," whispered d'Orcel, decimated.

Maupassant searched through the drawer without success. The weapon was no longer there. The comte raised his eyebrows in horror.

"I-I don't understand," he stammered. "It was there. It's always there. Nobody ever uses it. I keep it in the drawer as a matter of habit. I haven't ever fired it. Not once."

"Where do you keep the bullets?" demanded Lola as she removed the bloodied casing from her pocket, opening up the handkerchief so the comte could see.

As she did so, she heard the key in the door turn twice. They were now locked in.

38

REVELATIONS

Andréa d'Orcel, whom nobody had been paying much attention to for several minutes, had walked slowly over to the door and ensured none of them could leave.

She held d'Orcel's gun, with its dark walnut handle, looking at each of them with a sinister expression.

"What are you doing with that, my dear?" asked the comte.

"You will not get mixed up in this!" she said.

Lola could not believe the dramatic turn of events. She had to come up with a solution quickly if they were to all leave the suite alive.

Maupassant appeared to be detached from the situation, as though he weren't quite living it in the same way as everyone else in the room. Was he taking mental notes of all the goings-on for his next novel?

"Miss Fletcher is on her way," declared Lola, her voice rising. "We asked that she meet us here. You won't get very far if you fire that revolver, you know, and when she learns that you have us all trapped in this room, she'll go straight to the police."

The mention of the police had no visible effect on Andréa. She laughed bitterly. "There's nothing Miss Fletcher can do to me! I'm absolutely convinced of that!"

Maupassant suddenly left his trancelike state and entered one of cold anger. He threw himself at Andréa in the clumsiest of moves, and she banged the heavy weapon against his temple, grabbing his cheek at the same time. He was completely at her mercy.

"You're an impulsive one, my dear. You clearly don't know the strength of a woman, especially a mother!" she screamed.

"Where is Miss Fletcher? Is she in danger?" asked Maupassant.

"She's another one with pretensions, is she not? Did she truly believe I had no clue? I gave her what she had coming. She's out of the game now."

"You are speaking in clichés!" said Maupassant.

"Hush now, or I'll shoot, and you know I will. You're so very vain with your ideas of women! You believe me incapable? Well, why not ask Lambert's opinion on that? Ha! If you can find him, that is!"

It was at this moment that all became clear for our heroine. She sidled over to the bureau and picked up the framed portrait of the young uniformed gentleman. Eugène immediately came to her mind. Emotion soared through her body. *I've got it now! It's her! And it wasn't done to protect her husband . . . but her son! The murderess!*

"This is a madwoman we have here," said Maupassant.

"I told you to stop opening your stupid mouth," retorted the comtesse.

"No, she is far from mad," said Lola. "Don't you recognize this for what it is?"

"If you insist on speaking, I will pull this trigger," said the comtesse. "And the famous writer will be the first to fall. I need some time to determine what to do here."

Her voice was loud and cutting. She had transfigured entirely. She no longer played the part of the pretty wife of a comte. Her airs of nobility had disappeared without a trace. She was now a determined, strong, and wronged woman.

In the thick silence that followed, Lola made signs with her eyes toward Maupassant, who understood not one of them.

Finally, Lola spoke up. "Clara must have been in love with the young d'Orcel. What name did you bestow upon your son, madam?"

"Maxime," stated Maupassant.

"Don't you dare embroil my son in your sordid entanglements!"

Lola went ahead, not allowing the protestations of the comtesse to slow her down. "Maxime, in turn, was in love with Clara. Well, as much as a spoiled child from a rich family can be. They had intimate relations. It's as good a way as any to spend one's youth. Love of this kind with ancillaries is common enough among the nobility, and as a general rule, any results of such passion are swiftly dealt with, are they not?"

"Are you quite finished with this comedy?" exclaimed the comtesse. She stared at Lola, just as would a snake at its charmer. She barked, "That girl . . . that nobody . . ."

"That's right, is it not? What an impudent girl! She got it into her stupid head that the man might do the decent thing and marry her when she discovered she was with child! An innocent little fool she was! How did you get wind of it in the first place? Perhaps you are sufficiently close to your son to have sensed in him an altered mood? Or is it something to do with money? I fancy that to be far more likely! You had your eye on his accounts! You must have known what he was doing with his money! His bills and notes are all addressed to you and your husband, no doubt. I imagine he started spending a little more than was customary? Little trinkets, silk fans with mother-of-pearl, items of that sort? I'm just hazarding a guess, of course."

"That type of girl knows exactly how to maneuver herself! She found herself on her back all too easily. He won't have had to promise her much," she shrieked.

Lola, shocked by the comtesse's words, said, "But she wanted so much for him to be a part of her future!"

"She said Maxime adored her!" said the comtesse, mockingly. "And she didn't take to it too kindly when Maxime obeyed us and told her where to go with her demands! What did the silly little bitch think?"

The parallels with Lola's own recent worries with Eugène sickened her, but she said nothing, feeling humiliated.

"This is unbelievable," she whispered. "All women fall into the same trap! Every time! Do they really always believe it? Does it never fail? I have a lot of experience with men, and even I believe every word they pronounce! We all hope for a better life than our mothers lived before us! But can that really justify our own stupidity? I can picture well how deceived my Clara must have felt, for she always lived by the rules."

"Oh! She made such a scene here! To me!" the comtesse said. "Can you conceive of the insolence?"

"What would you have had her do? She was in a state of panic! She knew what lay ahead of her as a young woman on her own with a baby. She'd be sent away from the hotel, banished from all society, and forced to work the streets! Even her own people would disown her."

The comte was having difficulty following what was happening. "Andréa, my dear, please explain this to me! I follow not a word of it!"

"That's enough, Charles! Don't play the serene innocent! We can all see through it!"

"And so, it's true? She was expecting Maxime's child?" said the comte. "I can't even remember what she looked like . . ."

"She was very pretty, monsieur," said Lola. "And intelligent. And she had a name. Clara Campo."

"Quiet!" howled Andréa.

But Lola pressed on ferociously, "She was distraught at the situation she found herself in. She didn't want to deny her love for Maxime, so she decided to threaten Charles—in accusing him of having seduced her and impregnating her."

"I happened upon her in this very room! She was writing her dreadful list of threats here! On my own bureau!"

"Which explains her ink-stained finger," said Lola to Maupassant.

"Charles never knew a thing about it—not any of it," said the comtesse. "Whether the scandal involved him or me, it would have impacted our son's future in the same way. I couldn't let her get away with it."

"And so you spoke with Clara. You talked to her of a solution so often practiced in families such as yours. If the arrival of a child should be declared, you give a dowry to the girl and have her marry some local boy instead. And that's done and dealt with!"

The comtesse made no response.

"No? You didn't even try that? Oh! You went further still? A nice little concoction with the means to abort the child and a little money on top of that to stay quiet about it?"

"And what's wrong with that? What a windfall for a girl such as her! You cannot begin to comprehend how arrogant servant girls are these days."

"But Clara didn't want to abort her unborn child, did she? She said it was a sin. She was a practicing Catholic, Madame d'Orcel. A pious girl."

Andréa looked like she had forgotten where she was and what she was doing, but a part of her was still keeping up with Lola.

"And that's when you decided to kill her. But how did you learn of the lethal nature of the laurel family? Did you know of the way rats are traditionally poisoned in this region?"

"My husband has an incredible knowledge of botany," she declared triumphantly.

Maupassant added, "She knows her husband's works well, for she transcribes his notes for him. Yet I still fail to comprehend something. Transcribing is one thing, but how did you manage to get her to drink . . ."

The comtesse smiled bitterly.

"You wrote her a letter. And in the process, you stained your dress with ink, didn't you? You fixed a time and place to meet with her," said Lola.

"If you say so. You're certainly a headstrong young girl. Is that a trait of all women in this part of the world?" she said coldly.

Maupassant and the d'Orcels all stood facing Lola.

As the comtesse continued to speak, she held the revolver up against Maupassant's temple. "It's a good thing you're all exactly where I want you."

39

Nerium Oleander Laurus Rosa

And so, I reacquainted myself with the Sacré-Cœur cellars.

I found myself lying among a pile of dried leaves that had escaped from a large broken jar. I was in some sort of storage facility with labeled flasks and boxes on shelved walls. From what I could gather, it seemed I was in the orphanage apothecary and infirmary.

I started to wonder whether or not Andréa had played a role in Clara's death. Why had she toyed with me so? Did she even have a lover, or was it all just a story? And if so, why would she have told me a lie like that? I understood less than nothing.

And this whole time, as events were unfolding in suite 327 of the Hôtel Beau Rivage, I had no idea what was happening. I felt too weak to stand and was sneezing incessantly. My head spun, and I crawled along the floor, fear stricken, desperately assuming that my fate would be similar to that of poor Clara. But after several minutes, I was able to lurch to my feet.

I brushed off the dried leaves and powdered substances from my clothing while holding my breath before running over to the door and banging on it wildly. Nothing happened. Nobody heard me. The noise from the building site was so loud that I feared I'd be trapped in there for some time. After what seemed like an eternity, I heard a key turning in the door. It was pushed open with a rush.

"What are you doing in here? Who are you?"

It was a nun. She looked at me in what appeared to be a mixture of bewilderment and terror. She glanced at the floor and the broken jar and leaned in to examine it more closely.

"Watch out!" I cried. "It might be dangerous to inhale!"

She picked up some of the broken glass and threw it into a far corner before calmly wiping her hands on her robes.

"Indeed, it is quite dangerous," she said. "It's a poisonous powder. *Nerium oleander laurus rosa*. How long have you been in here breathing it in?"

"I cannot tell you. I-I fell asleep. I was sneezing quite violently when I awoke."

She stared at me worriedly and then helped me back outside to the garden. "Don't move. Please just sit here awhile. I don't know how much has entered your system, and so I'm going to have to give you an antidote that will cause you to be sick. It will stimulate your gag reflex. We need to do this just in case."

She disappeared for a few minutes and returned with a bottle of castor oil and made me swallow several large spoonfuls. She dug a small hole in a flowerbed, and it didn't take long for the oil to work its magic. I emptied my stomach into the earth. She covered everything up with fresh soil. I felt so shaken by the experience—never had I felt so ill. I couldn't stop my body from trembling.

"I want to go home."

She tried to stop me, but I broke free of her and stumbled off into the distance as fast as I could. I heard her shout, clearly hoping to reassure me, "If you feel your heart start to slow down, you must drink alcohol and inhale mint or ether! Try Mariani wine! It's recommended by the pope."

I left the grounds of the orphanage and reached Les Pavots in less time than I'd anticipated. I felt sick to my stomach as I ran, spitting onto the road as I passed the entrance to the Hôtel Central, hoping beyond hope that nobody would recognize me. I knew not to enter the house and shuffled instead to the outdoor privy. The castor oil had made me feel worse than I could have imagined, and I was hardly able to contain myself.

"What's going on out there?" shouted Rosalie from the kitchen window. "Have you caught the cholera?"

"No! I took some castor oil. It seems I might have been poisoned! Where's Mademoiselle Lola?"

"She went off with that letters man to the hotel. They're laying some sort of trap for the comte," cried Rosalie. "Charles, I believe his name was. They think he's the assassin! They met with that Paul fellow."

"Paul Antoine?"

"That's it! He was sent out to look for you. It was his mission!"

I felt momentarily relieved and headed to the kitchen to wash my hands and face in hot water. I asked Rosalie for a glass of Mariani, and just as she was pouring it, Paul Antoine appeared in the doorway.

"But where did you come from?" exclaimed Rosalie. "People are in and out of here like there's no tomorrow, and I can't keep up!"

"Oh my God, Gabriella! I've been looking for you everywhere! Lola was so concerned! Where have you been?"

"It's too long a tale to tell. I have to go. Rosalie, do you have anything mint flavored?"

She handed me a bottle of crème de menthe.

"That's just perfect! I'd like you to accompany me, Paul Antoine. We'll go and find them presently. I know now who killed Clara. It was the comtesse d'Orcel! This means our friends are in danger."

I hurried as quickly as I could down the hill to the Croisette, followed by an overemotional Paul Antoine.

40

A Tonic

With the revolver pressed firmly against the side of his head, Maupassant exchanged a look with Lola. They had to find a way of gaining some time. With every second that passed, they were closer to the comtesse completing her desire to murder them in cold blood.

"When all is said and done," Maupassant ventured, "I must declare that this is all quite ingenious and very daring! I can't even begin to unravel my thoughts on how you managed to kill Clara."

"Well, you lack imagination, my dear. I doubt very much that your disappearance will leave much of a hole in the literary world."

"That's very unkind," sulked Maupassant.

Andréa felt empowered. "Do you believe I'm about to give you your whole storyline for your next novel? I'm sure if you were to live to tell the tale, you'd make some money out of this!"

Lola stepped in with bitterness in her voice. "That night, there was a play held in the comte's honor at the Cercle Nautique. The comtesse showed herself out and about in society and talked with several of her acquaintances. And in her purse lay the vial, ready and waiting."

Lola shivered as she spoke, feeling repulsed.

"You installed yourself at the back of your box so your movements would attract fewer attentions. You left the building, and out into the cold you went in your evening dress. Is that right? You must have had some way of covering yourself, for you would have been too easily noticed otherwise," Lola continued relentlessly.

"You're quite clever! Yes, I wore a long-hooded cape. It covered my entire ensemble."

"You must have exited the building from the back door and walked . . . or run . . . from the Cercle via the Rue Bossu."

Andréa was by now hypnotized by Lola's words, correcting any slight errors, modifying specific details, and filling in the gaps. Almost indifferently, she explained, "The girl told me how to find her. I knew she shared a room, and I knew the other maid was out visiting with family that night."

She still seemed unable to pronounce Clara's name.

Maupassant came in at this point, inspired. "You knocked lightly on the door and waited, for she was expecting you! The *crumpled letter* . . . She must have let you in fairly quickly."

"Indeed, for they do not have the right to receive guests."

"And that's when you pretended to show her nothing but goodwill!"

"Ah! Here comes the novelist now," moaned the comtesse.

"It's just that I've heard so many stories like it! It really isn't all that original! You reassured little Clara and told her that it served no purpose at all to try to blackmail Charles. You said you understood her distress. You said you would speak to the comte on her behalf and force him into accepting her plight. After all, her child also belonged to your son!"

Lola listened to Maupassant with tears in her eyes, revolted by the duplicity of the comtesse and distressed to hear how her friend had been so duped in the last remaining moments of her life.

With disgust, the comtesse gave her response. "I managed to calm the girl. What credulity! She was no longer afraid. She sobbed in gratitude, falling into my arms."

Maupassant seized his chance to pursue his thoughts. "You told her that from that moment, she had to pay very special attention to her health and that of her child. She had to do everything she could to stay in excellent form. You declared that you would have a little house made ready for her until you could find them a better situation."

"And then you gave her . . . ," whispered Lola.

"A tonic," said Maupassant.

The comtesse finished the story, almost boasting. "Yes. A potion that had a dreadful taste, but which I had taken during my confinement with Maxime. It was a simple enough lie. And she believed me!"

Her condescending tone was difficult to hear as it resounded throughout the room.

"Clara gulped it down without ever suspecting it to be a concoction that might kill her," Maupassant continued.

The comtesse shuddered, possibly reliving the scene. Her state seemed more than perplexing.

"I didn't realize she'd suffer such searing pain. It all happened so quickly. She went into a convulsion almost immediately. She was moaning so loudly. I was very afraid someone would hear such a noise. I didn't want her to wake the other servants. I begged her to come with me, that we would seek out a doctor. I snatched up a bottle of absinthe from her neighbor's bedside table and supported her weight as we walked. My idea was to finish her off under the Pont de la Foux. I thought I'd pour the alcohol all over her and that it would be assumed that she'd died of a drunken episode."

"But she didn't make it even as far as the garden before collapsing, did she?" whispered Lola, tears now running freely.

Maupassant wanted so desperately to walk over to her, to console her, but the gun was still being pushed into the side of his head, and he dared not move a muscle.

"She fell. And so you dragged her over to that bush where I saw her. You doused her in the liquor. And you left her there. She was still alive," Lola continued.

"And when you came back to the theater and said you'd had a turn . . . that was what all that was about?" asked the comte. "And you sent me home ahead of you! You said you needed to take some night air! You were so agitated! I knew something was wrong!"

"It was! I had to go back! I didn't know whether she was dead or alive, did I? All I could do was hope we were finally rid of the filthy thing!"

As his wife finished her speech, d'Orcel looked at her with something of horrified admiration in his eyes. He threw himself at her feet, his eyes watering. "My dearest love! You are so brave! A genuine heroine! You killed to protect our child and our name! She is no assassin, I can assure you! She is as high and mighty as they come! Never will I ever be able to thank you enough for this!"

Maupassant watched this next act unfold with interest, but Lola looked down in contempt.

It was at this precise moment that Maurel attempted to enter the scene, knocking gently. He had been listening for some time from behind the door. This meant he had heard the comtesse make her admission of guilt and that he now knew Lola had been correct. But it hadn't been the husband . . . It had been the wife. *Cherchez la femme,* he thought, satisfied with his cultural notions, just before tapping softly on the door again.

Andréa d'Orcel kicked her husband as she reprimanded him, saying, "Get up, you scoundrel! What ridiculous behavior! You're trying to distance yourself from this, aren't you?"

After several more tentative knocks, Maurel refused to delay any longer and unlocked the door with his skeleton key. He failed to announce his imposition. The comtesse jumped in surprise when she saw him and pulled the trigger of her revolver at the same time. The bullet hit Maurel, and he screamed in agony as he collapsed to the floor.

"Oh no!" cried Andréa. "What an idea to arrive just now, my dear Maurel! I want no witnesses to what I am to do here."

"This plan of yours is getting more and more ridiculous!" said Lola. "He'll betray you. You'll swing for it, my dear comtesse! And I'll be in the front row!"

Andréa d'Orcel turned to Lola and shot her weapon again. Lola fell to the ground, wailing. Maupassant wanted to run to her aid, but he was next in the comtesse's firing line. Nobody dared move.

"My dear," she said to the comte. "Go and lock the door, if you would."

D'Orcel complied.

"Now go and take a look in that chest on my desk, and you'll find another revolver in there. Bring it to me."

The comte did so and handed her a small-barreled silver gun with fine engraving and a pearly ivory handle. So she had a second weapon she intended to implicate in her morbid death scene. A pool of blood was forming under Maurel. It was fast becoming a glossy sea of red, a glistening mirror of scarlet. His eyes were rolled back into his head, and he was shaking uncontrollably.

Andréa walked over to Lola, who, too, was quivering violently on the floor.

"This is the moment," she said to Maupassant. "I'm going to place this jewel of a revolver in your harlot's hand, and then she's going to shoot you with it, with my guidance, of course. As she shoots you, my husband will have the justification he needs for having shot her with our Devisme."

She thought out loud, looking down at her hands, a gun in each, and pointed toward Maurel with her foot.

"He already had to kill Maurel, because he entered the room and threatened us all trying to rescue this bag of filth, for he, too, had been having relations with the little whore!"

She stepped over to Lola and placed the pearly gun in her right hand. Lola allowed her to do it while maintaining her dying-swan act, for the bullet hadn't actually touched her.

She followed every single gesture the comtesse was making, her eyes half-open, and when the comtesse placed Lola's own finger on the trigger and pointed the barrel toward Maupassant, Lola jolted upright, wrested control of the smaller revolver, and knocked the comtesse off balance. But the older woman managed to pull the trigger. She missed her target, and the bullet hit a vase at the other side of the room, causing it to shatter into a thousand pieces in a loud burst. The water puddled onto the floor, surrounded by a mess of tulips, hyacinths, and lilies.

Maupassant hurled himself toward the comtesse in an attempt to grab her weapon, but he slipped on the water, which was spreading slowly across the wooden floor. Lola pointed the smaller gun at Andréa.

Andréa screamed in fury and threw herself at Lola. Maurel lifted himself up onto an elbow and started to panic about the amount of blood flowing from his injury.

"Can't you see this is over?" shouted Lola as she struggled with the comtesse.

The comtesse fired another shot, this time hitting the mirror above the fireplace. Maurel's body shriveled in pain. He reacted more strongly than when he'd actually been hit. The reason? The pain of seeing one of his best suites destroyed, no doubt. Lola broke free of the comtesse but lost her footing and fell onto Maupassant. He took her into his arms and threw her onto the sofa as the delirious and wild Andréa d'Orcel looked on.

It was at this point that the door opened for a second time.

41

HURRY!

I hurled myself into the suite followed closely by Madame Davies and Paul Antoine. The scene was indescribable. It took several moments before I understood.

Lola had a trickle of blood running from her forehead down to her cheek, pooling on her chin. The sight of it almost brought me to my knees. The manager, Maurel, was bathed in his own blood. I was overcome by what can only be described as the most violent emotion.

The comte d'Orcel, his face wet with tears, was slumped on the ground, powerless to do anything against his wife, who was now loading the last of her bullets into her revolver. He turned his head toward us, and upon seeing Paul Antoine, his cheeks flushed. He then turned away, as if he had no further interest in his presence. Although I had registered that initial sense of shame, I didn't understand the reaction. I turned to look into the eyes of Paul Antoine and noted that there was amazement and confusion there as he exchanged looks with the comte. It must have only lasted a mere fraction of a second.

The comtesse was evidently distracted by our sudden arrival. She gawked at me as though I had risen from the dead. Maupassant took this as an opportunity to jump on her, knocking her off balance and pushing her to the floor. Her weapon slipped out of her hand and slid across the polished parquet.

I dashed over to them and kicked the revolver further out of arm's reach. I undid my belt as Maupassant held her down by the waist. He helped me tie her hands behind her back, knotting the belt tightly.

"You!" screamed the comtesse, appalled. "How did you do this? How is this possible?"

Lola made her way toward us and helped us attach the comtesse firmly to a chair. During this time, Maurel studied his injuries and noted that they were but surface wounds. His face showed the relief he must have been feeling.

"Madame Davies," he said. "Please run and fetch Dr. Buttura. I presume he must be at the hospital at this hour. And you must keep what you have witnessed here a secret."

The housekeeper left the room in a calm and orderly manner, duty bound. Lola stayed within close proximity to the comtesse, who had walled herself in the deathliest of silences.

"Madam," she said to her. "You took the life of a young lady in her prime. And not satisfied with her death alone, you repeated the same murderous act with Amédée? Why?"

"Ha! He had every intention of blackmailing me! He saw me in the gardens that night. He was entering the hotel and must have been about to start work."

"Ah! And that's why you sold a necklace to Siegl's! You needed to make some quick money so you could buy his silence! But you had a second plan! You didn't want to give in to his blackmail attempts, so you took him to the slaughter!"

The comtesse's eyes moved toward a small mauve satin clutch bag sitting atop a trunk. I felt a desperate need to walk over to the bag to check its contents, but nobody in the room dared move, including myself.

"That's his poor luck! He found himself in the wrong place at the wrong time."

"No, he didn't! That was you! You were in the wrong place at the wrong time, because these acts of yours will forever haunt you."

Maupassant added, "The dead always return. Clara and Amédée will come back to you every night of your life."

"This is all very Edgar Allan Poe, isn't it? Do you really imagine I believe in all the *'Le Chat Noir'* nonsense?" She shrieked icily and spoke like a woman possessed. "You're all fools if you believe these were my first kills! That stupid girl . . . and a horseman?"

She stared at me in triumph.

"What are you trying to tell us, madam?" asked Maupassant.

I answered for her. "She means the orphanage. Poison. I went to my meeting with the comtesse at the bathhouse, and then I followed her. She went as far as the orphanage. She has her own key, because she's one of the patronesses. Someone struck me over the head. Well, when I say someone . . . ," I said, staring at the comtesse, who had a satisfied smile on her face. "I woke up in the Sacré-Cœur infirmary. They keep a lot of medicines in there. A lot of poisons too."

Lola and Paul Antoine whispered at the same time, *"Nerium oleander laurus rosa."*

Maupassant barked angrily, "Just stop with the mystery of it all!"

Lola took over, expressing what I had certainly never dared to imagine. "How was she so sure of herself when it came to the specific use of this plant? Do you think she relied solely on her husband's research? She tested it first! A real-life, full-scale test! How practical it is to have access to that many young children as a . . . great patroness! She managed to set up the experiment *in situ* on living guinea pigs!"

"The orphans . . . ," whispered Maupassant.

The comtesse rolled her eyes. "Well done! You got it right the first time!" she howled.

"The orphans?" I screamed. "That's why in January they all . . . My God!"

This disgusting discovery turned my stomach and reminded me of the castor oil I'd swallowed. The overwhelming feeling to vomit was too strong, and I had to run to the bathroom and their luxurious sink. I could hear Lola muttering in devastation.

"Anna and her friend Adèle. Anna almost died . . ."

"No!" cried out Maupassant in horror, his hand held to his mouth. "It's impossible. Have you no conscience at all, madam?"

"I most certainly have one, my dear! It's just that I know what is important in life and what's not! I make a real contribution to society. These little vermin are quite capable of spreading cholera and the like wherever they go! The mayor should be thanking me!"

The tears now flowing from Lola's eyes met with the blood on her cheeks to form a light-pink liquid, which she tried to wipe away with her sleeves. She hissed, "Your name will be forever sullied by this, and I will walk to Paris if I have to, just to watch you swing."

I approached Maurel, who was now sitting on an armchair, looking very pale. His shoulder looked to be bleeding heavily.

"We need to make a tourniquet of some kind," I said.

Lola, not taking my words into account, marched over with determination toward the door.

"Where are you going?" asked Maurel.

"To find Valantin, of course! It seems that everyone has forgotten that what has been happening here in this room is, in fact, a matter for the police!"

Before leaving, Lola glided toward the comtesse and stepped behind her, taking the older woman's hands into her own. Was this compassion? If so, I found it rather unsettling.

Their hands intertwined, and something that looked like a miniature lightning bolt passed from Lola's hands into those of the comtesse. Lola had given her something. A small object . . . Something shiny . . .

What was it? It had obviously been hidden on Lola's person, perhaps in the folds of her dress. The comte stepped over to join his wife and shooed Lola away impatiently before attempting to put a comforting arm around Andréa's shoulders. The comtesse leaned forward, almost collapsing into him as she sobbed.

We left them to their intimate torment and walked out of the room. As we passed through the doorway, I was surprised to see a final, almost masked glance between the comte and Paul Antoine. Lola followed us out into the hallway, groaning under her breath with sourness, contradicting her very recent caring gestures toward the comtesse.

"She's crying because she's failed, not because she regrets the horrors of the acts she has committed."

In his office, Maurel lay on his Louis XV chaise longue, taking care not to stain the fabric. Dr. Buttura had arrived by this point and was seeing to the wound with the greatest of attentions.

"Strangely enough, I was talking to my friend Isnard about dressing gunshot wounds earlier," said the doctor.

"The revolver went off by accident," said Maurel.

Lola, annoyed, opened her mouth to speak, but Maupassant hushed her up, and I took her by the arm and pinched her.

As none of us contradicted this version of events, Buttura asked no questions and continued to see to Maurel's injuries.

"It is only superficial. You won't even be able to see a mark here within the next few days. Now the wound is disinfected and dressed, you should take some time off. Please adhere to these recommendations."

As he stood to leave, he turned to us and said, "And if you're still interested in the fate of the little Campo girl, it turns out she was poisoned. Everything is written in my report, and I've signed the burial permit. The case is still open, however. I believe the police still have much work to do."

As we all failed to react to his words, he further clarified, "Don't any of you want to know what poison it was?"

After yet more silence, he stated, "*Nerium oleander laurus rosa.* It's a poison that we all have quite readily available to us should we so wish to use it! For it grows in most of our gardens! I will take my leave of you now."

He left, visibly saddened by what he assumed was our lack of interest in what he had told us. As Maurel dressed himself, he asked that we all keep the whole business about the shootings a secret and not breathe a word of it outside the hotel. Everything would work out just fine. His hotel would be safe from ruin, the future of businesses in Cannes secure, the protection and reputation of the town intact.

But Lola wouldn't hear anything of it. She fought against him, refused to be convinced by his ideas on the subject. Even as Maurel tried to support his view by stating that Lola wouldn't be able to happen upon a richer clientele if the winterers were to flee Cannes, she wouldn't budge.

"I couldn't care a jot!" she shouted.

"But you'll lose everything!"

"I don't have anything to lose, Maurel. Do you really believe that my house or my jewels even compare when it comes to the life of my dear childhood friend? And the short lives of those orphans? And even that of Amédée, who had but one wish in his life: to cherish Clara?"

"I think you're going to have to be flexible," said Maupassant with a slightly sharp tone to his voice. "This is simply the way of the world."

"I expected so much more than this from you! You really disappoint me! But I guess you're more a part of their world than mine."

"That's not true! It's just that I know how the music goes! I've seen this played so often before, *Belle Amie!*"

I walked to Lola's side and took her hands in mine. "Listen, this is about justice, not vengeance. Don't allow your feathers to get ruffled here. Let's leave it now to the professionals. We have good policemen and judges, and they will get to the bottom of all this. I know they don't always act as we would wish, but they can take over now."

She resisted me somewhat, but I felt her calm under the caress of my soothing voice. She looked to Maupassant in sadness, and to Maurel with a feeling of powerlessness before leaving the room and, on her way out, kissing both cheeks of Paul Antoine, who, in turn, failed to react one way or another.

I followed her, linking her arm into my own. I felt that she required the presence of a friend, and I was proud to be one to her.

She turned and slammed the door to Maurel's office in defiance. It was perhaps her way of having the last word, but I was sure she would do as she had been asked and not breathe a word of our experience to anyone.

Before leaving the hotel, we took a detour to the basement so she could collect her dress from the laundry basket where she'd left it. She quickly changed, not speaking a word, before we set off together homeward.

42

JUSTICE?

We ambled slowly down the Rue de Cannes and crossed over the railway line.

Lola vented her anger. "I don't want you to think that I believe in the whole 'eye for an eye, tooth for a tooth' thing, Gabriella, but for once in my life, I would like to see some real justice done here. The scales are too far tipped in the wrong direction. We need to balance them out, don't you think?"

To hear her use my given name like that provoked in me a quite devastating sensation. It felt like vertigo. A dizzying happiness. My knees knocked beneath my skirts.

I know how ridiculous that sounds! As if I were nothing but a fifteen-year-old girl. To be in such a state just because she had uttered my name?

I tried so hard to remain calm, to take control of myself, but my pulse was so quickened, I felt like I was soaring.

"But you reached your aim nonetheless, no?" I managed to say. "You made a promise to Clara that you would uncover the truth, and we now know who killed her. That is all down to your determination and your courage."

She glanced at me, the sadness so clear in her eyes. "You are so kind. Of course, I am contented that we understand the truth behind Clara's death. But I am still so grieved that it will not be fully avenged. I don't believe that murderess will ever really pay for her crimes. Not with our justice system. Don't you see how unjust that is? All those babes . . ."

I could find no answer for her. Truth be told, I was focused on mastering my own sentiments and did not yet feel ready to partake in such a serious debate. We walked the rest of the way to Les Pavots in silence.

Rosalie had prepared a hot soup for us, and we perched ourselves around the kitchen table, eating quickly and with relish. I sensed that Lola was enjoying Rosalie's attentions and had almost reverted to a childlike state, for it was Rosalie, although often harsh with her words and short-tempered, who reassured Lola the most in this world.

I helped Lola up to her bed and placed Anna in the satin sheets next to her. They were both so cozy and warm as I tucked the covers in beneath them and blew out the lamps.

I climbed up to my own bedchamber under the eaves and, with my ink and papers, set about writing the novel that you read now. I started with my meeting with Mademoiselle Filomena Giglio and Monsieur de Maupassant, and then decided to begin the work with an imaginary reenactment of what might have been Clara Campo's final moments in this life. It's what I had envisioned had happened, before the truth was revealed.

As I later lay in bed, the rain on the rooftop kept me from falling asleep.

The monotonous symphony forced images into my mind. Clara's body, the corpses of children in the gardens of the orphanage, Amédée and the dark-red hole in his head . . .

As I rose the following morning, I looked out the window to see that the torrent of rain had turned our street into a veritable river. But as I descended the stairs, I was surprised to see that Maupassant had managed to make his way to our home, despite the despicable weather, and was sitting opposite an exhausted-looking Lola at the table, enjoying breakfast. Anna was joyfully serving them hot chocolate.

As she saw me, Anna flew up and jumped into my arms before hopping down and disappearing from the room. She clattered down the stairs, hollering with excitement as she did so, "A pot of tea for Miss Fletcher! She's awake!"

"You're an early riser!" I said to Maupassant. "And quite soaked, I see. I can hardly believe you braved this storm! I suspect the news you have must be worth the effort."

"She's dead," said Lola frankly, although with a glazed look on her face, as if deep in thought. It was as though she were saying, *Finally, we have justice.*

Maupassant explained. "When you left, I admit to feeling bewildered and ashamed of Maurel's attitude. It is one thing to know and appreciate what happens among the upper classes but quite another to participate in it. I knew I couldn't be a part of that. Those foul people simply brush everything under the carpet, and the police help them.

"And so I decided, without allowing Maurel to know anything of my plan, that I would let a few of my journalist friends in on some of the details of what had transpired. For my friends certainly have a flair for scandal! I mean, it's how they earn their crust, after all! I knew that I'd only have to let slip a couple of morsels and that they'd be all over the affair like a rash. They would uncover enough to embroil the d'Orcels in the biggest story this town has seen in some time!

"Just as I was about to leave Maurel to his own devices, the door to his office opened, and in walked Charles d'Orcel. He was haggard-looking, a broken man. He was crying, full of intense remorse, but also in a wild panic that hadn't manifested itself until this point.

"His wife had just taken the very same poison she'd administered to Clara and had died in his arms in total agony. He couldn't fathom how she had found the liquid, as she hadn't moved from the seat. As he rested his head on her lap, she broke free of him, managed to untie the knots around her wrists, and swallowed down the liquid in a single gulp. It means the poison was already on her person. In her hands.

"After hearing this, I decided to help Maurel and do things his way. I accepted that I wouldn't need to add any fuel to the fire. I believed that Andréa got her just deserts. And so, here I am this morning, to find out what Mademoiselle Lola feels about all this."

I observed a keen triumph in Lola's eyes. She glanced at me, challenging me to open my mouth. *And what of it?* she seemed to say. *I didn't force her to drink it.*

So that's what she'd gone into the bathroom for! It wasn't for the towel at all! That was the miniature lightning bolt I'd seen.

"Paul Antoine had the exact same reaction as I. When he learned of the comtesse's death, he, too, promised to keep the event hushed up," Maupassant continued.

"If you're asking for my opinion," said Lola, "I don't mind giving it. I would have much preferred a trial. The comtesse d'Orcel in the stocks. She was a murderess of the very worst kind, and it would have been a good opportunity to let the general public know what day-to-day life is like for maids!

"As for Clara, I feel as though her death has been avenged. I am glad that that dreadful d'Orcel woman went the same way as her too. I'm delighted it was the same poison and the same torment."

43

OBITUARY

In the *La Revue de Cannes* obituary section, there appeared two very different announcements.

One mentioned a young Italian woman from Cannes who was well known on the Suquet, dying of cardiac arrest, and it spoke of her brilliance at the La Ferrage. There were just two lines for the death of Clara Campo. It made no mention of the fact that she worked as a chambermaid at the famous hotel on the Croisette.

The other, in the most elegant arabesque print and outlined in a black frame, evoked the sad and unexpected passing of Madame Comtesse Andréa d'Orcel de Montejoux following a long period of sickness. Added was a vivid description of the ever-beautiful blue skies of the French Riviera under which she spent her final few days in peace.

Both obituaries failed to note the address at which these women died.

The deaths of the orphans of the Sacré-Cœur never made it into any publication.

44

BURIAL

The comtesse's funeral service was discreet. Well, as discreet as a full mass at the Eglise du Bon-Voyage could be. As the curate drew his homily to an end and the large walnut coffin with mother-of-pearl insets was lowered into the freshly dug earth, another burial was taking place at the far end of the cemetery in an area separated off from the rest by a small hedgerow. It was the communal plot. The paupers' grave. A few families from the Suquet had come to see Claro Campo off on her final journey.

Over the hours that followed, there were a great many comings and goings at Les Pavots, including from Maupassant, who had a fantastic tale to tell. At the comtesse's funeral, Maupassant had kept close to the comte, under the guise that he was lending his support. At the end of the stilted ceremony, d'Orcel took Maupassant to one side. They stepped inside the front carriage, away from prying eyes.

"Do you think anyone will divulge anything?" He needed promises from him that Clara's family, Lola, and all other witnesses would not make the truth public.

"I cannot speak for them," said Maupassant.

"Do you imagine a little nest egg might do the trick?"

"Oh no, not a little one. Think of the value of the name d'Orcel! How much is that worth?"

"That's what I thought," said the comte bitterly. "It always comes down to a question of money in the end." He pulled out his papers.

"You are right. It is a somber state of affairs," declared Maupassant, laughing to himself at the irony of it all.

"I'm going to sign over two bank orders," d'Orcel decided as he wrote. "There will be one for the girl's mother. As for that whore that you mix with . . . well . . . I imagine she wants even more than the mother! This whole business will bleed me dry, but I would like to respect the last wishes of my wife."

He showed Maupassant the sums he had written. Maupassant hadn't wished to enter into such bargaining at first, but a thought suddenly occurred to him, and a plan began to form.

Maupassant noted the amounts on the bank orders, sighed with disappointment, and made ready to step outside the vehicle. "You can contact me again when you're ready to make a genuine gesture."

"Wait!" D'Orcel held out his hand to stop Maupassant, quickly added a zero to the end of the figures, then showed him the new amounts.

Maupassant gave another passing glance at the numbers and shook his head. "Below a certain amount and there is little purpose in wasting my time." Again, he made for the door.

"Is that what you really feel?" d'Orcel asked, angered.

Maupassant paused and waited. Finally, d'Orcel blew out a heavy breath and added another zero. Delighted, Maupassant took the notes and gave the comte his word of honor that nothing of the events that had taken place behind the closed doors of the Beau Rivage and beyond would be uttered by any of them in the near or distant future.

The atmosphere at Les Pavots was decidedly cheerful. Maupassant had had the orders cashed and had given both envelopes to Lola. There was a real fortune in those envelopes. It was not only enough to help out the Campo family, but also enough to buy the house from Philémon Carré-Lamadon.

Maupassant was boasting. Rosalie and I clinked glasses in celebration. Sherry was jumping from one lap to the next, and Anna was giggling in delight. Only Lola remained quiet.

Finally, she announced, "Please excuse me. I have a letter I must write." Then she returned to her bedchamber mysteriously.

45

FACTITIOUS JOY

Upon our return from Madame Campo's to deliver the money and posting Lola's letter, I helped Lola with one of her hats, pinning ribbons and silk flowers to it and talking happily of our newfound fortune.

"Just picture Philémon's face when he finds out you've bought the house!"

"Come now, Miss Fletcher."

The way she said my name sent a shiver down my spine.

"Do you really envisage I'm going to accept the money? This death money! How many people had to die for this? This money is supposed to compensate for Clara, Amédée, and all those dead bambinos? You know me so little!"

"What? I am totally at sea, Lola."

"I'm going to put the money in the bank for safekeeping."

"But you could buy this house!"

"No. The money isn't mine." She looked at Anna, who had joined us and was now playing with the cat. "Anna, go and see if Rosalie needs your help."

Anna jumped up and hurtled down to the kitchen, with Sherry sprinting to keep up.

"I don't follow when you say it isn't yours," I said.

"I'm putting it in a merchant bank in the name of Anahita Martin. You see? I remember her official name. It will be her dowry. I believe it right that the money we have as a result of Clara's death should go to save a little orphan. I mean, we're adults, are we not? Why should we need d'Orcel's charity? We'll manage well enough without it."

Taking the d'Orcel money to live a better life, to pay for her house, to pull herself out of the misery she was in, was beyond her.

"But . . . but how?" I stammered.

"I have plenty of ideas! You see all this furniture? Well, I'll sell them! And then there's my soap! Paul Antoine has agreed to let me borrow a workshop. I can make and store them there! It's right next to his house."

I noted her use of the word *I*.

"How exciting this will be! I've never been inside a bank before! But now I have come of age, I can do whatever I like! Life can be so exhilarating!"

I turned my face away and put the hat back in its box. I didn't trust her. Yet she was one of the best people I'd ever met. But I couldn't help dwelling on the fact that she was putting her generosity toward others above her feelings for me. Did she think so little of me? She knew that without the house, we would be separated.

She laughed giddily at me, and I returned a smile, but it was factitious joy. I couldn't comprehend this sudden madness from Lola. Why was she behaving with such wild abandon when she knew we would soon be without a roof over our heads?

"Why the long face?" asked Lola. "Come on! We need to live in the moment!"

That evening, I managed to express some optimism following several glasses of champagne. There was something frenzied in the way I spoke. I laughed too loudly. I sang. Maupassant gazed upon me in awe. But I knew that these were my final moments of happiness with her. I wanted to drink to forget.

46

DISCREET GOODBYES

We knew that Maupassant would be taking the express 14:44 train to Paris on Tuesday afternoon. With further rumors of cholera spreading throughout towns in the southeast, Maupassant had decided he'd spent more than enough time in Cannes.

"Besides, I've had it!" he'd declared. "I can't even walk two steps down a street without having to take my hat off to someone, bow to another, greet someone else. There are so many dinner invitations. It's all quite tiresome. My next book is about to come out, and my presence is required in Paris. I believe we're set to have the most pleasant of springs, and it's about time I was out of my woolen coat."

Lola and I took Anna to the station so we could all wave him off. The little one was up front in the landau, for she adored being as close as she could get to the horse.

Lola had decked herself up in her most flamboyant red finery. She took up most of the space in the back, for the dress had to spread out to avoid creasing.

We parked the carriage behind all the other vehicles awaiting or dropping off passengers in front of the station.

There was a real crowd gathered on the platform.

François spotted us from a distance and waved at us to join him. Well, he waved at me, in any case, for he wouldn't lower himself to acknowledge Lola. He was still vexed with her for having forced entry into his master's house as he was writing, for it just wasn't the proper thing in his view.

Several admirers had come to the station to say their adieus to Maupassant. A whole host of upper-class women surrounded the young writer in addition to his mother, Laure le Poittevin, and his brother, Hervé, who had returned from his trip to the mountains.

Lola must have felt intimidated, for she expressed a desire to keep her distance from the gathering. Maupassant was so occupied with his friends that he failed to see us. When he did finally catch sight of us, he signaled us to come forward. His mother observed his gesture and turned to look. She appeared inquisitive and sardonic in equal measure. Lola demurred, and Maupassant was soon caught up in saying further goodbyes to more friends.

I focused solely on the pleasure I was feeling at being out and about with Lola and Anna.

Though my future remained uncertain, I marveled at how very far I'd come.

I recalled that desperate time, and yet it seemed so far in my past, as if years and years had gone by. That fateful night, I had walked beyond the Villa des Dunes and La Réserve restaurant to the tip of the peninsula just in front of the cross opposite the fort on the Île Sainte-Marguerite.

It was a clear evening; the moon was full, and its reflection shone on the surface of the water. A sea breeze stirred the dry grass beneath my feet. There was nobody else present at that late hour. Perhaps a few fishermen were spending the night in their huts, but I didn't spot a soul. The odors from the surf mixed with the pittosporum invaded my nostrils. It tickled them slightly.

I was determined. I bent down to the ground and started filling the pockets of my clothing with pebbles and rocks. I would drown. Hand my body back over to nature. The fish would make a feast of my corpse. But I was a good swimmer, and so I had to take every precaution to ensure I wouldn't resurface.

And that was when a sheet of newspaper, *Le Littoral*, blew toward me and got trapped under my foot. It was as if destiny had spoken to me. I screwed it up into my fist, but suddenly, I faltered, spun around on myself, and plunged into the water. It was so very cold.

I struggled to the surface and gulped down air as my body dealt with the shock, and the waves splashed around my hips, trying to engulf me before the tide pulled me farther out to sea. The weight in my skirt pockets started to pull me under, but the stones were slipping out . . .

I did everything a person is not supposed to do in a situation such as this. I coughed, spluttered. I panicked. I felt an unforeseen urge. I didn't want to die. The sheet of newspaper balled up in my hand . . . I had to read it.

My foot touched the bottom, and I pushed myself to the surface, swimming as best I could to the shore and pulling myself out of the waters. I was drenched, miserable, and in a pitiful state.

I attempted to open the scrunched-up piece of newspaper, but my hands trembled too much. It was impossible to read in the light, despite the moon being bright, for there were no gas lamps on that part of the coastline.

But this had now become vital to me. I needed to know what message destiny had sent my way. I managed to run to La Réserve restaurant without being seen. I got close enough to read under the artificial lights dotted around the building.

Among a list of the latest winterers to have arrived, advertisements for a range of medications, and rental announcements, they were there—the words that were to set my fate in motion. The position that needed filling at Les Pavots with Mademoiselle Giglio.

I went back to my rented accommodation via back-end streets and unlit passageways, as far away as I could from the well-trodden paths of Cannes. I no longer wanted to die.

The very next day, I presented myself to Lola.

I no longer resembled that woman who'd tried to take her own life that night. Thoughts of death never crossed my mind these days. A lady with a heart of gold had replaced one who had more gold than she knew what to do with. I had so many aspirations now. I wanted to write what we had all lived through, and I felt I had a mission. I also had every intention of staying near Lola and saving her from herself.

I would make sure we both had our feet on the ground, but I did wonder how I would do it without a home, a job, or any money. There didn't seem to be any clear solution to my problems. They were impossible to resolve. Inextricable. They could be summarized in a single question: How was I to stay with my Lola Deslys?

47

A RISKY GAMBLE

The next morning, several police officers and a state bailiff stood outside the front door, banging on it wildly. The order had come from Philémon.

They had come to sequester all the furniture, for it now belonged to Carré-Lamadon, the proprietor of the house. It had come into his possession at the same time as he'd acquired the property. He had stated that he wished to protect it from theft—theft perhaps committed by his tenant before her notice period was complete. They placed ribbons and labels on almost all the items of furniture as well as the soft furnishings. After they had left, Lola sat cross-legged on the floor, refusing outright to use a single one of Philémon's armchairs.

I kneeled by her side and tried to add a spark of humor to the situation, but my irony reserves had run dry. This meant she couldn't sell her furniture, and it was the only concrete plan she'd come up with so far.

Anna snuggled into Lola, and Sherry jumped up onto her shoulder. The three of them were so closely intertwined that it was difficult to distinguish who was who.

Suddenly, I heard a horse and carriage draw up noisily outside. It must have been traveling at some speed. I shivered and thought immediately of Philémon. Had he come to provoke Lola?

But it was an anonymous carriage.

A woman climbed out, helped by the horseman. She was alone, veiled, and dressed in black. She looked around, and even though her face was covered, it wasn't difficult to feel the condescension and scorn emanating from her.

Rosalie was in the pantry, trying to pack up the soaps into crates, and hadn't heard the carriage pull up. And so the children took it upon themselves to rush down the staircase to meet her.

Lola and I looked at each other. She seemed somewhat relieved, and I couldn't fathom why she should feel such a sentiment. She strode to our office, placed herself in the seat behind our "bureau," and picked up one of my quills.

"Do exactly as I say. And don't be dazzled by anything that might happen. I'm going to say very little, but I'm going to try to look inspired. Do as I do. Try to speak as little as possible. Don't sit down. Be confident."

I felt quite astounded and went to stand by her side. I watched as a slight smile formed at the edge of her mouth.

"Come in, madam!" we heard Anna cry, clearly very proud of the responsibility of her new role.

In a wave of citronella and the rustling of brocade, the high-class gentlewoman walked into the lounge and appeared revolted at what she saw. She hesitated, seeming to regret having come. It didn't look as though she'd be ready to remove her veil any time soon.

Lola didn't move from where she was sitting but called the woman through.

I stepped out of our little room to greet her with the assurance of the woman I had been in a previous life. I took both her hands, attempting to put her at ease.

"Come in, come in, my dear. Allow me to present Mademoiselle Deslys, our . . . expert. My name is Fletcher. And for what reason do we have the honor of your visit today?"

"I am Maria Alexandrovna, the grand duchess . . ."

I couldn't believe it! I stared openmouthed before remembering myself and curtsying with reverence. The probability of seeing her at Les Pavots was so infinitely small that I hadn't recognized her. And I had so often seen her portrait in the paper and even met her once at the Clarences'.

Lola remained motionless, her brow furrowed. She was playing her role quite brilliantly; it's just that I was baffled as to what role it was.

"Say no more, Your Imperial Highness," I said, and turned to Anna. "Go ask Rosalie for a tray of tea and scones."

I felt so nervous. I invited the lady to follow me farther into the room and pulled out a chair opposite Lola for her to take a seat. She hesitated, and I leaned in to Lola's ear and whispered, "She is sister to Alexander III, the tsar. She's Bertie's sister-in-law. But make no allusions to it!"

Lola looked at me with a knowing smile. I was very worried that she wasn't taking this visit as seriously as she should. I offered the grand duchess the chance to take a seat again, but she refused.

"It is a great honor that you should call upon us. How can we be of assistance to you?"

She launched into a speech that I found rather confusing, for it was something to do with a letter.

"I'm sure you can only imagine the secrecies and mysteries in the microcosm that is the world of the winterers here in Cannes. We're talking state secrets that touch every royal family in Europe! Rumors circulate incessantly, but we more often than not are able to separate truths from lies. Don't forget that we have the very best informers money can buy."

She inclined her head slightly toward Lola.

"This is all about avoiding scandal. For attempting to cover a blemish with face powder never really works, does it? It always shows through, in my experience."

Lola rose and walked slowly out into the lounge and over to the window, looking downward to the Hôtel Central as if she didn't have a care in the world.

The grand duchess made a gesture, almost in supplication. "Madam . . ."

Lola clearly savored the moment, for I watched a shiver run over her body through her thin and dusty cotton blouse. She must have adored being called madam. What was I seeing here? Where had this newfound ease of Lola's come from? I believe I was still in a state of shock as I spoke.

"Please explain the purpose of your visit, and I am certain that Madame Deslys will find it within herself to be of service to you."

The grand duchess seemed to lose all her confidence. She lowered her head and removed her veil. Her voice was shaking as she appeared to become irritated.

"You said you had some precious information for me?"

Lola waltzed back into the small room with an assured step and addressed our guest.

"I need some information from you first," she said decidedly and, to my ears, quite insolently.

I could hardly stand to watch the scene unfold. She waved her hand in front of Lola with negligence.

"I will attempt to answer you, I suppose!"

"How is it you find yourself in such a precarious situation?"

Oh my! How did she dare? Where was she going with this?

"It is rather embarrassing . . . ," replied the grand duchess, who seemed to be following the situation with full comprehension.

"And what is its value?"

"I cannot put a price to it. It was offered as a gift to Catherine of Aragon by Henry VIII in 1519. It was to demand her forgiveness for a bastard child he had fathered with his mistress. I was foolish enough to wear them to one of Baron Lycklama's balls."

Destiny takes us down such sinuous roads, does it not? I remember Lola having talked about the baron's famous masked balls when I'd first met her. There was something about it in the paper. A picture of her! Yes! The grand duchess had been there with her husband! And she was wearing Catherine of Aragon's jewelry! Beautiful diamonds and other precious stones.

I understood that a ferocious deal was about to be made and decided that I could serve no greater purpose than diving in at the deep end and getting involved with the figures. I had to give the impression that I knew what I was talking about. I didn't have much of an idea, but I knew that when it came to money, I would fare much better than Lola.

"When you say you cannot put a price to it, you mean it's priceless, don't you? And how much does priceless actually represent to you? I must insist on your putting a number on it, because, you see, our commission here . . ."

She looked so relieved to be done with the airs and graces and to finally be getting down to business.

"You name your price. This is a question of honor for me. Of course, these days, honor can be monetized."

Even the smallest stone in the crown jewels had to be worth a fortune. I couldn't keep up with my own thoughts. I wondered how much we could ask, still not knowing how and why we were in such a position.

The grand duchess was now sitting on the old straw chair and had abandoned her arrogant demeanor entirely. Sherry was sitting on her lap, playing with the black taffeta fringing on her dress.

I took a leaf of vellum paper and dipped my quill in the ink. I wrote down a six-figure sum, my heart racing. It was the amount it would cost us to buy Les Pavots and added on to that the cost of a landau and horse. I showed it to Lola, and she batted her eyelids—her way of telling me she approved. I slid the paper over to the grand duchess.

I exchanged a look with Lola, my eyes full of hope.

A stillness ensued. The only noise we could hear were the swarms of swifts outside that had invaded the town only the day before.

Lola moved back into the lounge and pulled out a wooden box from one of her trunks. She searched through it calmly at first and then turned it upside down, scattering the contents on the floor. She fumbled through the mess of jewelry—bracelets, necklaces, faux diamonds, tiaras, brooches—trying to separate precious metals from gaudy fakery.

The grand duchess rose to her feet, almost suffocating in anticipation and apprehension. Lola picked up a gold pendant earring between her fingertips, its huge diamond swinging in the light.

The grand duchess and I both returned to our seats in surprise. I had to force myself to take on a neutral tone of voice. I couldn't show our new client that I was in as much shock as she was. It was here! An earring purchased by Henry VIII! In front of our very eyes! *Oh my! How did she do it? How in the devil did she do it?*

Just then I remembered! It had happened a few weeks earlier. I'd seen her putting something shiny in that wooden box of hers! And what about the letter she'd sent the day before?

The grand duchess removed a banking draft from her bag, already signed and stamped with a royal seal, but left blank. She pulled herself together and picked up my quill, copying the number I had written out for her.

As we heard the grand duchess's vehicle move off into the distance, we all stood there, not daring to utter a sound.

Suddenly, Lola giggled mischievously. She gave Sherry the loudest kiss on his nose, and he, in turn, protested by jumping from her arms and running off to the other side of the room. I imagined how good it must feel to have a kiss on the nose like that from Lola!

She must have read my mind, for before I knew it, she threw herself into my arms and started singing wildly, attempting to dance the polka with me at the same time!

She fell into a chair at the table, where Rosalie had taken the time to set out the teacups, and devoured a scone greedily.

We grouped together, openmouthed in astonishment, as she explained how she'd happened upon the lone earring in among the bed linens at Madame Alexandra's as she'd been getting dressed.

"How in the world had it got there? And who should I have returned it to? For I knew it might create quite the scandal! And we all know how vital it is to avoid scandal in this charming little town of ours, do we not? And so I kept it, without breathing a word of its existence to anyone. It was only later, upon reading the newspaper, that I saw the jewel on the grand duchess and learned that it belonged to the British crown. I saw her when I was out on a walk on the Croisette. Do you remember when I asked that I be left alone? I went out to find her. I told her that I knew of her most embarrassing situation and that I could help her if she thought there was a little money in it for me. I later wrote her a letter describing the object and where I'd found it, and I told her to meet me here today."

I snorted with laughter, but Rosalie showed her anger.

"When I think that you made me believe we might all be out on the street! And all that time you knew . . ."

"I didn't know a thing, Rosalie! My gamble paid off! I had no idea whether or not she'd show herself here today! And I had no intention of giving you any kind of false hope."

I turned to face Anna. "Well, Anna! I feel it's safe to say we can make some different choices now in terms of your well-being and your education. Isn't that right, Mademoiselle Lola?"

"Yes! It's exactly right!" She looked around at us, beaming. "My darlings, we're home! Gosh, that was nearly the end of me. What an adventure!"

Epilogue

During the weeks that followed, I would sit in my office at night, pen in hand, and write down my narrative, detailing everything that had happened to us throughout our investigation and adding annotations and corrections where necessary.

One moonlit evening, when I finally felt satisfied with my manuscript, I wrapped it up carefully in brown packing paper and tied it up with fine string into a tight bundle. That night, I slept like an infant, so overjoyed with the end result of my work.

The next morning, I woke up before the rest of the house and made my way to the post office, first making a stop at Madame Alexandra's. I felt my skin burn as I walked into the boutique, knowing that the bookseller must have been watching me with keen interest, wondering whether or not I would venture upstairs. He was a young man, with a fashionable mustache and a shabby-looking jacket, worn at the elbows.

I must have disappointed, for I stayed among the stacks, searching through the books carefully. I was looking for the name and address of an English publisher to whom I intended to send my first great work!

I found the English-language section after a few minutes and closed my eyes, ready to choose a book at random. Chance would have it that the book I pulled off the shelf was by Mark Twain. The publishing house was in America. The shipping costs would be far more expensive, but I didn't want to go against what destiny had dictated. I felt superstitious about the whole operation.

I asked the seller if he would allow me to copy out the address of the publisher onto my parcel.

"Oh! Are you a writer?" he asked in admiration.

"How did you guess? Yes! This is my first novel. I'm sending it off today!"

He smiled at me kindly and made some space on a counter so I could write down the details on my parcel.

As I awaited my turn at the postal office, I scanned that day's news in the paper.

The front pages told of a suicide in the fields just beyond the Boulevard de la Foncière. The man had borrowed a great deal of money for a building project and had been ruined following the collapse of a local bank.

What a contrast there was between what I'd read in the article and the emotions I felt inside. I was happy! Thoughts of suicide couldn't have been further from my mind. The fortunes of Cannes seemed to be crumbling, whereas I felt I was going from strength to strength. Little did I know what the future had in store for us. We had thought the matter of the crown jewels had been put to rest, but they would soon reappear in our lives in the most unexpected way.

At the window, I asked for the safest way to send a package of value across the Atlantic. As I handed my pages over to the postal worker, I whispered a prayer. "Go, little story of mine. Go and fulfill your mission. Go and tell the world of all the little Clara Campos."

And with a flutter in my heart, I made my way home to Les Pavots.
The End

Acknowledgments

The writing of a novel doesn't start the day you sit down at your computer to write the first chapter.

It is the result of a long process of maturation, and those you meet along the journey are essential to this result.

This is why I would first like to thank history and literature teachers Bernard Gassin and Sylvie Giordano, with whom, thanks to Maggy Wollner, I taught creative writing classes within the national education system. My role was to help teenagers write crime stories that took place in Cannes during the belle époque, walking by their sides along the streets of my city as they did so. I so wanted to be in their shoes, so impatient was I to be writing my own story. It was at that time that the characters in my mind started to take form.

It was Christophe de Mendoça, a history teacher, who, from the very start, helped me fathom all the chronological and geographical details imposed upon me by the presence of Maupassant. I also want to extend my thanks to Joséphine Saïa at the Cannes municipal library, who guided me in my historical research of Cannes, as well as Jean-Luc Fabron, Patricia Arnéodo, Jean-Luc Frizat, and Annick Legoff. They all welcomed me and helped me with such warm smiles. They guided me throughout the jungle of local bylaws, real estate funds, and regional papers from the period. The Association des Amis des Archives de Cannes was also of great help to me. Thank you to Jacqueline Leconte.

Lhattie Haniel, a historical romance author, helped me to lift the barriers that were stopping me from launching myself into the language required to write a novel of this genre. And Laurent Bettoni, author, publisher, and friend, helped me to construct this novel, better allowing me to target those words I needed.

My beta readers, Julien Biri, Lionel Cavalli, Catherine de Palma, Bernard Gassin, Danielle Boulois, Audrey Alwett, Amanda Castello, Xavier Théoleyre, Hélène Babouot, and Brigitte Aubert, each gave me their personal views and feelings on my work, enabling me to make important adjustments to the text. Warm and loving gratitude to them.

I also wish to extend warm thanks to Monsieur Claude Marro, a historian, former teacher at the Institut Stanislas, and vice president of the Société Scientifique et Littéraire de Cannes, who not only allowed me to access the records of the Société—of which Maupassant *himself* was a member—but also took the time to read the first draft of the novel with a view to spotting any possible anachronisms in terms of Cannes and its history. His article on the education system in Cannes was essential reading for me when it came to determining what sort of school Lola might have attended. He helped me enormously. His view of my work was most precious to me. It was also in looking through the 2016 records that I came across an article written by Nina Deschamp, a PhD in history of law. Her text revealed to me the tragic and unexplained deaths at the orphanage in Cannes, which incited me to further explore the subject.

In the same way, Madame Noëlle Benhamou, a specialist in nineteenth-century literature, and particularly in Maupassant (and who created the site www.maupassantiana.fr) offered her kind services to me in reading a draft of the novel to verify if everything written on Maupassant was correct and that what I had imagined could be deemed to be reasonable. She cowrote an article mentioning *the mysterious woman in gray*.

Amanda Castello, a French Italian author, adjusted my Italian phrasing, and Reinat Toscano, a Niçois poet, passionate about Nissart and Provençal language, helped me translate a number of phrases used in the text. Thanks to these incredible specialists and great lovers of language.

And so to Yves Lavandier and Benoit Fourneraut, who, upon reading my work, helped me to deepen the characters of the main protagonists and change a few aspects of the storyline. I wish to thank them with all my heart. Carole Chicot added the finishing touches in French. Thank you, Carole.

I feel so fortunate to have crossed paths with Gabriella Page-Fort and Jeffrey Belle. Without them, this novel would never have seen the light of day, possibly forever remaining a work in progress. My gratitude is infinite. It is also to them that I owe the existence of the English-language version of my novel. Great thanks must go to Alexandra Maldwyn-Davies, through whose magic my story has come to life in English. She gave the voice to Miss Fletcher, the narrator, and made the French text sing in English. Andrea Maldwyn-Davies and her sharp eye for detail, as well as the ever-listening Baby Meredith, helped her in this task.

Warm thanks to the Amazon Publishing France team, Clément Monjou and Emilyne Van der Beken, who were both so patient with me—I know I can be tiresome at times! They supported me faultlessly.

All novelists have a dream: to find themselves at home in a real library, a natural shelter away from the world. It's thanks to Frédéric Thibaud, from City Éditions, that *La Lettre Froissée* has been brought to a French readership. I found him to be so empathetic, kind, and free-spirited. I also wish to thank his enthusiastic coworker Alice Serverin, who was a joy to work with.

About the Author

Alice Quinn lives on the French Riviera, surrounded by her family and cats. After achieving great success with the Rosie Maldonne mystery series, featuring *Queen of the Masquerade, Queen of the Hide Out,* and *Queen of the Trailer Park*—which was a #1 bestseller in France—she changed her register and plunged with delight into historical intrigue in Cannes in the belle époque, an era full of intriguing contrasts. *The Crumpled Letter* is the first novel in her Belle Époque Mystery trilogy. For more information about the author, visit her at www.alice-quinn.com.

About the Translator

Back in 2001, after having read philosophy and French at the University of Leeds and realizing that being able to write a decent essay on Kant's categorical imperative didn't leave her with a great many career options, Alexandra Maldwyn-Davies decided to move to Paris, where she embarked on a career in writing and translation—working on projects including widely enjoyed video games (*Game of Thrones*, *In Memoriam*, *Shiness*, and *Men of War: Assault Squad*), top-rated apps (Human Defense, Le Déserteur, and Chocolapps), best-selling fiction (the Rosie Maldonne series: *Queen of the Trailer Park*, *Queen of the Hide Out*, and *Queen of the Masquerade* and *The Crumpled Letter*), and seductive travel books (*Fermes-Manoirs du Bessin*) and contributing to translation guides (*The Book of Standing Out: Travels through the Inner World of Freelance Translation* and *The Bright Side of Translation*).

She is currently working on two projects of her own: her first novel (see her blog posts for further details at alexandra-maldwyn-davies. com) and a sourcebook, *Women in Translation* (a collection of writings and articles on translation from the female perspective).

She has steadily built a successful freelance French-to-English literary translation business and can now boast that she does what she loves every day of her life—she tells stories.

She lives in rural Finistère, France, with her daughter (a future bilingual genius if ever she met one) and a motley crew of thirteen rescued dogs and cats.